TIBURON

Tiburon

Additional copies may be ordered from the publisher for educational, business, promotional or premium use.
For information, contact ALIVE Book Publishing at:
alivebookpublishing.com

Book Design By Alex P. Johnson

ISBN 13
978-1-63132-270-9

Library of Congress Control Number: 2026926700

Library of Congress Cataloging-in-Publication Data
is available upon request.

First Edition

Published in the United States of America by ALIVE Book Publishing
an imprint of Advanced Publishing LLC
3200 A Danville Blvd., Suite 204, Alamo, California 94507
alivebookpublishing.com

PRINTED IN THE UNITED STATES OF AMERICA

10 9 8 7 6 5 4 3 2 1

TIBURON

PATRICK J. HAGAN

Alive Book Publishing

MY *TIBURON* BACK STORY

by Ronan O'Neill

PLEASE FOLLOW ALONG as I, RONAN O'NEILL, take you on a tour my life from my being a first generation protected suburban son, through a glance at my college career at Georgetown University, to my brief, but eventful active duty career in the U.S. Coast Guard. Then, on to law school in San Francisco, and my dual careers in civil litigation practice for almost forty years, and my USCG Reserve career often linked to the law. Along the way, meet those with whom I formed significant relationships over my life's journey.

My legal career is marked, over the years, by imagination, perseverance and resilience, mostly leading to clever, sometimes novel, relationships and winning results. As you can see below, if you choose to read the more detailed Back Story to this point in my life, you will get more detailed glimpses of how I moved fairly quickly from defending more straight-forward civil litigation to far more complex matters, some with potentially billion-dollar outcomes, across a spectrum of mass personal injuries, to giant property cases, including class actions, and not limited solely to California.

As my successes mounted, I was appointed lead counsel for all of my main client's cases throughout the United States (National Coordinating Counsel, or 'NCC'), my areas of responsibility and arenas of practice changed and I took on other forums well beyond the California state trial court system, to federal courts at all levels and governmental agencies. Then, on into the world of insurance, both in the United States and in Europe, notably becoming deeply involved with the iconic institution, often referred to as Lloyds of London, and its multi-national principals and its varied agents.

As these decades evolve, I have shared those aspects of my personal life which are germane to making me into the man I become over all of those years. You will meet the women I come to love, including some I lose, and my family as it grows and changes. FOLLOW these decades of these divergent lives based around, but not in, San Francisco. SEE how it all starts in *SAUSALITO,* and continues four books later, here in *TIBURON.*

— — —

To more fully appreciate my continuing story as presented here i*n TIBURON,* the reader should be aware that many of its characters first emerged in my four autobiographical sketches chronicling significant events of my earlier life as suggested by my deceased psychiatrist and friend of many decades, Dr. Margot Arnaud. *SAUSALITO,* featured me as a young Ronan O'Neill, my family, and a number of my formative experiences, with considerable focus on the women in my life. My second effort, *MILL VALLEY,* emphasized my legal career growth, as well as my own family, and other people close to me, in new or changing relationships. *ROSS,* my third novel, focused as much, or perhaps more, on my evolving familial relationships and friendships as it did on some of the biggest challenges of my legal career which included an increasing recognition among the leading American civil litigation attorneys on the defense side, and the forging of relationships in, and about, the United Kingdom. *SAN ANSEMO,* my fourth novel, discusses our efforts to influence the US EPA while interacting mostly with British experts and other influencers in the UK, particularly in relation to the Lloyds insurance market. Our family expands, or seemingly so!

— — —

ADDITIONAL DETAILS follow which might help acquaint first-time readers:

SAUSALITO began with me, Ronan, arriving in that Northern California bayside town in 1971 as a junior Coast Guard officer assigned by its Headquarters to observe a major oil spill investigation. I had recently returned from the Viet Nam War, was highly decorated but still suffering the traumatic emotional effects of combat. On my day of first arriving in Sausalito, I met Carolyn Tyne, an aspiring young model with whom I almost immediately became somewhat romantically involved. Later and fortuitously, we began sharing what became her Sausalito apartment.

My reactions to the 1971 Golden Gate oil spill investigation and my Sausalito friend Joel Tinker's being in law school led to my decision to leave USCG active duty and to try to become a lawyer. While attending UC Hastings Law School in San Francisco, I fell in love with a school mate, Sandra Allen, and we became engaged. Her father was the managing partner of a large San Francisco firm where I clerked during law school and was expected by that family to start my law career. However, my engagement ended abruptly when Sandra reacted explosively to my decision not to join her father's firm. Immediately thereafter, I experienced a serious emotional crisis, which might have proven fatal as I stood on the Golden Gate Bridge pondering unclearly very negative thought patterns about my future. But the fortuitous and timely appearance of an old college girlfriend, Mollie Phelan, brought me through the worst of that crisis. With the initial help of my psychiatrist, Dr. Arnaud, my mother Kate, and Mollie, I became better at confronting my emotional fears, slowly gained confidence, and moved forward with my life.

Following law school, my friend Tinker provided me with an opportunity to join Klein Kelly, a small Oakland law firm, and I quickly began to thrive there as a defense litigator hired mostly by insurance companies to defend the entities they insured. I married Mollie, who was then an IBM systems analyst. She very quickly became a much sought-after computer applications developer. I achieved some initial significant prominence in the Northern California defense bar at a time when asbestos was fast becoming a medical and legal pandemic. As a result, within less than fifteen years after my initial arrival in Sausalito, I was becoming a central figure in nationwide high-stakes litigation, often collaborating with my friend Tinker who had relocated his practice to Washington, D.C. As *SAUSALITO* ends, Mollie, our four young children and I had relocated to the nearby town of Mill Valley, from which my second novel draws its name.

In *MILL VALLEY*, Mollie and I enjoy an almost blissful decade with our family. I continued a sporadic, mostly long-distance relationship with Carolyn, never actually meeting our son, Patrick, until the latter part of this book. Meanwhile, Carolyn had become an even more successful model, rising to an *haute couture* international level. Mollie's career as a computer applications designer became incrementally more successful. After leaving IBM, her job became bi-coastal, slightly complicating our lives. All of this occurred while I was leading a burgeoning practice of huge, potentially high dollar outcome civil legal actions, some on a national scale. During that same time, our firm's local asbestos caseload increased markedly in size. I was able, over time, to expand my diverse legal team to include a beautiful woman lawyer who also had a scientific background. Soon, I fell into a long-term romantic relationship with this Martha Walsh, who became our team's resident expert in Science and Medicine, and my frequent travel companion.

Desert Mutual insurance Company (DMIC) designated me as National Coordinating Counsel for all of its asbestos litigation targeting CAL Board, its largest target insured, which became national in scale. I continued to litigate against, and at times with, Sandra Allen, my former *fiancée,* and her father who represented a larger target defendant in many of these same cases. Also, with input from various members of our national CAL Board defense team, I was designated to undertake the development of a novel defense to the massive U.S. Environmental Protection Agency-driven litigation designed to require defendants to pay for removal of all asbestos-containing products installed in buildings, which gave rise to more than a few of those mega-cases. In the face of some political duplicity, I tried the first phase of such a case brought by the Los Angeles Unified School District (*LAUSD*) with mixed results.

My work in attempting to facilitate our quest to defend CAL Board and develop that novel EPA defense allowed me to meet key figures on the international stage of public health. These assignments led to my travelling even more extensively; and, in the case of several iconic European scientific experts, providing high-end hospitality as entertainment. (These leaders of their respective scientific communities (J. Corbett McDonald, M.D. in the UK and Canada, for Epidemiology, Julian Peto of Oxford and the University of London in Quantum Mechanics and Mathematics, and Jean Bignon, M.D., Paris, as Chief of INSERM [French equivalent of NIH], all of whom were rarely expert witnesses and would accept no fees for their time because they believed that doing so might appear tantamount to being bribed.)

I was also retained by DMIC to coordinate and manage a London search for their missing older reinsurance policies of many years, placed with Lloyds syndicates, and to secure payment to them to assure that DMIC maintained its continued liquidity. Under the loose supervision of DMIC's COO, John O'Sullivan, my team successfully negotiated a search protocol with Cheshire & Booth, DMIC's London Placing Broker, which stored the files of the thousands of its coverage placements, and allowed us to identify the reinsuring syndicates for most of the missing years. This complex assignment also involved starting up a small company to act as a go-between with that broker and the many reinsuring syndicates, called Long-Tail Litigation, Ltd. (LTL), utilizing DMIC's lead solicitor's executive assistant. On our first meeting, that assistant, Madeline Myles, promptly seduced me, and we became entangled on an "as available basis" whenever I was travelling alone in London.

This continuum of my life, as I set out in ending *MILL VALLEY*, devolved bitterly as Mollie was suddenly taken seriously ill, not long after she met and befriended Carolyn and her son Patrick when they came to visit Carolyn's long time West Coast apartment home in Sausalito. That book ends with Mollie being rolled into emergency oncological surgery.

ROSS commences where MILL VALLEY ends by tracking the agonizing last days of Mollie's survival and her living blueprint of our family's future life for me and her children after she succumbed. The days and months after Mollie's passing are portrayed closely as I saw a great deal of Dr. Arnaud during that time. After conferring with my children, I acquiesced in Mollie's dying advice and asked Carolyn to marry me. Having come to care about Mollie deeply, Carolyn too was guided by Mollie's dying wishes on the same course which I was asked to follow. She accepted my marriage proposal forthwith. Together, we decided that we needed a new home to replace Mollie's in Mill Valley. Carolyn purchased a huge house in Ross, not far from St. Anselm's parish church. The work to restore that house, the turmoil of moving four school-aged children, my mother Kate agreeing to move in with us, and Carolyn along with her Patrick becoming Catholics before our marriage were all occurring simultaneously.

Meanwhile, my team at our law firm took care of my work and our clients during my travails surrounding Mollie's demise and my dark grief-driven period thereafter. Our big-ticket caseload continued to increase and another client, Haney Pumps of Auburn, New York, insured by Cayuga Mutual, located nearby in Seneca Falls (actual site used for the great Christmas movie, *It's a Wonderful Life*), sent a potentially devastating Bodily Injury case located in Calaveras County in California's Sierra Foothills. Their general counsel, by then an old friend, requested that I handle that case personally and I did.

My expert development work continued from *Mill Valley* in the United Kingdom and France, as did my work as National Coordinating Counsel for CAL Board as appointed by Desert Mutual Insurance Company with much of that work taking place in the Eastern United States. These massive asbestos property damage cases remained the largest share of my workload. Reggie Fox, one of the partners on our firm's team managed the massive litigation of the Northern California Asbestos BI cases. Meanwhile, our partner, Phil Hassard, having relocated to Glendale, just north of Los Angeles city, undertook to litigate all of the CAL Board BI cases in the south of our state. (Phil was quite taken by our *au pair,* Ingrid, having met her at my wedding to Carolyn. He proposed and she volunteered to Carolyn that her younger sister, Elsa, could replace her. They were Swedish, spoke English perfectly, and Carolyn met Elsa in Paris for an interview.)

Something novel: being married to Carolyn opened all sorts of non-legal doors in New York, Paris and even London. Our whole family actually became involved in a magazine fashion shoot in Paris during the Christmas season. On that trip, Carolyn and I decided to adopt each other's children. Meanwhile, my daughter Maeve's voluntary participation demonstrated a proclivity for the staging of those fashion shoots, which was noticed by Robert, a very senior French executive producer for *Vogue.*

Beginning SAN ANSELMO, Maeve is in her last year of high school, while Carolyn's Patrick is in his third year at Princeton, where he is evolving into a star player on that university's basketball team. He also has an eye on Ingrid's sister, Elsa, our new *au pair*.

My mother Kate is trying to keep up with my sisters living on the East Coast while she has reinvented a life for herself in suburban Marin County.

Carolyn, with Robert's podding eventually recruits Maeve to intern in Paris and New York as part of his team (becoming her mentor). She starts in at Stanford, and ultimately splits time at the *Sorbonne* (thanks to another mentor, Jean Bignon while living with his family when in Paris). My older children continue to excel academically, socially, and in sports, especially Robert in basketball who is several years younger than his step-brother, Patrick Tyne, and already two inches taller. (I am 6′ 5″ and look up to my two oldest sons and my young Patrick is only two inches shorter than me with a least three or four years of growth soon to follow.)

Much of this novel is given over to evolving a methodology for putting an end to more than a decade of litigation involving the removal of asbestos containing materials from buildings throughout the USA, pursuant to EPA Rules, especially schools which have become the key target of our defense. While that is on-going, the Lloyds' insurance institution in London is beginning to fail under the weight of USA litigation in two huge fields: a massive volume of asbestos injury cases (first called Mass Tort) as well as environmental damage under federal statutes, e.g., CERCLA, generating enormous clean-up costs.

Having created a mechanism to allow DMIC to recover its decades of reinsurance, I become involved in any number of initiatives at Lloyds, as does DMIC.

SAN ANSELMO chronicles these Lloyds business developments in detail as well as my expanding and evolving familial machinations; including our coming to the aid of the Johansson family from Stockholm when Ingrid and Elsa's mother is seriously injured in a vehicle collision and needs highly specialized rehabilitation available at few places world-wide, one of which is in Kentfield, adjacent to Ross and near-by San Anselmo. We facilitate her admission and have her family stay at our San Anselmo second home while she receives in-patient treatment, and also when she moves into an out-patient status.

Substantial amounts of emphasis are dedicated to preparation of an impeccable authority to approach the US EPA on changing its In-Place Asbestos Rules; as well as preparation for, and the actualization of a mass-gathering of concerned entities with varied interests on the continuation, or reconstitution, of the Lloyds insurance markets in London which are seen as beginning to fail, even as this convocation takes place. John O'Sullivan of DMIC and Gerry Dwyer of Connecticut Indemnity have jointly retained me, and we become deeply involved in this reconstitution which continues throughout TIBURON.

DEDICATION and ACKNOWLEDGEMENTS

These tributes go hand-in-hand for this fifth in the Ronan O'Neill/Marin County Towns series. First & foremost, to my longest surviving friend, long-ago mentor, frequent working companion and the editor of this series, I cannot thank Bruce McDonald enough, but I try to do so again, here and now, and whenever we speak or write, for all that he has done to encourage and assist me over the years, and especially with this project.

Also, Jane Wells, my former partner and continuing friend, always willing to pitch in with assistance, especially when my technical competence becomes insufficient. Thank you, as well!

PROLOGUE

Starting what might prove to be my last installment on what has become a series about me, and evermore about my family, I commence with a sense of trepidation.

The years have been generous to me, and to most of my family. I have more than fifteen years of law practice left to highlight, but perhaps fewer matters of noteworthy substance than those discussed already. Thus, I shall do my best to find those events I deem worthwhile in those remaining years. Still, I do plan to shift my focus somewhat more to my family and those with whom I have interacted for much of my life, mostly consisting of work and family. Of course, my children will all be featured as will some of their associates. But Carolyn will be more of a primary focus, and some of what I write, I learned only because of her.

Rather than flay all the details of the "You bet your Company Case…" of Haney Pumps brought by the Environmental Defense Fund and the Natural Resources Defense Council (EDF/NRDC) under California's Proposition 65 (PROP 65) which ended my SAN ANSELMO novel with the issuance of an Alternate Writ by California's Supreme Court to those two environmental entity Plaintiffs to Show Cause as to why it should not enter its Writ of Mandamus compelling the Alameda County Superior Court to enter its Order Sustaining the Haney Pumps Demurrer to those Respondents' Complaint on California Constitutional grounds that its PROP 65 legislation violated that state's constitutional separation of powers provisions.

Negotiations between Haney and the EDF/NRDC commenced within a very few days of the receipt of that Order. The California Supreme Court went on to grant four multi-week continuances to those Plaintiffs to respond to its Alternate Writ while staying all of their PROP 65 litigation in California at their request. Settlement was ultimately reached for much less than $100,000 between those parties. Near the outset of those negotiations, Haney introduced its new line of stainless-steel submersible pumps which instantly became the state-of-the-art for that industry. Haney Pumps stock price shot upwards. The California Legislature ultimately revised its implementing legislation for Prop 65 to cure its earlier enacted errors highlighted in Haney's writ petition. Thus, PROP 65 cases continue to be filed until the time of this writing. Finally, I could not pay for a drink or a meal in Auburn, New York, or nearby Seneca Falls, for a good ten years (not that I got back there all that often) after we won that case.

To put this narrative piece about our lives in perspective, let me begin with the observation that somewhere as I approached fifty years, I began to view life as a journey of uncertain duration with mostly unspecified goals. Self-observation was never a strong suit with me. Hence, my continuing need for Dr. Arnaud. Moreover, with the loss of my mother Kate, that need seemed to intensify. But as Mollie, our young daughter grew, and I worked somewhat less, I found myself sharing more of my insights with Carolyn. (My youngest children with Mollie, the Twins, Patrick and Meaghan, eventually got up the gumption to tell me that they were uncomfortable with their Baby Sister being called Mollie. I allowed that her real name was Margaret Mary. Meaghan asked if they could call her "Margie" (Mar-Gee'), instead. Thus, Mollie had two family nicknames. Never seemed to bother her.) This pattern of budding independence in our family life can be seen to intensify hereafter. I only wish that I knew more about what Carolyn thought on the earlier "other aspects of her life," which she never chose to discuss, or minimized, when that seemed needed.

1

ROSEVILLE

Although this matter was dealt with on a day-to-day basis by my partner, Martha Walsh, her pregnancy caused me to pay more attention since she had announced a plan for a post-natal leave of uncertain length. Also, there were on-going issues of major potential insurance coverage conflict avoidance between Great Western Foundry (GFW, the actual client) and Cayuga Mutual Insurance Company (Cayuga, GWF's insurer and the entity retaining our firm to defend GWF), an area of my specialization.

As the new year began, these two entities had reached an agreement to use our services for matters which extended beyond the actual defense of the ever-increasing volume of lawsuits brought by, or on behalf of, minors claiming exposure to toxic substances in the land where waste was dumped reflecting the use of the sand-casting method for creating brake shoes for railroad cars and engines. We suggested immediate fencing of all such properties under the control of GWF. We also suggested No Trespassing signs and a generalized warning about substances potentially having unspecified health impacts. This advice was followed promptly.

We located a soils expert that understood materials and the aging of toxins over time in soil, who was willing to opine about the issues in these cases. We realized that we needed two experts of this ilk: one to advise the litigants, retained by our firm to act as our consultant, never to be disclosed under the attorney-client privilege; and another highly qualified, to serve as our testifying expert. We held off hiring that second expert until we could learn who the plaintiffs' side would disclose, if anyone.

Julian Peto was kind enough to identify an expert at the University of Wisconsin who was well-versed on the evolving state of causation research for lead. We retained this woman Ph.D. as our consultant, at least initially. Strom Nordquist, Cayuga's Western Regional Claims Manager, approved of all of these steps and agreed to compensate the experts whom we retained.

I was present for all of the separate initial expert meetings at our office, run by Martha along with Felicia Clarke, a senior associate. (Joshua Small had relocated to Glendale as a junior partner, seconding Phil Hazzard, who was much pleased with that arrangement as he was with his wife, Ingrid's pregnancy with a second child.) Andrea Parsons and Stuart Brock, VP of Finance and GC of GWF, were also present. Having hired these individuals sight unseen, and having very different agendas for each, we were quite pleased with the outcomes of our first meetings with each of these experts. Of particular import, but not surprising, were the opinions on lead causation of IQ deficit which paralleled my conversation of many months ago with Julian Peto, that all of the studies on this topic to date were inconclusive when read together; and, were unlikely to yield anything to create consensus because of all of the known variables associated with contributing to IQ. Dr. Gwen Franck appeared extremely self-assured. I found her persuasive. But we were in the California state court system which had looser control on foundation of expert opinions than did the federal trial court system.

Our consulting soils/materials Ph.D., Martin Sheen. a professor at Stanford, suggested testing in stages. We asked him to assemble his team to begin forthwith. We asked the testifying consultant only about the viability of the testing suggested by our consultant. Her essential agreement allowed that testing process to move forward with the knowledge that we were using state-of the-art techniques. (The use of double experts was intended to avoid the possibility of a testifying expert running a test which could be used against the client. Thus, the consulting expert worked as part of the legal team, but was never intended to be disclosed.)

This causation expert was opining on a meta-basis, i.e., being familiar with an entire subset of a given research area. If her opinion could become harmful, we would merely replace her. Then her potentially adverse testimony would be silenced by her having been part of the legal team under the Attorney-Client Privilege.

It appeared that in an unknown universe of these types of potential Mass Torts, the only "safe harbor" for a target defendant was to defeat the claimed causation at the very outset of the litigation. That was our plan for defending GWF!

———

While all of this intense legal work was on-going, Patrick Tyne was having an amazing basketball season in the Ivy League leading Princeton to a one loss record in league play and a bid to play in the thirty-two team NCAA Tournament field. Meanwhile, our once *au pair,* Elsa, was making her initial steps with Carolyn's agency by participating as a young model in a *Vogue* layout being staged by Maeve in the Hamptons on the Long Island under Robert's supervision. Patrick and Elsa's relatively close proximity allowed them to see each other on occasion, but they kept that very private.

Playing in the NCAA Tournament was a "very big thing" as only one Ivy League team was invited annually. I let John O'Sullivan know right away because if Princeton advanced far enough that might jeopardize Patrick playing in the Post-Lloyds Convocation golf tournament in Ireland. (John had his son playing rugby as well. I also had my son Robert signed up to play in Ireland along with Patrick Tyne. We were five of the twelve Americans who would be taking on the British in a Ryder Cup format across the south of Ireland over four days. We needed those young players as they were among our best!) John's son at Minnesota was a highly skilled ice hockey player. The Gophers needed to win their last two games to secure the Big Ten bid to that NCAA tournament.

Quincy Frandin-Jones (Q) and Wilfred Smythe, the Clerk for Twenty King's Bench Walk, Barristers, were making the actual arrangements for the golf tournament itself, including transportation to Heathrow, hotels, golf courses and food (pubs underway were optional!), ending the first night in Killarney. They were trying for twelve per side, with no guests. Our solicitor, Bradley Campbell, despite his disavowal of any golfing skill, was planning to play.

As for the Lloyds Convocation itself, there was to be a Reception, Cocktails and Dinner the first night, three two-hour sessions with a 30 minute hiatus between each on the second day, and a two hour session with questions, comments and networking on the third day, followed by cocktails and a smallish dinner. The event itself had golf or horse racing on the fourth day. Our Tournament get-away was from Heathrow at 6:30 that fourth day evening with a destination just west of Killarney, via Cork Airport that evening.

As for my presentation to Reinsurers and Retrocessionaires at the Convocation itself, I was scheduled to be part of the keynote lead-off group while coordinating my lead-off first hour presentation, which was to forecast potential areas of concern for new plaintiff liability initiatives in the Twenty-First Century. I was granted permission to ask Corbett McDonald, M.D., a world-famous epidemiologist to participate with me. The Convocation Committee agreed and Corbett accepted. As mid-April drew near, we had settled on Tobacco, Food (especially as formulated by chemical processes and genetic changes), Telecommunications (especially hacking and deceptive fraudulent schemes), government reimbursement claims (for funding health care or remediation), and new heretofore undetermined Mass Torts, perhaps potentially created by California's PROP 65. We prepared to speak on each and have fifteen minutes for any needed interaction. No paper was being offered!

Carolyn and I were discussing the children and their futures as another school year was moving rapidly to its close. Robert would be going into his third high school year at

Branson School. His sports of choice were now basketball and golf. He was by then very good at the first, and almost phenomenal at the second, considering how little he practiced (but he did read a good deal and made a great effort to understand the physics of that game). Academically, he was excellent; while socially, he tended to be on the quiet-side, but not bashful. He very much wanted to go to Princeton! The Tigers coach was very much aware of him, and perhaps thinking about postponing retirement a few more years.

Carolyn wanted Robert to consider other schools, like Stanford, where we could see him from time-to-time. My response was why not take the Twins and Robert on a Colleges tour? Having never done so, Carolyn thought for a few minutes and decided that would be a grand idea for the coming Summer. She also added that perhaps stopping for a few days in Longport, NJ, to visit my sister, Rose Mary, could be part of that project. I allowed that it sounded sensational and why did she not see what she could fit into her work schedule, as well as to talk about it with the Twins mostly.

Two days later, Carolyn reported that Robert gave her a list of seven universities: three on the West Coast and four on the East. When Patrick and Meaghan became aware of this potential foray, they allowed that they might wish to be part of it as they were only two years behind Robert in going to college. That appeared a game changer since Robert did not wish to be "bogged down" with his younger siblings or to see schools of "no interest to him." When Carolyn put this dilemma in front of me, I thought for a few moments and then proposed a compromise.

Only have the Twins go East and they could each pick

two more colleges, if needed. Or, Robert could perhaps spend a day or two on his own doing other things if he did not wish to see their choices. The Twins were a bit too young to give them the same option, especially with some of the destination schools never visited by me.

— — —

All of this transpired while Mollie was going to nursery school nearby for her early years.

By then I was becoming more active in my honorary Society, especially in the area of Environmental Law. In a matter of a few years of activity, a number of my fellow members suggested that I volunteer to head-up that group for two years. Not certain that agreeing was the best idea, but as always, my saying "NO" to a request proved difficult. So, when they persisted, I agreed. Now, my turn as Practice Group Chair was to begin at the Summer Meeting at the Greenbriar in West Virginia this coming July. That meant coming up with some thoughts of what can be accomplished by this group over the next two years. (My partners all being environmental experts in their own rights, I sent them a memo asking for input in terms of ideas. Their responses gave me much to consider, and I thanked them at our next partners' meeting.)

With all of these tasks, especially speaking to the Retrocessionaires at the Lloyds/Grey's Inn Convocation, I found myself speaking at least once almost every month with Corbett McDonald in London. Although his team studied a wide variety of substances for potential carcinogenic or toxic effects, many of them were not far enough along to have some assurance of scientifically provable concern.

Corbett was aware of California's PROP 65 and its list of toxic chemicals. He pointed out that although many of them were unproven as a threat to humans at the banned threshold detection level (e.g., parts/billion in many substances in many instances), he felt that challenging their toxicity itself was a waste of time and resource. Moreover, he agreed with me that the size of California's economy meant that those entities which sold product into that state needed to be on guard so as not to run afoul of that statute.

Another area of his on-going concern was in the structural changes to the genetic make-up of foods and the food-chain. Many of these examples were the subject of some level of government oversight, but neither of us were at all confident that most governmental entities had the skill, staffing and over-all where-with-all, or even the will power to oversee the incredible range of substances being modified using a wide array of methodologies made available by modern science.

Each area of potential concern needed to be vetted by me before placing each in line for discussion before my London audience. This proved time consuming. Thankfully, I engaged my partners at a sufficient level that they were fully aware of my broad topic and the need for diverse levels of input to assure its basic accuracy.

— — —

As we wound toward London, I was making various plans with different people: Quincy Franden-Jones, one of the convocation organizers and Wilfred Smythe, both running the follow-on golf event in Ireland; Bradley Campbell, DMIC's solicitor and Madeline Myles, his one-time assistant and now COO of Long-Tail Litigation, Limited (LTL), the joint venture for collections and other tasks which might appear from London-based sources of forms of re-insurance for DMIC and Connecticut Indemnity, Gerry Dwyer of CI, and John O'Sullivan EVP and COO of DMIC for London matters, also the captain of the American team in the Irish golf tournament. Seemed I was spending one-two hours per day on all of this planning.

— — —

The Roseville case was taking up most of my billable time. Andrea Parsons, the CFO of Great Western Foundries (GWF), was taking a very hands-on position step-by-evolved-step in the process which we were creating to abate the sources of their historic pollution (or at least isolate them from the public) which she saw as a continuing opportunity to minimize her company's costs (Neither side thought this represented an insured loss). She was relentless. She drove Martha a bit crazy. I tried to get Martha to understand GWF's cash position. (Cayuga was unsympathetic since GWF 's historic conduct essentially created their potentially huge exposure.)

Martha really wanted to get GWF's defense position into the courts before the science on lead causation got to a point where it became sufficiently strong to appear as some kind of a scientific consensus on its alleged dangers. Toward that end, Martha and Felicia Clarke were working on a joint Demurrer (Motion to Dismiss under California law) to the first fifty-six Complaints based on the theory that no compensable injury was being pleaded for any of those individual plaintiffs. Since this tactic had the capacity to short-circuit this entire litigation, Cayuga Mutual (GWF's insurer), through Strom Nordquist, the West Coast Claims Manager, strongly supported this approach.

This process led at times to Ms. Parsons staying overnight in Oakland. One night, Carolyn was in New York with Mollie, working with Robert (in from Paris), Maeve, and using Elsa for her first time as a lead model on a 18-22 page Fall high fashion layout utilizing Broadway theatre openings, as well as the Opera's and the Symphony's Opening Nights. Martha had a night out with Mary planned. So, she bailed out on dinner with Andrea at her hotel. Martha asked me to step in. Big mistake on my part: I drank a bit too much. Next thing, Andrea suggested that we get some coffee. But the restaurant was closing, so she suggested we go to her room and she would make a few cups. We did, but while waiting for the water to heat, Andrea excused herself. When she returned, she had her hair down and was wearing a bathrobe. I took that as a cue to leave, got up and started to put on my suit jacket. Andrea put out her hand to block one of my arms, and said, "Please stay awhile longer? I get so lonely here some nights."

I paused and she leaned in and up, kissing me on the lips. I reached for her shoulders to push her back, but she snuggled closer before I could act. Things were on the verge of going even more wrong, at least for me, maybe not for Andrea. But near the last second, my common sense got the best of me, and I pulled back from the kiss while holding her at almost arms' length. I shook my head. Saying, "Andrea, we both really know better than to do this. You are the client. I am your lawyer. We might enjoy ourselves, but it would create a damning cloud on our relationship moving forward. Stopping now, we need never mention this again.

Oh, and do not think I do not appreciate you. You are extremely beautiful. Now, I really think I better go."

She smiled shyly, looked downward, then with her eyes barely visible said, "You really are a terribly nice, smart, sexy man. Can you forgive me?"

Me, "For what?"

By the time I left her room, I was very sober, and more than a little shaken.

— — —

The next day, five of us met in our conference room. The good news: Andrea acted as if nothing had happened that night before. We proceeded to agree on the entire theme for the text of the Demurrer to be filed in the Sacramento County Superior Court; also on some discovery to the parents of each minor plaintiff, almost all of them had one or more parents as a *Guardian ad Litem* (Minor children could not appear on their own and these "Guardians" were among statutory categories of individuals who could apply and be appointed routinely to represent the children until they became adults.), as suggested by some research on lead and IQ undertaken by Felicia with guidance from Martha. Martha also reported on some potential experts who might serve as additional consultants for the defense, with a view to not being disclosed to testify.

We had a working lunch for a second straight day. Stuart Brock, GWF's General Counsel was also present. Before we started, Andrea announced that she wanted to leave by 2:30 to beat the bulk of the commute traffic headed east-bound on I-80 toward Sacramento. We met her goal and they were both gone a few minutes after two. When Martha and I were alone, she said, "Andrea sounds like she had to wait for you to be sober enough to drive home. I've never known that to be a problem for you in the past. Is that really what happened last night?" Martha turned and left the conference room before I could answer.

— — —

Within a few days after our office served GWF'S first written discovery on plaintiffs, one of their lead attorneys called me with no warning. At first, he was cordial and polite as he explained that the guardians and parents of the actual plaintiffs were not really parties to the lawsuits, merely filling a statutory role for minors. I was non-committal to that tactic. Next, he suggested that generational lineal IQ testing was next to meaningless as a predictor of the IQ of off-spring. I responded that any number of scientists would not agree with him, rather viewing it as a potential, some even a strong, predictor. Goodness! That somehow triggered the gentleman and the next thing I knew I was getting an earful about being a racist, and prejudiced because all of the plaintiffs were minorities, mostly African-Americans. My response when he paused for breath was, "That's nice. Next time you wish to communicate I suggest your office do so in writing. As to you, please tell your partners you are *persona non grata* in communicating with our office until we have your written apology." With that, I disconnected him. Then, I dictated a memo, attempting to recall with precision the specific language Attorney Fred Young had used in the call he initiated. In doing so, I realized that he never got to any specific goal in his call.

I gave my dictation to Lily and asked her to transcribe it,

so I could make any edits while my memory remained fresh. When we finished, I called Martha and Felicia into my office, and Lily handed them my one-page memo. When they both looked up, I asked them, "What should we do about this, if anything else for now?"

Felicia responded first, "We all believe that this is an African-American firm in Sacramento; and, they appear to have a pretty good reputation for professionalism. I suggest that you both authorize me to send this memo to their named partners on the Complaint, also to Joshua and suggest that he address its contents with their designee. Ronan, I have seen how you deal with difficult situations in the past and how you often have used them to your side's long-term benefit. Here, I see an opportunity to do something like that. I feel that Joshua as an African-American is best positioned of all of us to carry this off."

We talked for a few minutes, got some details and agreed that Joshua and Felicia should circulate a draft quickly. They did. We made a few minor suggestions, and he caused his letter, with my memo attached, to be faxed to that plaintiff firm's office about ten minutes before 5:00, their nominal closing time.

The next morning, Joshua asked if he could meet with Martha, Felicia and me at 10:30. He came into my office. The four of us sat around my small conference table. He passed out a one-page letter from Attorney Young who apologized unreservedly, and apparently sincerely, for his outburst of the day before. Martha asked, "How did you close this so quickly?"

Joshua, "Well you read the letter and he talked with his partners last evening before calling me this morning. As you both surmised, he started with a round-about foray to see if

I was our firm's token Black. Before he got himself into that quagmire, I called him on his tactic. Then, I said, 'There are no photographs in Martindale-Hubbell {A national digest of law firms in America, published annually}. But just so you know Mr. O'Neill is White and Mr. Foxx is Black.' I paused for a few seconds. His first response was unworthy of repeating. Then, he said I shall send an apology forthwith, and thanked me. When I got his letter, I called you all."

Martha, "We doubtless have achieved a major credibility advantage. We mustn't waste it. Let's see what they do next?"

Mr. Young called me a few days later. He thanked me for having Joshua get in touch with them, then praised him. I interrupted just long enough to say, "Please do not try to recruit him. We are very fond of Joshua and his father. We see him becoming a full partner soon and being part of the future of our firm."

We then had a professional discussion. I explained that Martha was the lead attorney on the case, and not me. He asked for an additional five weeks to respond to the discovery we had served. Seemed reasonable to me, so I agreed. My parting thought: I hope Martha gets our Demurrer heard before she gives birth

---

In order to maximize Long Tail Litigation, Limited (LTL)'s position and whatever market leverage it had created, I put together an outline of my topics for potential new environmental/toxic tort substances, suitable for annotating with new points. I talked with John O'Sullivan and Manny Garcia at DMIC and requested the 'go-ahead' for a long week in London to work on preparation there. I would stop in Scottsdale on my way back for any additional input. Madeline of LTL volunteered to assist me in putting my draft speech together. I got two half days with Corbett. Julian Peto was up in Oxford working on a paper and allowed he was sorry to miss me, but he had a deadline to submit for peer review pre-publication.

So, I spent a long week finalizing my initial draft outline of our first hour, planning that I would split time with Corbett on the toxins themselves, while I would do the introduction and wrap-up myself. Bradley and Madeline were able to secure invites so LTL would have a presence.

When I stopped at DMIC in Scottsdale, John O'Sullivan and Manny (who was also attending and golfing) were pleased with the outline. Also, I intended to make my trip for the Convocation in April two days shorter by virtue of this preparation.

Carolyn and Mollie met me at SFO. The trips were starting to wear on me more each year.

After a day back in the Bay Area, I was able to get forty-five minutes with Dr. Arnaud, I needed to see her to express my frustrations about how my processing of my work was beginning to take me a bit longer and my stamina was beginning to feel more than a bit taxed at times. She let me ramble for a good twenty minutes or more as I covered where I had been and what I was doing. Then, "Ronan, you seem very excited and very psyched. It's been three months since I last saw you and you appear to be going non-stop. You have turned fifty. That does not make you old, but trust me, age is more than a number. Age is a short-hand manner to describe generally the stage each individual is going through in life in a general, somewhat overarching fashion, sometimes physically, sometimes mentally, or sometimes emotionally. It's that last context on which I think you need to focus. Your recent event with that woman lawyer from Sacramento, albeit a close call, presages some maturity in your decision-making at last. Perhaps having realized all that your life entails, you will begin to realize that you cannot afford to take on any more emotionally taxing activities at this time. There. That's my take-away for you today. Is the beautiful Carolyn at home?"

When I nodded YES, she added, "Go home to her. It's time you let her become your rock. She may already think she is, but you need to let her know that she really is! Oh, and please give her my best wishes. I like her ever so much for you!"

2

LLOYDS LONDON CONVOCATION

The SHERATON Belgravia was located considerably closer taxi-time-wise to Grey's Inn than was the Grosvenor House. John preferred The Berkeley; but to many of us attending, its pricing was just too much. So, the bulk of us stayed in this charming smallish, very tall, very narrow hotel across Belgrave Square from the German Embassy. My room was on the sixteenth floor with a glorious panoramic view of countless London roof tops, many of them world famous, e.g., Big Ben or Westminster Abbey. A very real treat! It had been years since I stayed there, following my first trip to Paris.

Patrick Tyne's Princeton team had been eliminated in the Eastern Regional Final of the NCAA Championship Basketball Tournament. He flew first to Paris for a few days with Elsa, then joined us two nights before the Convocation's Closing Events. My son, Robert arrived the night before the Opening Session, as did John O'Sullivan and his rugby-playing son, Sean; so did DMIC's Manny Garcia and Gerry Dwyer of Connecticut Indemnity. Bradley Campbell would be attending all of the sessions in his capacity as a Name Partner of Thornton, Campbell & Thornton, Solicitors, while Madeline Myles would be present on behalf of LTL, as its COO. Both announced their availability for the Irish Ryder-Cup Play, immediately following the Convocation's golf tournament in Surrey. Our grouping was well-represented at these events, especially considering Quincy (Q) Franden-Jones' role as one of the Convocation primary organizers, along with his Clerk of Chambers, Wilfred Smythe.

Much to my consternation, I made certain realizations in those last few days leading up to that huge meeting's kick-off: although virtually all of these people were "players" in my years of working in London, they had never been all together in one place at any single time, and two of my sons would be part of it. That I was the connective tissue that had brought so many of these unique individuals to bear on the divergent weighty issues which we had all helped to resolve successfully dawned on me as I readied myself to speak. Now, here we were all preparing to do what we could to facilitate the reformatting, or would it be reformation, of one of the world's critical financial institutions. When I spoke of this with Dr. Arnaud on my first visit following these various events, she paused, then said, "You will doubtless come to think of this outcome as one of your life's crowning achievements."

As I write this years later, I now think that she got that observation right on the button!

The overarching goal of this entire exercise was to create an environment, or perhaps platform, to replace a world class insurance institution's very structure of conducting its business in the face of what had amounted to a colossal financial failure. For centuries, businessmen formed syndicates to place insurance to indemnify business risk-takers in the event certain calamites might occur, e.g., the 1906 San Francisco Earthquake, for certain risks, e.g., fire, inability to conduct one's business and the like. The lead underwriter ("Lead") for a syndicate would take on as many named investors (called "Names") as he deemed appropriate to cover one or many more insurable risks. These Names would agree to be part of a syndicate and the Lead, through brokers in London and elsewhere around the world, would place coverage, primarily casualty coverage, or if some other insurer had written that primary coverage, the lead could sign on to provide "reinsurance" for some percentage of each loss. (Policies, in most instances, would contain a total amount of loss for each individual loss and an aggregate amount of loss in the policy after which no further payment was owed ("Stop Loss"). If the amount of coverage in the primary policy was exhausted for a loss, then a Lead may have placed an "excess" policy above the primary to cover any loss exceeding the primary policy, and so on. For large business ventures, these policies would be of many different types and cover many different potential losses.

The Names would agree, in return for an annual premium through the Lead, to pay its share of any loss, historically without a Stop Loss. This exposed the Names to "unlimited liability," but because catastrophic losses very rarely occurred, and so many names existed diversifying their risks, Names hardly ever went broke, or paid exceedingly large amounts. UNTIL the dawn of mass environmental torts in the USA. These took two major forms at first: environmental contamination of the waters of the USA in violation of retroactively created federal laws; and second, tens of thousands of asbestos personal injury lawsuits ("Bodily Injury") or property contamination ("Property Damage") with indemnity for jury verdicts and settlements quickly mounting into the hundreds of millions of dollars, and then there were all of those attorney's fees. In some instances, those Syndicates at Lloyds had primary coverage; but in most instances, they had reinsured American or

European primary carriers. Massive losses followed, then bankruptcies, suicides, and other unthinkable outcomes. The money to pay those vast array of indemnity obligations at Lloyds, under their time-tested working model, had dried up.

A new business model, or models, was needed to replace that centuries old model of Lloyds in order to keep the world's economic countries financially viable. Hence, this Convocation of those interested in bringing a new multi-billion-dollar casualty insurance market into being.

I was to be the keynote speaker and, along with Professor McDonald, we were to advise on the potentials for new Mass Torts threatening the capitalist economies during the early decades of the Twenty-First Century.

Corbett and I met twice to finalize our outlines, key points and observations. I met with the panel for the opening session and was given a small role, with less than one minute to fill. I spent considerable time with John, Manny & Gerry discussing business. Then one evening John and Gerry hosted a private dinner at Brown's Hotel for those mentioned above following the Convocation's Opening Ceremony and Cocktail Party. Most of us repaired to the bar at the Sheraton Belgravia for a night cap. My son, Robert, attended all of that evening and shared a few beverages. I made certain he limited his alcoholic intake (did my Dad thing!).

More than four hundred invitations were issued for this Lloyds Convocation. About two hundred replied, most accepting, but many of those were unclear on whom would attend. On the Opening Morning for Registration (about one hundred having registered at the cocktail event), there was a level of surprise amongst the organizers when more than an additional two hundred were in lines to register. More poured in as the morning moved forward. The weather was sunny and warm. Inside Grey's Inn's Main Hall, the one-foot-thick stone walls kept out the bulk of the heat. Chairs for one hundred and eighty had filled about half of the hall. One hundred more were brought in before ten o'clock, and they were filled. Some stood. Others leaned against the walls.

We began with the Opening Panel and spent twenty minutes, per schedule. Then, I took the floor for the first substantive session and introduced my co-speaker and world-famous scientist, Dr. J.Corbett McDonald. We outlined the categories of toxins we were going to discuss, explained how we chose them, and then proceeded to discuss each: Tobacco, Hybrid Foods, New Mass Torts (particularly California's PROP 65 as a starter laboratory for that state's aggressive plaintiff bar), government condemnation of evolving chemical compounds, and technological piracy. We pointed out how each of these could take many forms, e.g., for Tobacco, a process called Vaping was beginning to burst onto that scene, all with no known research. How long before lawsuits would follow based on uncertain science?

Many questions were left unanswered. As Corbett told me the moment we ended, "Better left unanswered. Most toxin topics ended with the most we could say was 'a great deal of research will be needed to achieve any form of scientific consensus.'" Then, Corbett added, "but that will not stop the greedy from suing, especially in America."

Robert waited off to the side while I answered questions and conferred with a good many attendees. Based on some things he had said at dinner the night before, and granted he was tired/jet-lagged from his eleven hour flight, I was not even certain he would make the earliest presentations (all mine). Yet, there he was, "That was amazing. All the people around me were taking in every word the two of you spoke. Some of them were in awe that you had Dr. McDonald as your 'live co-speaker.' At least one thought he was dead. Where do he and you come up with all of that information? Or, is some of it speculation?"

As we walked to lunch to meet up with our bigger contingent, I told him, "A great deal of what we said is highly refined predictions based on our careers in different scientific research and, in my case, the law involving cases based on toxic substances (or words to that affect). We would make up lists of topics, some we discuss first between ourselves, and then on those which we agreed, with appropriate types with whom we work or associate whose opinions should prove reliable. We rewrite. We test out our theories on others. That was the nature of what these people want to hear. They do not want to be surprised by accidentally underwriting a risk they did not know might exist. Did you read those two papers I gave you for background on the people who would be attending this meeting?"

Robert was impressed. He spent so much of his time listening all of that day and the morning of the next. Our group stayed together for about forty minutes at lunch and then split up with a promise to meet up at the Convocation's Cocktail Party and Dinner. Patrick Tyne arrived that afternoon, and gravitated to Robert ever so quickly. (Princeton had lost a very close game in the NCAA Eastern Regional Final, and was eliminated. Everyone at that school was utterly delighted with their showing, especially Elsa and his mother, Carolyn. Patrick's coach announced that he would return for one more year!) Bud O'Sullivan, John's son, also arrived in time for cocktails.

Although "the boys" had each other, each of three saw this event as a giant learning opportunity and spent a great deal of time listening to our attendees' conversations. Gerry Dwyer of Connecticut Indemnity was impressed with Patrick Tyne, and for that matter, with Robert, saying, among other things, "They are so tall. So handsome. So avid at listening. John told me that Patrick is so good that me might be able to play basketball professionally. Is that really true? And, how did you, then your sons get to be so tall? I don't think of the Irish as a particularly tall race."

I begged-off from answering that first query, but I knew Patrick kept being approached by would-be agents. He went to his coach for first tier advice, but I expected his mother would assist in that regard before this coming Summer was at an end. I only told those who asked, "It might turn out to be true. As for the height thing: we all know that Scandinavians can be quite tall. But you may not know that for centuries the Norsemen paid mostly unwelcome visits to the Irish coastal areas, some settled there, others were less kind. Either way, that may have contributed to the height thing, or it could just be a natural genetic progression."

The weather continued to grow warmer as the afternoon wore on, but the one-foot thick stone walls of Grey's Inn kept its main chamber coolish. Perhaps that outside heat helped the attendance inside to grow almost to overflowing.

The sessions had changed from risk topics to those dealing with potential future financial structures which might prove beneficially available to support revisions of the London Market as the continuing underpinning for a world Property and Casualty Insurance marketplace through the layers of risk assumption needed to create the confidence to buy the products marketed around the world to the consuming public in its various guises. In other words: how could a more reliable system of reinsurance and retroceding be established if the "Old Lloyds" business model was to be superseded?

Some of those sessions were shorter in total program speaking and participation time, but broke up into segments to allow discussion of the concepts being evolved among the attendees who moved about and interacted in accordance with their respective interests. Much of the smaller group dynamic occurred outside the Great Hall on the grounds of the Inn.

On a short break between sessions, I encountered Gerry Dwyer who could not wait to tell me that this might be the most important financial meeting "in the history of 'our insurance world,' as we know it." She allowed that she wished she could clone herself to be in more than one group at a time so she would get a better grip on the concepts being espoused, and especially those that might be gaining favor. She was not alone in that mindset.

At the conclusion of that first day's sessions, Quincy Franden-Jones saw me, then John O'Sullivan saw us both. Although we each had various follow-ups still to complete before repairing to change for the evening events, they both were ecstatic about the manner in which the attendees morphed into groups and began to react in ways that indicated a willingness to be creative to assure that a flexible working model of a "New Lloyds" would evolve in the near term. On that note of optimism, we all went our separate ways.

I met my sons at the appointed meeting place. Bud O'-Sullivan asked to join us and we taxied to the Sheraton Belgravia together: a relatively short ride. Bud allowed that his father did not plan to change and was staying at the Inn and continuing to interact with other attendees. To be sure we maximized our attendance, I asked the taxi driver to return and fetch us promptly at 6:30. He agreed. We all planned to be back at that point for the return. I quickly read two short faxes, then called Lily at my office and gave her some instructions for dealing with the faxes and to check in on any other significant developments. There was an expert issue on the *Roseville* matter needing my attention. While I freshened up and changed outfits, I thought about it. Martha was unavailable, so I left a message for her with Lily. Then a quick check-in with Carolyn and back to the taxi where the "Boys" were all inside awaiting me. Returning to the Cocktail Party on the terraced lawns of Grey's Inn, we found a massive imbibing activity was in full swing with the buzz of conversation creating an enveloping sound almost having a life of its own! Bud advised on our return ride that his Dad had reserved table 46 for ten of us in the main dining hall. We also decided to mingle individually to see what, if any, developments were being discussed in this seemingly very wide open forum.

The number of bars on the lawns was more than sufficient; each had a wine, spirits and other beverage sections. The first two sections each had two lines which moved fairly well. Thus, the amount of alcohol readily available called into question the number of cocktails to be consumed.

After an hour or so, I ran into Patrick Tyne who was drinking from a bottle of water. He allowed that with basketball season having just ended, he was not in condition to drink anything like he might be able in the months ahead (assuming he would not be playing any ball on his return to Princeton from this trip and where he would be taking some courses to ease his final year's workload, assure he graduated with his class, and could marry Elsa shortly after his graduation). All the while, Patrick was grinning, and on his leaving to join another group, said, "I assume you do not live like this all the time. Mom tells us some stories of where you stay over here and what you do. Plus, we have all seen your Paris lifestyle. So, all of this does not come as a complete surprise. What it does tell me is how highly you are respected by so many of the people here, especially your clients, John and Gerry."

At the end of a somewhat overlong drinking fest of almost two hours for me (every other beverage for me was water), we all began to gather at Table 46 in the mid-point rear of the Great Hall but looking across the room directly at the Speakers Dias, but seven tables-for-ten away from us. Each two tables had a waiter whose job was to sell and deliver beverages. Quincy, sitting on the Dias had alerted our waiter to be extremely attentive while John had doubtless supplied a stipend well ahead to smooth any wrinkles. Bradley Campbell, Solicitor, and Madeline Myles, COO of LTL, joined us for the first time, and they brought Stanley Booth, Chairman of Cheshire and Booth, one of the largest of the London Placing Brokerage Houses, and his son, Frederick, well-known to many of us for his role in locating so very many missing reinsurance policy files in their vast subterranean floors of paper gathered over centuries.

Young Mr. Booth who was more than a few inches taller than six feet, took one look at my two sons: Patrick almost nine inches above six feet and Robert, perhaps an inch taller than his older brother, and gravitated over toward them, engaging by asking, "Are you both going to be playing for the Yanks' golf team in Ireland in a few days?" When they answered in the affirmative, Frederick disengaged from his father and joined the three younger men announcing that he too was to play as well, and he was the UK's team's youngest by far. He also allowed that Bradley and Madeline were to play, and neither of them had an actual handicap. He then said his was eleven which made him above a mid-level player on the UK team. In the course of discussing that tournament, Bud O'Sullivan allowed that Rugby was his main sport which created a lengthy digression as that sport originated in the UK. Getting back to the main topic, Bud allowed that he was a twelve but had not played much lately. Patrick Tyne, looking a bit peeked, added, "I'm afraid I'm a four, but Robert is better. He's a two. But like Bud's rugby season ending, basketball just ended for me last weekend. So, I have not played even two or three rounds this year.'

Robert chipped in, "My high school season ended two weeks ago when we lost in the California semi-finals. But, I played four rounds since then."

Frederick asked Patrick, "How come your season lasted so long in college?"

Bud jumped in, "Patrick may not blow his own horn. I live two thousand miles from Princeton and go to university almost four hundred miles away. In the USA college sport systems, each for men and for women has an end of year tournament to decide the National Championship. The Biggest Tournament of all is Men's Basketball. All of those games are televised nationally and into Canada as well. Forty-two teams were selected to play for the basketball title. Princeton did not get a bye, so it had to play and win six games to win it all. Ohio State did not get in, and we were pretty good. When my Dad told me that we would be meeting Patrick Tyne who played for Princeton, I decided to watch in our fraternity gathering room. It's an athletic fraternity, you have to play a varsity sport to belong. Other members watched as well. The Tigers, that's Princeton, blew out a small conference champ by maybe forty points in its first game. Then, they drew a good team from the Philadelphia area, and won a close game. In the last minutes of that close game, when things got nip-and-tuck, the ball for Princeton kept going through one pair of hands— Pat Tyne—rebounds, assists, a steal, and four baskets. One of the announcers ended that broadcast by saying, "We have an Ivy League star on our hands. After a very long wait for Princeton, that would be Patrick Tyne!"

Somewhere during Bud's praises, the other conversations around Table 46 stopped. When Bud paused, his father, from several seats away, asked, "What happened next?"

Frederick added, "Yes, please go on"

With that little prompting, and having a stage, Bud went on, "Part of the advertising on TV for the next set of games, the Sweet Sixteen, which were staged in four markets, winning two games to get into the Final Four. Featured in the Eastern venue, Madison Square Garden in New York City, the only team of those four from that regional area was Princeton. So, the TV advertising showed Patrick in split seconds making two big plays from that last Princeton win and the camera turns instantly to these two beautiful women who are going simply nuts, jumping out of their seats, and then onward to others. My fellow frat members by now knew who Pat Tyne was, but they wanted to know about the two women. I called my Dad. He called Mr. O'Neill. Turns out they were Pat's girlfriend and his mother, Mrs. O'Neill.

"Anyway, The Tigers won their first game in the Garden and Pat Tyne was again a standout. And, the camera found those same two women again. Now, they got into the papers, things like "... a star is born...." Then along came Duke two nights later. Patrick's play was heroic. Despite a really great team effort, Princeton lost. But fans in orange and black poured onto the floor. That joy, even in a losing cause is why that Sweet Sixteen TV weekend is the highpoint of the college basketball season."

Patrick just sat there as Bud kept going on and on. He did turn a slight shade of pink. Robert was taken aback by some of Bud's descriptions, especially the two women that were singled out by the TV cameras. Gerry Dwyer, smiling ever so slightly, spoke first, "Patrick, I had no idea you had become a celebrity in the last few weeks. But, of course I have met your mother and know why she is. Has the media connected who she is with you, as yet?"

He had to answer something, "I guess I got a certain level of recognition among U.S. college basketball fans, but I cannot believe it will be any more than that."

Robert jumped in, "I play against Patrick quite a bit and I know how good he is—REALLY Good! My good news is I get to play with him next year because freshmen are eligible and Princeton has admitted me early based on Advanced Placement."

I let out an audible gasp; two Princeton tuitions and one

Stanford. Yikes!! To Robert, I said, "Congratulations! I didn't know anything about this entire process."

Patrick quickly responded, "Mom wanted to surprise you, I guess the five of us succeeded," and with that he was smiling broadly, adding, "and Elsa and I plan to announce our engagement when I return at the beginning of next season."

Bud looked at him, jaw dropping, "How lucky can one man be!" His remark brought those five minutes to a humorous conclusion, and we all then moved on to other topics, most of us trying to sort out the rumors and speculations abounding from the day's events. Quincy dropped by Table 46 and spoke with small clusters, longer with his UK compatriots. We all agreed that a trend appeared to be forming that corporate members would be allowed to participate at Lloyds for the first time in the history of that market, but HOW?.

The final morning of the Convocation tried to give some life to the speculation of the night before as the last panel attempted to sift through some of the many concepts advanced and called for those interested in continuing participation in one or more of those concepts to form into committees and to work through a central coordinating group here in London with committee participation open worldwide thereafter.

We returned to Table 46 for the closing lunch and speeches. Attendance was notably lighter than the second day's sessions and more departed as the luncheon wore on. Quincy left the dais moments before the meeting's conclusion and made his way to Table 46. He spoke to all of the official attendees, describing potential committees and suggesting participation by each entity present except LTL.

When he finished, I mentioned that omission to him. He said that at some point that might make some sense, but that entity might be objectional to some of the funding entities based on its role in collecting from so many syndicates. I allowed that he had just given the very reason LTL should be part of the mix as transparency and credibility were going to be bye-words for any new entity and LTL was one of a very few entities that fairly and fully understood the nature of collecting funds from reluctant reinsurers and retrocessionaires.

Quincy not having participated in LTL, but doubtless having been a source of counsel to reluctant putative payor names (not forgetting for a moment that barristers did not have conflict of interest rules in the sense of the American Bar), apparently was not going to back LTL to his colleagues in London, perhaps a critical omission. I glanced at John O'-Sullivan who bobbed his head once and turned to Gerry Dwyer who did the same.

"Quincy, you have been most kind in including all of us in this Convocation and the ensuing golf outing, would you be ever so kind as to include me as a member of your London Steering Committee, preferably with a voting right?" Before he could answer, Gerry and John both spoke seconding my request, to which I added, "Surely your experience would indicate that a few American insurers should have a role in this overall process as they will be a primary potential purchaser of the products put forth by the New Lloyds group, not to mention possible investors depending on all of the schemes coming together (I chose the British vernacular for that point. Q's nod told me it was taken). What do you think, Stanley?"

The managing partner of Cheshire & Booth, a major

Lloyds Placing Broker, thought for a second, then, "I can see both sides of the issue when it comes to LTL, but that entity had a very significant role in keeping the entire collection process civilized, and bringing all of the people here for these meetings. If Mr. O'Neill is a participant on the London Committee, I will volunteer Frederick here to participate for our firm and other smaller brokers. In the event issues arise where LTL's advice is needed, between the two of them, Ronan or Frederick can seek their advice or even produce Ms. Myles to confer. I believe that would be a reasonable compromise."

Heads nodded affirmatively. Quincy, putting a good face forward, allowed, "I shall get back to everyone on this request in the very near term. Those of us 'Off to Surrey' tomorrow should be fully packed and meet at the west gate of the Temple tomorrow a.m. Our motor coach will wish to depart by 9:15, so please be early, if possible. We shall go from Surrey directly to Heathrow and depart from there to Cork on *Aer Lingus*. A motor coach will meet us there and take us to Killarney for a late dinner and a good night's sleep."

Quincy departed, spoke briefly with one or two others, and disappeared. Stanley Booth bid us a farewell as he was no longer golfing with back problems. That left nine golfers: six Americans and three from the UK, the latter three residing in London and the rest of us at the Sheraton Belgravia. We parted company outside the front entrance to Grey's Inn where a virtual taxi stand was fully functioning. John O'Sullivan asked Manny and me to join him for a nightcap in the hotel's small bar, having abandoned The Berkeley for one night. He allowed we could discuss the meeting more on the morrow when taxing to the Temple west gate. With our clubs and clothes, we ordered three taxis for 8:30. Then, John wanted to talk about the golf match. The Killarney Golf Club was to be a four-ball event. The other six Americans were all handicapped in the 15-20 range. The three of us were among the highest handicaps, and played very little. So, John suggested that each of us join one of the youngsters and play as a team for one round. (Quincy had provided John with seven handicaps. Neither Madeline nor Bradley Campbell had a handicap. So, those two would play with a 36, but it was not clear what we were up against otherwise. The next day's round at Surrey might help clarify some of this, but some of the UK team was not playing in Surrey!) As a result, we went to bed somewhat timely, but uncertain of our golf and underfed with no meaningful dinner.

The best parts of the coach ride to Surrey that next morning were the black coffee and the bacon sandwiches!

3

THE IRISH GOLF TOURNAMRNT

A proper Irish breakfast had at least one more item on its plate than an English one.

We all were starved by the time we had our morning constitutional and some attempt to locate the bellowing red deer (looking ever so much size and shape-wise like an American elk) which had howled in its mating ritual seemingly half-way through the preceding night. A long, exciting day, followed by travel, Guinness, and a small dinner, and all of the glories of travel, especially our golf clubs not coming off our aircraft. Mercifully, Quincy and his clerk, Wilfred Smythe, worked tirelessly to assure that all of the twenty-two sets of clubs were aboard last night's last flight and were outside our hotel even at that moment. The Cahernane House was a mile or so west of Killarney town, by the time we returned from our walk into the town proper, our clubs were in plain view. Everything was so green, on that walk: so many different shades and shapes of plants and trees in this hilly, soon to be mountainous, gateway to the Western Coast of Ireland around the oceanside view of County Kerry on a road network known as the Ring of Kerry.

On the trip over, we learned that two Englishmen had come over a few days earlier to play Killarney and Salt Point, the first two courses for team play. We also learned more about each other's golf in Surrey. The younger generation hit their balls so much further than any of the rest of us. It was truly shocking. No one's short game was great, and their iron games were shaky at times. Still, everyone was within shouting distance of their handicaps.

A hole in one at Surrey was the pride of a Nebraskan Convocation attendee who insisted on Champaign for everyone. He had never been to England. That meant his prolonged celebration led to a rushed trip to Heathrow and probably contributed to our golf clubs missing our flight. Ah, but this Irish Tournament, with its Ryder Cup format, was to be a once in a lifetime adventure!

Our motor coach trip to the Killarney Golf & Shooting Club was uneventful. Earlier that morning we had worked out the pairings and set our team's order of play. John O'-Sullivan as the USA Captain felt he should go first to allow him to finish earliest and be available to encourage his other teammates. With his son's agreement, they were the first twosome to play. Wilfred Smythe, advertised as a 15 handicap, and a young partner from one of the solicitor firms, as their opponents, teeing off at 1:20. We put Patrick Tyne with Manny in third position and I was partnered with Robert in the number six slot.

The course was on gently rolling hills with creeks in play as well as drainage ditches. Much of the course was defined by Killarney's lakes that divided the club's property for its disparate uses. Five or six holes, depending on the player's first shot, brought that water into play. The weather was lovely as was the course's condition. Two barristers whom we barely knew from Twenty King's Bench Walk were our opponents. For the first three holes, they complained of the effects of their drinking exploits of the night before.

We teed-off at 2:20 and won two of those first lake holes

and halved the other. That seemed to get their attention and their play improved noticeably. Unfortunately, for them, my younger son, Robert, was warming up as well. On hole number 4, he had a drive of more than 300 yards, stuck his second shot within three feet of that hole and made the birdie putt. We halved the par three hole five, but Robert barely missed an eagle putt on hole 6. When they conceded his birdie putt, we were ahead by four holes. We won the front nine by five; and our match was over after hole 12 with Robert and I having a seven-hole lead with six holes left to play (7 & 6).

The rest of our team had varying results. Patrick and Manny managed to win after a par on the 17th hole to go up two holes with one to play. Gerry and one of her senior managers in London won as well 3 and 2, defeating Madeline's team. But John and his son Bud drew the British pair with Wilfred as their star player, put up a fight, but lost 3 and 2. Quincy's pair also won, 4 and 3, as did the pair on which Bradley was the B player. So, it ended tied with three points apiece in the Four-Ball Round. We had a late afternoon match the next day in what had been changed to Kenmare. The motorcoach took about half of the players back to Killarney House, but my two sons and I got dropped with some others in downtown Killarney where we shopped for souvenirs for half hour and then met the Scottsdale threesome in a pub for a pint before getting taxis back to our hotel.

Dinner that night was tables of six: three from each team. Quincy was one of the UK people and I knew no one else, except Bud O'Sullivan who sat across from me. Quincy allowed that he had spent most of his time since returning from the golf on the phone from London with some of the steering committee members. He asked me if a short meeting right after dinner would not be inappropriate. I excused myself and was back in less than five minutes. "I told them it would be about New Lloyds. I hope I was correct?" I asked him.

"Yes," Quincy responded. "They have an idea and they want to run up a test balloon on some Yank companies. They know what I'm up to, and they know you and who all of you are."

As others broke into different groups following Port wine and cheese, John, Gerry, their number twos, along with Bradley, Quincy and me sat around one table, off to the side of the dining room. Three pints of Guinness and a bottle of Johnnie Walker Black Label, ice cubes and glasses were on the table.

Quincy began, "The issue is one of capital for the New Lloyds. Would your companies, or an entity under their control here in the UK be willing to put up original capital as a contribution to start a new enterprise. The details are ones that have been discussed on and off for years, essentially a limited liability corporate structure under English law. Perhaps hundreds of them, as underpinning for an enterprise with somewhat less grandiose returns than Old Lloyds, frankly uncertain at the outset and dependent on the overall success of the entire enterprise, including limitations on types of reinsurance and probably substantially different accounting and treatment of any potential long-tail enterprising.

"But for now, the key question is whether or not this is a concept worth pursuing as a serious avenue to bringing this new entity into being. We are not asking for a commitment at this point. More options need to be agreed upon and solutions created, but that's the very basic framework. Any questions?"

We broke at 12:30 a.m., agreeing we would try to have two or more answers by week's end.

I did not feel one hundred percent the next morning, but Manny button-holed me on the way to breakfast, saying, "Can you find out very quickly the thinking on what might be a minimum capital contribution?"

When I asked Quincy, he said too soon, but for planning purposes, maybe 5-10,000,000 pounds, or something up in that range. He also allowed that they were thinking about non-voting members with smaller contributions like one million pounds max. Manny left. John and he returned in about fifteen minutes. Gerry was with them. John said, "Those types of numbers beg other questions, like what kind of yield, how big an interest, what prevents dilution of interest, for how long, and more. Depending on those answers and others, it presents a potential pathway. Gerry, do you agree?"

She did, I took those responses to Quincy. By then it was time to begin the process of moving our troop from Killarney to Kenmare on the Ring of Kerry Road. With its spectacular views, frighteningly narrow passing spots, all on surfaces mountainous and sometimes poorly maintained, provided a jolly two-hour ride. The last few minutes took us through the Kenmare Golf Links where we would soon engage in our two-ball match. The Kenmare Hotel, located just beyond the starter's shed, was another of the grand Irish hotels undoubtedly constructed to afford the Anglo-Irish aristocracy a retreat from the likes of Dublin and Cork, reachable by hired transportation in a day, two at most. The charming village was just to the west, made adjacent to the hotel by a scenic footpath above, and along, the Kenmare River.

Following check-in and a late luncheon of sandwiches and salads, we began our match. John O'Sullivan, paired with Manny, opted to go out last and requested that I, paired with Patrick, go off in the first match. That gave us little time to warm-up. Our opponents were Quincy and Wilfred, two of the better UK players. Patrick scanned the course book to get a rough idea of its layout; and then, suggested that I tee-off on the first hole. He wanted me on the left side of the fairway. I wish I was good enough to have that level of control (If I did not know a course, I always aimed for the middle of the fairway.). On this shot, my aim proved somewhat true. Quincy teed it up for the UK team, hit it down the left side and outdrove me by a good thirty yards. Being a par five, my shot left more than 300 yards downhill to the green. Patrick took out his five wood and whispered, "There's nothing between the flag and your ball except grass. I'll see what I can do."

He drew his five-wood back and brought it forward in a shortish swing that seemed to end quickly. Our ball shot forward perhaps only twenty or so feet above the fairway following what sounded like a rifle shot of contact between club-face and ball. As the fairway sloped gently downward the ball seemed not to want to come down as its elevation followed the descent of the hillside. When it landed, the ball's first hop was not high, but sped it forward rolling rapidly toward the green, only slowing as it approached the flag itself. I had a putt of about a six feet for an eagle.

As Wilfred approached his ball, he said too clearly to Quincy, "We could be in for a very short day if that keeps up." He hit an excellent, but high, three-wood which came to rest about 50 yards from the flag, and said, "Better hit it close and hope Ronan misses."

I did not miss, mostly because Patrick saw the overall tilt of the hillside's effect on the putt's break as it would slow and set me a few more inches of break than I otherwise would have played. We conceded them their birdie. Patrick was to drive on number two, and when he pulled out his driver, Quincy asked, "Does that club have an extra-long shaft?"

Patrick smiled, saying, "All of my clubs, my Dad's, and my whole golfing family have customized shafts because we are all so tall. Otherwise. How could we swing properly?"

Patrick's drive uphill carried about 260 yards. Wilfred's went maybe 210.

We won the front nine by three holes and the match after number fourteen with a five-hole lead. Robert and Bud were the third match and they won even more decisively, up eight with seven to play, against Madeline Myles' team. They were most complimentary of her golfing outfit. At the end of the day, USA led UK by one point as we had six victories to their five; and, two matches were halved.

Dinner and our second evening were more relaxing and we had the day free on the morrow, with our motorcoach leaving for Waterville at noon. That afternoon was to be given over to a tour of the Skelligs for those interested, and adventurous enough, including a boat ride to Skellig Michael, the most preserved of those towering mini-islands.

As the motorcoach pulled away from the Kenmare Hotel, Wilfred, the Chief Clerk of Twenty Kings Bench Walk, picked up the driver's tour bus microphone, and introduced Ciaran O'Halloran, Chief Historian at Trinity College on

County Kerry, who began, "The Irish have been on this island and its extensions for a very long time. They were civilized for almost two thousand years as various races melded together. Kerry is among the most ancient intact counties still not fully modernized. Please allow me to tell you more."

On arriving in Waterville, Quincy allowed that he had received a call from the Steering Committee's secretary, and based on its history, albeit brief, the committee would acquiesce in LTL attending certain sessions as a non-voting attendee at the outset. (I thought, doubtless the interest of the American property carriers as potential investors might have had something to do with that concession. Still, let's see how far it goes?) They had also approved adding me, but were not clear on any guidelines for "voting members."

4

WATERVILLE

The Professor O'Halloran's recital of the Waterville area's history started by featuring its topography, mountains all around this cut-off *Imeragh* peninsula, with Ballinskelligs Bay to the south, Lough Currane to the north and the Waterville River on the west, gave a romance to its name, but only to be matched by my first glimpse of that wondrous area viewed from high up in the east as our motorcoach paused on its first siting from an outlook seemingly 1,000 feet above the Atlantic Ocean. Then down a twisting narrow mountainside road with occasional glimpses as Ciaran told us the story of the golf links upon which we were to play our singles matches the following day. They were built originally as ten holes to provide some amusement for all the men involved in the unending "eleven month task" of bringing ashore the first European connection with the Transatlantic Cable from America back in the late Nineteenth Century. The course was expanded to eighteen holes several decades later in the Twentieth Century by a group from Chicago who ultimately sold it to the town. The Waterville Golf Links occupies that last spit of land between the town proper and the Waterville River flowing southward to empty into Ballinskellig Bay before that body melds into the often-wild North Atlantic Ocean on this, the most western of the southwestern points on the Irish Isle. That location was the very reason why that cable came ashore there. Lough Currane, formed the northern edge of the village and was one of the most grand spots in Europe to sport fish for Salmon.

The Butler Arms Hotel occupied the west side of the Waterville Town Square (more of a trapezoid). Straight across from that hotel on square's east side was the Chaplin Mansion. (No mystery about it, as the entryway to the Butler Arms was a veritable photographic museum of several decades of the early "Chaplin years" as Charley and his second wife produced another family over several decades, including daughter Geraldine, a star in *Doctor Zhivago*, well before our visit. Information flowed freely from our hosts, the owners of the Butler Arms, John & Mary. The south side of the square was the Bay itself and the north side of the Square was the town's Main Street, replete with the usual Irish shops providing tourist goods and some necessities. My assigned room, a single, was on the ground floor with a view of the parking lot. (For an extra fifty Euros per night, I got a very nice room with a view of the mountain from which we had descended into town. The bath was modern and I was on the top floor. Others upgraded as well. My sons, both very tall, were pleased with the bedding arrangements in Ireland where most of the twin beds were about eighteen inches wider and ten inches longer than in the USA hotels. They shared a double twin room throughout the golf tour.

A tour with a boat trip to Skellig Michael, followed by a small bus tour of Valencia Island was available to eight brave hearts. My two sons and I were the first volunteers. Bud O'Sullivan went along, but not his father who was forthright about his fear of the North Atlantic (The Titanic and all those things!). Gerry Dwyer and Madeline Myles were the only other volunteers, just as well, and a bit of a surprise. The VW mini-bus was a bit crowded with the driver/tour director and we six, four of whom were relatively large individuals. Seamus offered us each a bottle of lager or one of water, as he mentioned that the boat ride could prove quite damp depending on "how the sea was running." Expecting a chill off-shore, we were all wearing our foul-weather golf outfits and tennis shoes. The ride to a small village of seemingly less than ten structures, called Kilrelig, took but a few site-filled minutes (many ruins and mentions of the devastation visited by Cromwell and his men on Ireland and especially its Catholics, not long after Elizabeth's death). "Quite a few of the area's inhabitants fled to the Skelligs at their coming, Not all returned when they left," a tone of bitterness having crept into Seamus' voice.

Seamus drove through the small town and out onto a jetty, ending just where the inlet lost its protection from the ocean waters proper. The vessel was about 45 feet long and had a somewhat wide beam. It looked a bit like a tugboat, but with higher gunwales. The tide appeared in and we walked up a gangplank with a rope handhold to board. Interestingly, Seamus boarded with us. We moved to the stern, quite open and found benches with cushions. Seamus introduced the boat's captain, Marcus O'Lynch. He spoke for a minute describing the voyage we were about to undertake. Then, he asked if any of us had been to sea, e.g., meaning the ocean, before this day? My sons and I allowed we had as did Gerry and Bud. He asked us about where we had done so. Most described resort towns, I went last and said, simply, "Down the Atlantic from Virginia to Nassau. Across the Pacific and the coastal waters of Southeast Asia."

O'Lynch to me: "Military?"

Me: "Coast Guard, Viet Nam."

Him: "Action?"

Me: "A few times."

O'Lynch: "How big was your boat?"

Me: "82 feet. Save you the trouble, I was the Executive Officer."

To everyone on deck: "This is my boat, Maureen, after my mother. I am in charge of everything on this voyage. In rare instances, I get to have a back-up. This is one. Your rank?"

Me: "Commander."

The skipper: "If for any reason, I become unavailable, you all, including crew, answer to the Commander here, Ronan O'Neill."

He turned and went up the ladder to the wheelhouse. He spoke into a tube and the engines showed signs of life. Seamus and a deckhand casted off and we moved sideways and slightly backwards from the jetty, turned ninety degrees and set off toward a stone pillar rising out of the waters of Ballinskelligs Bay.

As we drew nearer, Seamus said, "This first Skellig is 'Gabriel.' Named for the archangel. As was the case for some hundreds of years, monks, hermits of sorts inhabited these strange formations. They were literate and spent their days in prayer and reproducing the writings brought to them for that purpose. When Rome was about to be burned and looted as its western empire fell, some of that city's fathers sent their progeny by boat to Ireland and specifically to these Skelligs and some near-by monasteries to reproduce those writings and preserve whatever they could of Rome's history and culture. It is not safe enough to go ashore here for first time visitors."

We came up on Skellig Gabriel at a slow speed. The seas were relatively calm, and the Maureen rode low in the water. Seamus explained that a few of the Skelligs had a tie-up or a bit of an anchorage. Skellig Michael where we would debark and tour was the best, being maintained by the Irish National Park Service. After circling Gabriel twice, we pushed further out into the Bay and headed northward. We could see more Skelligs at various distances, each appearing somewhat different from the others in their craggy rocklike towering shapes.

Dead ahead standing taller and wider than any of the other Skellligs stood what must be Michael. We approached straight at it and began to move to port (left), and very slowly circled this monument, noting a landing with tie-up on the lea of this obelisk of an island. We came around a second time and Captain O'Lynch brought Maureen up next to the dock where Seamus and his younger brother, the deckhand, made the vessel somewhat fast dropping fenders over the vessel's side to prevent any damage from any water's sudden harsh action.

They put out the gangplank and, following Seamus single-file, we went ashore. A brief view of our surroundings added little. Seamus encouraged us to climb, and we did: up-and-up and around the monolith, until suddenly we were on a grassy lookout of greater than 200 degrees. Our view was so special, squinting across the Bay to make out what was probably the town of Waterville.

'Twas an awesome sight with all of the water around and below our perch, and a bit of a sea mist beginning to form. We were mostly speechless. Seamus allowed we could buy a snack or a beer, paying under an honor system. Madeline stepped forward and said, "This is a day I shall not soon forget. I was leery of coming on this bit of a detour to our Pub-crawl, but these Skelligs are an education unto themselves, and I suggest that we all share some crisps and raise a bottle to Archangel Michael. My Treat!" At the end of that little speech, Madeline held my eye for a fraction of a second as she surveyed her shipmates, or so it seemed.

Seamus explained that Skellig Michael contained the largest living area of all of the surviving Skelligs which for some period of centuries served as human habitats. Following his introduction, our guide/bus driver invited those willing to climb the ancient rough-hewn stone steps to the uppermost areas. Everyone followed, and I was assigned to bring up the rear. More steps than I think most of us expected were needed to make the winding assent to that essentially flat area, which had three large livable-looking caves.

When I came fully upon the viewing area, I was shocked by how high we seemed relative to the sea below, which was still quite resounding as its waves beat against this ancient rock tower, yet it was the view outward to the north that took my breath away. Skellig Michael, unnoticed as we descended into Waterville had the most astounding view of the very road we had travelled earlier in that day.

I was so taken by the shapes and colors that all I could do was look. The silence was eerie. No one was speaking. Finally, Seamus broke the mood, "Your reaction, each of you, is not at all unusual. When first seen, following that climb, the panorama appears otherworldly." (Those words came back to me years later as I watched the next to last *Star Wars* sequel and the discovery of the reclusive Luke Skywalker's "place of respite" at its inception: there, on that very shelf above the Atlantic. Having been to that very spot myself only made that film all the more magical.)

When we all got our voices, the enthusiasm, and appreciation, of undertaking this foray was made all the more worthwhile by sharing it with my sons and my friends. I knew as I stood there that I would need to return to this very spot one day soon with my whole family!

The adventure of the boat ride back to its dock, the tour of Valencia Island with its ancient dwellings so well-preserved, not to mention its ancient cemeteries, followed by the late onset of the sunset from a most-western point in Europe, the cumulative effect of that day was ever more exciting (also making a lasting impression on the rest of my life). Listening to Seamus' recanting of the Skelligs history and scaling Skellig Michael gave me a sense of renewal in my faith in God.

Changing and meeting in the hotel bar with our twenty-four, Quincy greeted us with the news that there was sufficient enthusiasm from Western insurance carriers to undertake a share of underwriting the new London casualty market that a subcommittee was being formed to persuade Parliament to change some of the laws surrounding Lloyds and its charter (a necessary predicate to a change in unlimited liability). Moreover, there as a sense that this foundational funding would provide the impetus to further creative structuring permitting individual entities to invest in Lloyds. All that said, one central question remained: what form would the new entities take in that new market?

That topic was discussed repeatedly during the remainder of our tour.

The next day's singles match, in which I drew our Welsh Barrister Quincy as my opponent in the lead-off position for the U.S. team, proved time-consuming and wet. The weather varied between wind, rain, and both. Our all-weather clothes were not really up to the task and a shortage of caddies made the day even more tiring. All things considered, we would probably be fortunate to win.

Gerry Dwyer fell on the Seventh tee box and had to be assisted off the course (this created a win for Madeline Myles, a beginning golfer!). John O'Sullivan's back was not up to all of the activity nor the weather, and he had to withdraw (creating a win for Bradley, our Solicitor, another not very good golfer). So, despite my eking out a win, the three lads winning their matches, and two halves, we lost the day 7-5. With our 6.5 to 5.5 lead from the first two days, we lost the tournament 12.5 to 11.5.

At dinner that night, Quincy had Wilfred present him with the Twenty King's Bench Walk Jug, saying in effect, he would have it engraved and the winning team could have possession for the next year (one month/member). A great deal of cheering, drinking and teasing ensued as we had a private dining room for our final night's event. I spent time with everyone to a greater or lesser degree, but knew many of us would be on the same bus to Cork Airport on the 'morrow. As I bid Madeline good night, she whispered, "Your adjoining door goes to my room. Please come over when you finish your calls. I will be pleased to await you."

I made all of my calls, then checked, hoping Madeline had fallen asleep. She had not, and she had a few new wrinkles to which she introduced me.

— — —

Most of us flew to JFK outside Manhattan. On landing, Patrick took off for Elsa's apartment in the City. Robert went to the Waldorf and checked us both in for that night. Bud went with him for John. The rest of us went to Gerry's regional office in Mid-town. First we conferred with Quincy by telephone on that Monday's developments, then we met among ourselves, and at two o'clock we broke into two groups and spent upwards of two hours reviewing "New Lloyds developments" with our respective executive committees. Tentative decisions were reached and we reassembled in Gerry's conference room to discuss them with each other. At five o'clock, we decided to go our separate ways. John and Bud had portable phones and John called Bud to advise we would meet in the bar at the Bull and Bear on the Lexington Street side of the Waldorf for drinks and dine there.

On arriving, I saw my old friend Andre on duty behind the Bar just below the huge metallic sculpture of the Bull and Bear locked in mortal combat towering upward from the center of that huge oval bar. The boys saw us and headed our way. Andre whispered something to two gentlemen and we had four seats together at his section of the Bar. My Stoli, four fingers high with ice, but not too much, appeared in a giant red wine tumbler, with a twist on its rim. John took one look at my drink and said to Andre, as we engaged in introductions, "I would love to try one of those!"

Another drink appeared almost as if by magic and the boys both had Heinekens. We stayed right there and went to the dining area, shared scrumptious shrimp cocktails and two giant bone-in rib-eyes, and a bottle of good California Cabernet. At the end, John declared the entire effort a spectacular success and off we went to our beds. It was not yet nine o'clock New York time when I reached Carolyn to wish her a Good -Night, and to have a few words with our Mollie.

On the way to Newark Airport the next morning through the Holland Tunel, Robert could not stop thanking me for that whole trip and the opportunity to have that level of experience at his age.

On the plane to SFO, Robert slept non-stop. After all, he was still a teen-ager.

———

5

MY WORLD AFTER WATERVILLLE

In the weeks to follow, I found myself rejoicing in being home with my family, extended family and the firm. One overarching matter, however, continued to dominate my thoughts, and I began to feel keenly that multi-level funding for its operation was the avenue to a successful "New Lloyds," at least for casualty. Part of my issue was an inability on my behalf to get "our people" to focus on this concept. Most of my clients only seemed concerned about protecting their investment, and not the context of operating in the actual universe of casualty reinsurance.

Carolyn and Mollie met Robert and me at SFO. They loved the souvenirs we had brought for them and shared them admiringly on the drive home, especially the woolen Irish scarves in their various shades of green (there was fog on the Great Highway so they could try them on in comfort). Patrick and Meaghan were delighted to see us. While Elsa's parents and brother were preparing for their return to Sweden, they too wanted to spend some time.

The weather in Ross was a pleasant seventy-five degrees, and the beginnings of a cook-out were underway. In seemingly no time, we were gathered in the rear yard around the bar-b-que grill with conversations covering a variety of topics, not the least of which was Patrick Tyne and Elsa—alone, but together, in New York City.

Her parents were not exactly concerned, but they missed

having Elsa nearby, especially Ludmilla, Elsa's practically recovered mother, still an outpatient at Kentfield Rehab Hospital. Moreover, with their daughter Ingrid in Southern California expecting a second, their son Helmut protesting his trip back to Sweden, and the potential for Gustav's working in the U.S. becoming less of a reality, their whole "trip home" appeared fraught with uncertainty.

— — —

The firm was running very smoothly: as managing partner, Reggie Fox, with his military background including a huge emphasis on planning and communication, kept all of our litigation on track (even mine). I was blessed to have him and told him so frequently. He spoke to me of loyalty, showing in his every action that he meant it. All of my partners were solid professionals, even the youngest. Moreover, the addition of the Connecticut Indemnity work had stretched our staffing to the point where we were adding both lawyers and support staff. Space was about to become an issue. Reggie, Mary and Phil had considered a number of options and a few weeks after my return, we met on the entire expansion issue to accommodate our growth.

Phil felt that Joshua should be made a full partner and that our partners would be needing more help as their work was becoming more diverse and they could use another lead attorney. We talked about a lateral hire, as we had only three junior partners, the other two for less than one year each. Martha wanted to have Felicity Clarke become a junior partner on October first. We agreed on those two promotions and that Phil should start looking for a lateral. With Martha taking an uncertain maternity leave, Felicity was not a candidate to go anywhere, and she was proving to Martha and me to be much better than just good.

Space for four to six more lawyers and staff of about the same number meant either a move, a separate building, or a separate office location in the Bay Area. None of the three were that attractive, especially another office (not enough full partners to support that). Reggie had been in contact with our landlord. A building about half a block away was for sale and would need some build-out. The landlord wanted to buy it, but was thin on capital. Reggie had broached a partnership. The landlord wanted a limited partnership with itself as the general. (I felt that was a bad idea: put up the money, but lose control? No. Just a partnership, but how much/for what percentage?) Or, we must move. (How big was that new building? Not big enough for all we wanted.) What about the floor below in our current location? (Reggie said he was told 'NO' on that one by the landlord. I asked what if we tell him that we would rather move and be all in one space, and see what he says?)

Finally, we decided to start hiring and to shoehorn people into current spaces for the short term. Reggie and Martha would head that up for Oakland and Phil and Joshua would work on Glendale.

Meanwhile, our Roseville client's case was moving forward. Martha was imparting some of her Science & Medicine background to Felicia who had an undergraduate first two years of Pre-Med. In doing so, Martha had Felicia doing the detailed research in case law on lead causation found in appellate decisions as well as reported cases of federal first impression. The concept, suggested in part by our consultant focused on all of the conjecture on potential causation where no scientific consensus was suggested in the opinions, or if contradicted in other decisions. The most certain of causation relationships was lead poisoning, usually in the young, capable of blood testing, known side effects, scientifically explainable, most usually found in contaminated water and lead paint cases. That key method of causation being ingestion.

There was virtually nothing of a legal nature on lowering IQ by virtue of lead exposure. What was raised in those lead cases is whether the plaintiffs had blood tests and what were those results; in other words, was there a sufficient reading of lead poisoning to begin to suggest unusual exposure. Being California state court cases, and because of our state's peculiar rules on medical discovery and required causation pleading, this was an issue which could be deferred until late into these cases.

Plaintiff counsel had begun responding to all of the written discovery which our office had propounded in each case. Other than the threshold questions about relatives and relationships, the balance of the responses dealing with hard facts about the soils, claimed amounts of exposure, and all of the questions about education and IQ were the subjects of discovery objections that they were premature under the California Code of Civil Procedure as they arose from scientific testing, were intrusive on privacy (especially of those who were not parties to the lawsuits), and were without known scientific connection to the subject matter of the lawsuits. Almost without exception, the responses repeated themselves as to each plaintiff. We met, talked briefly, and I made certain suggestions. Martha and Felicia left.

We gathered in my office the next morning. In twenty minutes, we three had agreed to start the beginning of the science battle now by coupling a discovery motion with a

Motion to create a Special Scheduling Order to circumvent the need for deposition discovery of the parties until the key underlying medical data as to each was disclosed. Martha ran our plan past Strom later that day. I got the three key GWF players on a call, went back over our overarching strategy, then explained why we thought the time to get started was now (even if the motions were not granted in their entirety, the theme of a denial might play a heavier role in the future on the ongoing motion practice we anticipated). Andrea Parsons and Stuart Block were fascinated by the process we were planning to use by combining what was almost a Demurrer technique to criticize the lack of any pleading with any scientific basis to support their IQ claims (we felt these to be scientifically weak and full of too many variants to sew further judicial confusion).

I called Attorney Young and asked him to have his side join in a Request for Single Judge Assignment, beginning with this motion practice. After conferring with his partners, they rejected that idea; however, he did acquiesce in a four-week extension to bring our motion practice. So that refusal yielded a third motion: Single Judge to go with Case Management and Discovery Response Compulsion. Felicia was charged with the first two and Martha with the third as it had the most science and was the most controversial. Both had associate help. Strom was nervous.

The GWF in-house lawyers were beside themselves. Andrea Parsons was getting close to wanting a role in the case. It was my job to assure that did not happen.

———

While all of this was transpiring, the UK movers and

shakers in the Lloyds Casualty Market were negotiating among themselves on finalizing a business model for the "New Lloyds." I had one or more conversations every day, or so it seemed, pressing the concept of muti-tiered capitalization in order to protect the potential capital of Desert Mutual and Connecticut Indemnity, our firm's clients. Clearly off the table was the concept of unlimited liability: with the rise of Mass Torts in the United States and perhaps elsewhere, limiting the upside risk had become ever more the keynote. So, the greater problem in bringing about change was incentivizing the actual reinsurance underwriting while also creating the diversity of investment so as to not be trapped in a single type of risk, e.g., asbestos or tobacco.

Bradley believed this diversity of placement for reinsurance was where the London Placing Brokers could become even more effective by devising systems to recommend specific actually diverse placements, and LTL could find a role in that process by tracking all of those placements, of all of those enrolled in real time, and by advising of the areas that became overfunded or underfunded to assist its subscribers in guiding their placements. (This step was an example of not "burning bridges" to all of those brokers during that collection phase of the "old Lloyds" meltdown.) Coverage tiers into the "catastrophic sphere" would enable further levels of reinsurance as the "New Lloyds" felt its way to understanding the new casualty insurance underwriting market which it was creating.

These steps forward in planning for New Lloyds were fast becoming more concrete as the monied interests, e.g., the retrocessionaires, whom I had addressed at the London Convocation wielded enormous influence at this level as their money might be viewed as the foundational building blocks supporting this entire structure of risk minimization, began to agree with this entire system in principle.

One major stumbling block was that the UK did not allow Lloyds or many other financial entities to utilize limited liability corporations. Moreover, this change represented perhaps the biggest diversion from "Old Lloyds" built on the Names' unlimited liability: whereas this new model's pivotal proposal had some form of risk minimization at virtually every level. Quincy, Bradley and any number of other influential legal types, together with all of the broker enterprises began a carefully scripted lobbying program with both major political parties to get a positive vote from Parliament to create the legal framework for the UK to maintain its position as the central focus of the Casualty Insurance Business World.

When Parliament passed such a bill bilaterally to fairly little media fanfare, the New Lloyds entered the final phases of its creation process. Next to come was the highest hurdle of all; would there be sufficient funding and credit to support this entirely new structure. DMIC and Connecticut Indemnity were among the first to pledge the requested funding for each institution.

Interestingly, my son, Robert, took an on-going interest in this entire process which he found utterly fascinating. This interest certainly gave me high hopes for that son.

6

CAROLYN'S COLLEGE TOUR

Carolyn, with her usual careful planning, put together two college tours for our three youngest of Mollie's children. First, before the hottest months, she wanted them to go back East, and starting with University of Virginia (UVA), then Johns Hopkins (seeing Fort McHenry), then four or five schools in Philadelphia, a visit to Princeton, and up to Hartford for Trinity College and Boston for Harvard, Wellesley, and Boston College. Carolyn was very resistant to anyone's going to college in New York City (enough mean-spirited things had happened to some of her friends, not to mention the crime plaguing the city at that time), that she just would not hear of it. (I always felt there was more going on there than she wanted to discuss, but she wanted "our Kids" to spend some time on her Connecticut farm and to visit Vera (as a base for Hartford and Boston).

Robert, after Ireland, and so much time with Patrick Tyne, appeared fully committed to Princeton, and although they did not offer athletic scholarships, his academics were such that he would receive significant financial grants to go to that institution. (I later found that was how he planned to get early admission.) Nonetheless, he happily signed on for both tours. The Eastern tour travel was basically by sport utility vehicle once there, while the West included more flights.

In the West, Both Carolyn and I wanted them all to look at the University of Washington, UCLA. UCSB and UCSD. They wanted to tour the University of Southern California (USC), University of San Diego, Arizona State and the University of Arizona. On both trips, smaller schools might fit into some cracks in scheduling. In all cases, the whole area of school location, not just the campus might matter, not to mention the regard for the school's degree in whatever career world they might pursue as their initial adult experience.

———

While I was engaged in catching up after the UK and Ireland, Carolyn took off to Seattle with Robert, Patrick and Meaghan. They toured the Seattle area and were struck by its beauty. Meaghan spoke to me on the telephone that first night and said the area with its water, islands and mountains, including the city itself, might be as, or more, beautiful than the San Francisco Bay Area. Upon arriving home the following evening, Meaghan had convinced herself that she wanted to go to "U-W" as that university was known to Washingtonians and its "wanna-bees."

Of course, the three of them were very familiar with Cal-Berkeley, Stanford and UC Davis (much more of an agricultural, science and engineering school—albeit quite excellent in those areas).

While briefly home, Carolyn spent real time with our Mollie and went over things with Esmeralda (Elsa would be home for the last four days the foursome would be touring). That would make Mollie very happy as she missed Elsa terribly. Elsa also had to confer with Carolyn and her parents on their plans. Then that following week, both Carolyn and Elsa were to meet Robert and his crew for a *Vogue* shoot in Venice lasting four days. I was not invited on any of these. The foursome's tour East was to start eight days after Carolyn returned from Italy and was to last two full weeks, including side-trips!

All of this planning took a huge bite out of that Summer. But I consoled myself with the concept that these tours were a once in a lifetime event and were a final stage in Carolyn's bonding with my children aiding her transformation from their step-mother to more of an actual mother.

— — —

In mid-June, I took a call from Tom Felix in Seattle. He and his firm had been our local counsel for Washington for more than a decade in the CAL Board Asbestos Bodily Injury (BI) litigation and he had become a member of the Society of Insurance/Civil Defense Counsel (SIDC) for about seven years having been nominated by me. He was an excellent business friend. His call was to let me know that he and his firm had joined a new network of small/midsized civil law firms, called American Civil Litigation Network (ACLN), being formed around the United States with specialty practices as a factor—all were litigation. It had four primary areas: Plaintiff and Defense, Bodily Injury or Property Litigation or Corporate. One Plaintiff firm by area and one Defense (two firms were possible, if only one area of law was practiced). Tom wanted to tell me he was their firm's contact partner, and they had only been members for a month. He had just returned from an initial get started member meeting in Naples, Florida. Fifteen firms like ours attended, none from the Bay Area. He had recommended our firm to the founders. I should expect a call as soon as the end of that day and no later than the next day. WOW! We talked more. Sounded intriguing.

When I got off Tom's call, I got Reggie and Martha in my office. Mary was at a meeting with Connecticut Indemnity's staff in Los Angeles. I called Phil and got him on my speaker phone. We discussed Tom's call. I told them about four of their member firms which I knew and that it sounded quite realistic and not too expensive. Moreover, as a firm network, it provided a pathway for all of our partners to be involved, and for the younger ones to develop their marketing skills.

As we were about to break-up, Lily buzzed me to say there was an attorney Finnerty from Jersey City on the line who was referred to us by Tom Felix. I motioned for everybody to sit back down, and asked Lily to put him through on my speaker phone, I answered it after one ring. "Hello, Mr. Finnerty, I hope you do not mind, but we just had a quick meeting of some of our partners about Tom Felix's call, and I asked them to sit down to hear us, if that's OK with you?"

Without so much as a pause, "What a pleasure to hear you all are so quick to react! Please call me Fulton. Cannot shorten that name and come up with any good nick-names. From what Tom tells us, your firm sounds like an excellent candidate to join us at this formative stage. However, as some of our members from populous states realize, we cannot tie-up a whole state, or one as big as California with one, or even two firms. We have a committee of three who are putting our group together. Talking among ourselves, we see California as having defense members in San Francisco with San Mateo and perhaps Marin Counties, and the rest of Northern California would be your firm's. In the South, there would be San Diego and Orange Counties, east to the state line. Above them, the same for Los Angeles County, and the rest of the state might go to a firm in a city like Fresno. But, first, can I answer any questions?

"By the way, one of our Plaintiff board members, from South Carolina, told me to sign your firm up today." No one spoke.

"Could that be Ron Motley, by chance?" I asked.

Finnerty chuckled. I held my thumb up to my partners. They were unanimous. I said, "Not all of my partners are here to vote, but by weight, we have enough. The San Francisco issue is OK for San Mateo, not Marin. I live in Marin and have for almost thirty years. Hope that's not a deal breaker?"

He jumped on that with, "No, we'll understand. You're here first. So, if you can let me know tomorrow that you're on board, we need several more board members and one more for the start-up committee, both for the Defense grouping team. We would like you personally to be both of those, if you accept tomorrow. Please let me know on that as well. Tom has provided your fax and all of the needed paperwork should arrive in your office shortly after I hang up."

We spent a few more minutes with introductions, then Finnerty was away. Martha opened my door and Lily was standing there with a bundle of papers, and said, "This all just arrived from Mr. Finnerty."

"Everybody, please wait. Lily will give each of you a copy of everything. Martha, would you discuss this all with Mary. Lily will you see that Mary and Phil each get a copy. Please call me tonight with anything urgent. Please let me have a short memo early tomorrow, Reggie would you speak with Phil and Joshua? If any of you or the others would rather me not do those committee jobs or would prefer to have one or both, please do not hesitate to speak up. Thank you all."

Based on this call with Fulton Finnerty, following my call from Tom Felix, I was willing to conclude that this was a bona fide start-up network that might very well fill our future marketing needs with our other high-end individual member organizations. Moreover, this opportunity to get in on the "ground floor" as a start-up director of an organization that could provide at least another decade of new business success through networking to obtain new client referrals. I was hoping my partners saw it that way.

— — —

The next morning, I called Tom Felix back for a few clarifications. Reggie showed up with two black coffees and we talked for about thirty minutes. After my drive home, I needed to talk to Carolyn, but she was in Seattle at the UW touring event. I waited until nine o'clock and called her. We talked for almost an hour. Even though I was only entering my early-fifties, I knew burn-out could catch up very quickly with lawyers like me. Plus, I needed to think more about the future for my partners. When we finished, I felt almost ready for the next morning. When Reggie and I finished, my plan was done, but needed my other partners' assents, and then Fulton Finnerty's.

My partners all assembled in our conference room or on its speaker phone. I began with my recommendation, then a short outline of my plan, and opened the floor to comment by saying, "So, if we are to do this, I see each of us having a part in doing so, and that mine should make way for Reggie and then whomever you all decide will be our next main contact."

Phil and Joshua were concerned with how they would fit in as were the rest of us. Tom Felix told me that morning multiple offices in the bigger states was an open issue. Moreover, some of the firms were in more than one state. The start-up board would have to grapple with those issues, and doubtless others. Other questions were raised, but the opportunity itself seemed to dictate moving forward on a positive note. We agreed that Reggie would be on the call with me to Fulton. We scheduled it for one o'clock PDT.

When Fulton Finnerty answered his phone, he allowed that he had forty-five minutes for our call; then, he needed to engage the other two co-founders constituting the start-up committee of the organization's board. He provided a little more detail about each than he had the day before. We had read more about them in the materials he supplied, yesterday. When he took a moment to breathe, I allowed that Reggie Fox, our managing partner and head of our largest litigation group, was on that call with me. Next, he wanted to know if we had questions, some of which he tried to answer, other issues were undecided.

Then, he turned to my willingness to participate in their network per his request of the previous day. I allowed my answer was slightly complex, saying, "I would be pleased to serve in the start-up capacity. I do believe I could be quite helpful in that regard. But for the Board, we would request that I have a shared term with Reggie, with a probable concept of his continuing in that capacity after the start-up phase is essentially complete. At my life's stage, my spouse is worried about my health and not spending enough time together. We are not getting enough of that time now, and my participation will mean even less. We hope that this will meet your needs."

"We are finished early, so it seems. Please allow me to call Mark and Liam and I shall get back to you both in a few minutes or we'll give you a time to call-in." With that, Fulton Finnerty was gone.

As Reggie and I talked for no more than two minutes, Finnerty was back with the other two on a conference call. We joined, introductions were made, and a few threshold questions answered. Whereupon Mark Westhoff said, "As the Acting President of ACLN, I should formally like to invite O'Neill Fox to join with us and you two gentlemen to serve in the capacities as you have suggested."

We accepted and the call then continued for almost an hour as we discussed states and firms, and our role to help fill the Western United States memberships.

After the call, Reggie and I compared notes and set up a partner call-in the next day to get everyone's input.

Last thing I did was ask Reggie, "ACLN will need a firm like ours in San Francisco, I believe we should try to get one we can trust. What would you think of Allen Boswell? Sandra does owe me some allegiance for helping her get started when her father died and his firm imploded from greed of some partners and too much debt."

Reggie: "Let me think on that tonight." He paused, then added, "Maybe you should run that idea past Carolyn tonight and get her insight."

Later that night, I took Reggie's advice, even though it was after ten and they were due to fly home tomorrow on an early flight from SEA-TAC. I re-explained the new network to Carolyn as best I could with today's additions, what they had offered our firm and me, and the success of her suggestion working on my future role and engaging Reggie in more external management and politics where he could potentially shine. Then I broached the subject of potentially adding Sandra Allen's firm as "our San Francisco competitor." Because of Mollie's views on Sandra, Carolyn had always been extremely cool toward her, despite Sandra's efforts to become friendly. I reiterated that "the hurt' from our pre-marriage break-up and my following break-down had been buried under years of cooperation in the overarching defense for our respective asbestos clients wherein we often shared similar issues, plans, and target outcomes. Moreover, when her father was dying, despite our differences, I had honored his request for help and aided Sandra with a bail-out plan and by providing an avenue for her to help create a new, smaller defense firm. All of which had created an abiding sense of loyalty to me on Sandra's part, not only personally but also how her firm conducted itself toward O'Neill Fox.

Carolyn listened carefully, asked just two substantive questions, which I answered, seemingly satisfactorily. Then she offered, "To me, this sounds like something you are wanting to do because you are trying to create some form of safety net in the event that O'Neill Fox might fail. Or even something worse. And yes, I do understand that you see a great deal of loyalty running from Sandra to you. But the one thing I do realize is that there is probably no other competing defense firm which will have anything like the loyalty to your firm as Sandra's, not just because of what you have done for her over the years, but all of the decade-plus of benefits running to some of your business friends whom you counseled to join up with Sandra. When I look at all of those factors, I agree you should consider moving ahead with her firm. But please don't do anything that if I were to learn about it, would make me regret agreeing to this."

Those may not be Carolyn's exact words, but they are very close. After we exchanged endearments and hung up, my mind wandered to where it had visited in the past. Of course, Carolyn knew that I carried on a non-exclusive affair with her for years, but she had never asked me if I did so with anyone else. Something about her statement made me think that she knew about others, perhaps Martha or Madeline. But the actual gravamen of what she said, if that was true, was she did not care at a level of calling me on infidelity. Moreover, could that be a two-way street with her?

When I discussed all of this with Dr. Arnaud, my psychiatrist seemed to restrain herself from laughing, coughed instead, and said, "I imagine she knows some things, probably cares, but realizes you are just being you, and no real harm. Whatever she does know, Carolyn has made it clear that nothing untoward should happen with Sandra. I suggest you behave yourself with that woman. Keep it all business!"

From that night forward, I have listened to that joint advice. Reggie went along as well.

———

Over the almost twenty years of practice for O'Neill Fox and its successor entities, we enjoyed our relationship with the AMERICAN CIVIL LITIGATION NETWORK, receiving and facilitating millions of dollars in referrals with its member firms. Also, building a lifelong relationship with the three co-founders, Fulton Finnerty in Jersey City, Liam Callahan in Chicago, and Mark Westhoff in Atlanta, not to mention our longest-timed friend, Tom Felix in Seattle. Reggie served on ACLN's Board for eight years, the last two as its Chairman. He semi-retired two years after that term was finished.

My other partners from its start-up days were active ACLN members and it helped us all grow or maintain our individual practice areas as our firm's practice became more diversified. While writing this, I think how much I miss Fulton and Mark who have gone to their final rest before me.

Sandra's firm never got proposed as a member. A few days later, she called to tell me Wallboard, her firm's dominant client, finally had filed for Chapter 11 Bankruptcy.

— — —

Carolyn and the three touring putative college students spent one night at home and took off early the next morning in a super-sized rental SUV for Southern California and Arizona. They began by heading south to Santa Barbara on highway US-101, picking up that first great west coast highway just south of San Jose. I got a call a little after 3:00 to tell me they had arrived at the Biltmore and were going to the beach for a few hours, then perhaps in the pool to warm up. Carolyn got on the line next, "I haven't been here in years. It's so beautiful, but it is isolated here. I can only imagine the troubles that could follow."

Me. "Oh, My."

Carolyn, "I'll call you at bed-time. Love you!"

She called and we talked for a long while!

— — —

With literally no one home (Mollie, now four, was at Yolanda/Mercedes' house, visiting for a couple of days), I asked Martha and Mary to have dinner after work while my tourists were overnighting in Los Angeles. We decided to try Scotts' Seafood House, right on Jack London Square, and got a window table overlooking the wide and deep Oakland Estuary with a view of the of the eclectic shoreline of Alameda Island, about a third of a mile across that water. We started the evening by them asking me about when the US Navy had a huge base covering almost all of the north half of that island. I remembered it well and described how it was the biggest employer in the whole Easy Bay, with enormous traffic through the Alameda/Oakland Tunnel that connected with the island's north end. Since that base closure, that traffic was reduced to a trickle. Unemployment in Oakland went up. So did crime. But I pointed out that the south end of the island, albeit a little bit difficult to access, was a very desirable place to live and not as expensive as many of the Bay Area's nicer neighborhoods. That broke the conversational ice and we went from topic-to-topic with no mention of work, and no pressure to get things done.

That nibbling thought reminded me of our pressure-packed defense of CAL Board in the *LAUSD* matter: nights, even some weekends working on briefs at all hours, the three of us, sometimes in Los Angeles, or Oakland, or both, plus Tinker and his people, mostly in D.C. We talked about it for longer than I thought we would, and that chat produced a real sense of nostalgia. Sipping my Chardonnay, I felt almost sentimental. When I finished that glass, I ordered coffee. Our conversation paused. Should I ask Martha about her pregnancy/ I decided not to do that. (Maybe wait a day or two and ask in my office. She was beginning to look ready. We needed to plan for when it happened and for the follow-on uncertainty afterward which Martha had promised about six months ago.)

Driving home alone made me miss everyone. I thought about the absence of neighborhood friendships. All we seemed to do was work, with enough spare time only for family. Both Carolyn and me. Life was going by so fast and I felt we must be missing out on something. When I relayed these thoughts to Dr. Arnaud a few days later, she chuckled, then said, "What you are beginning to understand is the acceleration of the aging process. Many of us feel it. The accumulation of years creates an evolution making each year seem to go by faster. The more aware people are of their life experiences, the more they tend to feel this phenomenon. In the end, it's a state of mind. Some say, "Do less and enjoy more." Others think that's just self-delusion. I suggest not dwelling on it. Unproductive!"

— — —

A few days later, I asked Martha to stop by my office for a chat. She brought her Starbucks concoction of the day. I drank my usual office black. She spoke first after our exchange of pleasantries, "Two things: I believe the time has come for you and I to agree to go forward in an arms-length relationship, and mean it this time; and second, I want to go over my plan for maternity leave."

As I looked at Martha, my eyes widened ever so little, I smiled and said, "I agree to your first point. Please note I am not asking for one last tryst. As to your second point, that's why I asked to speak with you now. Please proceed."

Martha outlined how she was planning to adapt to

motherhood, rather clearly, she saw that as a more exclusive role than I had expected. Martha said Mary acquiesced in that attitude as a condition of Martha's getting pregnant. I was once again sorely tempted to ask if I was the father. Somehow, she beat me to it by volunteering that I was not. (I have never been certain that was not a 'white lie.') This process of transition seemed time intensive on her part. But she was clear this was her once in a lifetime event. At last, she got to our areas of work collaboration. The asbestos science and medicine, other than causation nuances was largely in the past. The "Vermiculite defense" had proven largely a failure due to Corbett McDonald advocating for the Plaintiffs' Bar on that issue. But that left the Great Western Foundry cases. We were to meet and confer telephonically with the plaintiff attorneys this next Monday. Her preliminary talks indicated that they saw many things favorably, except that one adverse ruling on a critical issue with a "single judge" and their cases could be lost before getting in front of a jury. ("Complex Litigation Judges" for larger counties, like Sacramento were right around the corner temporally, so they were correct. As things stood, the rotational judges could change from one day to the next on hearing the Law and Motion calendar, allowing a "second bite of the apple" in the event of an adverse ruling in the first instance.) I suggested we refer them to Ron Motley who might speak to that point about not running up time and expenses if your case turns out to be doomed from the outset as unsuccessful. Martha liked that.

But of greater import was who would run the GWF cases while she was on leave? Martha said, "Felicia Clarke can do it. But she'll need much more help from you than I would. I think that's the only thing that will work. I like our new laterals, but this world of Toxic Tort Science and Medicine is so specialized that you have to acquire the skills over time. Felicia has been doing that. Quite successfully, I might add. She has worked with each of our experts closely. The one thing that she will need your help with is Strom and the client's people. Strom will start to see her name on the reports, but he'll know you've reviewed them (he knows you always do, and bill almost nothing!). If something becomes major, you can step up. Felicia will copy me with those reports and that will be all for the first months. I am not sure how many months. At some point, I will begin to insert myself back into that case; and I will make myself available to participate on the critical briefing on the science-based IQ motion practice, whenever it occurs."

"Andrea Parsons told me you two had a wonderful dinner! Repeating that occasionally might help to keep the peace with her; and lighten Felicia's load. Andrea can be quite aggressive with those to whom she feels superior. That would probably include Felicia, at least for now."

"I know this asks a lot from you, but it will be my last BIG ASK. We all know you're getting older and expect you to start pulling back on your workload, and to concentrate more on marketing.'

We chatted for another twenty minutes on GWF and a couple of other matters. Then it was time for Martha to leave. She stood up, looking every bit of eight-plus months pregnant, and walked around my desk. I stood. She pulled my head down, kissed me deeply on the lips, and said, "If you had asked me to marry you after Mollie died, I would have agreed on the spot. I have loved you all these years. Now, know that the physical between us is over forever. But if you need me, I will always be there for you. See you on Monday!"

— — —

Martha had her baby on Sunday. I called Strom on Monday and told him about the event and our plan. Felicia, whom he'd previously met was on the call. He was fine with everything. The next day was the Meet and Confer with the plaintiff lawyers. I actually found them all to be very professional. They asked Felicia to pass their Congratulations on to Martha. We talked for thirty or forty minutes. They said they were not inclined to accept a Single Judge Assignment and all that meant, nor would they stipulate to our proffered Case Management Order which greatly reversed California's standard discovery system (which was not geared to novel scientific basis discovery).

At that point, I asked them if they knew of Ron Motley in South Carolina. They did. I asked them as a matter of professional courtesy if they would call Ron and ask him about his advice on novel litigation and how to proceed when my firm was on the other side, especially about saving time and expense. They conferred, returned, and agreed to call him. I told them that I would schedule a date and time with Ron at his earliest convenience and that I did not plan to be part of that call itself.

— — —

Attorneys Scott and Young called me thirteen days after our meet and confer teleconference. Attorney Scott said words to the effect, "Mister Motley seems to have great deal of respect for you. He gave us more time than we expected. He listened to us, but then he told us that the worst lawsuit for his type of plaintiff attorneys might have been LAUSD. He explained how in that case and others, lawyers like us could run up expenses and waste time on matters that might prove unwinnable in the end. 'Better to take the shortest road to whatever that critical point might be.' Also, he added that your firm understood how to map out that road. We will agree to the single judge and your case management order. But we will need to schedule a special hearing with the Presiding Judge for the county."

I said, "Felicia Clarke is right here. She will work with you all on getting that scheduled and the two of us, plus one or two client types will probably be there as well. I will leave you all to discuss whatever is needed. We'll take the lead to convert our motions into the Stipulations and Felicia will run them by you all for your thoughts."

Attorney Young spoke, "Thank you for all of this. We never expected this level of cooperation. Have you done this before?"

I answered, "It may be the first time for Felicia, but Martha and I have been doing versions of this for more than ten years now. We try not to waste resources. We do appreciate your willingness to cooperate. We'll look forward to meeting with all of you in person at that upcoming hearing."

– – –

I called Andrea and Stuart, GWF's VP of Finance and General Counsel (GC), to let them know about Martha's departing on maternity leave and how we would be staffing their matter in her absence. The first thing they wanted to know was how long she would be unavailable. I tried to reply by creating the sense that she would not be actively involved for "awhile," without saying indefinitely, and by pointing out that Felicia and I were fully up to speed on the case; and, I would be more active in my senior status. Then, to persuade them, I explained that the adverse plaintiff firm was prepared to stipulate to a Single Judge Assignment and a Case Management Order, drafts of which we would be faxing to the two of them for their comments, if any, by tomorrow. We would thereupon forward them to the Plaintiff Counsel, and finalize those documents before setting a hearing with the Sacramento County Superior Court Presiding Judge, the only judicial officer qualified to approve the first proffered stipulation.

"What did you do or say to persuade them to agree?" asked Andrea.

Felicia proceeded to explain our firm's and my connection with Ron Motley of South Carolina. They had never heard of him. I explained about his asbestos recoveries in the tens of millions and the beginnings of tobacco recoveries for more than half of the states in the billions; and, that we had been involved with various litigations where our firms were adverse, either directly or indirectly. So, having eventually developed a cordial, professional relationship with Ron, I asked him to speak with them. He did so, and they were persuaded to go along with our view of how to proceed as the potentially most expeditious and cost-effective manner of moving this litigation to a conclusion. Both of them knew from our prior meetings and conversations that Martha and I had used a similar strategy in the past.

Andrea responded, "We shall look forward to your faxes, and we will respond expeditiously. Thank you!"

7

THE AMERICAN CIVIL LITIGATION NETWORK

When I spoke to Carolyn that night, I asked if I should fly down south to be with her. She paused and suggested that instead I might visit Mollie on Saturday and take Yolanda and her daughters somewhere of their choosing for a treat. That's my wife: always thinking about others and being as kind as possible. How I loved her. How I missed her. So, I did what she asked. We all had a great time at the St. Anselm's Parish Fair with its games, the rides and the food. Mollie was wonderful. She got to talk with her Mom on my cell phone. Mollie even was happy going home with Yolanda and her girls, but wanted to know when they were all coming back: only five more days!

— — —

Between the GWF matter and many calls with the ACLN founders, I had little time to contemplate anything else of a business nature.

Felicia, two associates and I took Andrea's comments, rejected most, and made the needed revisions to accommodate a few of them. We then faxed that package to the Plaintiff legal team with a cover memo suggesting how we might narrow the field for a judge (Only after checking with

Austin Smith, CAL Board's GC, whose offices were in Sacramento, to ascertain those which would prove satisfactory and the sequence in which to rank them, as done well more than a decade ago in our *Mullen* case in Contra Costa County.) prior to the actual hearing with the Presiding Judge for the Sacramento County Superior Court.

In those first three days of that tumultuous week, between the four of us on the start-up member firm selection committee, we added thirteen firms and had two more considering membership in ACLN. Of those fifteen, five were suggested by me, all from the CAL Board Defense Nationwide Team. That made a great many people optimistic, if not plain happy.

That Thursday, I drove the family SUV to the office. After a light lunch, I checked that the family foursome's flight from Phoenix was going to arrive on time at Oakland Airport, left the office and met them at the curb with their luggage. They were all four of them much tanner than they had been at their departure. Once in the Mercedes M-class, each of the three gave me the list of three colleges to which they might apply from this western swing and each added two more from the East, except Robert who felt himself fully committed to Princeton because of its early acceptance of him. Each one had to have one UC school: Robert took UCLA, Patrick took UCSD and UC Santa Barbara, while Meaghan picked UCLA. They all liked Washington, but none thought they would get into it! All three of them felt Stanford was the best fit in the West, and Robert liked Coach Luke Olsen at Arizona, a lot!

When it came time to apply, what would it all mean? Carolyn was so pleased with the whole event. She had worked hard to put these tours together and I felt grateful that she had the opportunity to do all of that parenting since her earlier life provided no such opportunities for her.

Meaghan changed the theme with her next thought, "What do you think of our tans? Everywhere we stayed and seemed to go was so sunny. Arizona was like an oven! Carolyn bought me two great bikinis."

Robert chipped in, "My guess is when you see the one, your comment will be, 'Where's the rest of that!'" All four of them laughed over that remark!

Yolanda and Mercedes were at our Ross house with Mollie when we arrived home. Mollie was so happy, all smiles and a few giggles, to see her mother. Carolyn picked her up hugged her, whispered in her ear, and I saw the trace of tears run down her cheek. The whole day, that whole week, were made worthwhile for me, in that one moment!

— — —

The four members of the ACLN start-up committee were on another call. We added one member and had two more to consider, but that day's big consideration was moving forward as an organization: Organization Chart (circulated by Liam to us pre-call), By-Laws and Voting Process. The Summer was quickly ending, but the three of them felt the need for a larger scale meeting, with voting on the organization documents and first actual board meeting with additional members added. I reminded them that I had proposed Reggie Fox for that first board and they had agreed.

Fulton Finnerty spoke-up at that point. "Ronan, you have been everything Tom Felix said you would be and more. Moreover, you sound sometimes like you feel you are approaching the point of burn-out. We see why you want this to be a shorter commitment on your part. We see an executive organization of Chair of the Board, filled by the outgoing President, President, Vice President and Secretary /Treasurer. We thought of a way to transition you off the board quickly. If executive slots last two years, long enough to get projects completed, but not too long; and we install new slates in September, then the first slate would be twenty-two months. If Liam is our first President; I'm second, so VP; then Mark would be third, as S/T. We could be looking at Tom Felix or Reggie Fox as fourth in line. So, he would come on the Executive Committee at the end of the first 'two-year term' when you step out of the picture to the title of Chair Emeritus. To do that, you would be the first Chair, but then done! The three of us agreed to that already. What say you?"

The other two voiced their support. I was honored, but I knew Carolyn was not happy with how I kept taking on more tasks, not fewer. I said, "There is someone I must run this past? Can we restart at 4:00 Eastern?"

They agreed and I immediately called Carolyn who was on another call. I left an urgent voicemail, and she was back to me within twenty minutes, "Yes, Ronan, what is so urgent?"

I tried to lay out the start-up committee suggested staffing of the first executive committee. After Mark Westhoff as Secretary/Treasurer, she interrupted, "Well, Ronan, that leaves you as fourth in line. Is that a problem for you? It's not for me, just a long way off,"

My response took but a few seconds, 'No, fourth would be Reggie Fox. I would serve less than two years as the first Board Chair, if that's alright with you? I do not want to overcommit any longer. What do you say?"

"Thank you for calling me. What a great plan. Whose idea?"

"The other three start-ups! As soon as we have a meeting date, I will give it to you. What are all the dates through early November you have scheduled. I do want you there."

"Where?"

"Biltmore in Phoenix? Essex House Chicago?"

Carolyn, "Take the weather out of play. Late Fall in Arizona is its best season."

We were back on the call on time. I agreed, but pointed out that they did not want all white men as leaders. So, they needed Reggie as their fourth CEO, and a woman no later than sixth, if possible.

Liam had circulated a list of potential By-Laws before this call. We ran through that list, taking more than an hour with most getting a cursory discussion. I said, "If we are to have a meeting this year, we need to schedule it sooner rather than later. I was thinking the first week in November."

Mark said, "Weather starts to be an issue that time of the year. Where would you have in mind?"

I replied, "Well, after I finished my first call that I mentioned, I had my assistant call the Biltmore in Phoenix for a four-plus day meeting, maximizing at 200 people, thinking that spouses should be invited based on my other network dealings. That's 100 rooms. We can do a quick notice and get sign-ups. It's 2.5 lawyers/ firm. Depending on how we organize, that may not be enough. They do not have any huge meeting rooms available, but they can handle up to 250 or so. Still swimming pool weather there. What do you all say? If you agree, please send me a fax list of the member firms and I'll get my assistant Lily to send something out seeking a tentative commitment in the next day or two.

I'll send you all a draft of that announcement tonight before I leave, and you can send me your feedback on it tomorrow by noon your times. Oh! It's not quite their high season yet, so the basic room rate would be $155/night. Or, $170 if breakfast buffet included. Shall we do it?"

They agreed. (Each of the three said their wives would love it.) "What about your wife, Ronan? Will she come?"

Me, "Absolutely! That place is her idea. She gets around and used to follow the sun. My assistant is used to working with her and her team. I shall look forward to your comments when I get in tomorrow morning!"

Carolyn was delighted with the new organization when I got home that night. I took some time to explain how I would be the first Board Chair for ACLN, and then Reggie Fox would slide into the chairs to ultimately become president for two years in its years' nine and ten. Thus, my heavy lifting would be confined to those first couple of formative organizational years. Then, bless her heart, Carolyn said, "You know how the Society is very strong on spousal participation, but does not really get that many spouses involved. Maybe this group could be different, have a more active spousal role in the meetings, especially for involving spouses of clients."

"Would you have time to put something together on that between now and the meeting, maybe work with some of the other spouses? Something sort of broadly organizational?" I responded. We talked more over the course of the evening, even when we first lay in bed.

The next morning, we were both still enthusiastic. As I was leaving, I told her I would call her during the day if anything was decided.

By the time I arrived in the office, the word had already begun to spread, "Martha has had her baby, and it's a BOY!"

Lily was not at her desk. Deirdre was beside herself with joy for Martha. Mary was at the hospital and serving as the communicator of all news, great and small. His name was to be Michael Francis, after an archangel and the patron saint of the city across the Bay. He was completely healthy, but Mary would not be in that day. Felicia was the first person to cross my office threshold. She said that the clerk of the Presiding Judge of Sacramento County Superior Court had read the stipulations and orders we had filed. He wanted to schedule a call for two o'clock that day. I told Felicia to call the plaintiffs, see if they were on board and tell them that Martha had just has her baby. Ten minutes later, she was back in my office. The call was set. The court provided a special call-in number.

Lily appeared in my doorway, said, "There were only very minor changes suggested by the other three attorneys. Mr. Finnerty wrote, 'I think Ronan has done this before, and more than once,' on his fax cover sheet. So, I made the changes and here is the final draft. You know we have the internet. Perhaps I could send this Announcement by email? Mr. Finnerty sent it to us by both fax and computer. Only one firm currently in ACLN does not have an email address. I could fax them."

"Lily, why don't you ask Mr. Finnerty's assistant to find out, and if she says he's 'on board,' then we'll do it your way. Please ask the three for a conference call at eleven our time. Give them our conference number."

Our call got the threshold planning out of the way first. That left it up to me to speak to "the spousal issue." I began, "There is one other matter that I think needs to be addressed here at the outset. For the members who spend their few days with us, there will be a certain finalizing of how ACLN will be organized for going forward, but the spouses have multiple days with no real structure. My wife, Carolyn, has suggested that based on other types of these meetings which she has attended, it might be wise to have a spousal committee set up a few events that other spouses might like. Of course, there are always the pool and shopping, but a few other items might prove worthwhile. Do any of you think your wives would be interested?"

Mark spoke up, "My wife, Ellie, might be interested in helping out with something like that. We've been to Phoenix a couple of times, but never stayed at the Biltmore. Has your wife done this sort of thing before, Ronan?"

Me: "Well, Carolyn is sort of in the fashion/advertising business, so she gets to a good many nice places. My guess is that she gets to Phoenix/Scottsdale two or three times in some years and I get there quite a bit as one of my biggest clients is located there. She will have some thoughts and she knows how to organize and cooperate."

Liam chipped in, "My wife is a real pool person, but I imagine she would like to do a few things, if interesting."

I said, "Carolyn thought a tour of the Frank Lloyd Wright home, kind of a museum, might interest some of the ladies. Is that an idea you might want to take home to see if it would generate any interest?"

We decided to pick this up the next work day.

Judge Ezra Quinn's clerk called at precisely two o'clock. Felicia and I were in our small conference room down the hall between our offices, with the speaker phone between us. Judge Ezra Quinn's clerk announced that all of the parties representatives were on the line, whereupon Judge

Quinn welcomed us to the call, "Good afternoon to all of you. This looks to be very interesting litigation, made even more so by the level of cooperation evinced by your joint filings and the process undertaken-to-date. Frankly, if I were not so busy with all of my other duties, I might well have considered taking on this relatively novel series of cases for myself. However, that will not be the case here. Before I agree to sign all of the draft orders which you have presented to me, do any of you have any questions or comments. Please know that I see this matter as a blueprint for complex litigation here in Sacramento County, and I will enforce these Orders once I have signed them. You see that the Single Judge assigned to these matters will be working at my discretion as I am responsible for this Case Management Order and that judge's appointment.

"Yes, Mr. Little?"

"Your Honor, Is the judge to be appointed on both of our lists?"

"Yes. She is. Anything else?"

No one spoke.

"As you all know, Judge Helen Winters is the only woman on both lists. You may also know that she is my younger sister by a few years. We have conferred on this and see no conflict whatsoever. Any comments or objections?"

No one spoke, again.

Judge Quinn, continued, "Mr. O'Neill, Austin Smith and I play golf sometimes. Are you aware of that?"

"No. I have never discussed you specifically with him. We have discussed some other judges since he is from this area."

The Judge, "In case you do not know, any of you, Austin Smith is Vice President and General Counsel of CAL Board, located here in Sacramento. Mr. O'Neill and his firm have represented them for many years. I did not know this until we looked his firm up in Martindale-Hubbell, and it listed CAL Board as a client. I called Austin to ask about Mr. O'Neill. Suffice it to say, he was effusive in his praise. Does any of this cause anyone a problem?"

Again, no one spoke at first, then Attorney Young for the Plaintiffs said, "Mr. O'Neill has proven to be quite honorable. Twice, he has provided us with personal references who have influenced how we are proceeding in this matter. So, we are satisfied with these documents and will be able to function under the Case Management Order."

With that said, the Judge asked, "Mr. O'Neill, do you have anything else you wish to add?"

Me, "No. Thank you, Your Honor. Just that we are pleased with the attention you have given this matter and thank you for signing the Orders."

The judge then got our email addresses and caused his clerk to email the signed orders to us on the spot. Lastly, he advised that Judge Winters would hold an Initial Status Conference in four weeks, with any submissions to augment the Orders he signed to be filed and served two weeks before and counter-submissions one week later. With that the conference call ended.

I asked Felicia to gather the two associates working on the GWF cases, as well as our lead paralegal Deirdre, and to meet me in the small conference room. I opened, "What I hope we can come up with is an outline for a motion for summary judgment that will end this litigation, including all of the main items about proof that will support that motion. The three of you have worked with our experts and written numerous memoranda on the science involved here, and the impediments to these plaintiffs prevailing on the only real theory which they have pleaded, diminished IQ. Also, I would include a second topic they seem to have avoided, blood lead poisoning. I believe they avoid that latter injury because few, if any, of them have any of that symptomology whatsoever. Please consider all the options based on their complaints, but do not make up any potentially successful path for them. Let's try to have that by a week from next Monday. Please share it with Andrea and her people, and ask if they wish to attend, or call-in at 2:00 on that Monday. From that outline, we will need your suggestions of all, if any, discovery we will need to take. That is what we will be seeking in our filing and your outlines will support it." While looking around at all four, I asked, "Felicia, do you understand?"

We spent almost thirty minutes resolving various supporting issues. Olivia and Tom, the two associates participated vigorously. They obviously wanted to be noticed; and, they were!

— — —

The ACLN call of our foursome went forward as scheduled, with Lily setting up the call. When I came onto the call, the three of them were already talking among themselves, Liam Callahan was saying, "Now I don't know anything myself, but my wife Serena just passed that on."

Fulton Finnerty chipped in, "My wife Abby thought the idea of having some social events for the spouses was a great idea, especially being planned by the spouses. I heard a beep a few seconds ago. Ronan, have you joined us?"

"Yes. Good afternoon to all of you!"

Before I could go further, Mark Westhoff spoke, "Liam says his wife thinks that she remembers a big spread in *Vogue* magazine from a few years back where a top fashion model and her husband and some of his children were in a Christmas themed shoot in Paris and of all things, she remembers that because the husband's name was Ronan and he was a lawyer. He told her that was way too much of a coincidence. Good story though, don't you think?"

A moment of dead air, then, "Well that would be quite a coincidence, but then again they do happen, Liam. In that instance, Carolyn and our merged families had a marvelous time in Paris as we pitched in a bit here and there on one of my wife's major spreads. By the way, that's the correct term. Carolyn has been a model for about twenty years. She is less busy than she was before we married, but she occupies herself with other tasks, and she loves projects and meeting people in more non-public surroundings. I imagine that's why she suggested this. Also, probably why she suggested the Biltmore. She did some one thing like this there on an occasion a few years ago."

Liam interjected, "Does she still work as a model?"

Me: "Yes, but not just shoots; also, endorsements, not to mention career assistance to several young women. We also have a relatively young daughter to go with our blended family of five. She has help. Oh! She is also very smart. If you all agree with this as a project, why not send the contact info for your wives to Lily. I'll ask her to put it all together, circulate it, and work with Carolyn to set up a call-in for them. Do you all agree?"

They all agreed readily. I brought Lily on the call briefly. She took over. The three lawyers left. I hooked up Lily and Carolyn who were fast business friends, spoke for a minute, and left the balance of what we would do to them to see to all of these needed preliminaries.

The American Civil Litigation Network (Defense Group) was firmly underway with a four-day weekend organizational meeting set for the Biltmore in Phoenix in early November.

— — —

I kept Dr. Arnaud informed of most of what precedes this notation as well as other developments that I considered significant at the time, seeing her every two weeks or so. Despite my workload, the actual detailed legal work was lessening in favor of the marketing. I tried to keep her up to date, but I sometimes felt that a phone call here and there might help. Sessions tended to run on. Calls also dealt with any need for immediacy. I asked her about that idea. She thought about it and agreed generally. Then, she asked me how I thought it might work. I said I would have to think about it. "Great" was her response, "Why don't you call and leave me a message with your thoughts and a number and some time frames when I might call you back."

So, in a few calls, we had a new means for quick consultations.

8

THE ASBESTOS WORLD EVOLVES

Although in these pages, it might appear that asbestos litigation, as a whole, was drawing to a close, that was simply not the case. First, there was the slowly growing world of Bodily Injury (BI) cases handled by our Oakland and Glendale offices; second, there were the remaining Property Damage (PD) cases where expenses were actually being incurred to deal with the removal of asbestos containing materials (ACM) for legitimate reasons, e.g., repairs, remodeling, even demolition. Third, there were asbestos waste issues, not unlike Great Western Foundry (GWF) which included some small amount of asbestos when compared to the amounts of GWF's lead. The first group of BI cases was under Reggie Fox's operational control, including some of those outside California. The second and third, far less busy than the first, were under Martha's day-to-day direction. But with her unavailability, they reverted to me as I was in overall charge of all of the litigation for CAL Board, and a few other much smaller insureds of Desert Mutual Insurance Company (DMIC) and Connecticut Indemnity (CI). More than I could undertake. I contacted Phil Hassard and Joshua Small in Glendale, or Walnut Creek (at times, for Joshua). When finished, it became clear that they were both willing to help out in Martha's absence.

When next our partners met, we all agreed, we needed more partners, and more lawyers.

The case load increases we had sought were continuing to happen, and our active case count was on the rise. All of this in spite of the CAL Board asbestos PD litigation classes and consolidated cases shutting down. Our marketing efforts were paying off. Now our management, planning and staffing needed to keep pace.

Later that week, I had a call from Sandra Allen. Since the demise of Wallboard, Inc., her largest client, we rarely worked on the same cases. In fact, I hardly saw, or for that matter, even thought of, her. She came to the point of her call after a few desultory pleasantries, "Ronin, I always enjoy catching up with you, but the real reason I am calling is that our case load has been seriously undermined by several client bankruptcies. Some of my partners are looking for a merger, but some of us just wish to downsize. That may mean one or two of our less productive partners may not stay on. But we also have too many associates by four or five, maybe even six. Just seeing your firm's growth, I wonder if you might wish to interview some of them? If so, I would like not to project our potential contraction publicly, at the moment."

I asked Lily to find Reggie Fox and ask him to step into my office. He did. I quickly caught him up on where we were in our conversation.

"Sandra, you know Reggie. He works locally and knows a great deal more than me about a great many young attorneys. Why don't you tell us whom you have in mind?"

She started going through names: six altogether. She indicated that they needed to eliminate three, and maybe four. She could not guarantee that they would work in Oakland, but she was trying to give us first shot.

Reggie picked four of the six. Sandra told us what each

earned and their levels of experience, both time with her firm and the areas of practice (mostly asbestos BI cases for three of the four). Reggie and I caucused. Their pay was doubtless higher than ours (we would need resolution for that), but the job market was tight. We asked if Reggie and perhaps Mary could interview each of the four at Sandra's office, if she was willing. She declined on her office, but did offer her apartment in the City for this coming Saturday. We agreed they could use her living room and kitchen to allow two interviews, separately, one by each partner. A half hour break between pairs would allow them to finish by one. The three of us tentatively agreed on that plan. We thanked Sandra. Mary agreed with the whole plan even though she was not at all certain that any of the four would prove useful in her very different policy coverage litigation and its highly specialized underlying analysis.

— — —

When all of the partners met by phone that following Monday afternoon, Martha asked if she could participate. Being Mary's significant other, she was perhaps better informed than some of the others, especially those in Glendale. Each of them spent about fifteen minutes giving their respective thoughts on each. They agreed that only one of them might prove useful to Mary. We all agreed to put that young woman aside for Mary. The other three, two third year men and a second-year woman, appeared to have spent virtually all of their time in the defense of Wallboard BI cases, and a few of their smaller clients, becoming far less busy after the bankruptcy filing. The three of them appeared largely interchangeable except for the slight gap in experience and salary.

Reggie allowed that if Phil and Joshua wanted to try one in Glendale, any of the three might work out. Whatever two were left, if any, Reggie would use here in Oakland. (We had been able to rent a half of the first floor in our current building when a tenant moved out. Only two relatively small spaces rented by other tenants were left in the building. We suggested that Mary approach her chosen associate forthwith, while I would talk with Sandra about the willingness of any of the other three going to the Glendale office. We agreed to call-in at five the next day.

Before wrapping up, I spoke for a few minutes about Felicia Clarke with whom I was working intensely on the GWF matter. We had promoted her to Junior Partner the past January one. We needed more partners, I suggested that we move ahead and offer her a full partnership at the end of the year, and that they come up with two more to become "juniors" at that time.

Martha backed me up on Felicia and Joshua offered to vet all of the other associates with Reggie. We agreed to resume this all on Thursday. Clearly, the sense of our being a firm in transition had taken hold on all of my partners.

While Martha remained on the phone and Reggie in my office, Lily was able to find Felicia in the tech room and brought her to my office. It was near the end of her day and she had been working on drafting discovery to the Plaintiffs in GWF. She looked tired, and more than a bit nervous to be summoned to my office at the end of the day. Reggie suggested that I lead-off, "Felicia, sorry to interrupt you toward the end of your day."

She smiled demurely, "I'm afraid we have at least another hour to go before we can call it a day. We have made a breakthrough in wording for our interrogatories, but we need to test it with the claims of the different plaintiffs. We are in the middle of doing that now, and I would prefer we do not put it off until tomorrow, lest we lose our momentum."

"Great," I responded. "Martha is on the phone as she wanted to be part of this meeting. We'll be quick. The partners just finished a meeting. As you probably know, the firm is going through some changes, mostly growth. You've been a junior partner for less than a year. Joshua was the first of those and he spent two years getting up to full partner. Very little precedent. Martha and I have been very impressed with your entire work ethic, capabilities, and demeanor. The same for Reggie. As a result, the partners would like to welcome you on board as a full partner this coming January one."

Felicia looked as if her jaw literally dropped an inch on hearing those words. I shall never forget it. Martha spoke up from the phone, "So, Felicia, what do you think?"

"Oh My God! I was so worried when I walked in here and saw Reggie sitting there. I thought maybe I was getting sacked. How exciting! I cannot wait." Then, she was all smiles!

Reggie chipped in with some congratulatory words, then said, "Felicia, we are going through a growth spurt and the timing of your promotion is geared to the fiscal year of the firm and not our desire to delay your new role. So, there will be a call-in partners meeting this Thursday at five. You might wish to attend in the small conference room next door. Please, go finish up. Oh, and this is not a secret!"

— — —

Some of the new firms added to ACLN were because I had become familiar with them either as members of the Society or they were part of the CAL Board defense network of local counsel. One of those was Mason Eggars of Charlotte, North Carolina, a few years younger than me, and a US Army Judge Advocate General Reservist (JAG). Our wives got on well and he was very entertaining and appeared to be an excellent lawyer. He called me late one morning in the first days of real Fall weather in the Bay Area: grey clouds, enough breeze that those skies seemed to "scud."

He had the need of a high-end corporate defense on a very difficult matter. His firm did a good deal of work for a very diverse holding company with a wide range of subsidiaries. Each had its own set of leaders. Most were corporations with a usual structure, but some of the services, risk management, legal, some technology or intellectual property, and others were supplied by the parent. Thus, he worked with their Assistant General Counsel in charge of Litigation. But the subsidiaries were so diverse and so plentiful that not all of them were as responsive to the centralized control as would appear prudent. This appeared to be a case where a contract was made in an intellectual property area without several levels of their appropriate review, and the dollar damages were mounting rapidly on multiple fronts. I allowed that we could do business litigation, but had no actual IP capability *per se*. Since IP law is essentially federal, Mason allowed that his firm could do whatever IP work was actually involved. It all sounded good, but I wondered where I would find the talent for the needed day-to-day lawyering. I decided to bring that up at the Thursday night partners' follow-up on Sandra's associates.

I told Carolyn about the new matter referred by Mason Eggars from North Carolina; and, the likelihood that I would have to take the lead on that case. She was not at all sympathetic, nor particularly empathetic, with words like, "You really have to learn to say 'NO' sometimes… or…you are going to ruin your health… or…why don't you tell Martha she needs to get back to the office." So, I got to thinking how I could share some of my workload, and having told her about Sandra and her sudden surplus of associates, suggested, "How about if I associated Sandra to work on this one case with me? She does not sound very busy right now."

That got Carolyn's full attention, "Do you remember what I told you that Mollie told me about Sandra and what she almost did to you?" Staring at me as if I were a naughty child, deliberately misbehaving, "DO you?"

"Well, that was a really long time ago now. We have worked together cooperatively on quite a few matters over twenty-plus years. She has never made any type of approach to me in any manner other than on a professional level in all that time with the exception of when her father was dying, and that was at his request."

Still staring, wide-eyed, no blinking, and, "You helped her start her own law firm. Please do not tell me that she is only just a friend. A long-time ago, you were planning to marry her, not your Mollie. I think it's a very bad idea. A truly horrendous idea. But, I'll tell you what: spend a few days, see what else you can come up with. If you cannot find the right person, then if you let me meet with her alone, before you get her commitment, that will give me a chance to assess her attitudes and to honor Mollie's deathbed wishes to me."

I talked with Martha. She was at least a month, maybe quite a bit more before returning to practice, but she did not think much of the Sandra-idea. With their current workloads and experience, the new young partners were not candidates. Mary had no spare time at all and Phil was finally growing the Glendale workload, while Ingrid was expecting their second child.

I decided to talk to Reggie who was in daily contact with Sandra over her surplus associate issue, which appeared to be working out with our firm having to adjust our holdover associates pay scale somewhat to create a temporary alignment of sorts. Reggie allowed that Sandra was helpful in all of this, as were her remaining partners, down to five from eleven. The loss of Wallboard to Chapter Seven bankruptcy had proved devastating for Allen Butler what with their uncollectable Wallboard legal fees of six months, along with those costs advanced by her firm; and then, no future business for the foreseeable future. (All of these past expenses were claims in the Bankruptcy filing, and there was still insurance; but working out the actual sequencing of what policies would pay and when, could take as much as years. Moreover, the attorneys' fees to do so, would come off of the top of the cash that might become available. As I said, above: devastating!).

Reggie agreed with me that using Sandra could prove an excellent stop-gap, especially in Martha's continued absence. Carolyn was in New York, then Miami Beach for an eleven-day business trip. She returned my call that night. I explained all that I had done. She was peevish at first, but when I told her what Reggie had said, she became more pleasant, albeit still in her all-business-mode. She gave me several days the next week, asked if I wished to be present

(I did not see how I could stay away) and asked that I have Lily set up a 1:00 luncheon meeting in one of the curtained back rooms at Sam's Grille on Bush Street in the City. I followed her instructions and Lily got back to me with the day, cleared it with Carolyn, and asked me to call Sandy.

I did that right away. Sandra took my call immediately. We thanked each other about her associates and she heaped praise on Reggie, with some for Felicia as well. Then, she asked why the lunch. I told her that although she may have met Carolyn in passing, my wife did not feel she knew her at all. Also, Carolyn was aware of our engagement many, many years ago, and that when I talked to Carolyn about her, and our business connections, Carolyn felt a need to get to know her better. Hence, the Sam's luncheon invitation. A pause followed, then Sandra asked, "Does she hate me?"

I thought for a second, then said, "I am not certain about that, but my first wife, Mollie, held you in the lowest esteem possible. They became friends in the year before Mollie died. I am certain Mollie told Carolyn about you, but I never discussed it with either of them."

"Is this about a future joint working arrangement?"

Me: "That seemingly depends on the luncheon, then you."

———

I told Carolyn about that phone call. She was keeping her cards pretty well hidden as to how she planned to play things and what she had to say to Sandra at that forthcoming lunch.

With a great deal already going on around me, I received several boxes of files from Mason Eggars. His note inside said simply, "As received from the client. Copied, Bates-stamped (numbered consecutively), and forwarded to you. We have a copied set as well. Suggest you organize as you see fit and advise if anything seems missing. We'll await your call. We currently have forty-six days left to file our responsive pleadings. Thank you!"

I called Deirdre, our head paralegal, and asked her to have someone make two sets of the copied, numbered documents from Mason's client, Neptune Enterprises of Wilmington, NC. I asked her to hold them. Our lunch with Sandra was the next day.

Carolyn was at Sam's waiting at the bar for me, a glass of water in hand. We had agreed to meet fifteen minutes before Sandra to be seated. I got the last booth toward the back and requested that three sides be set with dining places, sourdough bread and butter along with water, and a bottle of Rombauer Chardonnay. Carolyn and I were led back. I suggested that I sit between the two women. Carolyn agreed and took the chair facing the back wall. Mine faced the tan curtain on the entrance to the plain dark brown stained wooden cubicle. The walls had no decorations and several plain coat hooks. We made small talk about Mollie. Sandra arrived, dressed in a blue business suit with a light pink blouse, slightly ruffled. Carolyn wore a designer dress in a muted green. Although I thought they must have met in the past, I decided to introduce them as if they were first meeting. I did so.

Carolyn did not allow the silent pause that followed to linger, "Sandra, I hope you do not mind my calling you that, though when I first heard of you, Ronan referred to you as Sandy. But then you were just becoming his girlfriend."

Sandra had started to nod her assent to her name's use, but stopped. Her eyes widened,

"But how did you know Ronan when he was first starting law school?"

"We met on the first night when he first came out to San Francisco for the Coast Guard to visit Tinker. I showed him to Tinker's unit, and we had a drink at the No Name Bar later that night." Carolyn spoke in an almost monotone, at a clear, deliberate pace, "When he returned to go to Hastings many months later, my roommate was moving to Paris, and I needed an adult as my co-tenant. We met on the rooftop lot right after he arrived and in five, maybe ten, minutes, he agreed to be my roommate and to be the adult on the lease. I travelled a huge amount of the time when he was in law school, so it worked well for both of us. For all those years, we had separate lives."

"Oh my, what a surprise. Ronan was very circumspect about his roommate mentioning a need for privacy, I never considered it could be a woman, a beautiful woman," Sandra seemed almost in awe of Carolyn.

"You need not think much about it. My roommate before Ronan was a very successful model. She gave me my start. I was very young. I was her protégé. She taught me to be a lesbian. I took over the *Cote d'Azur* lease from Ronan when I turned twenty-one, as we had agreed. I essentially practiced lesbianism, except for a Navy pilot killed in Viet Nam, who fathered my child. He was raised by Vera, my significant other, and me on our farm in Connecticut until my child and I moved out here when Ronan's first wife Mollie died. I tell you all of this because it was Mollie in her last months who told me about some events that occurred during her missing Ronan years: your break-up with him, and the aftermath of that event. Shall we look at the menu and order, then we can get back to why I asked for this meeting?"

I had been silent so far and thought about intervening, but realized with where their conversation stood at the moment, my speaking could change the dynamic which Carolyn had carefully crafted up to her self-imposed break. Our orders placed, Sandra spoke first, "You do know that after our break-up, I did not speak with Ronan for more than a year and then only in our roles as lawyers."

I decided that based on how this was going that I should excuse myself. I did and went out to the bar to eat my lunch meal.

Carolyn smiled, ever so slightly, "Ronan's version of your break-up starts with him telling you that he had decided not to take the offered position with your father's firm. Followed instantly by your losing your temper and screaming a blue streak at him, as if he had somehow destroyed your world. He left immediately while you were in mid-rage. Do you disagree with any of that?"

Sandra shook her head negatively, but did say, "The next day, I called him and left a message asking him to call me. He never did."

"Did you ever find out why he decided not to take your father's job offer?"

Sandra, frowning. "No. We have never discussed any of this until today. By the way, you would have made a great litigator. You do an excellent cross-examination."

Carolyn. "At this point, none of that matters. Suffice it to say: Ronan was emotionally on edge in those days. His time in Viet Nam with the Coast Guard had left him scarred emotionally. Bad things were happening when Mollie fortuitously happened on the scene. She had flown to the Bay Area to tell Ronan in person that his widowed mother was going to marry her father, those two having grown close after her mother died. Instead, she found Ronan emotionally destitute. She stayed with him. She transferred here with IBM where she was a star software creator. He moved in with her. Mollie found Ronan a psychiatrist, a woman, Dr. Margot Arnaud. He had passed the Bar examination. In a few months, he was recovered enough that when he spoke to Tinker, he ended up with that same firm in Oakland. By then, Mollie and he were married. You see, she was his first love, not you. And Mollie detested you!"

Sandra's jaw seemed to drop. In moments, "Why?"

"You didn't know Ronan. You never learned about his wartime experiences and how they had made him emotionally vulnerable. Your reaction to his decision was totally self-absorbed, apparently in line with your personality of those days, according to what Mollie told me based on her early discussions with Ronan and his psychiatrist. You upset Ronan so much that he found some drugs, used them, and that triggered his drinking, and he almost killed himself. If she had not stumbled on to him, he very well could have. That's why!

"Mollie told me you were toxic, and to keep Ronan away from you. I believed her. No reason not to then, nor now. But my husband who is a good, well-intentioned man, has helped you professionally in the past, and wants to help you more now, as he'll explain after I eat my salad and leave. But for now, please tell me how you feel about Ronan these days, two decades after those events I discussed?"

"Wow! Not what I was expecting at all," began Sandra, "He's a very generous, brilliant man and lawyer. He has helped me in my law business over the years and has never had an unkind word for me. I have not thought of him on any level other than as a friend, just as a very good, even valuable, business friend, for many years now. Well more than a decade."

Carolyn, "Is that all?"

Sandra, moved her chair, so she looked straight at Carolyn, spoke slowly, "I married too, soon after our split. Perhaps the wrong man. Simply put he was not what I wanted anyway. When I did not see Ronan for those few years, I was uncertain about myself. But when I would see him from time-to-time in the corridors of the City Hall Courtroom floors, and listen to him speak, I began to form some thoughts in the back of my mind. Then somewhere about when our clients were both brought into a potentially huge class action in Contra Costa County, and there was a defense meeting in our conference room at my father's firm, the thought suddenly sprang into my brain, fully formed: I had been a fool to fly-off the handle when he told me about my father's job offer! I spent years thereafter, even today, with that thought in the forefront of my mind every time I saw Ronan."

Carolyn, "Do you still feel that way?"

Sandra, "Yes and No. I will go to my grave knowing that I had acted as a fool. So, yes. I guess I do. But I no longer harbor any thoughts about resurrecting any form of romance with him. I remember at a meeting in Philadelphia, I was positioned where I could watch Ronan who was often very active in those meetings. I was doing so, when I realized that his associate Martha was watching me, watch Ronan. I suddenly shifted my gaze away, and realized that Martha had seen me do that. I was mortified! Embarrassed! What if she told him?" Sandra looked at Carolyn.

"Martha told him. Ronan told Mollie. When the time came, Mollie told me. That's why we are here." *(An accurate quote of Martha's words as I had recited them to Dr. Arnaud, more than fifteen years ago.)*

Carolyn turned to face Sandra, "I loved Mollie like the sister I never had. I changed my life and married Ronan because she asked me to do that as she was dying. She asked me to protect Ronan from you. He wants to, feels he needs to, work with you. I have my doubts about that, but I want to hear that you will have no designs on Ronan. If you cannot promise that, then we have nothing left to discuss. If you can, I will leave you two now."

Sandra looked squarely at Carolyn, and said, "My God! How you must love him. I don't know if I could ever love like you seem to. Yes, I can promise you those feelings will never come to the fore in any relationship that Ronan and I have in the course of our professional lives."

Carolyn rose, extended her hand toward Sandra, who took it and shook it, saying, "I feel certain we will be seeing more of you in the months ahead. Please never forget."

Sandra agreed to associate with O'Neill Fox on the Neptune matter.

9

MY WORLD ACCELERATES EVER FORWARD

Between the Neptune matter and Great Western Foundry on top of Martha's Asbestos Abatement Property cases, I was developing the sense that we were taxing my limits of concentration and our associate skills. *(Our firm had many other more mundane pieces of litigation. My focus here is limited to those of significant interest in their factual content.)*

Moreover, Reggie and I agreed that we should limit Sandra's participation to the Neptune case. After all, we had a written agreement on that. Sandra and I began by both of us reading that Complaint and its exhibits, primary among them being the licensing contract itself. After reading that contract, we both felt it had not been authored by a large commercial law firm. Some of the topics, including Liquidated Damages, Punitive Damages, Attorney's Fees, Choice of Law and Choice of Forum, all appeared most unusual in their language and drafting style. Also interesting were slight inconsistencies between dates of signing various attached exhibits, including the contract itself. Among the client's own documents, we were able to find very little by way of written communications concerning the drafting, or even the execution, of the contract. Since that document might ultimately control the entire dispute's outcome, we felt the urgent need to get back to Mason Eggars and have him contact the client on this threshold issue, perhaps have us all on a teleconference.

The next morning at ten Pacific time, four of us talked including the lead associate in Mason's office. We started by saying the identification of which person's files were sent to us was a bit unclear. Mason's associate, Regina, allowed that was how the files were delivered to their office and there was only a Post-It on each box identifying the producing person. Those two were Mildred Gamble, Treasurer of Neptune Fishing, and Brett Small, its head of production. Their contact person was David Pounds, Assistant General Counsel for Litigation and Human Rights for Neptune Enterprises, the parent of a number of somewhat diverse subsidiaries, only one of which had its own lawyer, and he was that sub's CEO. Pounds had supplied those documents to Regina Isaacs and assured her they were all the files they had.

Sandra then asked if Mr. Pounds had a file. Mason said he was certain he must. Then, what lawyer reviewed the contract? Also, if Neptune Fishing's President, Everson Harris, signed the contract, did he have a file? And, did either one of them participate in negotiating or reviewing the contract before it was signed? Finally, I asked about exchanges of draft contracts or provisions, and were there any transmittal documents or cover sheets? Then Sandra asked what about e-mails and attachments, noting that there were no printouts of anything electronic. Ms. Isaacs said she assumed Mr. Pounds would have included any and all e-mails in response to their office's request for all documents and files. At that point, Mason intervened and said they would follow-up on all of our questions right away and would get back to me, hopefully tomorrow.

Sandra and I talked for a few more minutes: we did not understand the actual science involved in the chemistry reactions leading to the product manufacturing failures that gave rise to this suit; and, we were both uncertain if some of the provisions of the contract were unenforceable as drafted under California law. I asked Sandra to look into all of this and whether any of these provisions could be attacked by Demurrer or Summary Judgment. Also, I mentioned that Mason had told me that the owner of the plaintiff tech corporation licensor had written some of the contractual provisions himself. A few well-researched legal memos should provide the basis for a requisite analysis for each provision in question.

Sandra and I agreed that there was a paucity of material on the drafting and execution of the contract and that the contract attached as an exhibit to the Complaint did not match the one produced by the client and provided by Mr. Pounds. All very suspicious!

Sandra asked if she could come to the office tomorrow if Mason set up a call and we could have lunch after that call. I agreed.

– – –

I managed to get Martha on the telephone later that day. I began by asking about her baby. That was fifteen minutes (because I had waxed on about Mollie not that long ago, I was much more understanding!). Then I told Martha about the workload imbalances and the new lawsuit which might generate very large fees. She was "happy for us." I explained that the complexity of all of the now pending matters made having a lead role in one too many to be taxing my abilities which were beginning to be less flexible as I was aging and that all of the stress took a cumulative toll on my psyche and my energy. She appeared sympathetic, but made no offer of her assistance. Finally, I asked her flat out: "Do you know when you will be coming back to the firm?"

Martha made a sound, like the indrawing of breath, "I don't know that at the moment, but I can tell you, I've begun the search for a satisfactory nanny for Michael Francis. Once I have that person and am satisfied that our son will get the appropriate care, I will return. As I tried to convey many months ago, I have no idea how long that will take. Sorry!"

I felt like I just took a fist to the solar plexus. I sucked it up and said, "Martha, I wish you well, but be aware, the Firm needs you now and so do I. Thank you."

When I told Carolyn about my call with Martha that evening, she seemed probably more sympathetic toward Martha, than me. But then she turned back to me and said that Sandra's candor had impressed her, and she might turn out to be less of a threat than Mollie thought she might be. Her wry smile after that statement was supplemented, as she moved toward the kitchen, by mumbled words concerning a zebra and not changing its stripes. I found that last phrase quite amusing!

— — —

Sandra and I proceeded, with senior paralegal Deirdre' s help, to have all of the delivered Neptune Fishing documents Bates-stamped for ID and production purposes as well as to track their sources. Our independent reviews of what we received seemed to raise more questions than to solve much of anything, including building a viable time-line. We were both mindful by that point in time of the potential to use parent Neptune's legal staff as a source of more documents. Our time for filing a responsive pleading to Ester-Tech's Complaint, already with one voluntary extension was moving rapidly toward the filing date. I called their lead counsel, Amanda Tatum, and asked for another thirty days. She seemed unhappy with that request, but when I explained that we only had the client's documents for six days, she gave me three more weeks.

Sandra and I put in a call to Mason Eggars and requested him to check with the Neptune staff counsel for all of their files and whether or not anyone else at the client/subsidiary had any other files. We also explained the need for more of a sense of urgency. Lastly, we went over some of the holes in what we had been provided and pointed out that their subsidiary's president's version of its contract with Ester-Tech was not the exact document produced by its CEO Everson Harris, not to mention all of the holes blocking any creation of a timeline in the process of this transaction. Mason allowed that he would try to get resolution by the end of our day today, or their East Coast day tomorrow at the very latest. When we finished that call, I turned to Sandra and Deirdre, saying, "You know I have a bad feeling about this case. Maybe it's just me, but I sense that this corporate giant runs on a legal shoestring, and may not keep accurate or complete records. Please keep that in mind as we go forward on this matter. Sandra, assuming our client produces no other contract by tomorrow, why do we not consider filing a motion objecting to their pleadings seeking to secure an explanation for that 'clash of contracts,' and its resolution. Please both of you think about it tonight. We'll meet over coffee here at nine tomorrow morning. OK?"

I did think about my proposed motion on several occasions before our 9:00 meeting, but decided to await the comments of Sandra and Deirdre. After we got beverages, we settled down at the small conference table in my office. I remember Sandra taking a chair that allowed her to look out the floor to ceiling window at the Oakland Estuary flowing slowly past us, like a tidal river, on the ebb tide seen from a block away. She ate nothing and asked, "May I start?" Dierdre and I both nodded YES, and she went on, "We have a call from Mason coming up soon. My fear is that we just do not have all of the client's paperwork, making any motion very high risk. I think we should wait and see to find out what else he discovers."

"I agree completely. I do not trust their paperwork so far. This whole matter seems to spell trouble!" was Dierdre's take.

"I concur. Rather than waste tine now, I'll call Mason in ninety minutes and see where he's at," was my input.

Sandra asked if we had a space where she could work on her own firm's other matters. We had a larger conference room between Reggie's office and mine and I suggested that she could wait there. After they both left, I asked Lily to come in. Besides being our senior assistant, working for Reggie and me, Lily also functioned as our office manager under Reggie's supervision. We had recently taken on the last vacant spaces in the building to accommodate the new attorneys, including some larger offices for the recent promotions. I asked Lily who was running all of that, under Reggie, to see if we had a space for Sandra, or any other visiting counsel to allow them to work temporarily. She said we did not, but there were now some newly vacant rooms; and after pausing to think for a few moments, perhaps we could use the smallest office of these, on our top floor, the third, for that purpose. She would move the two paralegals who were a bit crowded in there now down into a larger office on the first floor, currently a vacant room, unsuitable as a lawyer's office (no window). Thus, it came to pass that Sandra would have space on the same floor as Reggie, Martha and me. Then, Lily added, "Maybe Sandra could use Martha's office while we get that work done?"

Me: "That sounds great, but please run it by Reggie to make certain that he's OK with it. Then let me know it's fine and I will call Martha and tell her, unless you would rather do that?"

"HA-HA!" was Lily's parting on that last suggestion. She and Martha were "friendly enemies."

— — —

Our call with Mason Eggars was everything I had hoped it would not be: he spoke of missed connections, excuses and a variety of what seemed to be evasions. We went over our need for action now, and how delays were the worst possible waste of our limited time to respond. After ten minutes of mild haranguing, I realized this was not about Mason, but his clients. I stopped and said, "Mason, this is not about you, but you do see the fix in which we find ourselves. From noon to three, Eastern Standard time, please arrange to have these people available for 30 minutes each. Please explain to them, that if they do not cooperate completely, we will resign for cause forthwith as their California counsel. Please have their parent staff attorney on the line the entire time as we shall be looking to him, or her, to ride herd on these subsidiary people. Please use whatever words you choose, but tomorrow's call will be a make it or break it, so please stress the adverse consequences."

We spoke for another twenty minutes, and Mason seemed to better understand our issues. I suggested that he start with the Neptune parent's AGC for Litigation, including that person being present on Mason's calls to those not providing their files. This request met with some resistance making me realize that David Pounds was probably Mason's client contact and Mason did not want to rock that boat. So, I asked, "Mason, do you want me to talk to Mr. Pounds?" Sandra smiled at my question. She was probably thinking the same as me (Neptune's subsidiaries might well take an 'ostrich approach' to litigation).?"

Mason asked. "Could we maybe both talk to Mr. Pounds?"

Me, "Sure, why don't you see if you can get him on the line now?" Mason agreed, and we were on hold. In less than thirty seconds, he was back on the line with David Pounds whom it turns out had not yet read the Ester-Tech Complaint. Deirdre passed a note on sandwiches and we all settled down for what turned into an almost two hour call. (During that call, I seriously hoped Mr. Pounds was taking notes. I did not want to have to go through this again.) At least twice, I asked him who from their internal legal would have reviewed the draft contract. He twice responded that he was not at all certain that anyone had reviewed the entire contract. When I asked if the parent required its subsidiaries to supply contracts to corporate legal for review in all instances, he said NO. Even with a draft above a threshold dollar amount, like one million, he still said NO. Then I asked how the parent controlled the terms of those deals undertaken by the various subsidiaries. His answer explained why we were not getting what we needed, "Well, you see, the heads of the various subsidiaries almost all have a relationship of many years with Adam Young, the CEO and founder of Neptune, and maybe Adam Junior as well. One of them generally approves deals of any consequence in consultation with that subsidiary's CEO. Doubtless that was the case here as Everson Harris, Neptune Fishing's CEO, goes back decades with Adam Young. So, then I ask the big question: do they have any documentation of what they do and decide? To which David Pounds responded with a rousing, "Sometimes."

This level of colloquy went on and on. Finally, Sandra and Dierdre had a list with seventeen names on it of those who might be witnesses or might possibly have documents on this contract's creation and execution. Dierdre faxed that list to them at my request. I closed with, "By the end of this week, that's three days, we need to know in as much detail as possible who did what in this contract formation process, and we need each person's documents which were retained on that topic. That gives us twenty days, weekends included, to come up with a plan of action and draft all of the documents needed to move our as-yet unformulated litigation plan forward. We really need this action now. If we cannot get it done with this week of trying, then we all will have to consider other courses of action. Are we all agreed?"

Both David Pounds and Mason Eggars agreed, neither sounding particularly enthusiastic. Finally, we planned a group call for Friday at three o'clock, California time.

After hanging up, Dierdre allowed that she had never

seen nor heard of anything like Neptune. I thanked her for putting together the lists of names by company and job descriptions. She smiled and left. Sandra, who had ducked out as soon as the call ended, had returned to my office. She shook her head from side-to-side slowly, saying, "Never seen or heard of anything quite like that. This thing sounds like a giant family entrepreneurship masquerading as a multi-tiered corporate giant. I'm wondering if they'll even get an audience with either of the Youngs, and all these others! Sounds nearly impossible. WOW! But you were right: if they do not give us enough to come up with a plan, then we'll just have to say, 'Good-bye and Good-luck!' Do you think those two'll get anything?"

My response was simple, "How many times did I say that the complaint asks not just for seven figure damages under the licensing terms, but has provisions for prevailing party attorney's fees and punitive damages. All of that creating a no ceiling verdict and no insurance for any of it under California law! As I told them, they need to lead with that, and I would appreciate your sending Mason and David a fax right away and suggest that we conferred and think that the two of them should try to start with the CEO father and son first thing tomorrow, get whatever they have, discuss the risks and downsides, and get their mandate for full cooperation forthwith from everyone on Dierdre's list in the parent and the sub. Also, point out that unknowns can be added to that list. Please sign it yourself and show me as a "cc." Lily can help you with the copying and faxing. I want them to know that you are fully involved in this matter!"

Sandra got up, lifted her things, said, "will do!" and walked down the hall to her temporary place in Martha's office.

Before heading home, I stopped in Felicia Clarke's office to see how she was coming on the written discovery on the Great Western Foundry Consolidated Cases (GWF) which was due to be exchanged in about ten working days pursuant to the Joint Case Management Order. She had been working with our experts to come up with discovering as many variables, as possible, to undermine any causative correlation between lead alone and reduced IQ, both from an environmental perspective as well as a genetic. The number of written Interrogatories was limited both by the California Discovery statutes and the Local Rules of Sacramento County Superior Court. Motion practice would be needed to seek relief from those limiting rules as this was novel science; and as such, all variables needed to be disclosed without any artificially imposed limitations.

At this point, Felicia had 23 sets of variables with six or seven questions about each one. But the additional questions only need be answered if the witness answered each foundational question affirmatively. Since most of the plaintiffs were still minors, the probability of 23 positive responses was so unlikely as to never occur, especially since some of those 23 categories were mutually exclusive.

I asked Felicia how the process was going. She allowed that she was deeply involved with our two "consulting experts," and was hopeful of having a draft set for me to consider by the close of business tomorrow. I wished her success.

I stopped at SF University High School at 3:30 to watch Meaghan, a junior outside hitter help her high school dominate its intra-family volleyball rival, Branson, where her twin Patrick was beginning basketball practice for the forthcoming season, hoping to step into Robert's shoes as an

ALL-BAY AREA player for his last year, at least. He was there cheering for both teams: his sister on the rival and his girlfriend, a sophomore defender for Branson. Afterward, Meaghan asked me for a ride if I could first give her fifteen or twenty minutes. I agreed, knowing that players needed time to decompress with their teammates.

In my MBZ SUV, Meaghan allowed that one of her friends, a young man, told her that his father who was an editor for the San Francisco Times newspaper had mentioned that several of their reporters were putting together a series of articles exposing how your firm is defending a variety of major environmental polluters. I asked him a few questions, but that seemed to be the extent of that son's knowledge. Changing the subject slightly, I began to discuss our trips to Europe, meeting Sir Richard Doll, Corbett and Alison McDonald and Jean Bignon, pointed out that they were reputable world-renowned scientists, and that they were assisting in much of my work.

Thinking further, I said, "Meaghan, I'll discuss this with Carolyn, but please tell no one else. Let's wait and see what they write. I'll tell you what I will do before I do it, so you will be forewarned. Please do not worry. Love you, and thank you!"

10

JUST AN OLD-FASHIONED BAR BRAWL

I was a bit mystified by what Meaghan had told me about the SF Tribune doing an *expose* on O'Neill Fox and those clients which it represented in its environmental defense practice. I did not have to wait too long for the first article. Two paragraphs in, I realized that the authors had adopted a tone which I referred to as "righteously pedantic" against our office. I searched the multi-paged article carefully, but could find no quotes from other environmental, or high-powered, Bay Area lawyers. I thought for a few minutes and asked Lily to circulate the article among all of our legal and administrative staff and asked for their comments in one or two pages, if at all, by close of business the next day. (A follow-on was promised for next Tuesday. That gave us some time.)

Meanwhile, the American Civil Litigation Network's initial structural meeting at the Biltmore in Phoenix was growing closer which meant that both Carolyn and I had tasks to undertake in connection with that event. Carolyn had to work with the other founders' spouses on a program for those non-member attendees. She pointed out that knowing the schedule for events was critical for the timing of her group's events to allow couples to appear at the evening events in each other's company. I conferred with my colleagues on the overall member structure and the needed sub-meetings to accommodate the varying perspectives of our members. We decided on a short welcoming gathering for all member guests and a very brief introduction by firm only, without speeches from all members, followed by a break-out into plaintiff practice and defense practice with separate breaks and the balance of the first morning in those groupings with agendas and time for idea exchanges as well. We needed co-chairs for that role. I was able to recruit Harry Wartnick's firm from San Francisco, and he agreed to have lunch with me about items for the agenda. I also provided him with a list of all member firms. The Board was making an all-out effort to recruit member firms that were not aspiring to geographic growth which could cause conflicts of interest in the future. I sent a three page draft agenda to the planning committee members and we agreed to speak early on that Friday morning to try to finalize the overall outline for the timing of all events, and then leave the final detailed agenda for each large practice area's chair, e.g., Harry Wartnick, an old friendly adversary in San Francisco, was a co-chair for Plaintiffs.

I also sent a copy to Carolyn pointing out it was only a draft, but we were meeting early on Friday, so Lily would get her that iteration as soon as practicable on Friday. I pointed out that what she just received might have some minor time block movement, but very little significant variation was possible because of the strictures of facility availability at the Biltmore.

By the time I got home that evening, I only had time to sit my briefcase down, pour a Stoli on the rocks, and Carolyn sat her glass of wine on the family room bar, ready to talk about what the spouse's committee would like to schedule. Based on her often subtle digs about getting a master schedule, I knew that "they" were ready to move forward to their final agenda. A few minutes discussion was all that Carolyn needed. She picked up her wine, headed for her office, and said over her departing shoulder, "We should have something for you all before you leave tomorrow morning." They did.

— — —

When I got to my fax machine that next morning, there were two faxes, one from Quincy at Twenty King's Bench Walk, Barrister Chambers, and one from Bradley Campbell at Thornton Campbell, Solicitors, both in London. Both conveyed the need for a meeting scheduled yesterday for the end of the first week in December to finalize the underwriting/financial underpinning for the "New Lloyds" at the Grosvenor House, Park Lane. I called Lily and asked her to get Mary, Sir Richard Doll's Assistant to make two reservations for suites for that entire week. A closer examination of the faxes showed that they cross-referenced each other and were addressed to John O'Sullivan, soon to be CEO of Desert Mutual and Gerry Dwyer, Senior EVP of Connecticut Indemnity. I called Lily back and asked for three suites.

First, I called Quincy to see what he had from an overview perspective, then Barclay who approached this new vehicle more from a service throughput/financial funding approach at each level of the process might need. Both were on committees working to have a fully ready process by the time of these meetings, with the ability to adjust so that a functionally operational enterprise would announce itself in time for the new year, and leading up to the new century. Each promised a point in time written update within a little more than two of their working days starting tomorrow. I was able to get Gerry on her line, just before she broke for lunch. She agreed to wait while Lily transferred John O'Sullivan into our call. My input was brief, but needed. We reviewed where these matters stood when last we had spoken some weeks ago, and the need to assess quickly with key staff in our companies for any new or different input.

They gave me a very short list of what they would need to get the appropriate discretion at the Second Convocation in December. We agreed that Lily, through Mary, would handle our stay needs, while each of us would see to our flights and ground transport. I then prepared a memo to Quincy and Bradley with our collective thoughts, needs, and goals. With some overlapping, this all fit on two double-spaced pages. I ended by asking for a call at 9:30 a.m. PST on the next day including our UK contacts. By the time I broke for lunch, all arrangements were complete, including the three suites. Lily said, we booked them just in time according to Mary.

Meanwhile, Lily had put together a revised draft ACLN Organization Meeting agenda. Once I approved it, Lily sent it to the other three for use at the Friday a.m. conference call.

After a quick lunch with Sandra at *Il Pescatore,* a few blocks away at the entry onto the pier in the Oakland Estuary with the Jack London fueling station at its end, I reviewed our first two sets of draft written discovery for Great Western Foundry to Plaintiffs pursuant to our Court-sanctioned Stipulated Case Management Schedule. One set was geared to cover generalized areas of inquiry, mostly about the alleged exposures, but also covering other exposures in the timeframes alleged, and other generalized topics which could be answered for more than one plaintiff. The second set was to each individual plaintiff and covered as many of the contributing factors, events and relatives which might have some bearing on causation, if any, for each plaintiff. Following service, parties had thirty-five days to object to any discovery; and then as to those with no agreement, to move to strike the inquiries, or for a protective order.

These were the first steps in obtaining leverage for the defense of GWF. Felicia had met multiple times with Andrea Parsons and Stuart Brock, the two senior lawyers at GWF, as well as our expert consultants to formulate the scope and targets for this first discovery effort. It was a long and tedious meeting, Felicia and her two associates had spent a serious part of the last two months putting all of our discussions and opinions into a legally written format to generate concrete results, if any did exist in fact. My job was that of vetting and I took it very seriously. After all, clients were not pleased if we failed to obtain critical evidence because we did not go about extracting it correctly. To do so, I needed to consider the relevancy of all that was sought to the plaintiffs' cases or GWF's defenses, and whether or not we went about asking the questions correctly and in a legally defensible form.

The four of us went at that vetting, virtually without break for two and a half hours. We early on established a few internal rules. Then, it became the volume of the inquiries that might raise objections from the Plaintiffs' counsel. The three kept careful notes of all of our discussions. Their preparation appeared meticulous. At the end of the process, I said, "I hope you all know how proud of you I am. This was a difficult and arduous process and you have performed admirably. Felicia, I do believe you are ready to lead this battle and be the point person in defense of your group's labors and to get GWF's defense off to an auspicious start. Thank you all! Can I buy you a drink now at The Fat Lady!"

That next day's call with the clients and our UK advisors laid the foundation for most of the planning options needed to be considered by them at the Convocation and how our clients might see various avenues to pursue to avail themselves of their needed coverages, while attempting to generate revenue on the money they invested in their acceptable portions of the overall Lloyds enterprise itself.

While Bradley and Quincy, particularly Bradley, who along with Madeline Myles, were principals in Long-Tail Litigation Limited, were aligned with DMIC and CI, whose interests might diverge at some point, the issue of conflicts of interest persisted in the minds of all of us involved in this Lloyds restructuring project. (Please know that although DMIC and CI had closed their books almost entirely on the reinsurance found through the placement records of London Placing Brokers, Wilshire & Booth, that missing records location business continued and was a very real revenue producer for all of the entities involved. But as to "New Lloyds," LTL was looking for the right spots to position itself for future revenue streams. Those streams would most likely be revealed by the choice of operating entities created for this new enterprise, e.g., acting as a buffer in replacing, or restructuring, the Names Syndicates of "Old Lloyds."

When our call began to move into this area of speculation, I could sense that John and Gerry were both becoming uncomfortable, and I suggested that we digest the thoughts and data exchanged to this point and await the next developments from London in preparation for this Second Lloyds Convocation.

John and Gerry called me back in moments. Both had concluded that although Quincy and Bradley were in theory on the "inside" of what was happening that might not be the actual case. They wondered about another source that might provide another stream of information.

Silence followed. I said, "Ideas?"

More silence.

I floated, "What if I happened to be coming to London and wanted to see my new friend of several years, Stanley Booth, who might be on a different track in all of this and might be willing to talk based on our friendly relationship through LTL?"

John allowed, "Does this require going through their solicitors?"

I said, "We could invite Mr. Pierce, if Stanley agrees to do so."

Gerry replied, "Why not? That puts the ball in their court."

John asked, "Wives?"

Me: "No. I don't think so. Carolyn told me last night that she is committed through January. The entities with whom she is affiliated have events starting this time of year and she is heavily booked. Would either one of you like to run over there for a few days?"

Silence again. So, "I guess I'll check my calendar and try to squeeze something in. John, I hope you won't mind if I call on Julian Peto or Corbett McDonald while there?"

We exchanged pleasantries and they moved on. I was building toward an ultra-busy year-end!

Around 11:30, Lily stuck her head through my doorway and asked if we could go to lunch. I agreed and we headed to *Il Pescatore,* my local favorite now that the Grotto had closed for refurbishment under new owners (one of the Grotto's three brothers died suddenly and the other two decided to retire and sell their business, lock, stock and barrel. They had been in business for more than forty years and were a cornerstone of the Jack London Square eateries on the Oakland Estuary, a short walk from our office). That Italian 'fish restaurant' had a memorable special that day: grilled Dover sole with a garlic butter sauce (another of my favorites from Wheelers on Curzon Street, just off Park Lane in London). It was just excellent with two glasses of Chardonnay from the upper Napa Valley. Lily wanted to know about the firm's direction as well as my role and hers going into the future. We chatted about that. But once we moved out to beyond one year, I found I was very uncertain (not befuddled, so much as my not foreseeing a presently discernible plan for more growth, and a leadership transition to a younger generation. I did not give voice to those thoughts. Rather, I embraced them, thinking this is something to discuss with Reggie first.). I did tell her that her ability to embrace, and move forward with the technological changes, together with her willingness to share her training and insights, was a gift which we partners appreciated greatly. (Lily seemed hardly to have aged in the almost twenty years we had been together. She was pretty in a youngish manner, always appearing neat and well-groomed and modestly attired. That was her look, but her efficiency and organization and execution of tasks was just exceptional.) I told her I would be "lost without her." At those words, Lily lost a touch of color in her face, her ever-present smile began to fade, and I thought I saw a tear or two forming in her eyes.

Lily made a sound in her throat that seemed to be the beginning of a cough. But then, she swallowed, her chest moved, and she sat up straighter. Her smile returned. Her eyes fixed on mine. She never did that, and she said, "I think what you just said, and the way in which you said it, is the nicest thing anyone other than my Mom or Dad has ever said to me. Thank you so very much. If I was seated next to you, I would want to give you a big hug, Oh my! That was so inappropriate. I am sorry." But Lily kept smiling.

"Lily, after all these years, if I can do something that makes you want to hug me, I think it would be just fine if you actually did that. I know Carolyn would not mind. She just loves every opportunity to work with you. You are such a delight."

With that said, I rose, stepped part way around our table in Lily's direction, and before I could move as if in slow-motion, Lily was in my arms, her arms around my waist and her head on my chest hugging me as hard as I had ever been hugged. We stood frozen like that for perhaps thirty seconds. It seemed longer. With me being thirteen inches taller, I could not see her face as we hugged. But when Lily let go and stepped back, I could see tears streaming down her face. She looked up at me, smiled, and said, "I hope you don't mind, but I need a few minutes to regain my composure. I'll be right back."

I paid for lunch while she was gone and had the waiter put her one half of uneaten Dover sole in a container for Lily's later consumption. She reappeared as I stood awaiting her near the entrance. We walked past the dominating Port of Oakland building, across the Southern Pacific train tracks, and past our original office building. Three short blocks or so, not a long way. When we got to the front door of our building, she stopped. I turned to look at her. She broke the silence first, "I wanted to have lunch with you since it had been so long since we had done anything like that. I was afraid you had stopped trusting me. That you might fire me. I had to know. I was going to quit first if you started to do that. I just could not stand the thought, and I was becoming obsessed with worry. Now, I feel so much better! I never want to leave this job, this firm. I love it here and now I truly feel a part of it. Oh, thank you. Can I have one more hug?"

So, I gave her the hug she wanted, returned by her, and I felt assured of a relationship to last a working lifetime.

— — —

Sandra and I were seated at my office table as we called Mason Eggars at his Wilmington, NC office, at our agreed scheduled time. He answered promptly, with an audible sigh, followed by, "I have roughly a box plus of new files from some of the people we discussed. Of those seventeen names, we seem to have five. Several others said they would be a day or two. Others were not sure thy had anything, but said they would look around."

Me, "Anything from either of the Youngs or their GC?"

Mason, "Well I sent your memo and list to Leslie Worth, Neptune's GC, who has to clear anything legal that gets to the Youngs. I am afraid, she has been non-responsive."

Sandra, "How many of the seventeen have David Pounds and you heard nothing from?"

Mason sounded like he was going to choke, "I am afraid that number is four others, including Neptune's President,

Everson Harris, except for the handful that I sent you at the outset."

"Mason, Sandra and I are hopeful based on the attached "pleaded contract," we can have some, if not complete, success in defending this lawsuit. But that will never happen if the terms of the contract were not actually agreed upon, especially since it has the signatures for both parties. I will tell you what, Sandra and I will have a letter for you, from us, spelling out what we might be able to do very generally, but the other options Neptune may need to confront if it will not fully cooperate. Please have your assistant supply Lily with all of the appropriate ID data for us to address the letters to each of those twelve persons not cooperating to date, please include both Mr. Youngs. We would prefer to send them directly, with a copy to Ms. Worth, Mr. Pounds and to you. We would prefer to do all of this electronically, if possible. If you want to send something after ours, please copy us. Friday is coming quickly."

Silence followed. Then, "I heard you have crossed swords with Ron Motley more than once, and never lost. Could that be true?"

Me, "Yes. We are cordial, but I am not certain we are friends"

Him, "That will give me something persuasive to write. He is 'the SuperStar Lawyer' in the Carolinas.' When can I expect your letter?"

"It's being written right now. So, we need that contact data ASAP. We will send at the close of our business today. You'll have it when you read your email later tonight. If you do not, then no later than early tomorrow a.m.," was my response.

Silence for a few seconds. I added, "Sandra, do you have anything to add?"

Sandra smiled, saying. "Not really. This is going pretty much as we thought it might. Good speaking with you, Mason."

Two hours later, Sandra and I had our final version of a three page *in terrorem* letter to our clients explaining generally all of the bad things that could happen along the course of the case where missing documents, or inconsistent disclosures could very well lead to a very bad verdict/outcome, possibly even punitive damages. At 5:30 PST, Lily hit her send button and fourteen people in North Carolina got our letter within seconds. Following my instructions, Lily shut her system down right away. She said GOOD NIGHT. Sandra and I went home as well.

Walking to our cars, she asked, "Do you think we can salvage this document mess?"

I replied, "I don't know, but something I really fear is thinking they have disclosed all of their documents and that proves to be wrong. I like Mason a great deal, but he appears to have almost no client control or influence at all. He's not making me feel reassured at this point. You?"

Sandra, "I think you have done an excellent job of describing my feelings."

— — —

Lily had given me a folder with comments on the SF Tribune article "exposing our firm as a guardian of some 'evil empire'" which had set out to poison society while enriching itself. I poured a Johnnie Walker Black over a few ice cubes and read through the comments. They were highly critical of our style in the absence of any evidence. Reggie and Mary suggested we do nothing to allow them to look as if we were truly interested in defending ourselves from the utter nonsense they had written.

Carolyn had read the article. She thought it seemed to lack any logical theme or actual factual basis, focusing more on condemning our client manufacturers without their having a right to a defense.

I thought Carolyn gave me the best hint as to how to approach with a brief response. I sat at my computer and put together two pages, titled *Even Dirt deserves a Defense*. What followed was a togue-in-cheek attempt to hold the co-authors of this *Expose* to a standard that they themselves had failed to follow, and by pointing out that professional litigators represented their clients, but were not themselves the client, much as Charles Dickens could create Scrooge and write about him, that work did not make him become Scrooge. I emailed my draft to Reggie and Mary. Then gave a copy to Carolyn who was reading in bed as she waited for me.

Basically, I went back to the Declaration of Independence and the U.S. Constitution for my background and legal authorities, starting with "… (A)ll men are created equal and entitled to life, liberty, and the pursuit of happiness…." Then the right to hold property, and to have that property protected, up through the Bill of Rights. This was not limited to criminal matters, but the vast bulk of civil law dealt with money, property and the protection of human life from harm in terms of monetary damages (at this point of my rebuttal, I did not get off into other forms of equitable relief). Thus, our clients, which had real employees and many shareholders depending on them for their livelihood, when those clients were sued for dollar damages, as in almost every case, we stepped in to defend them, when asked.

A few edits undertaken by Reggie and Mary the next a.m., and Lily sent it off to the Tribune asking it be printed on the 'morrow's Op-Ed page. That paper wrote back affirmatively. By noon of the following day, we had more than one hundred emails from lawyers and firms in the circulation area of the Tribune. All but two backed our position and most thanked us for what we said.

(After the Tribune's authors' second article of their series and our response largely dealing with the more than adequate representation available to their suggested victims among the many very successful Bay Area plaintiffs' firms which existed solely to represent them, the owners of the Times reprinted the two articles, and our rejoinders, with its limited comment, and asking for feedback from its readers. That action resulted in this discourse receiving evermore coverage locally in and into the south of our state.)

— — —

Our first call on that following Friday morning was with the ACLN steering committee to finish our draft of the overall AGENDA of the ACLN official INITIAL ORGANIZATION MEETING. Almost two hours later we had our draft which we agreed to have Lily send to the committees for the various practice areas to allow them to incorporate their differing agendas for their attending members.

Lily copied Carolyn on her transmittal of the agenda, read it, and sent a transmittal message to Lily to include with the cover for the agenda to her "Spouse" organizers. We were on our way to wrapping up the planning for that meeting.

At the very end of our call, I mentioned the SF Tribune's

articles attempting to villainize, if not demonize, defense firms like ours and my responses. My three compatriots asked to see it. Lily had already scanned the Tribune's request for comments page and forwarded it to them a few moments after our call ended. Its circulation increased markedly moving forward. Some of the ACLN Plaintiff firm members had a field day with the Tribune, literally mocking its writers for their failure to understand, and appear to have no appreciation whatsoever, for the American tort resolution legal process.

— — —

Later that Friday, before lunch, Sandra and I had a call with Mason Eggars, who allowed that our letter to the recalcitrant Neptune responders had its intended effect and that Adam Young, the CEO, had his secretary copy all of those recipients and order them to get their contract negotiation materials to Mason without any delay or excuses. He had already received the executive office materials from five different individuals and several of the subsidiary's people. The client's documents we had received so far were copies without any Identifier of the source person. Mason had retained those and they were segregated by producing source. We asked him to have 'as received copies' of each set made and put aside one complete set as back-up to the originals, then to take a second set and using the source ID codes we devised to have them Bates-stamped in the exact sequence received. This would serve as the production set of documents when the other side sought them in discovery. We then asked him to have those initially-stamped documents copied, arranged in reverse chronological sequence by date ("chron" or "chron set") and place a second folder coded Bates identifier on each. He was to retain those originals as an 'as copied' set, and each Bates stamped set; and, we would piece everything together to assure what everyone had and the time sequence in which they got it. He asked for an hour to call back.

Mason had talked to his primary vendor for major document reproduction who allowed that they would put a staff together and have a Saturday pick-up for Sunday delivery to our office of the complete sets, as requested, no later than 9:30 a.m. Sandra looked at me, smiled, and asked, "Would you like me here by 8:30 a.m. on Sunday?" When I nodded YES, she added, "May I have Deirdre and one other paralegal to help me to undertake that task?"

I responded, "You all will need to create one complete set in reverse chron, then flip the chron and finally get to analyzing what we have to work with. Can we meet here Monday at noon to assess what you have found out, then we'll call Mason?"

More boxes were to arrive from Mason that following TUE a.m., and we had a fairly good fix on the content of the pleadings we were going to file in response to the Ester-Tech Complaint, beginning with a Motion to Strike the document attached to their Complaint claiming to be the Contact at issue. The documents supplied by Everson Harris, CEO of Neptune Fishing, in the Tuesday boxes, however, threatened to complicate those issues. All of this while the due date to file a responsive pleading was moving ever closer. We prevailed on Mason to capture Mr. Harris and get him into Mason's office for an hour or so, as soon as at all possible (Preferably yesterday!).

The gist of Mr. Harris' version of things was worse than

we could imagine: he had signed the draft contract offered to him by Mr. Singh after much negotiation and sent it back to him by mail (the same one attached to the Complaint). The next day, he re-read that signed draft contract, and realized that the initial amount of product to be produced was off by a factor of ten. So, after calling Mr. Singh and leaving him a message, he redid that one page, wrote a cover fax sheet including explaining his error, and faxed that page to Mr. Singh to insert the redone page as a substitute in the contract he had signed and sent the day before; and then, gave no further thought to it!

Sandra and I both shook our heads and waited for something further from Mr. Harris, but we got nothing useful. Instead, "The next thing I know, we are getting sued for a great deal of money. I tried to get to the bottom, but I could not make heads or tails of what my people were trying to tell me. That's when I called Leslie Worth, our GC, and asked her to deal with the lawsuit. Next thing I know, David Pounds, who works for Leslie is asking me a ton of questions and is looking for documents. I gave him a quick nutshell view of that deal, and asked my secretary to give him whatever papers she could find that I had given her. Far as I know, she did that and the next thing I know, I'm getting a letter from a lawyer in California I never heard of, but with a cover letter from Adam Young that made it sound like this is all pretty serious business. Now, here I sit talking to four or five lawyers from here and California. That's all I got. Should we be worried?"

Since Leslie Worth was a woman, I said *sotto voce* to Sandra, "You tell them." She did, in a grave voice, "You should be worried. All of us should. Your explanation, Mr. Harris is very interesting, but what we need are your written or typed 'papers' that support what you are telling us. Or anything electronic? Did you keep a copy of your cover note and that corrected page with the lower quantity guaranty on it? We have not received any of those."

Harris interrupts, "Well, I'm sitting here holding the single page I wrote and had faxed to Singh, with my copy of the draft contract signed only by me, but not by Singh."

Sandra, "Mr. Harris, do you have the fax transmittal you sent with that?"

"Give me a minute, I'll see if I can find it." Pause. "No. it's not here. Probably misfiled or thrown away. If I could just get a dependable secretary, maybe things would be more findable."

Leslie Worth spoke next. She sounded very serious, "Everson, I'm going to come down to your office and we are going to go through all of your papers. Do you have someone to help?"

"Not really, only a temp, and she seems best at fetching coffee," was his response.

Me: "Ms. Worth, could you possibly call Mason if you find anything else that looks like we should have in addition to what Mr. Harris is reading from? Mason or I can put together another call if you think it's needed. Thank you!"

We called Mason back, "Hello, Mason, we see what you are up, against." Then we discussed what we might plead. Unfortunately, everything helpful or meaningful was fact based. We had or were about to receive more documents shortly. But it was all factual evidence (unless jurisdictional, as in the *Clemson* matter in South Carolina, some years ago. *See MILL VALLEY*), which made a law-based motion unavailable because the court could not decide contested fact questions. Mason concurred. We needed to spend our remaining briefing time on Affirmative Defenses to be pleaded in our Answer to the Complaint. Sandra started right there in my office on her laptop.

— — —

11

ONE LAST YEAR BEFORE THE TWENTY-FIRST CENTURY

Having launched the Great Western Foundry's written discovery to the Plaintiffs and filed Neptune Fishing's Answer and Cross Complaint against Ester-Tech as well as serving it with an Initial Document Production and Contention Interrogatories, I was off to the Phoenix area for a week: first to meet with the Desert Mutual people about the upcoming Second Lloyds Convocation; then, for final preparation for the ACLN Organizational Meeting. When I asked our Board if I could invite some client types to the second night cocktail reception, I was met with an overwhelming positive response. In turn, they suggested inviting my four putative guests and their spouse-types to the formal dinner on the final night. So, I conferred with John O'Sullivan, who agreed to bring his wife, Emily Anne, who went by "Emma," agreeing to come to both night's events and to join the Board for its dinner on Friday night. He suggested Manny Garcia and Esmeralda for those three events as well. Also, he said Angela Lenovo and Richie Goldberg for the Friday cocktails; while for the formal dinner, they could decide for themselves.

Next thing, John asked, "Will Carolyn be with you? Emma would really like to meet her, but Emma is very shy. That's why you have rarely seen her. She is put off by bigger groups, but I know I can convince her to come by telling her Carolyn will attend."

"Since I am the Chair for the meeting and the organization, Carolyn has volunteered to run the Spouses' Activities Committee, so she'll be there the whole time."

John, "Any chance she plays golf?"

Me: "Yes. Actually, she's pretty good."

John, "If I can get a tee time for Thursday morning at Phoenix Country Club, could we try to fit in 18 as a foursome. Emma would love that. We play pretty fast: so about three and a half hours"

"I will check the schedule. I know the Board has a final meeting that Thursday afternoon before the Opening Night Introductory Cocktail Party at 6 p.m. We'd need an early start!"

— — —

Carolyn seemed especially enthused about the new ACLN group meeting in Phoenix. She was especially fond of the Biltmore and loved that we would be staying in the hotel's older original section, completely designed by Frank Lloyd Wright. The views were magnificent and the late Fall temperatures were relatively mild. She was also excited to spend time golfing with my major client, John O'Sullivan, soon to be DMIC's CEO, and to meet his wife, Emily Anne.

Our daughter, Mollie, was a dream child: always happy, exceedingly positive, funny, and smart. She really wanted to come along on our trip, but virtually all of our time would be taken up with the events of the client meetings flowing directly into the organizational vortex of ACLN. Instead, we were having her join us, with Mercedes, at John Wayne Airport on the Monday after the meetings for her first trip to Disneyland.

The night before golf with the O'Sullivans, we were scheduled to have a small cocktail reception and dinner with the Board of ACLN at the Capitol Grille not far from the Biltmore Hotel complex in the Fashion Plaza. The four founders, along with Reggie forming the initial Board were in attendance with their spouses. Carolyn and I were the first to arrive in the private dining room. I wore a sport coat, but no tie. My wife wore a two-tone cocktail dress with a not-quite demure bodice: All-American woman, on the slightly sexy side. Liam Callahan, and Serena, were the next to arrive. They both greeted me very affably. When I introduced Carolyn, I thought Liam might feint. He could not stop "looking at" Carolyn. Fortunately, his wife was also interested in her, and enthused, "Oh Carolyn, it's just so wonderful to meet you in the flesh! (I hoped my flinch was not visible.) I am so looking forward to our events."

Carolyn right back, "Serena, we'll have a marvelous time. Think of all the new friends that we'll have an opportunity to make. I'll tell you about one in a few minutes." With that, Mark and Barbara Westoff stepped into the room, followed closely by Fulton and Abby Finnerty. The enthusiasm was peeking as Reggie and Ginger arrived. Mixing physical introductions and pleasant banter, over cocktails, got the evening off to an excellent beginning. The ten of us fit nicely around the oval table which was a feature of that dining room. We all made an effort not to overdue the alcohol. The other three "founders" were anxious to meet John O'Sullivan, while all of the spouses appeared ready to meet his wife, Emily Anne, also known as Emma. Of course, I had told them all about our golf match the next morning, making them only more enthusiastic.

We started dinner with seafood appetizers, served family

style, and two quality white wines from which to choose. One waiter was designated to deal with wines, and followed our suggestion of asking about refills, rather than just pouring to keep glasses full. The four co-founders knew quite a bit about each other, but a bit less about my partner, Reggie. He filled them in on his career in the service, including law school at NYU while stationed on Governor's Island, a short ferry ride from the Battery and Wall Street, followed by an easy subway. He explained how we met, and how he had fit him right into our practice, eventually becoming managing partner. He liked meeting new people and he was very committed to making ACLN a success for all of its members. (A great off-the-cuff chat delivered flawlessly.) Reggie then asked Ginger to say a few words. She did, but added more, "Although I do not know any of you, I am confident that we will all become friends. This is because of Ronan O'Neill. Next to my husband, I hold him in higher esteem than any other living man. He found Reggie, and me. Together with his first wife, Mollie, who died young, and then Carolyn, Mollie's choice for his second wife, we have functioned as working compatriots and friends for all of these years. He is smart, loyal and creative. Carolyn is unique, and I hope you all get a real chance to appreciate her. She is a brilliant businesswoman, tireless, and fun. She did all the work on this dinner, along with Lily. I do hope we have more time to chat after dessert."

Carolyn picked up at that point, laying out that some of the spouses were more familiar with each other than others, but that was the point of the spousal events and she hoped they would prove a success. Leading to their being a feature of future ACLN meetings of this type. When she tried to pass the speaking baton to one of the other wives, Liam

Callahan intervened, and asked Carolyn, "I do not want to date your career, but my wife Serena says you have always been a high fashion model, but I told her that I remember you from several years issues of Sports Illustrated swimsuit editions quite a few years back. Would you mind telling us who is correct?"

Carolyn smiled, that understated All-American girl smile, and said, "My very first job was in a swimsuit at a giant Auto Show in San Francisco. Someone noticed me, got me involved with their agent, and that gentleman had me posing for the Swimsuit edition when I was very young. It was so exciting and they were all so nice to me. You are correct, Liam. Eight years, including two covers."

Another question followed, and Carolyn tossed the verbal ball back to Serena Callahan.

That evening went well, and thanks to its early start, we had time to mill about after dinner, over light drinks, or coffee, getting to know one-another ever better.

Back at the Biltmore's main building, I held Carolyn's hand as we walked to the elevator to go up three floors to our suite, and said, "As always, you were so wonderful. You made the Callahan's comfortable, and the others were easier. I do hope you have plenty of fun over this whole trip." Alone on the elevator, we shared a kiss. Back in our room, we shared more. I did love my wife so much, more all the time!

— — —

The next morning, I had a fax from Felicia on the Great Western Foundry case. It seemed that the Plaintiffs' firm wanted a real meet and confer on the Interrogatories we had propounded to each of their clients and their Guardians *ad litem*. Felicia knew I had to leave for London after a short week in the office, and I did not know how long I would be there. I thought for a few seconds, "Why don't you ask them for their preliminary objections? If they can give them to you informally, that might help us to have a more of a meaningful preparation to meet and confer in this first instance. After all, they are not using this as their formal meeting, but rather it would seem in the spirit of cooperation we are hoping to continue employing in this case. You know, Felicia, I have implied, but I do not think I have come out and said it: this could be a very novel type of litigation with a great many issues based on areas of science which are by no means close to being fully resolved. A key to defending this case may well turn on our being able to take that missing scientific consensus and use it in a burden of proof manner to stifle their moving forward with their assertions posing as admissible evidence in the different causation areas they will try to prove up. Am I making sense?"

Felicia thought for a few moments, then, "I think I understand your points pretty well by now. We need to get great clarity on their positions, area by area for causation, for example what role do they say genetics plays in this whole thing? For another example: Is diminished IQ caused by lead exposure alone a viable basis to use for that? If so, how does that work as a matter of science? And, if not: what other factors might create a viable basis for causation, and what is your scientific proof for each?"

My response was straight forward, "Yes. So, what we want is some structure to what they will assert. Based on our experts' positions, they should not have anything viable. Ultimately, that's what we need them to face up to as they try to answer this discovery. Why don't you try to set something for an hour in that short week. Lily will help with fitting it into my schedule."

Golf at Phoenix Country Club teed-off shortly after dawn! Emily Anne ("Please call me, Emma.") seemed enthralled in meeting Carolyn and they shared a cart of the back nine, speeding up our over-all playing time by putting people at the correct tee box with a minimum of carts passing on the narrow cart-paths. The two women seemed to spend their entire 90+ minutes in rapt conversation. Nonetheless, they played very well. Emma's local knowledge of the course proved most helpful to Carolyn! We departed for our return to the Biltmore at 10:15.

The Board had a pre- luncheon meeting at 11:00 for final issues resolutions, then a wine and beer buffet lunch with the membership from 11:30 to 12:45, followed by the afternoon sessions commencing at 1:00 in the conference center rooms. Carolyn was coordinating tours, then was hosting a pool party, hopefully light on the wine, for the spouses (included 5 men!).

Much of that afternoon was given over to a discussion of organizing by the different factions which we hoped the ACLN would include: the first division would cover the largest divide along the court room aisle between plaintiff and defense. But the second was more amorphous; attempting to specialize within each of those two areas. The Board had suggested that they have a discussion, but consider not reaching a decision for one or two meetings while competing concepts could be sorted out: also, suggesting that one or two representatives be agreed upon for each concept and that interaction take place, as needed, between meetings. The issue of hiring an administrator was discussed, but I volunteered that our firm's Lily would go a fair distance, at least at the outset for organizing by specialized areas.

(I asked Reggie Fox to be one of these organizing intermediaries. We had discussed that not overly specializing at the outset might be the better start-up posture, e.g., not separating product liability from environmental law, nor property damage from personal injury; and, have one large start-up group for all forms of Transportation Liability. This might better encourage interaction at the outset leading to more, if not better, relationships among firms practicing similar litigation. After all, firms could be encouraged to join more than one of these large groups, with different members in each being highly encouraged.)

At the end of the first full day, Reggie reported back to me that "our idea" had found great favor among the majority of defense types, and that the number of groups at the outset would not be large. (I thought perhaps paralleling the underwriting set-up at Lloyds! I told that to no one.) The same concepts were shared with, and adopted by, the Plaintiff Congregation (their word!).

The many side-bar discussions occurring in the larger grouping sessions provided the networking we, the Board, had hoped would take place and volunteers aplenty stepped up in the course of, as well as after, those sessions. Having Lily attend made the gathering of all this data far simpler as she was incredibly skilled in data handling with her ever-present lap-top.

That second evening session with our DMIC client -types present was a success all-around.

The Plaintiff-types were gracious and never contentious. The defense-types were hospitable, but not at all aggressive in pitching their firms. Clearly, this boded well for future meetings. The cocktails and dinner went quite well.

Saturday morning, the last business sessions concluded, followed by a variety of social activities, all leading up to the Black-Tie event. For golf, or other events (some by the "Spouses"), there were box lunches, or a poolside bar-b-que. That evening's Black Tie was for all of those (most of the attendees/many spouse-types) who stayed on for a Sunday departure. Carolyn and I were at the top of the receiving line, which lasted almost an hour. She was marvelously gracious, hugging many of the spouses, treating each as if a best friend. This created a warm carry-over for me. John O'Sullivan and Emily-Anne stood next to us (our two wives having partnered for golf in the afternoon tournament). The two of them were thoroughly impressed by the entirety of their days at the three-day ACLN event. (Later that evening, John and Manny told me that they would consider coming to a future event, if invited, even attending any appropriate sessions, as well.)

John invited Reggie and Ginger as well as Carolyn and me to a private Sunday lunch with Manny and Esmeralda. He said Emily-Anne, usually so shy about these types of events, was so encouraged when she mentioned to Carolyn how much she had enjoyed their time together. He actually seemed quite overjoyed hearing his wife's remarks! (At cocktails early on in the Black-Tie evening, John mentioned to me that this event had done more than anything he had tried over the years to bring Emily Anne out of her reluctance to participate in the social aspect of his business life. This did set me to wondering how Carolyn had that effect.)

All in all, the ACLN seemed off to a successful beginning. Reggie and Ginger were thrilled with the reception they received. It was my plan to have him make all of our intrafirm arrangements for ACLN event staffing to ensure as much full partner participation as possible.

I had a brief discussion with John at that final luncheon as a final follow-up to our time in London. He had used the ACLN meeting to decide he really should attend that final Lloyds convocation on its reinvention efforts. DMIC was committed to moving forward with the current plans, but their Board was extremely wary of the unknown risks facing a startup of the New Lloyds magnitude.

— — —

Amid preparations for London and follow-ups for the forthcoming convocation, my time in the office was strained. Lily was right on top of what needed to be done for ACLN on its organizational front and Reggie was prepared to work with her to assure dissemination electronically to all of the meetings attendees and for the inclusion of the additional designees to be supplied in those weeks post-meeting. Our Board had approved the draft Dissemination Notice for initial assignments on the organizational breakouts on the Defense side of ACLN. A counterpart in Marin County was charged with the Plaintiffs' side and Lily had supplied that firm with the Defense's notice to use as a model. Cooperation at the outset, at least, was the order of the day for that Winter's ACLN efforts. We had scheduled a Summer meeting in Chicago with Liam Callahan running the meeting and his wife, Serena, in the lead on the Spouses' activities (Carolyn had volunteered to assist, as needed.).

Meanwhile, Felicia and I had to undertake the meet and confer with the Plaintiffs on their objections to the breadth and detail, as well as their privacy objections, to GWF's written discovery requesting background data on each claimant, and their relatives, especially parents and *guardians ad litem* covering the many variable factors potentially affecting IQ (factors reflecting the advice of our expert consultants and a survey of the speculative and hypothetic factors being advanced in the current scientific literature about lead causation and a variety of health issues). My stating the purpose of that discovery was the very basis for our undertaking it.

Sandra was very busy with the client documents in the Neptune matter. When I checked, she had secured an extra three-week extension to file a response, using the client's distance as a reason for the delays. Her judgment at this point was that no lawyers had been involved for Neptune in the contract negotiation or execution and that Everson Harris was proving evasive when it came to a telephone conference to go over the conflicting contractual creation documents finally gathered in her possession, and distributed to the appropriate persons per the directions of Mason Eggars in consultation with Neptune Fishing's President, Mr. Harris. I perused them quickly and met with Sandra for an hour a few days before my departure. (During this week, which appeared to go by at a frantic pace, I was also being besieged with conference calls from a wide variety of sources in preparation for the London meetings soon to commence.) Those added Neptune documents were either earlier versions of a licensing agreement never finalized, or unsigned versions of a "final agreement." Moreover, none of those matched the signed document attached to the Complaint claimed to be the agreed-upon Licensing Contract.

Missing were all traces of transmittals, comments, evaluations, or actual intra-action among Neptune's team, or, for that matter, interaction among the parties' personnel (no emails, no faxes, no notes, no writings) who negotiated whatever was the agreement under which Neptune created huge volumes of product utilizing the patented chemical compounds, which failed to act as the early Neptune testing showed it would. Thus, Neptune Fishing did not want to pay the licensing fees stated in the contract and reiterated in Ester-Tech's lawsuit, but none of that was supported by any documentation, at all.

At the end of our session, I asked Sandra to make up a list of documents, by type, that we would expect to see associated with a negotiation of this type (examples to be added by her); and run it by me by fax that night. Then, we called Mason and discussed our plan, and asked him to make sure that all of the potential witnesses for Neptune responded in writing within 24-hours and provided anything, and everything, that might meet what we were looking for.

Because this case was in federal court, a Motion to Dismiss, for three "jurisdictional situations" was never waived under federal procedural Rule 12(b)(6). This was to be our 'ultimate safety net,' if deployed at the correct juncture in the case.

12

THE SECOND LLOYDS CONVOCATION

John O'Sullivan was waiting for me outside Customs at the United Airlines Gates at Heathrow. He insisted I stay at his hotel, The Berkeley (pronounced: bark-lee), a few blocks from Buckingham Palace. He always stayed there (as did Carolyn when on her own expense account). I never did, preferring the Grosvenor House. However, since Desert Mutual was paying for my hotel, I felt obliged to humor its CEO. I asked John if he wanted me to bring Martha since she had been instrumental in earlier negotiations, but he wanted to create a different image for DMIC at these meetings.

John felt that with the work of LTL, Ltd. and the efforts of our English compatriots that DMIC and Connecticut Indemnity (CI) had fared significantly better in the wind-down of the "Old Lloyds Market" than most of the other primary insurance Lloyds clients. He was concerned that his company's image from that over-all fiasco might give it a place in these forthcoming negotiations where the prices sought for its participation could be raised out of proportion to its premium base and its relative place in the American Property/Casualty Insurance market. Thus, we were DMIC's entire contingent. Similarly, and albeit significantly larger, Gerry Dwyer and I would be CI's entire contingent. Of course, both of those companies would have the benefit of LTL's contacts and influence as well as that of Quincy

Franden-Jones and his helpers at the barrister's chambers, referenced by its address, Twenty Kings Bench Walk. John believed that these players would suffice for this matter. After all, John and Gerry were our clients; thus, our bosses.

John beckoned and a porter came forward with a cart to take charge of my baggage. John made a quick call and as the porter brought us to the curb, a full-sized British taxi-van pulled up to the curb. Its driver exited, loaded my bags in next to John's, a tip to the porter, and we were underway. My landing brought me in at the very end of the eastbound commute into the City. Doffing our overcoats, we made comfortable, and John handed me a cup of hot coffee, saying, "Black. Italian blend, French roast. I do hope you like it. It's what Madeline makes for us at Bradley's office."

I countered, "This is quite luxurious. What is it?"

"It's a Rover-customized van, made for The Berkeley and other high-end companies. As a very long-time customer of our grand hotel, they accommodate me with a pick-up whenever it, or it's companion, is available. Seems to me that we should clean-up when we get to the hotel, or perhaps take a walk-about to get more on British time? How do you refer to their time, again?"

Me: "Zulu-time. It's military for Greenwich Mean Time. All action messaging in the military is in Zulu-time, or at least, it was. Yes, I do agree with your idea of a walk-about. Drinks are at the Bar with our people at seven, but I told Gerry we could meet her at six-thirty if she's ready. She'll let us know on that. Gerry's staying elsewhere. Should I put everything tonight on my room, and she can take care of Brown's tomorrow night?"

John assented, then turned to his phone for messages. I did the same. We agreed to meet in an hour after check-in. I unpacked my hang-ups, then had some fruit as a snack to hold me until dinner, having eaten breakfast on the plane immediately before landing. My rule was better a little bit hungry than overfed when undertaking a significant time change. This day: eight hours.

We walked toward Harrod's (Didn't everyone in the Knightsbridge part of town?), entered and gravitated to the confectionary department on the Ground Floor (The food markets were such a favorite part of every visit to this "Monument to Consumption."). Each of us bought a single dip ice cream cone. John had milk chocolate and I had vanilla. We exited, walked on a few more blocks, crossed the street and into Hyde Park heading in the general direction of our hotel. The air was brisk, but not cold considering how we were dressed. But with the Winter Solstice weeks away, the sun was fading, and the air was beginning to chill rapidly. Perhaps the ice cream was not the best idea. Nonetheless, our walk was enjoyable, especially as we both took the time to rehash our golfing trip to Ireland. As we approached The Berkeley's entrance, John stopped, so did I. He said, "At some point, all of this project will end. Ronan, I want you to know that I have come to like you very much; and my wife cannot stop talking about yours. I do so hope that we can remain friends, and will take the opportunities to visit from time-to-time?"

With that, he took off his glove and offered his right hand. I shook it, thinking at that moment that John had become a real friend, and I had made so few of them over the years.

— — —

Cocktails and dinner at the Berkeley were a somewhat dressy occasion: Both Gerry and Madeline wore elegant cocktail dresses (Gerry in a deep green and Madeline in a darkish royal blue), while the men all wore suits, several with vests, white shirts, with regimental ties in almost total display. Between ordering dinner and doing catch-up, the cocktail time was largely consumed. John and I had arranged for seating cards at our table in a very private corner of the Berkeley's extremely tasteful Main Dining Room. John sat between Bradley and Quincy, I was between Quincy and Madeline, and so on. No two people were paired with a working companion.

We got right to the discussion of the latest scuttlebutt on the equity organization for the New Lloyds, Quincy leading the way. Almost everyone but me had an outside source, while those at this table were my sources. Rather clearly, there were going to be multiple different sources of equity, much of which was to create and assure continuing lines of coverage from reinsurance on all levels among all lines of coverages. The issue of whether or not the retrocessionaires would provide equity was unresolved and quickly became a source of conflict among our diners. Two major issues were present at the outset: first, the actual retrocessionaire entities were very often fronting companies for a money source not wishing to be identified (for many and varied reasons, some of which might not be legal, or worse, depending on the funding entity's domicile, or other issues), and there might be layers of fronting through uncooperative domicile sovereign states; and second, calculating the available equity in such a murky situation was nigh onto impossible.

Nonetheless, Quincy and I both argued that if equity contribution was to be the toll booth on the pathway to participate at the New Lloyds, then each category of participants should be responsible for its share of funding the enterprise's start-up as well as carrying costs and working capital, together with posting reserve funds in a prudent amount. Client carriers, brokers, and investors were all prepared to contribute. One of the main reasons for this convocation was to set those amounts by category, and types of member within each category, as well as agreeing upon a mechanism to adjust those contributions in the future; and, to decide how to compensate all of those which contribute the capital, based on the success (read, "profitability") of the enterprise as it matured.

Our discussions of these points went on through dinner and into a first round of post-meal cordials. However, jet lag was becoming a very real problem for three of us. It fell on me to bring matters to a "Single Voice" perspective for the meetings themselves as we all might be selling on these points and we did not wish to appear contradictory. Quincy, who had all sorts of clients, was an exception to this proposition. His main duty seemed to be to get this New Lloyds enterprise up and running, while leaving all of these details to the actual market participants most affected by them. Gerry and John for their respective carriers were the major players at our table, while Madeline for LTL would be an ancillary participant, making either a relatively small equity contribution, or perhaps paying an annual fee. Meanwhile, Bradley and I were advisors to participants and as such would pay nothing, and derive no direct benefit (unlike Brokers, such as Cheshire and Booth, who would participate actively at the enterprise earning fee after fee for its various services). Thus, the lawyers were essentially one step removed!

Much to my surprise, Quincy and I carried the night on the retrocessionaire issue, and we were all in agreement when we parted. John and I hurried to our rooms as we were exhausted, yet we wanted to call home.

First, I checked the voicemails at my office: Lily said nothing pressing, and no one had raised an emergency. Then, I got Carolyn on my first try. She seemed to breathe new life into my over-tired body as I went through my day with her. My primary focus turned out to be the kind words from John O'Sullivan at the end of our walk that afternoon (which now seemed more than a day before). Carolyn was extremely pleased to hear about Emily-Anne, John's wife; and suggested that perhaps we could get away golfing for a long weekend with them in the early Spring next year. Then, she told me that Mollie wanted to say "Hello," and she came on the line to tell me about her wonderful day at school. Carolyn recaptured the telephone, and we exchanged terms of endearment.

Less than ten minutes later, I was asleep!

— — —

The six of us were planning to have lunch the next day at a different Wheelers, just across Fleet Street from the entrance to the largest barrister chambers, The Temple, at 1:00 p.m. When I arrived, Madeline was there and seated at our table. Of course, I sat next to her. She smiled, looked around, and then leaned over and gave me a very sexy kiss (much to my surprise!). She looked into my eyes, saying, "Ronan, your wife, Carolyn, is so beautiful, I could not believe just how glamorous when I met her. And she is so nice. Somewhere I heard a rumor that she was gay. That's not true, is it?"

I looked at Madeline, then at the path to our table from the entry, squared myself around a bit toward my companion, and replied, "Why in the world would you ever ask anything like that?" It came out somewhat more strongly than I wanted, but still…

"Oh, I just thought that, or something else, might have affected our relationship. You haven't shown any interest in me in much more than a year. I miss you. I really do," was her response.

Me: "Madeline, you do remember what you told me more than a year ago, that after one of your dinners with Bradley and his wife, that you and she had hit it off, and that the three of you were engaged in a relationship. Do you remember that?"

"Well, yes. But that was only to see if you might be interested. In fact, I can't seem to remember what you said."

Me: "I see."

Madeline looked at me, strangely, "I'm not sure I understand what you're trying to tell me. Can you please explain?"

"When you told me about that 'three-way' back then, I said, 'I see.' Do you understand now?"

She perked up, John and Bradley were just at the front door, "Got it. Can I come over to your place tonight? Tell me later."

Gerry showed up minutes later. We never heard from Quincy. We all discussed the exchanges which we had that morning. There was supposed to be a briefing at 5:30 from the Coordinating Committee.

We were supposed to have dinner at 8:30 that night at Brown's Hotel. Cheshire and Booth were hosting as a THANK YOU for all of the business coming their way by virtue of our joint efforts on recovering long tail Lloyds coverage placement files, along with LTL, Ltd. We all agreed to meet in their bar at 8:00.

— — —

On our taxi rides back to The Berkeley, then over to Brown's, John and I talked about the briefing on equity given at 5:00 with a view to making any comments, as requested by the Committee. (Failure to comment would doubtless be taken as acquiescence.) We concluded that there was nothing much to add or change. The 'morrow was to be terms of coverages. The major issue would be whether to continue or abolish "joint and several liability" if there were to be syndicates, or to eliminate syndicates altogether, or allow some hybrid; and if the overwhelming majority had a business model that all coverages could follow. We both thought that unlimited liability needed to be eliminated (seemed to be a sure thing), and with that the more modern mode of doing business by "following form" in each jurisdiction would suffice.

We first conferred with Gerry, then the others at the Bar: all agreeing with our assessment. Quincy joined us at dinner and we never again had the opportunity to confer as a group, but he did seem amenable (sober?).

The dinner itself provided no novel broker insights. Their thoughts seemed so much in-line with ours that I began to suspect that one, or more, of our London allies was also in league with Cheshire and Booth, largely because sometimes their wording paralleled ours. Still, this was not a bad thing as these brokers were the entities which actually brought the coverage business to the Lloyds enterprise, perhaps even more so following this new organization, if it came to pass in the form we were projecting, as seemed probable.

Toward the end of the evening at Brown's, Madeline managed to isolate me, boldly asking, "Ronan, it would appear John is going to join the brokers for further drinks. Do you think you could get away so we could have some intimate time together?"

Much of my life had been given over to succumbing to such seductive invitations, and I had certainly done so with Madeline on numerous occasions. Yet, something about her arrangements with Bradley and his wife made me nervous: I was ever so certain that I wanted no involvement in a menage, especially one involving the potential of another man. This moment was not unanticipated, only the timing was unknown. Following a pause, I said, in a hushed tone, "Madeline, I do appreciate the invitation, but I have Gerry here as a client as well as John. This trip is really very much about them. I feel I must stay with them. You look like such a delightful package tonight. I regret I shall not be able to unwrap you."

The night went on in the Bar at the Berkeley. Some of the discussions became recollections of golfing in Ireland. Stanley Booth asked, "Ronan, any chance you could arrange another tournament like that Irish event in California, perhaps including Pebble Beach?"

Gerry and John were quick to endorse that plan. All I could say is, "I can try. When would be a good timeframe next year?"

I called Carolyn to tell her about the golfing idea. Her first thought: "Perhaps you could find a way Emily Anne and I could compete?"

That would have to wait, I thought, as I hung -up after saying a fond good-night to my family.

The meetings of those next three days were both intense and somewhat mystifying at times. The various groupings wanted different outcomes for their participation in the overall risk of the entire enterprise. One thing was absolutely clear: no entity, or groups, were willing to undertake unlimited liability. Caps, or stop-payment cut-offs, were required at each contractual level, and type, of coverage, Moreover, the heretofore ultra-high levels of catastrophic coverages, with huge exposure amounts, would not be the bargain-priced coverages of the past. Every form of coverage was going to be written clearly and all parties associated with each block of coverage would have full documentation from the outset, starting with binders.

Small groups started working on language to achieve precision. The General Liability policies of the past took new form. The months of preparation for this convocation began to pay-off as the "New Lloyds" began to take shape as investors and underwriters began to carve out the different coverage markets and to divide up the areas of their interest and to formulate a variety of final business plans for moving forward.

I sat in on that third night's meeting of the overall steering committee of which I had been an adjunct member since the First Convocation. As each Managing Sub-Committee gave its tentative final report, my overall impression began to form the optimistic conclusion that this process had worked and, somehow, all of the differing factions had achieved all of the needed compromises to cause a new comprehensive marketplace to come into being. One which ought to be successful as an on-going venture for the foreseeable future (even in the face of the American court system and its Plaintiffs' Bar).

Stanley Booth had one of his firm's cars drop us both at The Berkeley. Quincy said he would join us by midnight. It was after ten when Stanley and I walked into the Bar. John, Gerry, Bradley, Madeline and several others were gathered around a very large pair of tables. I bid Stanley speak first, but he insisted on deferring to me. I gave my impressions and he added-on wherever he deemed appropriate. My glass never seemed to become empty. We had a bartender as our server and he seemed to be listening ever so carefully, even when he poured. (A great deal of water and club soda were also being consumed. Ice was not an issue, with a bucket on our table.) In less than an hour we were finished, but as I pointed out the final product for the closing vote would be available by 6:30 a.am. on the 'morrow with the to-be-hoped-for closing vote being cast at 2:00 p.m. by all of those certified to vote by the Credentials Committee. (Strangely enough, despite all of my efforts, as an American lawyer, I was not qualified as my job was considered only advisory. Whereas Quincy, despite being a barrister, was given a vote because of all of the substantive work he had undertaken at the various committee levels. [Quite fair, actually.])

Quincy arrived a few minutes before midnight. The group was trying to break up to get the needed sleep to be ready for the next day, but all stayed to hear what Quincy had to say. He told of how the retrocessionaire faction, or at least a significant portion of it, were uncertain about all of the safeguards remaining in place under some of the different coverages and at the levels of coverage, especially based on the U.S. court systems. But Quincy and his allies among the "London lawyers" were able to convince those skeptics that they were misjudging the whole system. Nonetheless, the proof would be in tomorrow's voting.

John, Gerry and I retreated, full glasses in hand to John's suite for a quick consultation. We all agreed that an affirmative vote made sense, although the absolute "final voting" would be the notices of funding approval from the many participating entities which would follow in relatively short time-line, as the new entity needed to be poised to write new business by March one of the coming new year.

We agreed that if the papers showed up by 8:00, there would not be time enough to cover all of the materials in detail. I suggested that we all look at the Table of Contents and try to decide how to divide up the reading. Also, we should consider what, if anything, required being read by us all.

I called only Carolyn and we talked briefly for the third night in a row. I tried to be frank, but she was well ahead of me, saying only, "You are sounding more exhausted every night. Please go to bed and sleep as much as you can. Ronan Darling, you know we all love you. Please don't kill yourself doing this. Good night, My Love," and she was gone, like that!

———

The next day seemed anti-climactic: We received the papers, divided them as prearranged, read them, then met. We essentially had no comments as this presentation appeared as a *fait accompli*. John, Gerry and I went outside. We looked at each other. They knew their company's commitments under the plan (these were not circulated as the monetary commitment for each factor was referenced as a schedule by letter designation, which were private to the investor groups and select Lloyds staff.). I asked each of them, "Are you certain about moving forward?"

John spoke first, saying only, "yes."

Gerry, swallowed, nodded affirmatively, adding, "We really have no choice: the alternative is to proceed without reinsurance for the next calendar year. We each pay our money and hope that we all got this effort right."

We all got cleaned up, met for a late brunch and took two taxis to the final voting site. It was all over in less than an hour. The New Lloyds moved into its launch phase. We all went to the bar at the Hyde Park Hotel, had a few drinks, followed by an early dinner.

When I called Carolyn, I interrupted her workout. I told her I was exhausted and off to bed, and would be home tomorrow night for a late light dinner, and asked if that was OK with her? She was kind and endearing. I called John, he suggested one last drink. We met in the hotel bar and had a double. I told him about what Carolyn had said about his wife and herself and the next tournament. He smiled, but said he wanted to think about it.

That next morning, we taxied together to Heathrow, but took separate flights. Right before we parted, John said, "I think we need to get the sense of the others, I wonder if any other spouses would be interested in playing, or might just wish to show up for a good time? How about if we split the list and see what we get?"

Me: "Did you ask Emily Anne?"

John: "She was so happy that Carolyn had thought to include her. We'll have to do something together no matter what since Carolyn is bringing her out of her shyness shell. Actually, I'm overjoyed. Have a safe trip."

— — —

Carolyn brought Mollie to SFO to meet my flight from Heathrow. They were front and center as I emerged from Customs. (One of the first to arrive with no golf clubs!) Mollie was now old enough that she could appreciate that her Dad had been far away for a real amount of time and that I had missed them greatly. We had a three-way hug and several kisses. Carolyn had a porter with a cart for my bags standing bye. Mollie hopped on the front bag and rode to the elevators with Carolyn and me walking hand-in-hand.

I told them about London and a very short version of what had finally happened on the creation of the "New Lloyds," all the while maintaining that nothing was finalized until the British Parliament acted to create the enabling legislation for that new entity (which seemed like a virtual certainty). Mollie fell asleep in her seat as we rode through Golden Gate Park. Carolyn observed that, and said, "I got a call from Emily Anne, John's wife. The first time she has reached out. She was so excited when John told her about my thinking on your Ryder Cup-like golf match. Do you think we can go?"

"Well, I ran it by a few of the people who would play, and their reception to the idea of spouses playing was more than a little cool. I am not saying it's not going to happen. Remember women played in our first go-round in Ireland. Not all of the British men are married, and I'm fairly certain that several of those have a radius beyond which extracurricular activity is OK in their lives. I don't know that for certain. What I'm going to do is talk with Gerry at Connecticut Indemnity, then John, and try to see if we could expand to accommodate others on the Brits' side to encourage the whole thing as well as to decide if once every year is a good idea, or perhaps every other year would be better. John and I talked and he wants to get together soon: the four of us. I was thinking the Monterey Peninsula. What do you say to that?" Did I get it right?

Carolyn's face was full of shifting emotions as I was talking. In the end, she had a fixed smile, "You really are something. No wonder I stay so in love with you. You are actually kind and thoughtful with me. When do you think? After the PGA's Crosby at Pebble Beach? There and Spyglass? Two rounds enough and a third day down the Coast to Ventana for lunch and some sights, like that 'Picasso gallery?'"

I smiled, Carolyn was always so willing, at least it seemed so to me. "Would you like to make all of the arrangements? Why don't you come up with some dates when you could arrange it, and I'll talk with John soon to see if any of that would work?" I asked.

We continued on that course and soon enough we were home in Ross. As the tires scrunched into the gravel on our parking area, Mollie woke, and in the midst of stretching, looked like at a young woman, saying, "I'm so happy we're home. Dad, I want to learn to play volleyball.

What do you think?"

— — —

Over the years, Mollie became an Olympic team volleyball player; first the regular hard- court game, including a

Gold-Medal performance. Then three more Games as a beach volleyballer, medaling each time. She was a physical marvel!

13

THE WORLD MOVES EVER CLOSER TO A NEW MILLENIUM

Sandra and I were able to extract, then reconstruct, what Neptune Fishing claimed were all the documents ever in their possession on the issue of the actual formation of their licensing contract with Ester-Tech. What also became evermore clear was that Abdul Singh, the sole owner of Ester-Tech, did not so much negotiate those contract terms, but rather dictated what they would turn out to be. Almost all of this took place on-line, or by fax. In neither instance was it at all clear that our client had given our firm everything that had changed hands over a six-plus months span, especially e-mail strings and attachments as well as fax cover sheets for forwarding documents. Nonetheless, we had what they had saved with which to formulate a defense. We tried.

The initial filings for Neptune Fishing included an Answer to the Ester-Tech Complaint and a Cross-Claim against that same entity wherein we alleged that the Contract attached as an exhibit was not a contract under which the parties were operating. Rather, that Everson Harris' signature on that attached document was executed in reliance on certain terms being modified in the final agreement, which were in fact not undertaken by Mr. Singh.

The fact that Neptune had utilized the licensed Ester-Tech substance in the manufacture of its products for four months and spent almost $5,000,000 on fishing gear products, which included marketing to the fishing public and initial distribution to key wholesalers and large retailers, might provide a difficult burden to overcome. The Cross-Claim also lacked any kind of express warranty claim as the plaintiff had repeatedly refused to do anything which might create an inference that it had participated in the actual development, and testing, of Neptune Fishing's new product line. To make matters even more difficult, all of the products were now in warehouses for storage and analysis for any possible future use, at present unknown, since the new product line formulation began to fail when it was in plastic packaging, could not breathe, and was exposed on a continuing basis to temperatures above 75 degrees Fahrenheit.

In addition to the losses sustained by our client, Ester-Tech had received only one payment on its minimum monthly order formula of $0.16/unit at the rate of 1,000,000 units/month for a minimum of 24 months (this was the contract term which Neptune Fishing disputed), as spelled out in Appendix A to the attached Contract. Also, Ester-Tech sought interest on the monies owed at the legal rate, attorney's fees, and any liquidated damages as might be applicable, along with punitive damages. We dealt with all of these claims in the Answer. This appeared to be a very difficult situation.

Amanda Tatum called me two days after service of our responsive pleadings and written discovery. She was pleasant for about ninety seconds, then suggested that we might wish to dismiss our Cross-Claim or face a Rule 11 (Sanctions) Motion accompanying a Motion to Strike that pleading. I asked her what support she had, and she offered, "A complete record of the contract negotiation, whereas you have some desperate fantasy."

Sandra drew in her breathe so loudly I thought it might be audible on my speaker phone. I paused for only a moment. "You sound like you already have an existing record. We have not. Would you be willing to share what you have so we can explore an informed decision with our client?"

"I shall have to confer with my client on that," was her response.

"Well, if you are threatening a Rule 11 Motion and have something that would cause our client to rethink its pleadings, a failure to produce it to allow a negotiated resolution would seem to undermine the spirit, if not the letter, of Rule 11. I do hope you understand that my offer is in the spirit of cooperation. I hope to hear from you in the very near term. Thank you!" by me.

Sandra broke her silence at the sound of the dial tone, "That was very quick thinking. I wonder if Mr. Singh is a very scrupulous organizer, or even if he records things without notice. We can only await her response. Different topic/same case: I believe that one of us needs to meet and go over this whole process with Mr. Harris, and perhaps Mr. Young, maybe both of us. What do you think?"

Me: "Why don't you raise it with Mason and see what he thinks? You can tell him about that call as well."

Sandra smiled, nodded affirmatively, got up, and left my office, saying, "I've never been to North Carolina."

The Great Western Foundry matter had been collected into a single huge Joinder by order of the California Judicial Counsel on the request of Sacramento County's Chief Judge, Ezra Quinn, after a Notice of Request filing and a joint filing of No Opposition with several Stipulations from the parties to that case. The number of filings had slowed, but by that year's end, the plaintiffs numbered 316. The Stipulations were included in the Judicial Counsel's Order of Referral to Judge Quinn who planned to retain those consolidated cases during the remainder of his chief Judgeship and beyond. In a conference with all counsel, Judge Quinn had praised the handling of those cases to date as a model for handling large tort cases (Beginning to be referred to as "Mass Torts.").

Martha was readying herself to return to her practice, while Felicia Clarke had continued in her stead, using a crafty technique of taking her breaks when I was most frequently available, and we even began to have lunch together once a week when we would both be available. Lily had become very fond of Felicia in Martha's absence and she helped schedule those lunches, always near-by. We had gone through several meet and confer conferences with the Plaintiff Counsel achieving some minor resolutions, but the main issues were the total reluctance of the adult relatives to participate in discovery of their personal medical and educational histories as we had sought in our discovery.

In addition, our opposing counsel were very upset that GWF had destroyed so many of its documents over its long history. We had tried to explain that this litigation was completely novel, at the very least, to our client. Moreover, one of the very first things our firm had done was to instruct GWF, through its General Counsel, to institute a Litigation Hold on all document destruction under its historically followed Document Retention Policy. The COO had signed a Declaration to the effect that they had followed our instructions without exception since they were given. Nonetheless, the Plaintiffs argued that they should be entitled to all sorts of evidentiary inferences because so much potential evidence had been destroyed.

Finally, it became time for both sides to file cross-motions seeking those discovery responses being withheld by the other side. When we disconnected from our last fruitless telephone conference with the plaintiffs' counsel having agreed upon a briefing schedule for each side, I looked across my small conference table at Felicia Clarke and the two associates working on the matter with her, and asked, "You know Martha will be back in the office in less than seven working days. But she has been focusing primarily on her asbestos contamination/demolition cases while on her leave. To me, most of the discovery arguments in these motions have been honed in her absence. I will be pleased to provide guidance and some editing, but Felicia, I think you are the correct person to lead this level of task through the motion process. You know that it involves issues critical to the case outcome. Are you and your team up to handing these tasks?"

When I finished, I got up out of my swivel chair, saying, "I'll be right back," and as I left the room, added, "Talk among yourselves, but I would like your answer when I return."

With that, I went to the Men's room, stopped for a fresh coffee, then swung by Lily's desk for a quick update on any relevant office politics, new business, or just gossip. I returned to my small conference room through my office which caught the three of them off-guard. They were sitting in silence and had to swivel ninety degrees to see me as I entered the room. This put them a trifle off their balance, for just a moment. But Felicia quickly picked up her pen, sat up straighter, and I believe she looked me in the eye (She had never done that; at least that I had noticed: always scrupulously reticent.), as I sat. Then she seemed to smile ever so slightly, "Ronan, and I still have trouble calling you that. We conferred. We feel that the legal practice training and work we have undertaken here at O'Neill Fox has prepared us to carry out exceedingly difficult assignments. We know we are extremely knowledgeable on these discovery issues. We know we can rely on your guidance, and should it come to that, some guidance from Martha. We are prepared to move forward on these matters for which you have prepared us. We believe we will not let you down. We really do appreciate this opportunity!" The others nodded their agreement.

I tried to hide my smile (I wondered how often she had given that speech, or some version on it, in her daydreams.), then said, "Good. I am delighted. Let us take a few minutes on some initial thoughts on the structure of the issues for this presentation. I believe our opening remarks in the Introduction are critical, and without beleaguering it, we must stress the very novelty of this lawsuit, predicated as it is on unsubstantiated scientific theories, while jumping from facts to assertions, cloaked as consensual scientific conclusions without any reference to proof of sound scientific causative connection to support any recovery. This means explaining the difference between scientific hypotheses and a consensus of the scientific community giving rise to agreed scientific principles. Just remember: this is a case where a summary judgment may not be possible because of conflicts in scientific expert testimony. With that *caveat* as a given, we must use every opportunity to educate our assigned single judge of the need to gate keep this matter, indirectly here and now; and, creating nuances in every brief we file in any way related to Plaintiffs' continuing failure to set out actual provable causation through scientific consensus, and instead relying on substituting unsubstantiated assertions."

The three of them looked at me. And silence hung in the air for more than a moment or two. Then Felicia spoke, "We hear what you say. We know how you all write: on multiple levels, but with the end goals always in sight. We'll do our best to get right on this. Should we go?"

Me: "Yes. Please give me something in a week from now, whatever you have then will have to be our starting point."

– – –

Martha began a series of conference calls with me in which I brought her back up to speed on her property asbestos abatement litigation. Several states were beginning a pattern of suing CAL Board. They were states where that entity had a substantial market share of products containing asbestos either for its fire-resistant nature (certain types of wallboard) or its workability value in the application of lubricating moist product (joint compound or sprayed wall/ceiling coverings). These states employed either their own construction personnel or outside contractors, which retained either some purchase records of product actually used, and also had people who could recall that usage. Thus, CAL Board had potential liability; but how much of that material being abated was, in fact, our client's product? We discussed this with our client, CAL Board, to come up with formulae, testing, and any potential expert testimony available.

I had met with Austin Smith, our client's General Counsel, to discuss these cases in Martha's absence, and he had undertaken document searches, especially for sales to the state entities or their contractors, while pulling together one of his company's bright young engineers to be an inside expert in reconstructing the product history, usage, and a testing protocol to identify chemical signatures our client's formulae for installed product.

I had copied Martha as well as Felicia on all of these developments in the hope that the amount of work undertaken at that time would pay dividends in the future. However, the development with which Martha would need to contend going forward was that some of those states' abated product was definitely that of CAL Board. Could we find a means to use that seemingly negative evidence to our client's advantage? What needed to be done to assess the ranges of potential dollar damages? Need to advise Desert Mutual?

These would be Martha's jobs. I had a few thoughts and communicated them to her. But I wanted to leave the heavy-lifting on this project to her, if possible.

Other abatement cases were not advancing well for the Plaintiff's bar and the defense techniques we had used in LAUSD were still effective in bringing much of that litigation into a state of dynamic gridlock caused by the claimants' inability to come up with any viable methodology for identifying our client's products. Were any new techniques evolving? Another issue for Martha.

It would be good to get Martha back, but we would need to find another office for Sandra. I consulted with Lily. We only had a few associate and paralegal offices available. Sandra would need space to work, especially with all of the documents in Neptune Fishing. Finally, Lily and I hit on a compromise. A vacant associate office was just down the hall from our small conference room which I often used as if it was my own. I called Reggie and discussed it with him, and we decided to put Sandra in that smaller office, to make "My conference room" into a "Neptune Fishing war-room," and to ask Martha to accommodate herself accordingly. Reggie essentially agreed. Then, I gave Sandra our proposal more as a *fait accompli*, than a suggestion. She acquiesced on the spot, but added, "We need to talk, if possible tomorrow?"

I asked where, and she responded , "Sam's in the City, if that's OK?" I was pleased. It had been too long. My favorite fish restaurant in the U.S, trailing only Wheeler's on Curzon Street in London!

— — —

Sam's back room was a series of small, dark-stained wooden-walled booths, each functioning as a private meeting room in its own right, curtained to allow the liveried waiters to have access, but otherwise preventing casual observation and eaves-dropping. Sandra was seated and waiting when I arrived. I began, "Carolyn is jealous that I am joining you. Not because it is you, but she loves this Sam's and now-a-days never seems to get past Sam's in Tiburon or the Spinnaker in Sausalito."

Sandra tried to smile, but instead gave a wan expression that almost seemed to be that of real pain, "The reason I asked you here is because my firm, our firm, with your old friends and me is, to put it simply, failing. We cannot come up with enough paying business to remain even close to viable, and we are pouring our own cash into it. We have talked to the landlord and he has a tenant for our space. But, we need to vacate in nine days. Allan asked me to talk to you. He was, I think, too embarrassed to come himself. We want to ask you to please take the three of us partners and two associates into your firm. Between the five of us, we may have a bit more than two partners' worth of paying work: three good, not great, real clients. Wallboard was our life's blood and we have not gotten over losing it. There, I've said it!"

Me: "What are you drinking?"

Sandra tried to crack a weak smile, "Are we going to talk about it? If so, whatever you're having."

I did smile, told her a joke, our drinks arrived, and I raised mine in a mock, wordless toast, "I met with Reggie yesterday afternoon about something approaching this very thing. We've sort of been waiting for it to happen. Our partners will need to agree to whatever is ultimately decided downstream. But for now, you can all come. The accommodations, at least for now, may prove to be Spartan. The pay will be systemic based on our compensation system. Reggie, as our Managing Partner, runs that. At least, it should help you all to stop bleeding your own greenbacks. Carolyn agreed last night. She wanted me to tell you."

By then, Sandra was crying. She tried to say something, but could not. If we did not have a table between us, I might have held her. But the table was there and I remembered Carolyn's words as we held each other going to sleep last night, "No matter what, do not hold her. You are such a pushover for a crying woman, especially one you have loved in the past."

So, I reached over, held the tip of Sandra's chin, lifted it, and looking into her eyes, said, as tenderly as I deemed appropriate, "Sandra, this is the best we can do for now. Let's see how things go from here. Drink up, and let's talk about what's to come for Allan Boswell and you all at O'Neill Fox."

We did and after an hour and a half, I decided to call Reggie, then Lily, on my way home, via Margot Arnaud's office whereupon I poured out the news of my lingering lunch meeting. This was not altogether a surprise to my psychiatrist who was far from enthusiastic months before when I had told her of my initial plan to associate Sandra on the Neptune Fishing matter. Dr. Arnaud had been very firm on my clearing that whole thing with Carolyn. Almost half a year had elapsed and nothing even remotely untoward had occurred. That helped pave the way for a favorable view on that day's decision. Also, as we rehashed Carolyn's earlier lunch meeting with Sandra. It surely proved a touchstone for Carolyn in the form of Sandra's reaction to Carolyn's steadfast no-nonsense approach to the putative work arrangement. I recall the good doctor's final words that visit, "Ronan, never let your emotional guard down around Sandra. From what you have told me over the years, and recently as well, you appear to have been Sandra's first real Love, and she is not, and probably never will be over you!"

When I got home, after lifting Mollie up for a hug and a kiss, I repeated the same thing with Carolyn, then and now, the Love of My Life.

14

MY LEGACY: BUILDING A LASTING LAW PRACTICE

The Holiday Season was becoming ever-the-more complex, especially since Patrick Tyne and the much-beloved Elsa were to announce their engagement on Christmas Eve, with the Johansson's in attendance from Stockholm, as well as my partner Phil with Ingrid, Elsa's sister, up from greater Glendale, with their children, not to mention my three children from my first wife Mollie and Our 'not so little' Mollie. Only our Maeve could not make it until New Year's with work/play commitments in Paris.

Our houses in Ross and San Anselmo were both full for varying lengths of time, what with sports travel for everyone in our family, and various trips and appointments for work. Our Mollie took ballet and had a role in one of the chorus lines in the *Nutcracker*, staged at the Marin County Civic Center in San Rafael, down the hill from our County Hall Buildings. (All part of Frank Lloyd Wright's last major architectural project, featuring a series of structures to encompass sports, entertainment, even fairs replete with livestock. The actual County Hall and Courthouse [2 buildings combined in a single structure] were the most renowned of all of those structures, and world famous in architectural circles.) Mercifully, there were multiple *Nutcracker* performances, so all of our joint families had an opportunity to participate.

Yolanda and her daughters prepared and served some of the meals. We all did breakfasts as a communal cooking event, while we also ate some meals at restaurants in the immediate area. We had Christmas dinner at the St. Francis Yacht Club, where I had been invited to join many years ago when one of their leaders discovered that I was the only Coast Guard officer awarded the Silver Star during Viet-Nam, and lived nearby in Marin County. We very much enjoyed our occasional use of that club's facilities, especially for Holidays when we did not travel.

On Christmas Eve, Yolanda and her girls left us with an outstanding buffet of traditional dishes. We celebrated in Ross which house had more interior entertaining space. It was a cold night and we had a fire. The cocktail hour lasted a bit longer than planned. Then, before dinner, Patrick Tyne, holding Elsa's hand in front of the fireplace, asked if he could say a few words. They moved to the center of the assembled families. Patrick spoke, "We have run all of this past Maeve who wishes she could be here, and sends her love to all of you. As some of you may know, my mother as well as Ronan are romantics in hiding. Slightly more than a year ago, I became confused about my feelings for Elsa, and was afraid I was going to lose her. I went to my Mom. She felt that Elsa had loved me since she first met me. I never knew that until then. We had been careful, not at all aggressive about our relationship. My coach at Princeton had an unbendable rule of no married men on the team. I knew that rule. So did Elsa. A few times over those first years, we talked about each other as if at some point we would become more serious. But it was that visit with my mother that led me to believe that I loved Elsa deeply and wanted to spend the rest of my life with her. Elsa helped me formulate a plan, and after consulting briefly with Ronan, we put that plan into motion. Elsa began to work part-time in New York and the coach got to see her. His wife recognized her from some magazine shoots and before long everyone who mattered in my life in New Jersey and New York knew we were a couple of sorts, and that's the way it has stayed until tonight. I have proposed to Elsa on many occasions, but we both agreed we would marry that very first night when my mother gave me her Porsche and told me to go somewhere with Elsa and make sure that she knew exactly how much I loved her and what I wanted, and to persuade her to want the same thing.

"Of course, very little persuading was needed. Turned out she wanted the same things as I did. Now we are to the last part of my parents' plan. Tonight, Elsa and I announce that we are engaged to be married, and plan to do so in this forthcoming June, here at St. Anselm's where we have all of the needed reservations already made.

"But there is one more thing. Elsa cannot be properly engaged without a ring. My mother has given me her ring to place on Elsa's finger. Don't worry. She'll get a new one. But you must know that this ring was not just Ronan's to give to Carolyn. It was his before that and he gave it to his first wife, Mollie, who, when she was dying, persuaded my mother to marry Ronan as her last dying wish. And Mollie gave Ronan this ring to give to Carolyn, my Mom. Now, they want me to give it to Elsa, and all of my siblings have agreed.

"So, Elsa, My Love, the Love of My Life," taking her hand and kneeling, Patrick continued, "Will you accept this ring and take me as your husband?"

Elsa's tears somehow transformed into a radiant smile, looking down at Patrick, saying, "Patrick, I thought I might come to love you from the first time I saw you. You always will be the Love of My Life. So, YES, I shall be your wife." He slid the ring on her finger.

Patrick stood, they kissed. I look around and there were few dry eyes in our home. Happiness abounded, making itself known in those moments that followed. Champagne flowed and that Christmas party really got going!

— — —

I spent part of that Holiday Season on the question of a follow-up to the County Kerry Golf Tournament with a second such event in very late Spring on the Monterey Peninsula. Carolyn had talked with the hotel manager at the Highlands Inn, site of our time-share. They were anxious to host our international group, and their room rates were clearly less expensive than those of the Lodge at Pebble Beach. Of course, Pebble controlled the three courses most usable for our tournament. (They had a whole series of rules making a group of more than sixteen far more difficult to schedule, especially when only five months away.) I conferred with John in Scottsdale. He cared greatly about a renewal of that golf and did not seem much, if at all, interested in the room rate differential. Mostly, he was taken with the concept of playing Pebble Beach!

Next, I called Quincy in London. I no sooner said the words, "Pebble Beach," than I thought he was going to jump through our telephone line and appear next to me, he was just that excited. I quickly came to understand that this was "A Once in a Lifetime Event" for the Brits and cost would be no object for them.

Next, Carolyn and I spent time with a senior concierge

at Pebble Beach. They recommended a minimum of a four-day, five-night stay, but suggested an extra day and night might prove helpful to all of those with serious time zone changes (after all, it is eight hours earlier than the UK). I left the room rate negotiations to Carolyn and Lily and turned to the timing. After the Bing Crosby/AT&T Pro-Am PGA Tour event, they suggested waiting at least two weeks for the courses to become more playable after all of the trampling by the galleries during that tournament. Then, there was the *Concours d'Elegance,* Pebble's splendid antique car show, rendering another week unusable. Thus, we were left with the first weekend in April on which to finish as Easter week came second week, and opened the Spring Season.

I spoke with John at DMIC and Quincy in London; also called Gerry at Connecticut Indemnity to assure she was on board. We decided spouses or significant others should be invited, as optional. We agreed on the timing for the Tournament and we came up with a tentative list of needed invitees. John's college age son would be busy in school. Patrick Tyne, nearing his graduation from Princeton, was also preparing with Elsa for their wedding back in Ross. So, both would be unavailable. Robert O'Neill was the number two player on the Branson School's Boys' Golf team and had a tournament scheduled for that weekend. Thus, he too was not able to play, much to his chagrin. Thus, we decided to let each captain be responsible for his team's invitations, but stressed "no ringers." Finally, we had Carolyn, whose name carried more *cachet* than either of ours, investigate and make the blanket arrangements, while individual invitees would be responsible for all of their personal charges, including room bills. Group events, including all golf, would go on a master bill and be pro-rated by invitee, at check-out.

We ended up with five nights and four days as the core of the event, including eight players per side. We received our special group rate for up to two nights on either side of the core stay. Bookings for the rooms for the event were to be coordinated with John, Carolyn or me. Lily did the actual bookings and was our key contact because of her competence and her availability. A few of the player attendees doubled up for a room. Others did not. John, Quincy and I were upgraded. Carolyn got the nicest suite, near a main pool and accessible to the other guests for unscheduled events, and private cocktails on arrival night.

— — —

While billable events were more sparse during the Holidays, our partners held an end of year meeting scheduled to last a maximum of four hours on December 30. Deirdre and Reggie went over our tentative closing accounting numbers, and we approved their recommendations for a distributable bonus to each partner. Joshua, and especially Felicia, were shocked by their bonuses; and incredibly happy!

Then we turned to expanding the firm and succession planning: neither a project on which anyone looked forward to spending time. But we did. First, more space was becoming available in our building during the coming year. We could use more space to accommodate Alan Boswell and Sandra, especially when they grew their business loads. The same was true of our newer partners. Then there was the Glendale office.

Unexpressed in the discussion of space was the future of the firm and adding more new business, new clients, and perhaps new practice areas. Reggie was becoming more and more involved in employment defense matters and referrals from our network memberships which were working very well in that practice area, Mary's coverage work was ever-growing. She was hugely popular with the CI claims staff in Hartford and its regional staff in Sacramento. She had two associates whom she considered well on the partner path and four juniors. Reggie had one. Martha was interested in the increase in litigation that was taking place in the health-care areas, especially beyond medical malpractice. Then, there were the increasing areas of intellectual property and other contract matters. We turned these thoughts over and came back to Alan and Sandra. (Sandra's third partner decided to leave litigation to go with a real estate development firm where his brother-in-law was a senior partner.) Those two were viewed as potential business generating assets, but we had no certainty of their abilities to realize that potential. We agreed that for the forthcoming year: a modified version of partner compensation with potentially reachable incentives would be proposed; and, they would have the titles of partner, but for the firm's purposes, it would be a probationary stage. We would help them by involving them in ACLN. Reggie and I were to discuss all of this with them. We also agreed to retain both of their more senior associates.

When Reggie and I met with Sandra and Alan, we went to lunch at Kincaid's, a more modern-ish seafood restaurant that was attempting to replace the Grotto (one of the three brother-owners died and the other two felt too sad to carry-on in their iconic location). We got a slightly private corner window table overlooking the Alameda-Oakland Estuary. They both knew the agenda going into the meeting. They also knew that we knew they had virtually no bargaining leverage. After some limited back and forth about how our plan might work out for each of them, first Sandra, then quicky, Alan, accepted. We had a nice lunch and walking back to our offices next to Sandra, she said, "I don't know how you first came to forgive me, but I feel after all these years that the worst mistake of my entire life was my unfailing pride which gave me the shallowness of character to so unthinkingly yield to losing my temper with you that awful day. But, somehow you forgave me. Yet, I have never fully forgiven myself. What you and Reggie are doing for Alan and me is just further proof of what a marvelous person you are. I hope Carolyn knows what she has in you."

— — —

Early in the morning of December 30 that Holiday Season, I received a call from Quincy in London. He was highly agitated, and at first I was terribly worried. But then, his flow of words slowed as I kept telling him to Slow Down so I could understand him (when you are not around a Welshman for awhile, the accent can take a few sentences to bring back your needed listening skill set). "I'll repeat myself. We've done it! The draft agreement for the 'New Lloyds' just received an overwhelming endorsement in the House of Commons! It will go into effect on January 1, two days hence. I shall send John, Manny and you complete copies by FED EX for delivery to your Ross address as soon as practicable. Happy New Year!"

I wished him well, but he was anxious to call John with the news. I made some coffee and quietly went out to get the paper. When I returned, Carolyn was waiting for me, bundled in a warm looking robe and very furry slippers. I smiled. She smiled back. "Quincy?" she asked.

"Yes. News of a total success for the start-up of 'New Lloyds.' A great many people and entities have staked a great deal of capital and energy, not to mention their futures, on getting that institution in place. Just in time, I might add. Some of us were very concerned that if this was not completed by the New Year that Lloyds would have to go into run-off, bringing about a financial crisis of uncertain, but very likely huge, magnitude."

"Well done. Does this mean the golf tournament will go forward?" Carolyn was beaming. She did so much wish she had been part of the Irish event.

I smiled, looked into her eyes, held her at arms' length, and asked, "How about this coming year, as soon as their school years permit, we take a family Summer vacation to Ireland?"

With that, I pulled her close and we kissed for a long minute. "You two should be upstairs with that!" came from Meaghan. Nothing like a teen-ager!

"Coffee?" Carolyn asked her?

– – –

As the Holidays drifted along, one thing we had hoped to accomplish came to pass: the Johansson's had a long family weekend to themselves in Napa, heart of the California Wine Country. Over time, Carolyn had acquired several, once a maximum of four, rental duplexes at Silverado Resort and Country Club, all within the immediate proximity of the founder's Mansion, hub of the entire Resort with its added buildings, as well as the adjoining golf course with its pro shop, a main restaurant, and the Members' Club House. Since Patrick Tyne had both Carolyn's last name and mine, he was a full member. (Carolyn put each unit in its own separate trust for the children, and used the operating losses to shelter some of each trust's income. She counted on appreciation to increase those property values over the years.) She arranged for Elsa's parents and brother to have one unit, with Phil, Ingrid, and their children very close by her parents. Meanwhile, Patrick and Elsa had what we referred to as "the Honeymoon Cottage," far from the others, overlooking Milliken Creek. With day trips, restaurants, and wineries, there were plenty of activities for our Swedish friends to enjoy themselves.

They had four nights in Napa. Their first evening, we booked the group for a large table in the main dining room at *Bistro Don Giovanni,* one of our very favorite dining spots in the whole valley. Its charm, along with the warm hospitality of its owners, made their incredible Italian dishes more delightful. It was the only night that Carolyn and I joined them. My wife was a bit of a regular there. The wine and the food, and especially the service, were all marvelous; and, when combined with the changing sky shifting from a multi-hued twilight followed ever so slowly to total darkness settling over the surrounding vineyards created an ambiance nothing short of magical.

During the Holiday Season, many of the diners and the other clientele in the nicer eateries were locals, and many were first-or-second generation Europeans. Our Swedish in-laws-to-be were absolutely delighted with the chatting that went on at their table with so many people dropping by to greet Carolyn, sometimes me, and to be introduced to all of them, especially the newer generation with young children.

Patrick was known to a few of them as he was sometimes in the Sports pages of Bay Area newspapers, or he was known through his mother. A very few recognized Ingrid or Elsa as the "nannies" for our children. It was, all-in-all, a most splendid evening. We finished early enough, and since Carolyn did not imbibe, we drove home to Ross that night.

On the way home, Carolyn was talkative, "What a great evening! (pause) You know, I wonder if those folks we met at *Baja Cantina*, would help with our planning for the dinners for the golf tournament? He was Jerry, but I cannot remember her name."

I responded, "Samantha, I think. But how would they weave in with such a different crowd, like the U.S./U.K. golf group?"

Carolyn: "Well, Jerry seemed a bit more under control at Stephenson Ranch. Why don't I just try and see how that might play out, and see if I can get some help on reservations along the way?"

Me: "Well, if you want to take it on, more power to you. Please just keep me posted. I do think it's not so far away that we can let dinner reservations drift. By the way, after the final round at Pebble, it'd be great if we could get a private area in the Taproom. Can you see what you can do on that as well?"

Carolyn added, "I'll try. I know there's a bar and more space in Stillwater. We might just run everything into a final dinner as some of the Europeans will doubtless leave early the next morning."

The drive home was relatively easy during the Holiday as it was not a travel or commute night, and we left early enough. By the time we were crossing the Bridge, Carolyn was reciting our entire plan. I was hoping to call John and Quincy, the Captains, and get their approval on the 'morrow. That way Carolyn and I could move forward to secure all of the needed reservations.

— — —

That next morning, I spoke with Quincy who appeared somewhat in a daze until I started unfurling our tentative plan. Right away, he asked if we could get extra nights at Pebble at the Tournament rate. Based on my conversations with Carolyn, and knowing the hospitality business that time of year, I told him. He indicated some people might wish to stay upwards of a week longer. So, I mentioned the Highlands Inn, the Hyatts, and several others in Carmel. Quincy was delighted with the golf plan, except he preferred a practice round at Pebble Beach. I allowed the regular rate would apply if he could get a tee time, I pointed out that all of the times had been arranged with a senior concierge at the Lodge and the Assistant Head Pro in charge of all event scheduling at Pebble itself.

Quincy knew little or nothing about Poppy Hills, nor the Links at Spanish Bay, both difficult courses in their own right. Poppy Hills would be for the official practice round, Leaving the three main Pebble Beach courses for the tournament itself. Wilfred had once played Spyglass many years ago and Quincy sounded more than a little in awe of it. He knew nothing of the restaurants or the facilities and was happy with the arrangements we were planning.

John was another whole story. First, he had spoken to Quincy about wives playing and Quincy was not enthralled with the idea as the number of players was limited by the number of tee times. (I had pointed out to Quincy earlier when he whined about wives playing that the only two we were trying to get in were Emily Anne, the wife of the client who paid so many of his bills. Then, my Carolyn and I hired him in the first place.) This put John in a better mood. He listened without interruption as I explained everything to him about the Five Nights and Four Days. In the end, he suggested. "Ronan, you and Carolyn were great to do all of this and I understand that Carolyn had to go outside our group for some of these arrangements. So, I am going to suggest that you both proceed to lock everything in place. But, having said that, I believe that Emily Anne and I should fly up there for a long weekend so I can be certain about all of the arrangements. We would do it soon: weather notwithstanding. If I really do feel we need to change something, that way we could still try.

I suggested to John that I would check with Carolyn to see if we could arrange something, and then get back to him on that idea. Thinking about John's idea made me wonder if it was more of a desire on his, or his wife's, part to spend some quality time with just Carolyn and me. That, in itself, did not seem a bad thing. Still...?!

I waited until getting home that night, fixing my drink, pouring Carolyn her glass of wine , and greeting/ discussing her day with young Mollie who had become quite a chatperson, before taking up John's suggestion with Carolyn. She appeared uncomfortable getting seated in her regular patio chair as I explained what had happened. After no more than a minute, I was finished, and waiting to hear from her.

Then, she made a bit of a face, and began, "I'm not at all sure about what I'm about to say, but I'm going to say it because I need to have it out there. I think you know I have been unerringly faithful to you since we married. I hug and kiss Vera, and less frequently Lisa, from time-to-time, but there is no overt Lesbian behavior. Not that I don't miss some small bit of it. But that's not what this is about. Many, if not most, models think that their genre is composed largely of Lesbians. Moreover, when one of them is 'on the make for another,' both parties appear to give-off non-verbal signals. On a few occasions when we have been alone, even though I am out of practice, I felt I might be getting those signals from John's Emily Anne. There now I've said it. Do you understand?"

I was more than a little flabbergasted by what Carolyn had said, and thought before answering, "Has she said anything directly, or actually done anything?" I was not at all certain I was asking the right questions. After all, I had no real expertise in that area.

Carolyn sipped her wine, and fixed me with her gaze, "That's why I was so uncertain about telling you, Emma has done nothing overt, not a thing; moreover, it's not a feeling that's always there. But it does arise only when we're alone. Now, you might think I find her attractive and this feeling is actually a transference on my part, a work of my overwrought imagination in finding her attractive?"

This was unsafe ground, so I tried to go forward slowly, "Carolyn Dear, only you know what goes on inside you, and God knows you had an exceedingly trying life in your early years, and I am not in any way judging you, but this 'transference thing,' it's not something I understand. So, I guess I have to ask if you think that might be true? And, if it is, what does that mean about going forward with John's suggestion?"

Carolyn finished her glass and got up to pour herself more, as she turned to go back, she stopped, and looked at me with a vague look in her eyes, "I don't know. I guess it could be me. Maybe I just subconsciously find her attractive. After all, she is many years John's junior, probably twenty-five, or a bit more; and, she is an absolutely stunning specimen of a woman. Not too thin, like me. But again, she has said nothing. I guess I want you to know, just in case something untoward should happen, if they come. Does that make sense?"

Me: "Up to a point, but what am I supposed to say? What will you do, if she does do something?"

Carolyn, "I have no idea. I suppose it would depend on what, if anything, she tries or does. I just want you to be aware. I realize John is a hugely important client for your firm, and I want no surprises; and certainly nothing to damage the business friendship relationship that the two of you have established. After all, the only thing John told me about her, and I think you too, was that she was very shy; and that seems true enough."

I decided to try a different tack, "Why don't you call Emily Anne and tell her the tentative plans for the tournament and see what she would like to do on a four-night long weekend, if you can arrange something? That might relieve any pressure on you. "

Carolyn smiled. "You really are a creative person. That would put 'the ball in her court.' I like that, I like it a lot. Let me call Pebble and speak to my Concierge, and see what's available. In fact, I'm going to see if I can get him right now." She pulled out her cell phone, touched a few buttons, and in seconds was asking for Geoffrey, the Concierge. In little more than ten minutes, she had a four-day weekend with three rounds of golf for a four-some, and a dinner at Still-water Cove restaurant on the final night.

"That appears to be the only weekend when we can arrange something. So, I do hope you can juggle your schedule. I know mine is OK. I shall call Emily Anne tomorrow morning. I would not like to interrupt their dinner."

"You could text her right now and see if she wants to talk at the outset tonight, especially since only one weekend is available. If those are the critical dates, we want to give John a chance to make whatever changes he might need to make first thing tomorrow."

Carolyn smiled, a wry smile, sexy, and said, "You really do want to see how this plays out for now, don't you?" With that she sent a short text.

Within five minutes, no more, Emily Anne called back on Carolyn's cell phone. I only heard one side of the conversation, but I could make out that Emma (as she liked to be called) was excited by the general prospect of our foursome weekend. Carolyn went through what she had tentatively put in place, stressing that the need to act promptly as this was the only opportunity which would provide the leeway to make any changes that John might deem to be necessary. Next thing I knew, Carolyn was holding, creating the impression that Emily was talking to John.

"Yes, Emma, that is literally the only weekend when we could stay at the Lodge and play all three of those courses. (A pause.) Also, I have some major commitments this Spring that I cannot move for my major clients and for *Vogue*. But I can squeeze this in. (Pause.) No, Ronan is fine with this. (Longer Pause.) Yes, Emma, that will be great. I'll have Geoffrey send you a copy of the Agenda when he sends it to me. (Pause.) Good, let's talk tomorrow, late morning."

Carolyn looked at me. Emma made John promise to free-up that weekend. That was what took so long. She may be shy, but her tone sounded highly persuasive!"

I smiled my wry smile. Carolyn smiled hers back at me. I finished my drink, got to me feet, put out my hand to Carolyn, checked to see no one was within ear-shot, and said, "Let's go right to bed. I'm not sure why, but I found that all to be very sexy, especially that look you got in your eyes more than once."

Carolyn smiled again, "Do remember that look, Big Boy!" She dropped my hand and bounded up the steps to our bedroom suite!

— — —

The New Year rang-in and the family drifted back to its non-celebratory life-style. Only Helmut Johansson stayed with us, rooming with Patrick O'Neill who had helped him get a Spring semester scholarship to Branson School which would allow him to play soccer. The two boys quickly became that team's top scoring threats!

My partners all agreed to the tentative plans for the forthcoming year as did Sandra and Alan, as "not-quite-equity partners" for the forthcoming year, at least. Alan was aided by playing to a six handicap. (John was pleased to add him to our American team.)

The courts were back into the swing of business. Carolyn was off to Paris, then back to New York doing planning for two *Vogue* layouts and a cover, also undertaking several appearances for her endorsement clients. Her trips always sounded glamorous, but I could tell from her somewhat frayed condition after being gone nine full days, that she arrived home utterly exhausted. Amazingly, in less than forty-eight hours, she was back to her fully-energized self with her Mollie every step behind her when not in school.

Carolyn had a brief shopping tour with Maeve when in Paris, they did some planning together (*Vogue's* Robert was also there), and she caught up on Maeve's social life. I got a call from Maeve, the day after the two of them had dinner. Maeve advised that she had met someone and they were having a relationship, but taking it very slow, Carolyn had not been invited to meet this person, but knew of her and would doubtless discuss this with me. It was not a comfortable call, but she was very verbal in her good feelings toward me.

I heard from Patrick Tyne to tell me that if he was available in the National Basketball Association (NBA) draft, the New York Knickerbockers (the Knicks) were planning to make him their first-round draft choice. (That front office still recalled Senator Bill Bradley, Princeton's greatest basketball player, with great fondness as he was a main part of the only Knicks' Glory Days!) Patrick had also been contacted by other teams, as well. He discouraged one or two of those other teams, not wishing to be part of a "building process."

He was still living in the Athletes' Dorm; still, he was spending all of his available free-time (not very much of it) with Elsa. They were planning a very early June wedding at St. Anselm's, much to the chagrin of the Johansson's. However, they were to honeymoon in Stockholm for several days, cruise to Oslo, then fly south to Venice, then Florence as a time for contrasts, and end where Elsa would be a first-time centerpiece of a *Vogue* spread on autumnal Italian fashion. Meanwhile, Patrick would await the NBA draft in New York alone.

— — —

After a preliminary findings order, and further briefing, meet and confers, as well as supplemental oral arguments, in February, Judge Ezra Brown entered his Order allowing most of the discovery requested by GWF, and very little of that sought by the Plaintiffs, who changed their positions to add asserting the willful destruction of potentially adverse documents by GWF. However, Judge Brown did allow the Plaintiffs to depose the last five years before this litigation was initially filed of whichever persons were ultimately responsible for implementing GWF's Document Destruction Policies. The Judge also would not compel any other non-party, except the individual plaintiffs or Guardians *ad litem*, to produce any IQ test results, or submit to IQ testing, unless a relative admitted to having done so in the past. These various foreclosures and guidelines for moving forward threatened both parties' plans for the litigation. As a result, we met and conferred with our adversaries and agreed to seek a stay order from Judge Brown while both sides filed briefing seeking intermediate appellate protection under the California Writ process to facilitate the needs of both sides in the on-going discovery phase.

Our client personnel and their carrier, Cayuga Mutual, were pleased with this overall course of action as it was delaying the much more expensive deposition discovery phase of these cases. (The Meet and Confer process had made very clear that Plaintiff counsel would want to hand pick three to five plaintiffs as exemplary trial samples. I worked with our younger lawyers to stress that whenever the other side wrote such a brief, these associates needed to be factually ready to demonstrate that no appropriate scientific consensus existed for any of the plaintiffs' putative theories of diminished IQ.

The net result of all of this jostling for advantageous positioning was the beginning of judicial gridlock, a circumstance which had proven quite helpful in achieving our client's dismissal in the LAUSD case, many years before (gone, but not forgotten!).

— — —

Following the highly successful Opening Organizational Meeting of the American Civil Litigation Network at the Biltmore in Phoenix, our Board was pressing forward with assistance from more than a dozen other firms in the recruiting and vetting of prospective firms to join ACLN. Reggie and Lily, highly energized by her administrative roles, were deeply involved in all levels of this rapid, efficacious build-up of ACLN's membership. At the January Board Meeting, we discussed amending the By-Laws to increase the number of Board Members.

Between our firm's memberships in the Society and two other individual member admission networks as well as our network for the defense of the CAL Board asbestos litigation, we had to move slowly so as to leave room for other firms to bring in new members to ACLN who might provide our firm with referrals for new work, or clients. Reggie was a very quick learner and he was great at evaluating which firms to start down the ACLN membership path.

Lily brought a home-made lunch for us to have an office meeting on ACLN before our first call of February. The lunch was almost fun, and ninety minutes flew by as we brought all of our records current and put together an agenda for that call.

Before going home that evening, Lily sent an email with the agenda for the next day's call to all of the Board members.

The last item mattered as we started the new year: tracking of new business referrals—a needed process?

———

Carolyn had several calls with Emily Anne about our four-day weekend at Pebble Beach.

Emma, as she often asked Carolyn to call her, was terribly nervous about her playing the three golf courses on which we were scheduled: Spyglass Hill, Spanish Bay, and Pebble Beach. Then, there was the issue of which restaurants to preview, and some sightseeing. I heard Carolyn's side of one call when I got home, "Emma, please calm down. You have been very clear that you are not confident in your golfing skills, but let me assure you, all four of us will be tested many times more than once on those courses. You hit the ball straight. That is the best thing you can do on all of those courses. (Pause.) OK. Please don't cry. John loves you. He won't get angry. (Pause. Longer.) Oh, Emma, that's hard for me to imagine. You're letting your imagination run away with you. I think I just heard Ronan come in. I'd better go. We'll talk again soon. (Pause.) Yes. Yes. I'll be there. I'll take care of you, if need be. (Pause.) Thank You, Emma. Bye-bye."

Turning to me, "She ended by saying, 'love you.' That's the kind of thing that makes me nervous. So, how are you tonight?"

"Maybe she's never had a friend as nice as you have been in dealing with her; and remember she is much younger than John, even younger than you. What have you learned about her background?"

Carolyn made a small face, and touched her nose, "You may not realize, but she does not like to talk about herself at all. I sometimes wonder if maybe she has something to hide. On the other hand, she does not seem to act mysteriously. I don't even know where she's from. I'll need to do better. I'll insist she be more forthcoming, the next time we talk. Now give me a kiss, then make our drinks. Let me go and get Mollie."

———

The three of us were going over Mollie's school day with her when my cell went off. Sandra, who was in North Carolina, was on the other end. It was after 9:00 p.m. there. She was agitated, "Mason and I just finished dinner with Everson Harris and some of his key people on this whole Ester-Tech deal. Maybe it was the alcohol, but of the four client people, none of them agreed about much of anything concerning the whole series of steps from contract negotiation to product development in what has transformed itself into a potential full-fledged disaster. We need a solid plan to start moving forward. Can we have a call tomorrow at 7:00 a.m. your time. Just Mason, you and me."

"Will I need any documents?" I asked.

"Not really. Just call this number and we'll be ready for you. Thanks!"

I told Carolyn that this Neptune case kept going from bad to worse. I took a cheese and cracker. Then refilled our glasses half-way, and sat back down to interact with our Mollie.

Later, in bed, as I pulled up my sheets, "I do believe this Neptune case just might be the worst thing our firm has ever had to deal with. I hope I do not have to go to North Carolina!"

Then I rolled over and kissed my wife Good Night.

The next morning, following a night of tossing and turning, I arose at 6:00, took a very quick shower, donned an exercise outfit, toasted a blueberry Pop Tart and made a pot of pressed coffee, fresh ground French Blend, Italian Roast beans from Bodega Bay Coffee. At 7:00, I called the phone number that Sandra had given me. It rang about ten times, without answer. I left a brief message and went out front to get the newspapers. I brought my cell. Three steps back into our house and my cell phone rang. It was 7:10 and Sandra. I left the papers in the kitchen and carried my coffee into my home office, closing the door.

"So, Sandra, How are Mason and you getting on?"

She spoke for about ten minutes, and when she paused, Mason picked up the verbal cudgel to use against our 'erstwhile client personnel.' Sandra jumped back on. I busied myself by writing down names of those at their client dinner last night. Finally, they stopped.

I took a deep breath, and went into my thought process from an essentially sleepless night, "Sounds to me that these people are in disarray and need some serious training and more than a little discipline. Mason, I am going to ask you, as you've had Neptune Enterprises as a client for some years to be the single contact point for organizing all of this. If you cannot get the needed cooperation, who will we be able to contact at the parent in order to get these folks onto the same page. Sandra, I believe that almost all contract cases are won or lost based on documentation. To date, Neptune Fishing has shown no proclivity for any type of document organization. Mason, at our office, we have taken all of the contract-related documents that have been supplied so far and, among other things, have created a chronological file of all of those documents. In some cases, more than one version of the same document. In other cases, a predecessor document described *post-facto,* is missing.

"Mason, does Neptune Enterprises, the holding company, have any document retention policy ("DRP")? (Silence.) "And if so, is that DRP in writing? Is it actually followed? What person, by name and title, is in charge of that DRP aspect of our client's business?"

As I was pausing, Mason spoke up, "Leslie Worth is the General Counsel for 'Enterprises.' She retained our firm about fifteen years ago because her father, who was becoming a now-retired partner of ours, had been their outside General Counsel for quite few years. She is very 'close' with Adam Young, Junior, the son of the founder and Executive Vice President of Enterprises. We provided her with several draft DRPs, probably close to ten years ago. She allowed she was going to implement one of them. I do not know if that ever happened, or which one they might have implemented. I was the junior partner on our firm's team servicing Enterprises at that time. I do not know if either DRP was implemented for any of the Neptune subsidiaries. Also, Ms. Worth uses outside counsel for almost all of the legal work of the whole Neptune family of companies. Only she would know the full scope of those services and what firm provides what service. They also have subsidiaries outside North Carolina."

Me: "You both can see where this is going. Sounds as if the Neptune parent provides the legal services either directly, or more usually indirectly, to its subsidiaries. Mason, can you corroborate all of this in the very near term, and especially open a door to Ms. Worth for our defense team, preferably without delay? Sandra, I'll have Lily box-up and send you a complete set of all of the Fishing contract documentation. The Fishing person providing each document is listed thereon. Mason, we need two things, a person to be the Custodian of Documents for Neptune Fishing, and that may turn out to be someone with Enterprises. Possibly, even Ms. Worth, but preferably not. But we also need a person Most Knowledgeable as to the documents and the transactions in this relevant timeline. Again, it may prove to be Ms. Worth, or perhaps more likely, Everson Harris? God forbid!"

"One other thing that needs to be done, and we'll need it to be updated as changes occur, is a schedule of each and every item of damage and the approximate dollar amount of each incurred by any party to this lawsuit. If we are able to get all of those numbers in one place, organized by potentially liable party, they may prove to provide the needed monetary incentive to get our client's people more seriously involved in this litigation. What do you think?"

We carried on for another twenty minutes or so. Sandra and Mason saw the need for the steps I had described, especially getting all of the potential damages displayed in one place. When we finished the call, I made an outline of matters that could be covered while Sandra was in North Carolina, dictated it to Lily's message machine, and asked to have a draft for when I arrived. With that, I went into the kitchen and greeted members of my family who were breakfasting before being on their ways to various tasks, most of them to school.

I went and hugged Carolyn who looked glamorous in a baby-blue silk robe, with her dirty blonde hair pulled back in a pony-tail. Esmeralda was about to take Mollie to St. Anselm's and then go to the market for our daily shopping. As those two were the last to leave, I apologized to Carolyn for being such a bad sleeper that past night. Then said, "I'm going to go up and shower, then run into the office for three or four hours. What are you up to?'

Carolyn smiled, came over and gave me a shy kiss, while saying, "I could use a shower about now myself. Mind if I join you?"

— — —

15

CLIENT ENTERTAINMENT: MONTEREY STYLE

We had been pressed to get all the arrangements made to entertain John and Emily Anne O'Sullivan for four nights and three days, much of it in Pebble Beach, which is a largely privately owned area, much of it sold and sometimes subdivided by purchasing speculators or developers. It is also replete with a great many service entities, and much of it is operated as a high-end town by its owners. Fortunes had been made and lost by those who owned that area and operated it. For many years now, it was owned by extraordinarily wealthy and brilliant trio of people who shared a common vision, including what seemed like its own Park Service which limited access by a series of gates, permits and fees. Very little, if anything, was left to chance at Pebble Beach.

Carolyn and I arrived in our family SUV, an M-class Mercedes-Benz, loaded down with golf clubs and a wealth of luggage. We pulled up in front of the Lodge. When we gave our names, within seconds, Geoffrey, our Concierge, appeared as if out of nowhere. He and the Doorman/Greeter sorted through our things. Carts arrived: Geoffrey and the driver sat in front of the first cart and Carolyn next to me in a spacious second seat. In seemingly two minutes we were transported to a corner building on the property, where Geoffrey escorted us into the living area of a three bedroom suite, while he explained, "This will be your suite for the forthcoming Tournament as well. As you all are the organizers and Mr. O'Sullivan is the team captain, we thought this appropriate, and since it was available this weekend, as well, our management felt it would be their pleasure to upgrade you four all to this facility for this weekend, as well."

We were gazing out the huge front window across a body of water, Stillwater Cove, following the ocean's panorama past the world-famous 18th hole with its oceanside fairway, then the Beach Club, to the famous hilly peninsula leading up to the Par-5 6th hole, then down to the superbly short Par-3 7th, and across to the eighth, ninth and tenth fairways running evermore distantly southerly along the cliffside and its beach well below, marking the turning point of this iconic golf treasure at the Club's southernmost boundary. Geoffrey's phone rang, just loudly enough that he felt a need to answer. The O'Sullivan's had arrived and he was needed back at the Lodge to coordinate. Carolyn went out with him, giving him a handsome tip in the process.

Carolyn went inside and returned with an ice bucket, champagne and four flutes. I opened the bottle carefully and returned it to its bucket, wrapped with a towel. We described what we saw in that very special view to each other, all the way down to the Carmel Beach, barely visible in the distance in the sun-generated haze. I put my arm around her waist, and at that moment the two carts appeared bearing the O'Sullivan's and their luggage. John jumped out and went around to help Emily Anne. They looked a bit tired, but nonetheless seemed excited. A sense of familiarity suddenly appeared and we greeted each other as if long-lost-friends, with handshakes and back-pats from the men; and, hugs and cheek-kisses between the women. They turned before entering, getting some sense of the view, while I said, "Geoffrey will see to your things. You may wish to give him some quick instructions. Please return right away so we can celebrate your arrival appropriately." I nodded indicating the ice bucket and the fluted glasses.

They went inside for only moments. I saw John slip Geoffrey two large denomination bills as he departed. As I started pouring, Carolyn began, "Ronan tells me that you played here once some years ago, John, and Emma, you've never been here?" They both nodded YES. "So, I'm going to explain that they have provided us with one of the most picturesque views in the world, including the entire golfing world, from this very patio."

I passed out the glasses before Carolyn began a detailed description, saying, "Welcome to Pebble Beach. We hope you all have a great weekend and find everything to your liking." Flutes clinked. We all drank. John heartily. The rest of us sipping. Carolyn presented a verbal picture of our view with a tour guide's familiarity, the afternoon colors on this hazy late-Winter sunny day painting what we were seeing as if in Van Gogh's colors. When she finished, "Do you all have any questions?"

John, said, "Truthfully, neither of us know enough to ask anything, as yet. Carolyn, that was just a magnificent job. I wish I could recall the holes with the specificity you described. Do you do television commercials?"

We all chuckled, but I saw a calculating glint in Carolyn's eye, as I began to speak, "Why don't we grab our car and spend the last daylight hour or so showing you both around 17-Mile Drive? That's the Pebble Beach official touring route.

Depending on what you want for dinner, and knowing you are an hour ahead of us, and travelled further, we thought about a casual dinner at the Taproom. No need to change, unless you wish? Being a Thursday night, I'm sure we could go either to some other casual place, or dress-up and go somewhere more fancy, as we'll be doing the next two nights. What say you?"

John and Emma conferred for a matter of seconds, and she said, "This is all so wonderful. It's like being in a dream. Let's just follow your suggestions. I'm sure we'll do that most of the time here."

We left through the Carmel Gate and drove through that town giving them both a chance to see some of its incredibly quaint architecture, and onto the Pacific Coast Highway for less than a mile or so, down through Pacific Grove. This was the home of California's Monarch Butterfly Sanctuary, then along its ocean view road, through the multi-million-dollar mansions lining the non-beach side, stopping briefly at one or two pull-overs to admire the rock formations and their crashing waves. Then, we turned into the Pacific Grove Gate, to Pebble Brach itself, circling into the Spanish Bay Resort where we all would play on Saturday, seeing enough so that they could understand that it was a completely separate resort from Pebble Beach Club layout itself, but all part of the greater entity itself. Then out to the Coast, past Cypress Point Country Club, the most exclusive club in the entire Resort, and onward for a few glimpses of Spyglass where we would play tomorrow, and back. (I have not attempted to describe everything else we pointed out.) When we arrived back at the Lodge, the Doorman allowed that Geoffrey had reserved a most desirable table for us in the Taproom.

As we all sat in the plush stuffed-leather-arm chairs, I got the sense that the ladies could use a break. We excused them after our beverage order. John and I talked some details of the upcoming tournament. But beforehand, he said, "I want to be clear. This trip was my suggestion and we shall be paying for the whole thing." Holding up a hand, he continued, "No. No. I insist. I cannot tell you how excited Emily Anne is to spend this time with Carolyn. You too, of course; but she has talked of little else for the last ten days. You've made me a very happy man with all of your efforts, both Carolyn and you!"

The balance of that evening was a good time, and the eight ounce Taproom Burgers were scrumptious!!

— — —

Not surprisingly, on Friday, play on the Spyglass course was slow. Our foursome had a chance to reflect on its first two holes while we endured a twenty-minute wait before getting our first glimpse of one of the most famous Par 3s in the golfing world. Emma, as we were asked to call her for the day, was overjoyed that she had shot a 7 on the Par 5 first hole: 520 yards downhill from the Ladies' red tee box, bending 90 degrees left toward the ocean at 125 yards from the center of an elevated island green, with no real landing area should you overhit it. The other three had managed 6's, with the men driving from the white tees at 605 yards (relatively steep downhill slope helps by adding at least 50 yards of extra roll if you stay in the fairway: all four of us did so!). The Second Hole was an uphill golfcart drive to its tee boxes, and the women got very little advantage on this relatively short, slightly uphill fairway to an elevated smallish green. Neither John nor I hit driver, instead hitting five woods to gain a decent approach shot to that pin. When our drives landed, their only roll was downhill toward the right, our balls moving away from the target flag on the green. Carolyn hit her three wood on a line left of the one chosen by John and me. With its slight roll to the right, she was considerably closer than the men. Emma followed Carolyn's lead, but pulled her 3-wood left behind a large bushy obstruction blocking her from any direct approach to the flag on the green, and perhaps to the green itself.

Ten minutes later, Carolyn's second shot was only about 10 feet downhill from the hole.

Mine was closer than John, i.e., about 20 feet to his perhaps 30 feet. Both had tricky breaks. Emma was on in 4 shots, with one very troubling third shot that only covered about 20 yards from a very bad lie in high grass, but by then she was closest to the hole. John putted first: misread the speed of the green and as a result got much more break. Suffice it to say, he did not lose his turn. His uphill second put got him to within two feet whereupon he marked his ball (doubtless hoping the women would concede his fifth stroke at some point). My first put was on a safer line than John's, but having seen what happened to him, I played too much break and left my putt a foot from the hole. Hearing nothing from the ladies, I stepped up and knocked my ball in the cup for a par. Carolyn had been silent while all of the activity on the second green was occurring. She strode to her marker, placed her ball in front of it; stood, then stooped and glowered at her line for a second, and removed her marker. After looking at her line once and two practice strokes, Carolyn calmly knocked her putt into the hole for a natural birdie.

As she reminded John and I, even with his conceded putt on number Two, the Ladies had a two hole lead on the Men. We watched the foursome in front of us, only one had hit the green, make an absolute mess of this beautiful Par 3 golf hole. Spyglass Number Three is "only" 140 yards, a drop of about 70 feet from the tee boxes to the elevated island green's surface. That green surrounded by sand traps for about three quarters of its circumference formed a tight landing area, and all the rest of what was visible was a jungle of seemingly unmaintained plant life. We could feel the wind blowing into us from the ocean located quite close behind the island green. Carolyn said something to Emma. The men went first: I hit a seven iron, playing the stiff breeze to add 15 yards to the rated distance. Wrong choice: the green was too dried out and my ball landed ten yards in front of the stick, but it bounced hard and rolled toward the far side of the green, barely stopping in time. John hit a six iron, landing it past the pin. One bounce and it was gone, never to be seen again. He hit a provisional with his seven and it came to rest in the sand to the right of, and below, the island green.

Carolyn's tee box was only about five yards closer than the Men's, making her seven iron the perfect club. Her swing was something out of a golf teaching manual and her ball flew toward the Spyglass flag coming to rest within twenty feet. She nodded, then turning to Emma, said, "No pressure. Just remember, not too fast at the very top. Keep your rhythm!"

Emma's practice swings looked perfect. She appeared somewhat more athletic than Carolyn, almost having slight muscle definition in her arms, and definitely some in her calves. She stepped back for a second, checked her line, then addressed her ball, and slowly began her swing, accelerating into the ball with her club face. That ball also flew straight and true, landed perhaps fifteen feet short of the pin and rolled gradually toward the hole, not coming to a stop until it was less than one foot from going in the cup. Carolyn turned to Emma, who stood motionless watching her ball, grasped her, giving Emma a little spin, hugged Emma, and exclaimed, "Emma, you almost had a hole-in-one! That was incredible!"

Carolyn just missed her putt, but the women were leading three-up, and had just played a great hole in a combined one under par. The day continued like that for a few more holes, not quite as badly for John and me. Carolyn was, as always, a very steady player, straight-hitter, good putter, but like most of us who rarely practiced, her short game could have used more refinement. ("Too many things in this life need doing," she would tell me when I suggested a morning of golf practice. Plus, one of the things 'worth doing' with Carolyn was fun!)

John and I won the Par-3 6th Hole, and the Course turned uphill, away from the ocean, plunging into the Del Monte Forest for the remaining twelve holes. Play speeded up: the men ultimately lost by one hole, and we retreated to the Taproom to salve our wounds and discuss that day's golf. After ordering our round, I asked, "John, what did you think of the Spyglass course?"

John frowned at first, then broke into a smile, "I think that most of our fellow players will feel about it much the way our front-running foursome's story unfolded as we waited to play on the number six tee box. When in a Texas drawl, our fellow golfer allowed, 'We were unable to book this course first, hearing it would be easier than Pebble

Beach. Well, I've got news for those folks back in Austin: We played Pebble yesterday, and it was hard. But I have never played five straight holes harder than this first five here at Spyglass. This is the hardest golfing in the world!'

"To me, that sums it up. Not unfair, but hard. Beautiful and so well cared-for. Emma, Darling, you played far-and-away the very best I have ever seen you play. Ms. Carolyn, Ronan was right, you are a little bit better than him and all of us. Did you miss a single fairway today? I think not. Where are we going tonight, folks?"

Carolyn interjected, "We only have four nights, and there are more places to see and go than we can get you both to visit in that time. So, I thought we'd take you all to *Baja Cantina* for a drink and some Mexican appetizers, then on to Clint Eastwood's place, Stephenson Ranch for a main course. A couple from *Baja Cantina* has made a reservation for us by his knowing the Ranch's owner. Is that OK?"

Emma chipped in, smiling and saying, "John, remember I said, 'no ties.' That's because Carolyn told me that 'Casual Dressy' is as dressy as it gets here' I hope you packed accordingly. I know I did. Let's go!"

— — —

That second night, after we met Jerry and Samantha at *Baja Cantina* was just about as much fun as you're allowed to have in this life. Jerry and Samantha were 'a hoot!' John and Emma liked them from the start. They had the big corner booth in the Bar at *Baja* all picked out. The four of us ordered drinks and appetizers appeared at the same time as the beverages. We had a fun hour, then had to scuttle to get to Stephenson Ranch before the night air got too cold to sit outside. That was not a problem either. Portable heaters, great wine and nice steaks made for an excellent evening. Plus, John was able to find out more about Jerry than we had when we first met them. Turns out he was a start-up investor, and he had achieved a number of very successful ventures, a couple of which were well-known, and publicly traded. He was still reluctant to name any of them.

What did become interesting, and secured Jerry's spot on the American team was his interest in what we had been doing at Lloyds, and after listening, he started asking about investing. Back at our suite, later that night as we all drank water, or otherwise sought hydration, John allowed that he had not foreseen that there could be a vast sea of capital from the Silicon Valley Start-Up investors. John wondered aloud, "Could Jerry possibly be the key that would unlock the door to some of that wealth which would add further credibility to the New Lloyds? Quincy and Bradley may need to be consulted ahead of time. What do you think, Ronan? Throw in Stanley Booth, as well?"

In our room, Carolyn whispered, "Ronan, they both love us. Do you really think Jerry could be a major business source? I never learned as much about Lloyds as I learned tonight listening to you three men talking."

The morning beckoned, and there were still two more fun-filled days and nights to go!

— — —

Our third day included golf on the Spanish Bay Course, replete with Ocean View holes, plenty of water and wind in play, and a testing layout demanding accurate approach shots to several very unusual greens. John played better. I did not. Emma was more erratic than at Spyglass. (Some of the carries over obstacles appeared to intimidate her, and she was out of play on a goodly number of holes.) Carolyn was once again the best golfer, but without any help from Emma, the men were able to win 2-Up. That left the Pebble Beach course as the deciding venue. Appropriately, that was the plan for the Tournament as well, where all players would be engaged in Singles matches. Afterward, it was just barely warm enough with a breeze off the ocean to sit outside at the Bar of the Clubhouse for a post-match drink. The ladies both chose Irish coffee, while John and I each had a very large Macallan's 18 year-old Scotch, neat with some ice cubes back.

I spent a moment or two regaling our guests with my stays at Spanish Bay when I would provide Legal Assistance for the Monterey area to U.S. Coast Guard personnel, and would get to book my stay there at an outrageous discount by my being under military orders, plus they would let me play as many holes as I could finish for $25/round after my time at USCG Base Monterey, a ten-minute drive away. "You may not have noticed, but I played the first six holes better than the rest. Those were the ones I got to finish most often." I ended with a chuckle.

Carolyn made a face, saying, "If that's so true, how do you explain paring eighteen less than an hour ago?" Then, she smiled!

I smiled back at her, "My best drive of the day, an incredibly lucky second shot, a miracle of a chip shot, and a good putt. It was my best, albeit luckiest, hole of the day. Thank you, dear!"

As we rose to leave, I tried to grab the check, but John would have none of it, saying, "Please (with emphasis) remember our discussion from when we arrived!"

Just then the fully-kilted Bag Piper appeared, and he began to play Danny Boy. I turned to John, "You are most gracious. (Pause.) Do you want to see Jerry and Samantha anymore while you're here, or do you want one of us to verify his background some more and test his actual business interest before the Tournament?"

"I'm thinking that should be you. As CEO of DMIC, it might appear a bit of a conflict to me, if I'm initially involved in any qualifying follow-up. Whereas you being our lawyer are better positioned to spin all of that process without divulging any of our involved entities' various business interests in London."

We drove back to the Lodge, and took a shuttle to our rooms. Carolyn had started talking about *L'Escargot* in Carmel for dinner tonight, explaining that the owner/chef had gotten his start in his home town of Mill Valley where my first wife Mollie and I had lived with our children for almost ten years. We all changed into business casual and were able to be on time for our 7:45 reservation.

The restaurant was simple, yet classically French in its *décor* and its choice of courses. The wine list was simple and was meant to compliment the classic French dinner choices which we indulged with time-honored snails and frog legs to be shared by the table, then the incredible French onion soup, and marvelous main courses. John and I shared *coq au vin*. With no appetite, the ladies split a Caesar salad. We began to tease each other toward the end of the night about the one common ingredient: garlic. Our SUV might never smell the same again!

We stopped in the Lobby of the Lodge, and had a glass of champagne on its balcony, overlooking the18th Hole and Stillwater Cove, all artfully lit to show itself as if by moonlight.

John and Emma agreed that our Tournament group would take over *L'Escargot* for one night and order from a reduced set of choices to allow Chef to do an excellent job of serving all of those present.

Carolyn was ready for sleep as I crawled into our bed, saying, "Ronan, you may not be getting too old for this kind of thing, but I may be. This will be two nights in a row with no sex. Please kiss me Good Night. (We kiss.) Love you!"

— — —

Our final full day saw us start with breakfast on the deck outside our suite. A temperature in the low 60's and little to no wind felt like an early Spring-like morning which allowed us to have a leisurely start to our day. We all walked past some other outlying buildings through the Lodge, and past all of the Resort shops. John and Emily Anne wanted to buy souvenirs for his children, themselves; and at Emily Anne's insistence, a Pebble Beach sweater for John's Ex, with whom she worked at trying to be relatively friendly and helpful, as possible, with their four children, the three youngest still nominally living with that Ex. Carolyn bought new golf gloves. I bought nothing (partly out of fear that John would try to pay for it!).

Our 11:30 tee time was preceded only by a few minutes putting practice. Then we teed off on one of the world's most famous golf courses (priced accordingly!). The first three holes are the least spectacular on the course, but then you come out to the ocean views, more breeze, and the awe of the scenery. The Ladies were up one hole. Following errant drives by both men on the first Par 3, they went up by two. We came next to the daunting Sixth hole, a Par 5, driving somewhat downhill, into a snakish valley framed on the left uphill by the top of a plateau-like ridge of the 8th fairway, then steeply uphill, somewhat over 100 yards to a long, narrow green on an ever-narrowing rising peninsula: I said to the other three, before lining up my second shot, "I always think this is the most diabolic hole here on the entire Monterey Peninsula!" With that, I hit a seven iron about 160 yards to where I hoped a full pitching wedge would get me on to the green (anything close to the virtually invisible flag would be a bonus!)

At the bottom of the rising fairway, the flag was not at all visible for the golfer's next shot. Carolyn's ball was not more than ten yards ahead of mine and John was a few yards behind. Our caddy had coached us carefully to this point. Emma lay three strokes and was away. As she had so far that weekend, she hit most of her shots straight. She did so then. But her ball failed to clear the ridge. Too bad.

John was next with a nine iron. His ball wanted to move right (not good: the ocean could come into play), but a fortunate gust seemed to hold it up as it cleared the ridge, hopefully on the green. My turn: I played my wedge a few degrees to the right of the line to where our caddy explained the flag would be. As it cleared the ridge, the northwesterly wind moved it a bit to the left. The caddy, "excellent shot, Mr. O'Neill, your best of the day, so far!"

Carolyn, easily within earshot, moved to her ball briskly, looked at her line and took one practice swing. As she does, Carolyn's swing seems effortless and without power. Nonetheless, the ball jumped from her clubface. The caddy moved to sight her ball crossing the ridge, and said, "That was an exquisite shot. Precisely correct for this pin."

Emma pulled up with their cart, and the caddy put their

clubs away, and we rode up to the top of the knoll. The flag was left of center, two-thirds of the way back on the green. John's ball was to the right of the green in the first cut. A good lie. Emma chipped up to within about ten or twelve feet. John chipped to within five. They were tied with net 4's. The O'Neill's two balls were lying 3. An examination found mine to be 8 feet or so from the hole, while Carolyn was inside three feet. My putt rimmed out, and Carolyn conceded my par. John and Emma both two putted. Carolyn looked at me, perhaps thinking I would concede her a Birdie, but that would put the Ladies up by three. So, I came straight out with it. She smiled, but said nothing. Her putt ran straight and true for the short distance to the cup and Carolyn had her natural Birdie four (net 3). As the caddie handed her the ball, she smiled at John and me, saying, "As Ronan said, 'That puts the Ladies up three.'"

Details of that day could fill many pages. Suffice it to say that John and Carolyn pared that magnificent little Par-3 Seventh, made so famous on television years ago, starting with the Bing Crosby Invitational at Pebble Beach (The first of the celebrity-hosted golf events which began to change the game of golf to more of an 'Everyman's Sport.'). Then came the infamous three hardest, successive Par-4s in American links golf, 8, 9 & 10 on the cliff's edge at Pebble Beach. The Ladies were only up one after those holes (only because Carolyn hit a miracle chip on Number-9 to halve with John and me at 5). I was fortunate enough to keep my ball in play as the wind was beginning to blow ever-harder as we made our way up the hill away from the far point of the course on Number-11.

Carolyn was playing as well as she ever played, as was I. John seemed to be tiring, but it was Emma that had us concerned. After Holes 8 & 9 where she lost balls over the cliffs onto the beach, she seemed to go almost into a trance of being demoralized. I asked our Caddy if he had any thoughts to help Emma after 11, which the men won to even up the match.

Hole 12 was a Par-3 to a slightly raised ultra-wide, but not deep, green surrounded almost entirely by a giant sand trap. Both John and I put our balls near the green, somewhat in line with the hole, but in the sand. The Ladies' tee box was a good thirty yards closer to that green. Carolyn hit hers almost next to mine. Emma took her six iron (Carolyn had played an eight, but she was a longer hitter.) As she walked to the tee, the caddy leaned over to her and seemed to offer her another club. She shook her head, but then he seemed to whisper something. Emma relented and accepted the caddy's proffered club. She took two practice swings, then her ball flew straight and unerringly toward the Twelfth green coming to rest on its grass surface no more than 18 feet from the cup. Emma turned to the Caddy, said something, and she was suddenly all smiles. We were all happy for her, with John seemingly revitalized. Emma missed her putt for a two, but made par. With her higher handicap, she was the only one of us to get a stroke on that hole, giving her a net 2, and putting the Ladies back in the lead, UP-1.

Carolyn's straight game allowed her to get a six on the ultra-long Par-5 14th hole, heading inland. That was a stroke hole for her and suddenly the Ladies were UP-2. The 15th and 16th holes were not terribly long Par-4s, but both had tricky approach shots. John hit an excellent wedge to twenty feet, and two-putted the 15th for a win. Ladies UP-1. We halved Hole 16.

Suddenly, while climbing up a rise, there it was: Pebble

Beach's last Par-3, the infamous 17th, where Tom Watson chipped in to win an Open from Jack Nicklaus, then, little more than a few years before. Walking up to our tee box, we could feel a stiff breeze quartering from the northwest. Our caddy said only that the full force of the wind could not be felt until we were almost to the green. John had the honor and decided to hit a six iron. He struck it nicely, sailing true and straight, then suddenly dropped almost vertically downwards. "Short in the sand," said our caddy.

I took a five-iron knowing I tended to pull it left, so I aimed out at the right side of the green although the flag was a bit left of center. I struck my ball with my maximum controlled force. It started toward the right edge of the green, not quite as high as John's shot, but then beginning to curve back to the center of the green as its descent accelerated. "Excellent shot," was the highest praise I got all day from our caddy. John slapped me on the back.

The caddy said, "Ladies, you need to take two clubs more than you would usually play this distance to offset that wind." They both did just that, but they did not factor the quartering nature of the wind. Emma was in the ugly rough to the south side of the green. Carolyn was in the trap that guarded the southeast corner of the green. John was buried in the sand, short of the green. I was about six feet from the pin. Emma picked up for a net-five. We conceded Carolyn's second putt for a Net-3. We all got one stroke except Emma got two. John had sand problems and was conceded a Net-4. I tapped in my barely missed putt for a Net-2.

So, it came to pass that we were All Even going to the world famous Pebble Beach Par-5 18th, its fairway bounded by the Pacific on its entire 540 yard left side, with a parallel sand filled waste bunker came into play between the seawall and the grass for the last 130 yards. My net Birdie accorded me the opportunity to play first. Experience taught me that my driver tended to pull left, if anything, which undermined my confidence enough that I chose my 3-wood for my drive. But it was good enough, carrying over the breakwater wall to the fairway, yet not behind the "fairway tree" that punished so many ambitious drives by blocking the most direct route to the green for the next shot. John's drive did end up behind that tree; in fact, almost under it.

Carolyn played a more daring line over the seawall leaving her ball to the left of mine and slightly ahead. But Emma's was the most exciting: her drive pulled left leaving her landing spot short of the seawall, but in amongst the boulders rip-rapped next to that wall to protect it from heavy wave action. We could almost hear her ball hit the rocks, but not see that ball until suddenly, a fourth ball emerged on the 18th fairway resting about 20 yards behind mine. "Marvelous!" screamed Carolyn, and Emma laughed loudly, perhaps in shock at her good fortune. (I recalled a client's ball having a similar fate leading to a par, net-4, and his winning 6 skins, worth $600 to capture that day's only profit in his foursome. An Omen?) John beamed.

John played around that infernal tree, but it took him five shots to be barely on the 18th green. Emma's adventure continued as she hit her second shot into the beginning of the narrow waste bunker running between the seawall and the fairway. Her third stayed in the bunker with a five wood. She had a good lie, sitting up on the sand, about 100 yards to the slightly elevated hole. Our caddy persuaded her to try her seven iron and to be certain to "pick her ball off the sand." She did just that! Suddenly she lay four about 20 feet from the pin.

I hit an OK second shot, followed by a lob wedge to six feet (lying 3). Carolyn, tried for the gap between the traps fronting the slightly elevated 18th to have an easy third shot chip to the flag. But she over-rotated on her turn and hooked her second shot over the waste bunker and the seawall, and into the waters of Stillwater Cove! She was so distressed. She dropped in the waste bunker and hit her fourth shot ending in the sand trap at the back of 18. Carolyn and John's score was net five, after both received concessions on not necessarily makeable putts.

Emma was visibly nervous, clearly worried that even though she received two strokes on this difficult hole with her handicap, that if she took three putts, the Men would win easily. Carolyn counseled her to relax, using the old, "This is only a game" technique. It did not work. Fearful that she would leave fer first putt too far short of the hole, Emma hit it well past the hole by five feet or so, leaving her a tricky curving downhill putt.

On my turn, I just missed a natural Birdie as my ball came up an inch or so short of rolling into the cup. I tapped in recording a net Birdie 4. John shook my hand and congratulated me. I whispered something to him quickly. He nodded YES, as I backed away to await Emma's putt. She did not seem happy as she approached her ball. I walked over to where she was standing and knocked her ball toward the hole, saying, "John and I are going to concede that putt, Emma. Your shot from the waste bunker was magnificent. You all should not be rewarded with less than a draw on this match, and for the golf overall. Congratulations!"

Emma was stupefied for a moment or two, not because she did not understand a conceded putt, but rather that her putt was too long, too difficult to concede. Carolyn took off her visor, walked up to me and planted a big kiss on my lips, then said, "You surprise me from time-to-time. This was one of those times. I know how competitive you can be. But also how you can be so kind and generous. Well done, Mr. O'Neill!"

"Well done, Ronan!" exclaimed John. Emma, by then was hugging Carolyn, and was perhaps crying. After a minute, the two separated, and as we prepared to vacate the green, Emma approached me, threw open her arms, and hugged me, saying loudly, "Oh, what an incredible thing you just did. John always talks about how smart you are. How patient, but you are so thoughtful of others. So is Carolyn. This weekend has taught me that there are some wonderful people in this world and we have been lucky enough to spend all of this weekend with the two of you." She was still crying when she finished.

I asked John to let me tip the caddy. He relented. I gave him $400, saying, "That seven iron advice was a day-maker for that nice Lady. Thank you."

We retired to the Taproom for a round of drinks and a bit of a rehash of the day's round. More than two hours later we would have a window table in the Stillwater Restaurant overlooking a well-lighted (and a few die-hard golfers playing) Pebble's 18th green!

Both of the women fully employed their efforts changing from golf gear to high fashion casual for our final night's dinner, looking striking, if not glamorous. Most of our talk ran to the Tournament which would be played slightly more than two months hence. We agreed that we should send out a newsletter-type e-mail to all of the invitees, generally describing our weekend (not too much detail). I would describe what the tournament would entail, while John would give an assessment of the restaurants and other entertainment. Carolyn would add a page on other local options for those who might wish to arrive earlier or stay longer, and the contact point for question resolution, namely the Lodge's Lead Concierge, Geoffrey.

After dinner we walked back along the path between the guest units and the 18th hole, stopping a few times to appreciate the Moon glimmering on the docile Pacific as it ebbed gently in and out of Stillwater Cove, occasionally glancing back at the lights of the Lodge as the night owls sat outside on its deck or stood at its windows appreciating the beauty of that night.

— — —

The last morning was all a bit of a blur: a buffet breakfast on our deck, the O'Sullivan's packing, Geoffrey overseeing their timely departure to assure they made their flight back to Sky Harbor, and then the "Good-Byes" themselves. Emma was the center of that morning as she was beside herself with gratitude, especially to Carolyn. They hugged as John and I were saying our farewell. It all lasted a mere minute, then they were in their cart and gone under Geoffrey's directions and care.

I hugged Carolyn and gave her a quick kiss in passing. Not before I could return to my suitcases, she pulled my arm, and said, "Emma, told me just now that she loves me. In all my time with Lisa, she never did. Only Vera. Oh, Ronan, I do not want to make any mistakes here. What am I to do?"

— — —

On our drive back, having thought for an hour or so, in minutes here and there, I said, "Carolyn, dearest. You must have had other women throw themselves at you. You doubtless have fending mechanisms, but if you ask me, I would say, "'Be kind,' but do nothing physical. Don't do anything to upset her. But do not respond to any physical advances. For example, limit her kissing. You know how to do that, no doubt. Hopefully, it will prove a passing phase for Emma."

Carolyn, "Oh, Ronan, how I do love you. I am sure glad I was on that car deck when you pulled onto it all those years ago. Not to mention being at that hotel bar in Paris. I cannot wait to see our Mollie!"

16

THE NEW LLOYDS KEYSTONE CONVOCATION

My inquiries about Jerry Milton met with nothing but positive feedback. I spoke to my broker and our bankers, both proved quite helpful. I conferred with John, and we decided to loop in *our* Gerry at CI to see how she might feel about involving him. We three agreed that I should meet with just him and gain a few assurances about the nature of our business at Lloyds, and what he might perceive as potential roles for himself, and would this potentially involve others similarly situated like him?

Jerry asked if he could bring Samantha up to San Francisco for the day, and she could shop while the two of us met for an extended lunch. I suggested Sam's Grille on Bush Street in the City. He thought that would be great, and he accommodated us by doing so expeditiously in order for us to meet before we had to be in London for the next Lloyds Convocation, a kind of formal kick-off/fundraiser for the whole new sprawling enterprise of many parts.

During the three couples time together on the Monterey Peninsula, John and I had been extremely circumspect about the New Lloyds itself as well as the DMIC related companies' interface with that new enterprise as well as its internal dealings. Once at Sam's, Jerry was very straightforward about what he knew of Old Lloyds, its troubles, and the

New Lloyds. As he described it, what he knew was superficial, but most of it accurate. His interest was mostly peaked by the rumor that Names, if they continued to exist, would not be subject to unlimited, nor joint and several liability, which would make risk-taking by professional risk-takers, such as himself, far more attractive. He elaborated on that in crushing detail to make his point, which I had understood when he first said it.

He had questions, some of which I was willing to answer, but not all. I mentioned the Tournament, and added the positions of some of the players, explained that we would be having meetings in London next week, and that we could let him know more details perhaps before the end of that week.

I paid, as he complimented our food, wine and my ability to facilitate total privacy, ending by saying, "When we met all those months back, it was mostly because I thought my wife would love to meet yours. Now, I realize how you were able to capture such a marvelous person as your wife. These must be exceptional people, and I do hope to have the opportunity to meet them."

After Jerry left to go meet Samantha, I called John and he patched Gerry in Connecticut into our call. I told them what had transpired, stressing especially his remark about "professional risk-takers." We all had the same thought: New Lloyds could use diverse sources of capital, and people like Jerry could be one very large such resource. (The next time we discussed that topic, we had all three, in independent reflection, come to realize that those types of risk-takers would not be easily, if at all, controllable, unless carefully managed at the inception!)

We had cocktails scheduled with Bradley Cooper and

Madeline Myles at Bradley's office on the afternoon of our arrival from New York (after briefly meeting with Gerry Dwyer and Phillip Stanczyk, one of her AVPs on our way there). That meeting went well, and they all were on board with meeting Jerry during "the golf," a term they often used in place of "tournament."

They were all somewhat surprised that Carolyn and Emma were to play for the USA team, but acknowledged that Quincy would be adding at least one more female on the EU team to even the pairings out. They deferred to him at dinner. Stanley Booth, Chair of Cheshire & Booth, was hosting dinner at Brown's that evening to share last minute briefings on the Convocation beginning tomorrow at 10:00 and to get the low-down on what "the golf" would entail.

My primary topic for this meeting was explaining Jerry Milton, and the specific type of capital source which he might bring to the New Lloyds venture, and how we all might steer it to be advantageous to our own entities as well. Everyone had ideas. John wrapped up as the time to depart for Brown's drew near, "Why do we not continue to discuss this during our stay and have a meeting of all of us on just this topic before we all fly Stateside? I'll set up that meeting. One additional point I would make is that until we have agreed on a relationship, and perhaps even afterward, that communications with Mr. Milton should run only through Ronan as it was he who made the initial contact and saw the potential for profitability in a putative new relationship, however it may come about."

That evening at Brown's was memorable to say the least: news about, and predictions flowing from that news, and perhaps wishful thinking, all abounded. We knew these invitees were among the group that should get the "full reveal" on all of the underlying capital structures and how that formation was perceived as functioning on as part of an on-going renewal basis (the asset/operational side of the annual ledger), while getting a view of the claims organization, and its set-up for each major line of coverage (A major recommendation of U.S. and some other countries was that lines of coverage including their reinsurance progeny should be separately accounted to understand the profitability of each line on an on-going basis. This was inspired by some companies which were utilizing real-time claims/reserve accounting positioned on a day-by-day basis to demonstrate their revenue needs and trend lines on a continuously available basis to show the need for potential rate, reserves, or even coverage decisions.)

Variations on these topics were openly discussed, while the UK attendees had a broader purview than the U.S. attendees. The onset of serving the sit-down dinner brought much of this discussion to a close and the focus shifted to the Tournament. Virtually everyone in attendance was scheduled to play as the teams were set to expand to twelve/side, subject to Carolyn's charm proving sufficient to persuade Geoffrey to undertake the needed steps to accommodate two more foursomes on each course, and adding an uncertain number, dependent on guests coming with players, for rooms and dinner reservation expansions.

John took a good twenty minutes to describe the three courses which would host the actual Tournament. He asked me to cover Poppy Hills for the practice round. I tried to do that by likening its holes to more like those of Spyglass, than Spanish Bay. I ended that by pointing out that the EU team should have the advantage as all three courses were created as links courses, far more plentiful in Scotland, Ireland, and even a few in Wales. My final comment, "Of course, if you have not played Pebble Beach before this event, television has not prepared you: the real thing is incredibly daunting!"

Stanley Booth and Quincy, two movers and shakers in the evolution to the New Lloyds spoke next, preparing this audience, in a fashion, for an underlying theme for the megaconference: lines of coverage in major category and sub-categories were to be the driving financial model for the entire enterprise. For example, major categories would include traditional maritime, aviation, pharma, corporate, property, errors and omissions, and so on. While an example of sub-categories for aviation would include manufacturing functions, airfield/terminals of all types, passenger companies as well as freight, and specific human resources, and so on.

The rest of the evening increasingly digressed into the Tournament and what to expect. John O'Sullivan allowed that Carolyn's advice to Emma had been exactly on point: dressy casual for clothing and style. I chipped in with a place we had not seen with them, but was an option for an additional night: *Baja Cantina,* which looked and sounded like a Tex/Mex honky-tonk, but turned out to be a hang-out for some of the indistinguishable very wealthy of the Greater Carmel area, and was the lower extreme of dressy casual.

The audience was far more interested in the three courses we would be playing, especially since only Pebble Beach got any coverage of what was for decades known as The Bing Crosby Pro-Am Invitational, recently evolving into the AT&T Pebble Beach Pro-Am. Many of the questions and comments from the UK guests showed a healthy respect for the entire program which Carolyn and I had put together, and to which John O'Sullivan gave his unconditional blessing (weather excepted!).

While I slept that night, I got an email from Carolyn advising that she had been able to expand the golf by two more foursomes, but the room count might prove a very real problem (there was overflow room at Spanish Bay. I passed that along to John and Quincy, the captains on the next a.m. They appeared pleased, especially Quincy.

The Convocation got underway a few minutes late at the Main Hall in Lincoln's Inn. The attendance was said to be more than 300, an incredibly diverse group, overwhelmingly male. They listened unemotionally as the members of the Steering Committee gave their reports, accompanied by state-of-the-art visuals. The presentations were recorded, and would be transcribed, available later in either form, or both.

Stanley Booth was one of the speakers, covering the actual pathways of various coverage placements in comprehensible language. Quincy was tasked as the final speaker of the first session. He gave a broad-based summary of the many operational changes, tying them back, as much as possible, to the now superseded methods/historical pathways used by Old Lloyds in the functions of its operation, and which played a major role in shaping the New Lloyds.

He appeared triumphant as he finished his summary to a standing ovation by those on the Committee and in moments by almost all in the Great Hall!

There was a break. Each member of the Standing Committee was thoroughly interviewed by invitees, including a very limited number of specific persons from the Free World's most highly regarded business news purveyors. The sessions for the rest of that day and the next were on a series of tracks: the first given over to the overall operation of Lloyds going forward by each major function; and the second, primary policy underwriting, its reinsurance, and claims handling.

John took the first track. Manny was puffing as he arrived in the nick of time to handle the second track, along with Gerry Dwyer, having delegated Phillip Stanczyk to attend the first. I, too, decided to attend that second track. After one session, a lunch break was declared (beating the first track to break allowed the three of us to get seats in a Lincoln's Inn pub, of sorts, while trying to save two more for our companions.).

Our topic at that lunch was one that remains viable even as I write about these events more than twenty years later: who are all of these people, and why are they here? We each strove to find those answers and made that a target for our Tournament two months hence.

After eating, and the others not showing up, we three separated more to meet first time attendees (different color name badges) as we made our way back to our Track 2 seats in the Great Hall. The first coverage of the afternoon session was Maritime, once long ago, the very *raison d'etre* for its initial investors to gather at Lloyds and issue a contract of assurance to a ship owner or a cargo supplier in the event of a lost ship or cargo, signed at the bottom by the "underwriter" being the agent for a group coming to be called a "syndicate," who were those who received the premium paid by the "assured" and would "indemnify" that assured for a loss should it occur and be proven up.

Sitting there listening to the Maritime panel's discussion at its outset was mesmerizing by the use of so many of the antiquated words; but, the discussion made a u-turn and a new procedure was pronounced which was meant to be more in line with the claims process on most of the other categories of coverage. However, the usage of the term "indemnify" by two of the five panel members might lead to a conclusion that the assured would pay for the loss itself, and be reimbursed by its insurer only once when all of its loss was fully known and documented. (Not actually very different at all from the historical Maritime loss compensation scheme.)

Because of the great attendance, the organizers were able to prevail upon the trustees of Grey's Inn to host the cocktails and dinner, essentially where the first convocation had occurred. With a three-hour break from the last program's end to the first cocktail service, the Black taxi drivers were to become enriched as many of the attendees sought to return to their hotels for a change of clothing and to undertake contact with their offices elsewhere in the world. Our group was not unlike so many others. John and Manny grabbed me and we made our way to a little known secondary taxi stand and got back to our hotel, the Berkeley, shockingly in a matter of minutes.

Lily was at her desk when I called. She said Felicia needed to speak with me and gave me the young partner's cell phone number which I loaded into mine then and there. A few other minor matters, and a few seconds of good-natured joking by me, and I was talking to Felicia, "Ronan, I am still having trouble using your first name. I am so sorry. On Great Western, Ephraim Scott called after hours last night right before I was about to leave. He was straightforward. He wants us to stipulate to stay the discovery order authored by Judge Quinn."

I thought for a second: some time had run since that discovery order trigger date. That meant to me that they are serious about whatever the issues. I asked Felicia if he talked about whatever the topic might be. She said he did not. (I did not want to ask her directly if she asked him that.) Finally, I suggested she put together a quick letter to the key client people and Strom Nordquist. Be sure to say we talked and I recommended that we stipulate because this is where the stretching of time works to our advantage. Have Martha explain "dynamic gridlock" from LAUSD. Please explain its benefits in that letter. I ended by asking her to fax me a draft in no later than six hours. I planned to look at it, edit as needed, and have her send it by fax to them today to show time being of the essence.

Felicia thanked me and went to work. I called Carolyn and began by thanking her for all of her work on "the golf." She chuckled. I told her that I had asked Quincy and John for the total attendee lists by the end of next week at the very latest so that Carolyn and Lily could finalize everything in addition to the increased number of foursomes. She reminded me of her many travel commitments coming up in the Spring. I was aware of her need to travel very extensively at that time of year. It was very hard on Mollie, and even me. But she would be seeing more of her Patrick, his Elsa, and our Maeve in that process. She asked about Lloyds, and I told her that its final make-up was about as we had discussed when John was visiting. The only thing left was to explore any additional business opportunities that might become available.

I looked at the clock and realized that it was time for me to change and get down to the Lobby Bar to meet John and the others for some quick preparation for tonight's event. (I also planned to spend time with Bradley and Madeline looking at areas which we might develop to add to the tasks now being performed by LTL. I planned to mention their getting to know Jerry Milton during "the golf" in the event that he decided to get involved investing in Lloyds and needed an agent in London.)

The taxis to Grey's Inn got us there fifteen minutes before the nominal start of the cocktail hour. We secured two tables for eight, then made our way to the cocktail area where we split up and engaged people hitherto unknown to us. That tactic was repeated often, and led to some interesting interplay at times, and a total inability to communicate at others. Finally spotting Bradley and Madeline, I moved off to join them and we began to explore the Jerry Milton "risk-taker possibilities."

Later, we met a few of the newer UK Golf Team members at dinner, including Oliver Martin, Head of Quincy's Chambers, and his sister-in-law, Mary Smith-Martin, Queen's Counsel and a ranking member in Lloyds Claims Office, both also to be players for Team UK. They were affable, but stiffer than Quincy (Who wasn't?). She asked to sit next to me at dinner. No one else had done so. I agreed.

After two rounds of drinks, most of us began to retreat to our tables. I saw John and mentioned that Mary wanted to sit next to me. He had no problem. Manny sat on the other side.

Once seated and having my white wine glass filled, I turned to face Mary who was attractive in a sleek, silver-blonde haired manner. I asked her to explain her role in the New Lloyds. She was obliging to a point, then said, "Let me be frank. I have known Quincy for a great many years. Although he can be annoying at times with his carousing, he is a brilliant, hard-working barrister. I value his opinions. Something new which we are considering in the assignment of U.S. cases going forward is using U.S. law firms that are not so monolithic. Too often in the past, we felt we were supporting an entire legal structure, at least fee-wise. Quincy has told me about what fees your firm charges, about the breadth of your work, and how you staff cases. It makes me feel that we are overpaying for a great many of the matters that we have assigned in the past, and that a change may be in order. He suggested that I talk to you."

"Mary, I hope it's alright with you if I use your given name?" She nodded. I went on, "If you are asking would we be willing to undertake work for members of this great venture, of course. But are you asking for more than that? I am uncertain."

She looked slightly upward and straight into my eyes, "You are very clever, Mr. O'Neill, ... Ronan. Quincy says you have more than one network of law firms with which you are associated. I was hoping we could discuss them briefly this evening....now, or later, as you might choose. But in more detail, if I feel positive about what you may have to tell me."

With that, I spent the bread and salad course telling her about our CAL Board network and how it came about, then the Society (just a bit as it was not firms), and during the soup and fish courses, describing the American Civil Litigation Network, ending with, "Is that what you had in mind?"

Mary Smith-Martin was a very good listener, rarely interrupting, and her mental wheels had little problem taking in what I was describing, she simply said, "Impressive. You must keep very busy. Can I buy you a meal where we could talk, but after I have the pause of a night's sleep to assure myself that this might prove a useful course?"

"Mary, I have clients and associates on this trip and have

committed literally all of my time, except breakfasts the next two mornings. Would tomorrow be too soon?"

She smiled, "You do understand that we English are somewhat late risers?" I nodded, she smiled (a first.) "However, for you, I shall make an exception. I understand you are at The Berkeley. Could we meet in its Dining Room at 7:30? That way we would have two hours and you could make a ten o'clock meeting in the City or the West End."

Taxiing to our hotel, I told John about what was happening and at the Bar, Gerry just a small amount. They were untroubled. I told Carolyn when I called her. She saw this as a great opportunity for our firm, and me. She even suggested that I could delay flying a day if that would prove helpful. I told her that I thought the best idea was to get through any threshold discussions during this trip because 'QC Mary' was being added to the UK Golf Team, and that event would not be an appropriate time to have an outstanding issue about a potential relationship. Carolyn agreed and reiterated her offer about my staying over an extra day. I thanked her and then whispered a few sweet nothings!

— — —

The next morning, Mary Smith-Martin, Q.C., was awaiting me at a table in a quiet corner of The Berkeley's Dining Room. She had ordered a pot of press coffee with accoutrements on the side for me. She was sipping tea. She stood as I neared the table holding out her right hand for me to shake, or so I thought. But when I gripped it, she tightened and pulled me effortlessly toward herself turning each cheek for me to give her brushing kisses, as was the British fashion.

"Please make yourself comfortable, Ronan. Upon reflection, I must tell you that you are one of the most engaging Americans whom I have ever met. That's based on our intermittent time together last night. You are very intelligent, but good looking and charming. I asked Quincy about your wife only to find out that she is an extremely well-known fashion model, working primarily for *Vogue*.

"Wow! That really impressed me. Does she know we are breakfasting? (I nodded YES.) Does she know what I do at Lloyds Legal?"

I stuck in a few words, "Not really, only that you are very important. You don't have to worry, you will meet her in a few months at the Golf. She has expended a great deal of time and some of her charm and reputation as leverage to add two more foursomes, including you, I believe, to that event in the last few days."

Mary, smiling, "You do seem to admire her. How long have you been married?"

Me: "Less than ten years, but Carolyn is my second wife. Mollie was my first wife with whom I had four children. She died from cancer, but beforehand, having befriended Carolyn, Mollie insisted that we marry and unite our families as soon as possible after her death. We did just that. Carolyn had one son, raised out of wedlock when her lover, a Navy fighter pilot was killed in Viet Nam. His name is Patrick as is my second son. We have one child, Mollie, named for my first wife, who is seven years old. That seems enough for now?"

We were sitting at right angles to each-other and Mary leaned closer, creating a feeling of some intimacy, and semi-whispered, "You are so forthcoming. Even for an American. The way you go about answering every query as if you are willing to do so. Your *curriculum vitae* is astonishingly polished, and Quincy and his people stand for you. Finally, I contacted a dear friend of my deceased husband, Sir Richard Doll whom I got from Quincy, and Richard could not heap enough praise on you, or your wife, for that matter. So, last night and this morning were to satisfy me that I could trust you because I want a *confidante* and highly competent counsel to handle our difficult matters in California. I think you are that attorney. Will you be my man there?"

I paused. Clearly, this woman, whom I had barely met, had researched me thoroughly, not that I hadn't been vetted before. It sounded almost too good to be true. I tried to think of any downsides, and came up with only one. I decided: present it to her now, "Mary, I am honored that you went so far in learning about me, and I want to say YES. Yet, there is one thing in the U.S. and many attorneys disagree about it on the defense side, and that is client allegiance: when retained to defend an insured entity, in the event of a potential conflict of interest, to which entity do I owe my primary allegiance? My answer must always be the entity which my firm is retained to defend. There are some exceptions, but that is my only concern. If you agree, then I am your man."

"HUH! You must be Hell on Wheels in a courtroom. You do know how to spin something just right. I cannot wait to hear more from you. Welcome aboard. O'Neill Fox is the first U.S. law firm retained by the New Lloyds. We'll have papers waiting for you to sign by the time you next reach your office."

Then Mary stood, offered me her hand once again, but this time we shook hands, firmly.

She sat, smiled, and said, "I have, of course, seen Pebble Beach on the telly. They even mention that other course,

Spyglass, with some reverence. Please tell me what to expect."

After a smallish meal, and another 25 minutes of golf/Monterey Peninsula chat, we parted. Her last remarks were different, "If I can get some time at one end or the other of the Tournament, I would love to spend a bit of time with you or Carolyn. Could that work?"

"For me, yes. But please understand, I cannot speak for Carolyn. So, all I can say is 'we'll have to see.'" We shook hands and she left. I went to my room and called the office, connecting to Reggie, our managing partner and our Lily, saying. "Reggie and Lily, I just finished breakfast with an extremely high-powered lawyer, Mary Smith-Martin, Queen's Counsel, and the Chief Lawyer at the New Lloyds Legal Office for all of its entities, and she is retaining our firm to represent them or their certain insureds in California. Papers will arrive in very near term directed to the attention of the two of you. Suggest we do not discuss this with anyone else at the Firm until all is signed and sealed. Gotta' run! Best wishes to you both!"

— — —

Those of our Irish golf group in attendance met at Stanley Booth's office to discuss among ourselves what advantages we might get from working with one another on the new entities besides being the allies which we had already become. A good many ideas were bandied about, some appearing worthwhile and others not so much so, at least facially. Several attendees were set to fly home that afternoon, so we broke up before 1:00 with the phrase, "We'll see you in a few months at Pebble Beach," on everyone's lips.

Our smaller group retreated to Bradley's office. Madeline did not race ahead to prepare food or beverage. I wondered, not out loud, "Did she delegate?"

On the short taxi ride, with John and Gerry (Manny and Phillip were among those departing early that afternoon), I decided to mention Mary Smith-Martin. Both of them had met her, but they thought she was there as Oliver Martin's sister and to be a female to help even out the gender of the golf teams. I conceded that was doubtless a main reason, but then pointed out her current job and that she had sought me out a bit last night, began to make a pitch, and finished doing so over breakfast this a.m. I wanted them to know about this potential new relationship. Instead of being concerned, they both congratulated me, but Gerry reminded me that historically Lloyds could be very slow in paying their lawyers. John seconded Gerry on that point, and said, "In fact, historically, they often placed obstacles to payment as you may know. So, be careful your firm does not get far in arrears on its collections. Some U.S. companies, I'm sure you know of one or two, build up their payables, then use that scenario as leverage to get concessions from their counsel. Ronan, beware that trap!"

No more was said as we arrived at Bradley's building right behind the other taxi. The balance of the day was set in motion by Monique, a recent promotion from elsewhere in the Solicitor firm whose mandate was to assist Madeline in the entire span of her duties from Bradley's assistant at the firm to all matters as Madeline's assistant on LTL, and for entertaining. She was ready to show off her entertaining skills on our arrival serving a variety of appetizer portions to go with wine or cocktails. The central business discussion shifted to LTL and potential new activities to expand its roles into New Lloyds as well as taking up new tasks, as yet unseen, in assisting clients less familiar with the ways and means of the London insurance establishment in its on-going evolution. Madeline, and now especially Monique, took copious notes. At the end of the meeting, I suggested that those two women put their notes into a single report broken down by suggestion types and circulate that for comments in several days after we all arrived Stateside.

Then, it was just John, Gerry and me taxing back to The Berkeley. We decided to stay in the Bar at a table with a cocktail, followed by three small dishes, one picked by each of us, three plates and a bottle of Bordeaux. We chatted briefly about the past short week's events, then moved onto Monterey/Pebble Beach. John promised to have the U.S. Team attendees sorted before the coming weekend. Gerry said that she would be alone and Phillip was going to fly his fiancé out on the last day and move to Spanish Bay for the remainder of that entire week. He felt more comfortable as a new person to the Team in not having his bride-to-be as a distraction until "the golf" was over.

— — —

17

THOSE MONTHS LEADING UP TO THE PEBBLE BEACH RESORT GOLF

With all of the different activities to cover in the weeks ahead, I made notes to myself on the flight home. Then, I slept. Finally, there were Carolyn and Mollie waiting for me as I cleared U.S. Customs and emerged into the International Terminal. There were hugs, kisses and kind words. Carolyn drove our SUV and Mollie sat in the middle of the back seat all the way home, updating me on all sorts of developments involving almost every member of her family. We were all so happy. The twins arrived shortly after our trio and the celebration of my return seemed to gain new impetus.

Carolyn was off to New York, then Paris that next week as the first trip of her Spring travels: some modeling assignments, some productions with Robert and Maeve, and some of her product endorsement appearances. These trips were becoming harder on her as Mollie grew older. (I knew it was any year now that she would want to start bringing Mollie along; she might even invite me.)

I took the rest of my arrival day and one more to calm my jet lag, and then returned to the office. Lily was pleased to see me (at least that's what she said). The Contract of Retainer of our firm from Lloyds was in a manila folder with a number of yellow post-its attached on the very top of my "To-Do" stack. I sat and pulled it toward me opening the file. There was a larger sticker with a note from Reggie saying he would be pleased to review any of his comments with me; and, that those with asterisks were especially potentially troubling.

The note also mentioned that Lloyds had failed to send its Billing Guidelines for Counsel, referred to in their proposed contract with some frequency. (I thought NOT GOOD and moved on.) When I finished, I asked Reggie to step into my office. He brought his own copy. We sat at my small table, across from each other. I began, "John and Gerry warned me that dealing with Lloyds could be difficult and not to let them put us in a position from which we could be held hostage by the outstanding fees they might come to owe us. I can see a big problem with their 'payment will be due 60 days from receipt of invoice for services or date of agreed-upon acceptance of invoice modifications...' No mention of interest, or even due diligence on their part, nor partial payment of undisputed charges. Do you think this might be a deal-breaker?"

Reggie fixed me with his stern expression, "Without their Guidelines, we do not have any real yardstick to measure our exposure. Just think of the differences between DMIC and CI's Guidelines and their both American companies."

I thought for a minute, then said, "I have Mary Smith-Martin's cell phone number. How about if I call her very late morning her time tomorrow and let her know where we might end up, using my request for their Guidelines as a shield to cover a few other comments about their timing of payments being too indefinite and skewed much too heavily in their favor? A bit of sounding her out, so to speak. No sense in wasting our time on this process if we are going to reject it in the end."

Reggie smiled, "Good to hear you say, 'reject it.' That's how I feel if 'it's take it or leave it.' Sure, why not try your tactic. Otherwise, how was the event?" He left and I put that file folder in my briefcase to take home.

Felicia Clarke asked Lily to pass along that she would like to see me when I had a free moment. She did not answer her phone, but Lily quickly tracked her down. Felicia, who could look pleasant at times, came into my office carrying a great armload of paper, and I barely recognized her. I guess the expression on my face gave me away. She spoke in a lower voice, smoother than usual, "I can tell from your reaction, Mr. O'Neill, that you noticed that I've had some changes made to my appearance in the last week or so. What do you think?"

I did not want to stare, but her hair was a brand-new style and color, and she looked healthy, almost glamorous. Felicia wore make-up, skillfully applied and her face looked so much more interesting, especially her eyes. Finally, she wore an outfit that made her look like she had a real figure, which she apparently had kept hidden successfully for several years. I almost coughed, then said, "I'm not at all certain that I should say anything? Oh, and it's Ronan, remember?"

Felicia smiled, even a slight chuckle, and bravely said, "Ronan, I'm not certain how old you are, but you are about my father's age. Please understand that I have met someone and he talked me into, and even paid for, some of these things I've had done, and clothes I've recently bought. He thinks that my 'new look' will be better for my self-assurance in the long-run, but I am finding it's making me very self-conscious. Your wife is so beautiful and so put-together. I told him that, he said to ask you. So, what do you think of my 'new look'?"

With that, I stood up behind my desk, saying, "Please put all of those papers over there on the small table. (She did so.) "Now come back to where you were. Try to relax. Shake your shoulders. Now slowly turn all the way around. Good, then in the other direction. (I sat.) You can sit or remain standing. Your choice."

She smiled, and her face looked more relaxed, she sat, saying, "I can tell you're married to a model. That was wonderful. My father could never do that. So, what do you think?"

"My guess is that there will be more than one or two other young women in our office who will look at you and say to themselves, 'If she can do that, why not me?' But you know what, I doubt any of them have underneath all of what you've been concealing all of these years. Your look has helped you become exceedingly attractive. I especially like your hair coloring and new style. Now, have I sufficiently served as your father surrogate? And if so, can we get down to discussing this draft appellate writ petition brief in GWF?"

When I glanced up at her from the revised draft red-lined brief she had handed me, Felicia was still smiling. I appeared to have made someone's day!

What followed were two productive hours.

Lily brought sandwiches for the two of us, and we worked through a stack of smaller matters and did some work on organizing ACLN. As three o'clock approached, Lily said, "Ronan, you look very tired. Are you OK?"

I answered, "Right before I left, I had a call from Sandra in North Carolina on the Neptune matter. We made a number of plans with Mason and at three o'clock, I'm due to find out where we stand from Sandra. That matter is making me very concerned, affecting my sleep. Not like me usually."

Lily's reaction was a frown, plus, "Oh, I'm sorry to hear that." Just then, a knock on my office door, followed by its being opened by Sandra. Lily took all of our lunch materials and left. Sandra joined me at my small table. She had a large stack and a yellow legal pad. Smiling, Sandra started, "Ronan, are you alright?"

Me: "Sandra, it's good to see you. No, this Neptune thing is lingering in the back of my mind like a bad dream which I subconsciously fear will end badly. So, maybe you can make me feel better about things?"

"I'm not at all certain that any outcome for our client on this whole matter is going to prove so satisfactory. Your idea of getting all of the damages aligned is proving worthwhile. The adverse has, at my request, sent a demand settlement proposal. It lists all of their claimed damages by category: licensing fees, attorney fees, and punitive damages, with the basis for each. I have put them all on my summary sheet here (indicating). Then, we have made an attempt to list all of our client's damages as well: spoiled inventory plus storage costs, lost ancillary expenses and useless advertising, plus wholesale and retail purchaser claims for reimbursement of their inventories. Those are here. (With that, she passed her summary sheet to me.) Both sides' damages approach eight figures, and they continue to accrue. Not Great!"

I looked at Sandra, and realized just how much she was aging with all of her stress, and said, "What do you suggest?"

She was ready for that, "As we discussed, some weeks ago when doing the client contract negotiation documents, it appears that Mr. Singh was doing all of his own drafting. His Liquidated Damages language actually starts that category by expressly saying it is present to 'penalize' a defaulter under the Licensing Agreement. That would potentially undermine all of the non-licensed manufactured product, with some very real possibility of success in federal court. Similar harsh language is used in connection with the Attorney's Fees provision.

"More grounds exist to eliminate punitive damages. Finally, all of this can be done with motion practice and is not dependent on proving 'no contract.' That can be saved as a fall-back. Also, no real discovery is needed. Like you, I do not believe that our client's people will do well as witnesses.'

"Other news: Mason has gotten in touch with Leslie Worth. Not a surprise: neither the parent, Enterprises, nor any subsidiary, including Fishing, has ever implemented any Document Retention Program. Nothing is documented at all. Documents are simply shredded. Mason believes that few, if anyone, at Enterprises see this as anything other than becoming a debacle.

"I see this as an instance where we should invite the client decision makers to our office to discuss the potential outcomes. I do not believe Mason has sufficient client control to affect an outcome acceptable to the clients. Being a woman means I probably do not have enough presence to covince all of those Southern men. That leaves you, and I sense that we need to get them out of their comfort zone of North Carolina to a place where a federal judge in her own courthouse might put some fear of God into their brains. That's the best I've got for you."

I consciously tried to relax my face, but I did not smile. I held the moment and raised my eyes to hers (something I had not done in more than twenty years), and began, "You have gone some way to making my day. Everything you have said, I agree with. Can you sell this to Mason?"

Sandra's eyes did not move from mine, "Yes, I have already started down that road. What next?

Me: "Easy. Tell him the whole plan and add that he needs to begin indoctrinating his client with the concept that they will need to pay serious money as well as write off their bad product as a total loss. They will need to consult a really good tax-lawyer now. Are you up to this?"

Sandra tried to fix my gaze, but I resisted. She did not persist, instead, "I feel like this is turning into a test of my full partnership readiness. But, yes, I am up to it. Shall I do this tomorrow?"

"Suggest you fax him a version of your Damages Summary Sheet for him to follow along as you explain to him 'what hog is eating what cabbage'." With that, I smiled.

So did Sandra. For seconds, I thought she came perilously close to hugging me. But I counted on the promise she had made to Carolyn and she did not break it. She gathered her materials and left. Lily came in, saying, "That was faster than what you expected, wasn't it? You need to go home."

After handing Lily a fax to send to Mary Smith-Martin, Q.C., I did just that!

———

The next morning at 6:00 a.m., I called that Queen's Counsel's number. On the second ring, she picked-up, "Good morning, Ronan. I trust this call is important from reading your fax."

"Yes, Mary, this is serious for our firm. Our managing

partner reviewed your retainer agreement before I got back to the office. As I'm fairly sure you know, Old Lloyds had a reputation for slow payment of outside counsel bills. Both Reggie Fox and I have been reluctant over the years to seek to undertake work from London for that very reason. There was nothing about your agreement to reassure us of payment being received within 35-50 days which is the range of payment delay from our slowest paying clients. Those clients may also withhold payment on any disputed amounts, but that's rare. Also, you did not send your billing guidelines. So, we cannot tell what specific billing texts may cause issues," I took a breath. She did not speak.

"Sorry to be so long-winded. I do not mean this as any form of criticism. In fact, if you are looking for a firm to work with on billing U.S. civil litigation defense cases, we are well-suited to help you out because of our working relationships with various firms in nation-wide networks. That's enough."

Then, I understood why Mary was a Queen's Counsel, "Ronan, you have hit our most troubling nail right on the head. We know we need to make changes, but all we have right now are our carryovers from Old Lloyds as you put it. Counsel billing and payments have been a source of concern in the past, especially with the syndicates making enough cash available for payments, with the primary use for that cash as the indemnification of our insureds, our expenses, and then lastly outside counsel. Even with funding changes, the amount of available cash is unknowable at this early stage, despite the cash flow models created by our planners. So, yes, I will listen to everything you have to say. Do you have any other thoughts?"

Me" "Well, two of the people playing for the U.S. Golf

Team in our Tournament in less than two months are the Heads of Claims for their companies. They both have Retainer Agreements and Billing Guidelines. O'Neill Fox does work for both, sometimes representing their insureds, and other times those companies themselves. Compensation rates may differ with the types of client, or the type of case. Those two sets of Billing Guidelines are quite similar, appliable to all legal work. I do not feel comfortable telling you more as those documents are the Intellectual Property (IP) of those companies. Both of those people were present in London last week. Did you meet Manny Garcia of Desert Mutual or Gerry Dwyer of Connecticut Indemnity?"

"Ronan, I'm being candid. I met so many people, I can remember only a handful of names. Neither of them are names I can recall. Sorry," Mary said, followed by a sigh.

I realized that a moment had arisen when stepping into the breach might lead to being a relationship-builder. I shrugged, saying, "Mary, how certain are you that you will play in our tournament for the UK Team?"

Mary began to sound exasperated, "Ronan, why would that matter at this point?"

I sighed more loudly, "Well, Mary, if I have your assurance, I will go to both of these people and ask them if they will share their guideline documents which could serve as a basis for your creating your own revised such documents at New Lloyds. Would that be valuable?"

"You would do that?" Mary asked, a credibility check?

Me: "Absolutely. They will not want your new venture to fail, even to stumble. Would you want a list of our comments as putative contract-signers?"

There was a pause, "Do you know that the way this call started, I thought our relationship would be over before it even started. Now, I feel as if I will be in your debt indefinitely. Quincy told me you knew how to get things done. I hoped he was right. Now, I feel he was unerringly correct. Please let me ask one more favor: could you and your partner, Reggie, make a redline version of our agreement as I sent it? On it, please indicate provisions requiring a complete rewrite, informed by what I hope those companies will send. Let me stop there."

I allowed, "Mary, I will try to have something from one or both of those carriers in the next few days. Please mention this to Quincy, and ask him to talk to John O'Sullivan about scheduling you to pair against both of those people on different days in the Tournament. No need to talk shop: better for relationship building."

"Ronan, Reggie, Carolyn and you need not pay for a single drink during that Tournament.

You are being such a help! Thank you!!"

When I got to the office, I told Reggie what had transpired. He acted delighted, saying, "Well, here's hoping something really good for the firm will flow from all of this. Now, I will definitely play. Better get some serious golf in over the next weeks! When are you going to make those calls?"

"Right now," was my response as I headed out to my office. On my way crossing the Richmond/San Rafael Bridge, I asked Lily to try to get Gerry on my line. She did.

"Gerry, just got off a call with Mary Smith-Martin, Q.C., whom I told John and you about back in London. She sent a New Lloyds Retainer Agreement to our firm. I won't get into it, except to say we could never work under the conditions potentially available under its terms for the very reasons which John, and especially you, set out."

Gerry: "Not a surprise. Maybe she was looking to get something else from you?"

"Gerry, how can you say that? Oh, wait, you would know about that," I said as I simulated a laugh, "but Quincy has her on the EU Team for the Tournament and you will get to meet her. But the real reason I called was to ask a favor on her behalf for New Lloyds. She needs some forms for retainer agreements in the U.S. to retain counsel for their insureds and for their own entities; and, billing guidelines as well. Any chance, I could get some of those to lend to her subject to whatever conditions you might want to impose on their use? Please recall, CI is investing in this venture."

I paused, Gerry took a few seconds, "Are you asking Desert Mutual for the same things?"

"That's the next call I'm planning to make. Called you first because you're on East Coast time."

"Ronan, tell you what: I'll do this for you and for the Lloyds entity itself, subject to the same terms and conditions proposed by DMIC. You can tell John or Manny, whomsoever you call what I said," allowed Gerry, "In the end, I do owe you a few favors. Keep me in the Loop!" She was gone with that.

I called Manny. He agreed readily. I had their forms the next day and let Gerry know. They both wanted me to be their conduit and to assure a "NO ATTRIBUTION" confidentiality provision, as well as a broad-based hold harmless, for the use of their materials. Both agreed to the provisions I drafted. QC Mary had everything within a week of our call. She wrote back to me to express her gratitude.

— — —

Our participation in the new, and then burgeoning, American Civil Litigation Network (ACLN) was incessant during those months leading up to the EU/USA Tournament. Carolyn was away much of that time and I liked to spend some time every day with our Mollie. (Esmeralda and Mercedes, Yolanda's almost adult daughters were much closer to their childhoods than was I. They pointed out that Mollie loved me, but she needed to begin spending more time with her friends [A/K/A peers] to improve and develop her social skills with her contemporaries [even using most of those words].) So, it came to pass that I had some free time on my hands.

One of those evenings while Carolyn was away and Mollie was with one of her *au pairs*, as a hard day's work was ending, especially for Lily, who was deeply absorbed in her ACLN Membership tasks, and as I was leaving, I saw that the time was past 6:00. I looked at Lily who was concentrating over her keyboard. For a second, a memory gripped me that some time ago, I had invited Lily to dinner and she had been so grateful. I stopped at the door to our suite, turned and looked at her. For no apparent reason, she looked up and straight into my eyes. How strange, I thought, and a slight chill ran through me. "Lily," I said, "Would you like to go to dinner with me?"

She paused in her typing, seemed to think for a second (knowing a great deal of my day-to-day life, she doubtless quickly concluded that I was heading home to be alone), her eyes glazing over, she answered, "Would you give me five minutes or so to finish this one entry and then freshen-up?"

"Of course," I replied, and while she did her things, I called Scott's Seafood restaurant on the Alameda Estuary and booked a window table. She poked her head in my door to show her readiness. I asked, "Did you drive in today?" When she said her car was in the shop, I allowed I would drive her home to Albany, on my way to Marin County.

We drove the few blocks to Scott's and a valet took my keys. The evening was cool, even though we were into Spring. Once inside, I took Lily's coat and gave it to the checkroom attendant. The welcoming hostess showed us to our slightly isolated window table overlooking the darkened waters of the Oakland Estuary, its lights from Alameda Island reflecting from the other side of its soft flowing. A waiter appeared in moments after we were seated, handed us menus, and said, "Good evening, Mr. O'Neill. My name is Albert and I have had the pleasure of waiting on you on a few occasions over the years. Can I get you both cocktails while you study our menu?"

With that, we ordered drinks and he departed. While looking at her menu, Lily asked, "Ronan, I still have trouble calling you by your first name. Is there any chance you might split a course with me? There are so many things here that I like."

Lily looked just lovely sitting there in the soft light. The thought passed through my mind that she was just young enough that I could be her father, "But, of course, we can. What did you have in mind?"

She smiled, "I just love their prawn cocktail. Would that be OK with you? That way, I can have two things."

"Just fine with me," I responded, "We could even split two more things, like this special, 'the Maine lobster roll sandwich,' and a salad, maybe a Caesar, or New England clam chowder?"

With that, Lily's smile grew so big, her face lit-up! "If we had the prawns, then the chowder, then the lobster roll, we'd have an all-seafood dinner. That would be so exciting!"

My turn to smile, and I did, while thinking, 'I cannot wait to tell Carolyn about this,' as I said, "Your wish is my command."

Albert had returned with our cocktails earlier. I looked for him and caught his eye after a few seconds. When he came over, I asked him to make sure that the dinner came in three courses, no rush. That way, we could savor each dish. I made sure we each got three prawns (he assured us they were very big), and I ordered a bottle of Rombauer Chardonnay, my favorite.

Lily was still all smiles, and said, "This is such a great treat. Can I tell you how much I love working on this ACLN membership project? Mr. Fox and you were so kind to think of me for this role."

I smiled in response to her gratitude, then said, "Lily, we have been together now for quite a long time, more than ten years. Believe me, when I came to appreciate the complexity and the need for diligence in getting this new network up and running, the first and only person I thought of as being fully capable to handle the entire task was you. Reggie agreed and that was why we told you to delegate some of our work if any of this should get to be too much for you. But neither Reggie nor I are aware of you delegating any of our work. We have such hopes for this new network and its being a massive referral source for new business, and by virtue of its start-up plan, you are a key person. Make no mistake about that. And, please know that we are grateful, ever so grateful, that we have you."

Albert had opened the wine and I raised my glass in a toast, "To Lily, the best Assistant any lawyer could ever hope to have!"

I thought for more than a few seconds that Lily was

going to cry. She stayed silent for more than a minute. Then, she sipped her wine, smiled, and said, "Oh! How marvelous! I do not believe I have ever tasted anything like that. It's so rich!"

Next thing, Albert set a dish in front of each of us with three of the biggest prawns I had ever seen west of the Bull & Bear at the Waldorf in New York. We each seasoned our own cocktail sauce to taste, a touch of squeezed lemon, and we enjoyed our prawns for ten minutes of delight. The rest of that dinner went just as well.

I had Albert put a cork in our Chardonnay bottle to preserve its last six-eight ounces to take with us. The valet had pulled my Mercedes SEL around, and he helped Lily into the passenger seat, whereupon I gave him a generous tip. I had never been to Lily's place, but knew she lived in Albany. She timely advised when to exit eastbound I-80, and a few turns later, with about a half-mile drive uphill, we arrived at her place. Her car deck was vacant, so she had me pull onto it. I waited for her to alight, but she hesitated. Finally, she asked, in a low voice, "Would you like to come in for a last glass of that wonderful wine?"

Having known Lily for such a long time, and how devoted she was to the firm, I thought nothing of agreeing. After a few seconds of her moving a few things around, she bid me to sit in her only oversized chair aimed straight at her television. She smiled as I sat filling that chair in its entirety. She took the bottle and sat it on the counter separating what appeared to be her kitchen/dining area from the living area where I sat. She started to exit to another room, saying, "I'll be right back in a minute or two. The powder room is next to where you are sitting."

I got up and looked around for a few moments, noticing

a sliding door leading to a deck just off the living area. I flipped a latch, then slid that door silently open, stepping out onto the deck. I moved to its front edge, staring straight ahead and slightly upward. The moon was on the other side of her condo, so the view was star-filled darkness. "Magnificent," I uttered to myself, not realizing that Lily was standing just behind my right side.

"It really is, isn't it? That's such the perfect word." Right next to me, Lily shivered, I felt it. She continued, "I was going to show you this when you were leaving. Even fewer house lights would be on then. Best is when I get up early in the Winter. The darkness seems deeper then. "I better go in," she said.

For some reason, I could never explain, I reached over and put my right arm around her shoulders and pulled her toward me to warm her up. The night air was getting quite chilly. I said nothing. "Oh, my. That's so much better. Thank you," Lily said as she snuggled into my warmth.

I thought for a second, then, "You're right, we better go inside." But, with that said, Lily did not move.

Then she said, "Please let me have one more minute." And, with that, she used her left hand to pull my arm down lower to make it a bit more snug as it wrapped around her shoulders.

As Lily started inside with me right behind her, she turned and said, "Ronan, I know you were just being nice and trying to keep me warm. You must know, by now, I have had a crush on you for years. That said, your gesture to warm me was a moment of actualization I never thought I would have. I never thought about doing anything with you. I know you are ever so happy with Carolyn. I love her too. She's so nice. A few sips of wine before you go?"

In that moment, I realized that if I left too quickly, it might convey that we had done something wrong. We had not; and, the last thing I wanted to do was to hurt Lily in any way.

So, I finished another two ounces, as did she while we rehashed what a fun time we had with our dinner, splitting the three courses. As I left, I said, "Lily, you are a most wonderful person. I count you as a dear friend, not just an employee. I would never want to do anything to hurt you. Please try to think of me that way. I want us to stay friends, and be more than fellow workers."

(I stopped short of uttering my next putative sentence, "In my own way, I do love you. I do not wish to hurt you.")

The next morning, Carolyn called me from Paris and I spent a couple of minutes telling her about the dinner with Lily, but I skipped the part about taking her home to her condo.

When I got to the office, Lily had a stack of papers on my desk: the latest roster for the Defense Counsel side of the ACLN. The sticker on top said, "Up to date and Ready to Circulate?"

I asked Lily to email it to the Board for Approval. She smiled and went right about doing so.

———

Not surprisingly, because of their involvement in the steps leading up to the New Lloyds, both John O'Sullivan and Gerry Dwyer were readily on board with providing their forms of Counsel Retainer Agreements and Billing Guidelines, through me, to Mary Smith-Martin, QC, in her official capacity. My cover email to Mary had pointed out that these were the intellectual property (IP) of those two entities and were meant to assist in her people creating their own Lloyds IP version of similar documents, as we had discussed.

After little more than a week, Mary sent me an email with an attachment of a draft Retainer Agreement to retain O'Neill Fox as counsel for Lloyds' entities themselves with details completed. I scanned it and passed it to Reggie to read (it was his job at our firm to do so). He came into my office that afternoon, and said, "This is sure a long way from the first draft of what they sent. I really don't see much of anything to negotiate. If you want, I'll go back and pick whatever "nits" which might be needed in a redline version."

"Reggie, that would be great. We do want them to know that we care enough to put in some work. Thank you!" from me, and he was gone.

I sent it back to Mary, just as Reggie had marked it up.

The next morning, I received a similar draft Retainer Agreement to retain O'Neil Fox as counsel for entities insured by Lloyds' entities, as well as Billing Guidelines, which were referenced in this document, but not the first one she had sent. I walked over to Reggie's office with his copies. We talked. He carefully made suggested changes to this agreement, and a few to the Billing Guidelines. I had Lily send those two redlined versions back to Mary with my cover note.

The following Monday, Ms. Smith-Martin sent an e-mail with three attachments and requesting us to execute those original documents and return them to Lloyds by expedited mail at its Lyme Street address. Reggie took care of the execution part, while I wrote a cover letter of thanks and requested fully executed duplicate originals be returned to us "...at their early convenience."

Two weeks before the EU/USA Tournament, O'Neill Fox executed those substantially modified Retainer Agreements with Mary's office at Lloyds Legal on Lime Street in London. Her Billing Guidelines were also remarkably similar to those of DMIC and CI. Our firm was fully aboard as a Lloyds Defense Counsel. Our partners gathered and we drank a toast to what we hoped would become a profitable venture for all of us.

— — —

I checked with Sandra on how she was doing with Mason and his identifying, then selling, the Neptune decision-makers on the need to meet, and to do so preferably outside their comfort zone. As we neared a week before I would disappear to the Monterey Peninsula for about ten days to deal with the Tournament and all of those attending for extra days, while seeking extra time with us (necessitating secondary arrangements for any grouping of greater than six), Sandra reported that Mason was having problems on all fronts. I had been fearing this failure of client control for most of our time on this matter, and the time to force some hard decisions was fast approaching. I asked Sandra to have a seat at my small table. I pulled out a legal pad. It was covered with my notes on Neptune (closely resembling Egyptian hieroglyphics). I began, "I have some suggestions. Why don't you let me get them out as a group, and then you can dissect them as you see fit. OK?"

Sandra smiled faintly, then gave me a nod in approval. I went forward, "Mason, no fault of his own, these are inherited client-types, probably no basis for loyalty, and years on end of their misfeasance, if not malfeasance. The result: no client control, and I doubt the client-types have any real sense of how badly this can all go.

"We have the opportunity to file motions to strike the Plaintiff's claims for Attorney's fees and Punitive Damages, based on the express use of the word, 'penalties' in connection with each of those contract terms. But it's not necessarily a clear winner on Punitive Damages as the other side will claim that the California law eschewing any claim built on a penalty is a nullity is procedural, and a federal court need not adhere to a state procedural statute. I happen to think that argument is a loser. So, we might have some leverage on that claim.

"We can take the same position on Attorney's Fees, but that one seems far less certain. Still, we have that statute. Some added leverage.

"We can argue that a contract was never finalized, but no one has ever written, more or less transmitted, anything to convey that to the Plaintiff. To me, this all looks like the parties thought there was a contract and operated accordingly, at least until things started to go really wrong! This seems a position more of desperation. Nonetheless, you should get all three of these positions researched, and create a legal memo on each, suitable to converting into a separate brief on each.

"So much for the relative strength of the positive side of where we sit as of now. Then there are the damages available to Ester-Tech, not to mention being suffered by the Neptune entities. You have done an excellent job organizing them. The language of the Licensing Agreement is crystal clear that our clients have the Non-exclusive use of the three patented substances, as described, and Ester-Tech has done nothing whatsoever about the use of those substances, but has made samples available to Neptune to undertake its own development and testing before entering into the Agreement.

"Moreover, we have not a single writing that disputes that express contractual representation. To me, that yields a loss on the Plaintiff's damages claims. Similarly, the Fishing Company has nothing but a loser on all of its claims. This amounts to no more than 'pouring good money down a dry well"' by chasing unrecoverable sunk costs. Everson Harris and Brett Hall created all of the tests and ran them. They did not expose their test samples to long-term heat or sunlight. Thus, several giant warehouses full of packages containing a gooey mess. Reminds me of a horror movie from when I was a kid—the Blob!"

"You have done a great job in creating spread sheets on all of these hard dollar losses. Now, we need a letter signed by me to the two CEO's , with CC's to all of those Mason and you think might be decision-makers, with your spread sheets as attachments, explaining our position and their need to face up to their losses and to meet with us here to come up with a plan of action before they pour good money after lost money by paying more attorneys' fees, in order to bring this matter to an end

"OK. Sandra, your turn to critique my plan."

Sandra had been making notes as I spoke. She asked for ten minutes. I took a break. She stayed at the table. When I returned, she asked some questions which I answered. Then, "Ronan, I remember that first meeting in the *Mullen* matter in my father's conference room. Your plan was novel. At first, no one wanted to follow your lead, but in less than an hour, you had convinced most of the older lawyers in that room to adopt your novel ideas. By doing so, the Defense won a victory no one would have expected in less than a year. I expect that might happen here too. We'll have that letter in their various hands days before you leave for the Tournament.

"Thank you for everything," Sandra said with a wistful smile.

18

PEBBLE BEACH: THE SECOND EU/USA POST-LLOYDS GOLF TOURNAMENT

Carolyn and I spent much of the days leading up to our departure to Pebble Beach trying to make our golf adventure and its many social accoutrements interesting and fun, all the while creating an atmosphere where relationships could foster and business might be transacted, all in comfortable social settings. Once our plans, and weather options, were finalized, we had to pack. By the time we finished, barely everything fit in our new Mercedes SUV with its second seat converted into a luggage deck. (Patrick O'Neill helped me pack the SUV, all the while bemoaning his inability to compete in the Tournament in which Patrick Tyne and his brother, Robert, had competed in Ireland the year before. With our clubs being the most difficult items, we were assisted in that we were not flying allowing all of the hang-ups to go into soft bags and lie on top of the other luggage. Carolyn monitored the SUV packing to assure her outfits were not being crushed. "Next time, let's ship the clubs, shoes, and other golf stuff. That would make this whole process far easier," was her advice.

I looked at her somewhat askance, sweat glistening on my forehead, but said nothing. She paused, then, "But Patrick and you worked so hard getting it all to fit. Thank you both so much!"

She gave Patrick, not sweaty, a kiss on the cheek. Then

turning to me, leaned in toward me, and whispered, "If you let me send the clubs next time, you will not be too sweaty for me to kiss!"

Carolyn's face lit up in a big smile, a kiss got blown, and I went to shower. Carolyn was waiting for me in bed. I got a reward.

Although Quincy was the EU Captain, he freely passed out my telephone number and Lily's to everyone on his team. We had circulated the Tee Times, including the practice rounds, and all of the "mandatory meals and entertainment" to keep everyone up to speed on being at the departure points in a timely fashion. Breakfasts or lunches were set aside to convene by sides to promote full attendance at the tee boxes for the announcement of the matches each day, just preceding the first foursome, the only ones known ahead of that time to assure that they had sufficient time to warm-up. Then, despite all of our explanations, the number of calls grew each day, as did the messages left from the UK, as the first day of appearing at Pebble Beach approached.

Carolyn became acquainted with Mary Smith-Martin, QC, who asked me who would address her wardrobe and entertainment questions and the like. I asked Carolyn who acquiesced. Thereafter, for about a week, those two seemed to talk daily as did Emily Anne from Paradise Valley. Even Gabrielle Campbell, Bradley's wife felt the need for multiple consultations with Carolyn. In all, I was sure that despite all of our planning, something would go dreadfully wrong.

Our drive down the Pacific Coast Highway (PCH, CA Route 1 or Highway One) was unremarkable with our early departure time on Sunday morning. Clear weather, warming as the Sun made itself felt, quiet ocean, splendid views, a few quick stops for appreciation, and McDonald's coffees in Santa Cruz. We chatted intermittently on our way. But by then, our relationship had entered the stage where we could enjoy comfortable silence. (Radio reception on the PCH could be very inconsistent with the cliffs rising immediately up hundreds of feet from the roadway.) As we approached the freeway segment of Highway One where Fort Ord, home base of the Army's Seventh Cavalry (George Custer's ill-fated outfit) for more than a century, was undergoing its decommissioning, Carolyn opined, "In a way it's a shame that most of those coming to this event will miss the drive we just enjoyed. There is so much scenery to enjoy, and history to know about, down here. The early and late arrivals need to be encouraged to strike out on their own and do some discovering. Don't you agree?"

Me: "After all the calls we've gotten, we really must encourage them to consult with Geoffrey, and we need to ask him to encourage that type of thing, especially to arrange private tours, which I think would prove the best thing. This can be a very easy place in which to get very lost!"

"You're right," she responded as I got off the main roadway for the entrance to Monterey. We took the creek side road down to the town's main street by the beach and turned left. The road headed toward the Presidio grounds but veered right, heading downward and through a tunnel into the easternmost part of town. We turned to the right and exited downhill toward Cannery Row. I slowed as we passed U.S. Coast Guard Group Base Monterey overlooking the Bay and its anchorage, then made a right and a left. We entered Monterey's Cannery section, made famous in John Steinbeck's writings, followed that road until we passed the iconic Aquarium, and emerged onto the coastal road that would lead through Pacific Grove, along the Pacific on our right, until turning slightly east through the Poppy Hills Gate to enter the Pebble Beach properties. Geoffrey had arranged a pass for us for two weeks which the Park Ranger provided on my showing my driver's license. We followed the Seventeen Mile Drive, past Spanish Bay, Spyglass, and Cypress Point, then into the Lodge itself. We were a few minutes early; but when we announced ourselves, Geoffrey must have been standing-by as he appeared in moments.

"Oh! Mr. & Mrs. O'Neill, it's so good to see you both again, to welcome you once more. Please, let's go inside the Lodge for a few minutes whilst I assure that all is in readiness before we take you to the same lovely facility you occupied a few months ago. My understanding is that Mr. O'Sullivan and his lovely wife will be joining you tomorrow and they'll depart on next Monday. You all will stay until that second Saturday. Also, to avoid moving you because of the make-up of this suite, another couple has volunteered to move in that Monday. That would be Sir Oliver Martin and his sister, Mary Smith-Martin, QC, from London, departing the same day as you all. I gather they will both be playing in your Tournament. Does this all meet with your understanding?"

I looked at Carolyn. "Did you know about the Martins?"

She looked bemused, "I might have said something about how we would have to move on that Monday in the course of all the things I talked about with her. She is very bright, you know. She buzzes from one topic to another without much pause. Still, I don't see it as a problem. After all, you have met them both?"

"Well, I've spent quite a bit of time with her, but very little with him. He's the Head of Twenty Kings Bench

Chambers. That's Quincy's place. I suppose Wilfred is technically his Clerk as Head of Chambers since he identifies as Clerk of Chambers. Yes. It should be fine." I added.

Geoffrey glanced away for a moment, then rose, saying, "Please finish your refreshment. Your rooms are ready and your things are being moved there now. It's so lovely outside. Perhaps we can finish our preparations on your veranda. I've ordered clam chowder for you both with some Rombauer Chardonnay to tide you over until dinner tonight.

In two more hours, we had wrapped up the last of the Tournament details as of that moment. Geoffrey left and we finished our wine, then retired for a nap.

— — —

The only people to show up on Monday were John O'-Sullivan with Emily Anne. Just as with our bedroom, an extra clothing rack had to be brought in for all of her outfits. Clearly, the women's sporty-casual dress code was being upgraded for the Tournament people. Quincy and some of the brokerage people were arriving on Tuesday as were Bradley and his folks. Gerry and Phillip from CI were due on Tuesday as well. By Wednesday, everyone, but two EU team members were set to undertake the practice round at Poppy Hills, the only non-Pebble Beach golf course we would utilize.

Sunday's cocktails on our veranda were a rehash of our stay with the O'Sullivan's almost two months before, but our dinner was a more eclectic catching-up on a wide variety of topics before winding around to the formal event structure of the Tournament. Tee-off times each of the four days started at either 1:20 or 1:30 which assuming six foursomes and a five-hour round would have the last foursome finish by 7:30, the starting time for cocktails in the Lodge's private bar, and dinner at either 8:30 or 9:00 depending on venue. We had asked Geoffrey to move our groups up to an earlier start time in the event of cancellations. Darkness could be an obstacle to everyone finishing (Not a usual obstacle for players from the UK which had later spring light due to its more northerly latitudes).

The first course in play would be Spyglass and we would be playing "Four-Ball." (Lower team's players' net scores against one-another, no carry-overs.) The second day would be Spanish Bay playing "Two-Ball," sometimes, described as alternating shot (Again, no carry-overs).

Lastly, Pebble Beach for Singles. As the co-hosts, Carolyn and I were to go off in the first three foursomes, or earlier. John and Quincy, as the Captains were to go off early as well.

Dinners were at *Baja Cantina* on Wednesday evening, with Stephenson Ranch on Thursday after Spyglass. *L'Escargot* was Friday night and the Private Dining Area of Stillwater Restaurant in the Lodge for our final night on Saturday. Transportation was arranged for all of those needing it (many of them).

As we discussed all of these events in detail, we had a marvelous evening in the Taproom that Sunday night. For Monday night, we allowed that due to travel schedules and jet lag for the EU-types, folks would arrange dinner on their own. (Jerry and Samantha Milton got together with the O'-Sullivan's whom they had met in March, and were joined by Quincy, Bradley and Madeline. Mary Smith-Martin and her 'husband,' Oliver, along with Gerry and Phillip from

Connecticut Indemnity joined us as we reprised the convenient Taproom for its excellent casual dinner choices and fine wine list.) For Tuesday night, we had a reservation at Little Napoli for a private party in their wine-tasting building immediately adjacent to their restaurant's kitchen in the heart of Downtown Carmel. On Wednesday night, Jerry and Samantha Milton had arranged for a private area on the deck immediately off the Bar at *Baja Cantina* for a big reception with a flavoring of Tex-Mex in combination with an American cookout, two of that house's specialties.

So, it came to pass that Queen's Counsel Mary finally got to meet my Carolyn and Gerry Dwyer. I was not certain what this upper crust barrister was expecting, but Carolyn had her charmed in the first thirty minutes as the three women, each near the very top of their professions fended with each other not to appear overly grand, but far more than merely competent. Easiest for Carolyn: she was the one most known publicly. Hardest for Gerry, known almost exclusively in the insurance industry, with little public notoriety. But they seemingly became friends before the night was over. QC Mary was most careful to seek out both John O'Sullivan and Gerry on an individualized basis to thank each of them for their "input" in assisting Lloyds Law Office to create its own American Billing Guidelines and Contracts of Retention for Representation. Oliver Martin, who seemed content to observe his 'sister' and those with whom she interacted, was doubtless brilliant in his own right, but hid his candle in his Mary's presence. I sat there much like the other two men, and paid attention to the women's discussions. I found it all somewhat enlightening.

After the meal itself was finished, our other four guests started to ask about the golf. They were familiar with the host course from the U.S. Open and AT&T televised golf events. None of the four knew anything about Poppy Hills or Spanish Bay. Some knew of Spyglass as an "off-camera" course in the AT&T televised event. Carolyn took the lead in discussing Pebble Beach, then chose to discuss Spanish Bay which she characterized as "target golf." I was going to contest that description, until I remembered that John and Emma both agreed with her on that point, especially John.

I suggested they ask John O'Sullivan about Spyglass, especially its first six holes, and then told them about Poppy Hills, describing it as more like Spyglass than the other two courses, but having a number of target greens, essentially true of most Par 3's, but especially on these Monterey Peninsula courses. The other thing I chose to stress was the absence of flat lies combined with the need to account for your shot's roll after the ball would land because of the slopes in the fairways and the greens.

At that point, Oliver spoke up, "Are you really warning us that these courses may be a bit of an overmatch for those of us playing as casual weekend golfers?"

I smiled wryly, "Just as much as I am forewarning myself, as a casual weekend golfer, not to go into this Tournament with any *Great Expectations.*"

"*Touche,* on that one," in an exaggerated brogue, as Oliver actually broke into a real smile, "I do believe that most of us will get along splendidly, although I do find much of Dickens overrated as he wrote for the masses."

"Very successfully, I would say, and you?" by me.

"His best work far and away was *A Tale of Two Cities,* which I admire greatly, and I have never been certain about his target audience for that one. Certainly not the House of

Windsor!" With that, Oliver asked about the First hole tomorrow on Poppy Hills.

I allowed that it had many of the attributes I had just described. Starting with a bending to the right slightly uphill drive onto a sloping fairway to the right, it was not overly long, but heavily trapped around one of the largest greens on the course. "Prudence" was the word I suggested for the first drive. Then I added a general warning for Poppy Hills, and added moments later for the other courses as well, "Beware going off the backside of any green!"

We walked back to our rooms, and all concurred that another nightcap would be one too many. Inside, Carolyn immediately sat down in the living area (John and Emily Anne had not returned as yet). She asked, "Please give me a Double Johnnie Walker Black." I complied, and made one for myself, as well. She continued, "You know that Mary-person is some kind of strange being."

I countered, "What is that supposed to mean?"

"When she looked at me the very first time, it was as if she was staring into my eyes and probing for my soul. I had to concentrate to break-off the connection she was making. She did not try that again until just as we were leaving. It felt like maybe an attempt at hypnosis, or even... Don't make fun of me, witchcraft!" and with that Carolyn shuddered. I put my arm around her shoulders, and gave her a hug. In that moment, I thought about QC Mary's breakfast with me in London, and asked myself, "Had she done that to me and I was unaware, and thus, non-responsive." I told Carolyn about that.

She thought for about a minute before responding, "Maybe it's some sub-conscious thing that she doesn't really know she's doing? But, it sure did not feel that way. Could it be some sex thing? Not in my experience. Very unsettling."

"You do know there are very few women. You will have to play against her at least once, and a UK man as well as Madeline. Don't be put off our game. That may actually be her *raison d'etre,*" was my riposte. I leant over, pulled Carolyn to me, no resistance, and kissed her.

We went to bed with no further discussion on that QC Mary point. John and Emily Anne had not yet returned!

— — —

The practice rounds that Wednesday proved more enlightening than I would have thought. Quincy asked to go out in the next to last foursome and asked me to have my foursome be last to allow us to confer from time to time. After consulting with John, our Captain, I agreed.

As it turned out, I spent verry little of my practice round practicing. I only completed five or six holes. Issues and questions dominated the day, and I got an extra cart to help me negotiate trips to many of the other foursomes, especially the EU team members since all of this was new to them and although some of them nominally played on links courses, for many that was not the case. Interestingly, Madeine asked QC Mary to ride with her for that round, and they had almost no questions. Their only concerns were Ladies' facilities and when could they get a snack?

I started out with Manny from DMIC and Gerry and Phillip from Connecticut Indemnity as a foursome. We all got along fine and they did not seem to mind much that I kept going off to tend to others. I noted that Gerry and Manny both had cleaner looking swings than during the

Irish rounds last year. Having played those links courses was helping them here on the Monterey Peninsula.

With many elevated greens, and my caveat about going over the backs of those greens, almost everyone made inquiries about how far they needed to "carry" their shots. (None of them thought to buy a course book. I called Geoffrey and asked him to be sure each cart was equipped with course books for the Tournament itself. Those books received heavy use throughout those three days of play.)

Madeline told me that QC Mary had a range finder which gave them excellent approximations of "carry" distances. (They did not know that the USGA did not allow range finders. That changed by the time I write this.) Still, that twosome got on quite well together. Madeline mentioned to me in passing that QC Mary seemed quite interested in me; and when I asked, that QC had literally nothing to say about Carolyn. (Interesting at the time.)

We were scheduled to go directly from this course to the *Baja Cantina* for dinner. Those without transportation would be on a van with the non-playing guests to get to the cocktails and cookout. That van was scheduled to depart Poppy Hills Clubhouse at 6:30, meaning that a few foursomes might not finish the course. However, Quincy was trying desperately to play all 18 holes. That led him to agitate me to force play to move along which I tried to facilitate.

Quincy's foursome had teed-off on Hole number 18 by 6:20 p.m., and they rushed to finish that Par 5, two of them actually making pars and the other two bogeys (perhaps an indication that first instincts are best followed when golfing!)

The Tuesday evening at Little Napoli had been much of an ice breaker for many of the players and their guests, but the dinner was served sitting at places, unlike *Baja Cantina* where after each trip to retrieve food, the guest could join a different group. That seating plan did lead to more new friendships being formed. Jerry and Samantha were everywhere on that deck that night seeing that everyone was well-fed. Plenty of waitresses and bar maids also were in attendance.

As that Wednesday evening slowed, I noticed Jerry spending a good deal of time with John O'Sullivan, Gerry Dwyer, and later Quincy. In all three instances, he seemed to be carrying out a somewhat opening investigative discussion on the creation and operation of a Lloyds investment vehicle, and what entities might qualify to be involved in creating or investing in such a venture. I noticed that Quincy asked Oliver to step into his conversation with Jerry. They were not whispering.

As people were drifting toward departure, Jerry came up to me, and said, "You may have heard what I have been discussing concerning the formation of vehicles and what is needed to undertake those steps. I am not even clear on whether an American citizen could undertake that, and what would be needed to qualify, and if being subject to the British legal system would be a firm requirement. Who could help?"

I smiled ever so lightly, saying, "What did Oliver say?"

Jerry responded, "He said words to the effect that such an inquiry was not 'his thing.' Then, he added something like I should talk to you. So, I am. But I am not sure where to start."

My smile widened a bit, "Jerry, there are people here who can answer what you are asking, but they get paid real money for that sort of advice. Oliver Martin is related to

Mary Smith-Martin, Queen's Counsel. She is the Head of Lloyds Legal. She probably makes the very rules you might wish to understand. Quincy was a major mover in the New Lloyds. He probably knows. Bradley Campbell is a London solicitor with whom I have worked in close proximity for the better part of a decade. Bradley has no potential conflicts with your inquiry pattern, he's the one with whom you should confer. Do not be shocked if he sends you a bill on his return to London. Good Luck!"

I walked Jerry over to Bradley and introduced them. It took some time for me to appreciate the scope and value of that introduction. (I continue to appreciate it as I write this.)

— — —

John O'Sullivan had invested a great deal of time and mental/emotional energy in his pairings for the three events. As our Captain, he felt it important to go out first and to be available to cheer on those behind him as each event wore on. For that first round, I suggested he partner with Reggie Fox, a slightly better golfer than me. He agreed. He wanted to keep Emily Anne close at hand. So, he paired her with my Carolyn as our second foursome. He placed me in the fifth foursome with our relatively junior partner, Joshua Small (so excited/ so nervous). I had not seen him play. He went out with Manny Garcia the day before for a very quiet practice round. Manny was playing last with my old friend, Joel Tinker, the only player to miss the practice round. But still, perhaps the best of all of our U.S. golfers!

Carolyn and Emily Anne drew QC Mary and Madeline, in an agreed-upon all-female foursome (one/day, every day of the three). QC Mary's handicap was one stroke lower than Carolyn; but, Emily Anne was three strokes lower than Madeline's maximum handicap of 36. As the lower of two low net balls/ foursome, those high handicaps could win some short holes and swing a match (at least that's what the two lower handicappers were hoping for!).

Much to Carolyn's pleasure, she brought her "A-game" to their match. After the grueling first six holes on Spyglass, her team was up 6-0. By the turn they were up 7-1, with one half. After 11 holes, they were up by 8 with 7 holes left to play. Our women put us up 1-0. Apparently, once it became clear that Carolyn was going to win most of the holes, all of the women loosened up and they had some real fun. Since the third foursome was not pressing them from behind, they played out the whole 18. And retired for a quick drink afterward.

Joshua was a hitter. His tee shots were like my sons. Some were hard to find, but we had a great time, winning our match: Up 4 with 2 holes to play. Manny and Tinker won. While John and Reggie took half a point with a tied match. We retreated back to our section of the Lodge for drinks on our deck with a pre-arranged bar, while folks changed to their best casual finery for the dinner at *L'Escargot.*

A fantastic meal, fabulous wines, a few speeches, and a great deal of self-deprecation after Spyglass had had its way with most of our golfers. The captains reported that there were only five gross scores of less than 100 among the Yanks and two among the Brits: whilst the net scores were seven and four, respectively, below 100. The matches themselves, stood three and a half to two and a half in favor of the U.S.A.

A great time was being had by all!

When the four of us got back to our deck, the residue of our earlier informal cocktail party was missing, so we decided to have one night cap rather than rush off to bed. Emily Anne, now in Emma-mode, could not stop gushing about how well Carolyn had played that day. She was one of the five gross and seven net less than 100 scores for the Americans. Tinker and I were among the others. We discussed who should be paired together for tomorrow of the three women. Gerry Dwyer was the third. We finally decided that for singles, the actual pairing was far less sensitive; and that for tomorrow in two-ball, Gerry should be paired with Carolyn to maximize the opportunity for a point. Emma would play with John, who would play singles with his son (who was able to arrange getting there) on the final day.

While the Ladies continued their own dialog, I told John about Jerry's inquiries into syndication at Lloyds and my referring him to Bradley Campbell as an entrée to LTL, Ltd., which might serve as a vehicle for creating a Lloyds qualified entity, or series of entities for those people otherwise not qualified by their residency, or some other disqualifying factor. Of course, any such entities must be real entities with real world value, and contractually subject to jurisdiction in either the UK or USA. We talked for another 15 minutes. Bedtime intervened.

The next morning, Bradley Campbell called me back. Jerry had been in contact. A brief discussion ensued. Gabrielle was with him at that time. Now, she was having breakfast with Carolyn and Emma. Madeline was with Bradley now. I called John. He would be here in five minutes, I asked Bradley and Madeline to come down to our place. We retreated inside for privacy when the four of us were together. We were finished in twenty minutes, all agreed on a plan of action to expand the role of LTL, Ltd.

For Spanish Bay on Friday, both captains used a similar strategy: pairing their very best players in twosomes for the alternating shot event ("Two-Ball" since each foursome only played two balls). John paired himself with me, and Carolyn with Tinker. His third best team might be our women's twosome or Reggie Fox paired with Joshua Small, my partner of the day before. We hoped to win at least three and a half points, for a two point advantage going into the singles matches on Saturday (With twelve points at stake that last day, no lead was really safe from a team that got extraordinarily-hot!).

The wind decided to blow harder on Friday, and increased in its gusting as the afternoon wore on toward evening when it quickly started to calm. Being very aware of this potential, I so advised John. Also, I suggested playing his twosomes in reverse order of their potential to win. When Quincy saw our line-up, he immediately invoked a special tournament rule: a playing captain could change his position on the day by swapping spots with any other player. (I thought that rule only applicable to singles, but Quincy swore that was not the case. After all, it was a friendly match.) His twosome had been first and probably would have crushed our twosome, Stanley Booth and his son, Edgar. Now, they got a much better chance by playing the two UK women. Meanwhile, John and I continued to have a chance to defeat Quincy and Wilford.

Between the wind blowing in off the ocean, the obstacles (ponds, several swamps, overgrown depressions and small canyons) needing to be carried, sometimes more than one per hole, and with relatively tiny greens, no one side had scores of which to be proud. Yet the victories by hole added up faster for our twosomes with three wins, two halves, and only one loss, yielding a two day score of seven and one half points for the USA, and only four and a half points for the UK!

(As noted above: certainly NOT an insurmountable margin!)

So it was that we repeated the evening of the day before: cocktails on our deck's bar while outfits were changed and everyone got refreshed, then off to Stephenson's Ranch, located on a knoll just behind Carmel's first mission of St. Thomas Borromeo, a fully functional Catholic parish, and an arm of Carmel Bay. With Jerry's assistance, we arranged for outside tables with space heaters and lanterns creating a festive atmosphere for our private party. From down below our plateau at the bar side of the deck, everyone got to observe the day's end herding by the only black of the resident flock of sheep into their barn about 100-150 yards away. Jerry and Samantha Melton were the last to join us on the deck as they brought a guest with them, the owner, Clint Eastwood, who graciously circulated among us. When Jerry introduced me, I responded to his greeting by saying, "Very nice to meet you at last, Mr. Eastwood. Our law firm is located in Oakland's Jack London Square (his eyes widened just a bit), and one of our neighbors for years has been your cousin, Don Kincaid, with whom you grew up in Piedmont."

"Call me, Clint. How is Don doing? He had that bad auto accident some years ago," he responded.

"I heard he retired a few years back and he may have moved away. His firm has been undergoing some restructuring since he left. I'm afraid that's all I know and some of it is speculation at its best." Standing a few feet away was Reggie Fox. And I gestured to him, saying, "This is our managing partner, Reggie Fox, perhaps he'd know more about Don?"

With that Clint turned away and exchanged words with Reggie before Jerry could continue the introductions. As that celebrity neared the end of our party guests, Samantha Melton was waiting for Clint and Jerry while arm-in-arm with Carolyn. Clint and Jerry stopped in front of the two ladies, and Samantha said, "Clint, this lady is the reason we have come to meet so many of these marvelous people from all across the world. Jerry called me from *Baja Cantina* when he recognized her and we met by coming here a few nights later."

Clint put out his hand to Carolyn and deftly pulled her close bussing her on each cheek, European-style, while saying, "Carolyn, It's so nice to see you again after so many years. I recall fondly having a few cocktails with you and some of your model friends at one of the hotels above the Spanish Steps in Rome while you were there for a huge fashion extravaganza and I was there for a publicity shoot. What brings you to this group?"

Carolyn, "It's terribly nice of you to remember me. I'm married now, to that very tall gentleman over there with whom you spoke briefly. I'm now Mrs. Ronan O'Neill, but I retain my work name of Tyne for all professional purposes. Are you in this area a great deal?"

Clint laughed, and said, "I'm the outgoing Mayor of Carmel." With that, he turned, kissed Samantha, and together, the three of them departed. The rest of the evening was a blur of conversations. Near its end, QC Mary wandered over to me as I briefly stood alone reflecting on this whole event-to-date. She was dressed very stylishly with a low-cut cocktail dress, "Very impressive! It would appear that your Jerry is a real player. Moreover, watching you deal with a celebrity of that ilk causes me to think that no lawyering role might be too big for you. Let's the two of us find a few minutes to talk tomorrow night before too many cocktails?" With that she reached over and patted my hands that held my drink steady.

With that, I thought, "Time to get back to the Lodge," and went about acting on that thought.

— — —

19

PEBBLE BEACH: WRAPPING-UP A SUCCESSFUL SERIES OF EVENTS

The first early Saturday morning indications of dawn caused me to roll over on my back and begin to try to wrap my mind around all that had happened on several different levels in our time in Greater Monterey: first, the golf; second. the business opportunities; and third, our, maybe my, social interactions with Emily Anne O'Sullivan and with Mary Smith-Milton, QC. This latter thought process was more a function of confusing, and sometimes contradictory, signals from those two women toward Carolyn, and in Mary's case, toward me as well. Yet, my self-conscious had divided them accordingly. But, as I stretched, and felt Carolyn stirring, I thought I'd have to await more sleep to finish, or at least move along, that process. When Carolyn's left hand and arm started reaching for me, I decided that making myself available to her was my best move at that pre-dawn moment.

That Closing Saturday was to be a completely Pebble Beach Resort Day. Geoffrey had prevailed upon the Food and Beverage Powers-That-Be at the Lodge to have the Taproom open for Brunch at 10:00 for our group (first tee time was 12:30). There was a beverage buffet on the Bar. (Early cocktails were discouraged by the team Captains!) A side-bar table contained cereals, fruit, milk and other side dishes (e.g., cheese-grits!). Main courses came from the menu, with the big seller being their Eggs Benedict. (Several steaks were special ordered!) The two sides and their followers were separated by a very pleasant floor screen.

Each team gave a player a number from 1-12 with the two matching numbers playing each hole while being paired against their same number on the opposite team. For example; John O'Sullivan was number one and Manny Garcia was number two on Team USA. Quincy Franden-Jones and Oliver Martin were numbers one and two on Team EU. All four would play all eighteen holes together, if need be, as a foursome with the same numbers engaged against each other in each singles match, yielding 12 points. Twelve and a half total points were needed for a team victory. Carolyn and Gerry were in the USA second cart, paired Carolyn against QC Mary and Gerry versus Madeline, etc. I volunteered to be USA Number 12 in USA cart 6 along with Emily Anne. Emma played against Bradley Campbell while I drew Sam Harmon from Twenty King's Bench Walk. The wind increased in intensity as it shifted from West-by-Southwest to North-by-Northwest as the afternoon wore on. That wind caused all of our players problems, but USA's bonus saving grace was the O'Sullivan's having played Pebble Beach two months before. John got half of a point as did Manny. Carolyn won her point against QC Mary (she admitted later just to me that it had proved a struggle at 2-1). Tinker won a point, as did I. Sam O'Sullivan with Joshua Small each played to a half, as did our Reggie. That was five and a half points after my win on Hole 15, by a score of 4 and 3. Yet, we needed aa half point from Emma who was down one with three holes to play, and Bradley Campbell was playing his best golf, especially for his maximum handicap of 36, that was three less than

Emma's that day. Only the two of them were left to finish, while all of our other players and guests were making their ways to watch that last match. Emma and Bradley tied with net pars on the 16th hole. That left only the dread 17th and the world-famous 18th where each of them had the same handicaps.

Emma had the same caddy who was on her bag back in March and she had me in her cart. No one, as far as I knew, had told her that her half point was needed for a clean USA victory. Bradley was first up on 17 by virtue of having to use the Men's tees. He studied the wind for a few seconds. The flag was in the far-left section of the irregularly shaped green (very wide, but not at all deep) at about 175 yards. He chose to hit a 5-iron. His set-up looked to be straight at the flag. As he had almost the whole day, he used a deliberate takeaway and an under-control swing. The ball came off his club with a good arc. However, when it started downward, it ceased moving toward the flag and instead began to move leftward, nose-diving the last fifty feet or so.

The caddy came up to Emily Anne as she exited our cart at her tee box and handed her the 5-metal wood from her bag. Her distance was 138 yards. She looked at the caddy, then at me, and said, "That's my 150 yard club."

The caddy smiled, and said, "With this wind this afternoon, that pin placement will play 155 yards. It's more than a one club wind from the north-by-northwest."

Emma turned and looked at me, quizzically. I kept my face unsmiling, only saying, "If I were you, for this shot, I would trust my caddy's judgment. The other thing I would do is aim at the middle of the green, not the flag."

Emily Anne accepted the club which was extended to her, the caddy saying, "Mr. O'Neill is correct on the aiming spot with this club. Make good contact, the club will do its own work."

She put her tee in the ground, then her ball on it, took two practice swings (she must have hit that club at least five or six times so far in her round), squared her stance, took a breath and went into her swing. The contact sounded good. Her ball headed toward the middle of the 17th green, but when it started downward it appeared to move to the left and came straight down the last fifty feet. Emily's shoulders sagged, saying, "It moved left."

The caddy smiled. She got in the cart. I took off, saying, "I think you may be OK."

As we drove up to the green, we both noticed that Bradley and Sam were not on the cart-path, but had headed to the left side of the rough to approach the green from the famous Tom Watson-side. They parked a way back from the green, exited, and began to search. Emma's ball was just to the right of the flag about fifteen feet away. I looked at her and said, "Two puts and you have a net one."

Her head went from me to the caddy. She smiled, and said to him, then me, "Thank you. Thank you both."

There were huge clumps of what is lovingly referred-to-as barranca starting 5 yards or so in front of that leftmost portion of 17. After searching for ten minutes without success, then conferring with Quincy, Bradley conceded the hole to Emily. They were tied going to the 18th tee. The entire gallery of player-attendees and all of their guests had assembled greenside to watch the last hole, as it would decide the Tournament. Bradley needed an out-right win for the EU to avoid losing the Championship to the USA.

Bradley had to give Emily almost 70 yards in teeing distance, plus his drive brought the ocean into play. His three-wood drive was safe, but short with the ever-present fairway tree slightly blocking his second shot. Emily Anne used her three-wood as well, but her contact was a bit heavy and she was only about twenty yards past Bradley's ball, but more toward the ocean.

Bradley's second, a three metal was well struck and went past the tree to the left and short of the ocean-side waste bunker. Emily's second, also a three metal just made it past that tree, but stopped short of Bradley in the short right rough. She heard those dread words, "Still your turn."

Emily conferred with our caddy, Jimmy, then me. She feared hitting a metal wood out of the rough, afraid that the longer grass might turn the club enough that she would pull her shot into the waters of Stillwater Cove. He agreed, and suggested a 6-iron. I nodded positively. She swung under control, but the ball did not exactly leap from its sticky lie. Instead, it seemed to float in the air going perhaps 90 yards and somewhat left to sit smack in the middle of that ocean-side waste bunker. Bradley would want to aim for the flag on 18 with his third shot despite the likelihood that he would not reach the green. But if he came up too short, he could end in the front of that same waste bunker, perhaps even under a lip. So, he hit a 7-iron straight up the middle of the fairway, coming to rest to the right, and short, of the 18th green. Each of them lying three and neither with an easy fourth shot. Game ON!

Emma was further from the hole and needed to hit first. Jimmy talked with her, as I listened, "When you were here two months ago, you had a shot a bit like this one and delivered a wonderful 5 metal wood to the middle of the green. This one is probably 20 – 30 yards closer, and your lie is good. Please try the 7-metal wood. Please try to hit down on the back of your ball as you strike it, driving your club slightly into the sand. Remember there is a slight knoll starting upward just behind the hole. You may feel the 7-metal is too much club, but if you hit it as I suggested, when your ball lands, it will take one bounce and then spin backwards down that knoll toward the hole; or, at worst, it'll stop."

They both looked at me. I nodded agreement, although my brain said, "That's a damn hard shot to execute," but I kept smiling. Jimmy had Emma take two practice swings. His final words were, "hold onto your club through contact."

Emily Anne was young and strong, a pretty good athlete. She lined up her shot, took one waggle, and went right into her swing. She did not hurry. There was contact and a puff of sand.

Her ball went straight toward the flag, and over it altogether. I could hear Carolyn somewhere utter a gasp. No doubt fearing going over the back of the green. Her ball landed a good 25-30 feet past the flag, took one short bounce, then spun backwards down the knoll in the general direction of the flag, coming to a stop about seven feet past the 18th hole. Emma had done it again on 18!

Jimmy went over to Bradley and conferred with him. Bradley later told me what our caddy said, "Jimmy told me he could not believe Emma executed that shot which she just made. Then he said, 'If she can do it, so can you.' So, he explained to me that my forty-yard shot over a greenside sand trap was much harder than Emma's shot because I did not really have that same knoll with which to work. From the angle of Bradley's lie, the green itself ran ever so slightly downhill toward the ocean making it difficult to stop his shot. His caddy said to play half a lob wedge. 'Be sure not to decelerate your swing and finish it smoothly.' He took three practice swings and he said the last two felt really good.

But we all saw what happened. Bradley decelerated his swing just enough dumping his ball into that intervening sand trap. Then, took two shots to get out. He missed his first putt, leaving him at seven. Emma was at four. He conceded the hole as Quincy conceded the match to Team USA!

I hugged Bradley and told him it had been great fun, and we needed to do this all again next year. By then, the crowd around Emily Anne was beginning to thin. She was the heroine of the Tournament with net Eagles on the last two holes at Pebble Beach. She might play another forty years and never enjoy that level of success again.

John O'Sullivan came over to me and asked if I thought it would be appropriate to invite Jimmy, the caddy, to our dinner that night. I agreed and John asked me to do it. When I asked Jimmy, he allowed that was very generous, but he felt the need to get permission from his uncle, Geoffrey, our high-ranking concierge. I told Jimmy I would like to call Geoffrey and I wandered off to do that. Not as easy as I thought, but when I fully explained the circumstances, he relented. I gave John and Jimmy the good news.

That final dinner of the Tournament overlooked the Pebble Beach's 18th green and Stillwater Cove just beyond it as suggested by that restaurant's name. The cocktail hour began early and ran 15 minutes late by design. The EU Team, all Brits at the moment, were good-natured in their praise of America's team. Quincy was at his finest in praising John and Emily Anne O'Sullivan as the winning team's Captain and its most valuable golfer, respectively! Then he waxed on in praise of Carolyn and me as the organizers of the overall event, ending with, "The O'Neill's have set the bar so high with this Tournament that any future matches will be extremely hard pressed to even approach the scenery, the courses, the refreshments, which still leaves companionship. Toward that end, our current plans would be to bring you all to a venue where few have trod, but is one of the most spectacular in all of Scotland, Royal Dornoch. One of the oldest courses in continuous play in the British Isles, about 30 miles north of Inverness on a Loch of its own name, and the town where having come to America to make his fortune, Andrew Carnegie retired to the castle he built on its shores. We hope that many of you can join us there. Stanley Booth is a member and he will see to finalizing that event so we all may make the plans to attend. John O'Sullivan tells me that he believes two years is enough for a USA Captain and he is planning to step down. I do not know if he has persuaded his successor to accept that Captaincy, and I hope I am making an agreed announcement that Ronan O'Neill will succeed John. Those of us from Europe wish you Yanks our best and hope to take our cup back from you on our shores next year."

Much cheering and applause followed. Carolyn took my arm, leaned into my right ear, and whispered, "Did you know anything about that Captaincy?"

I shook my head negatively, but smiled while saying, "I hope you can join me. The team needs your steadying influence, not to mention your peerless golf among these women players."

A public display of affection (PDA) took place, then Jerry Milton appeared at my elbow, followed by Samantha. He spoke in a low voice, "Ronan, I do not know how to thank you for all of this. You may have helped me to create an investment opportunity to diversify the use of accumulated wealth for people like me. I am hoping you will allow me to retain you and your firm to assist me in meeting the right people in London and introducing two of my closest associates in the use of venture capital. Before Carolyn and you leave, would there be a chance that the four of us could talk more about this? Thank you, again!"

I was not surprised by that request. I looked at Carolyn who nodded YES, and said to Jerry, "Please let me check with a few others, but I see no reason we should not be able to arrange something." (So many of the players were departing on Sunday to get back to work on Monday. Also, I knew John would like to have one last get together.)

Carolyn said, "How about if we did a late lunch on Monday. We need to get back on Tuesday, I have to be in New York for an assignment on Thursday. One of my clients wants me to make a television commercial and I need to do an interview about it on a news talk show on this coming Friday after we shoot it."

Jerry looked at Samantha who seemed to acquiesce, then said, "We'll arrange a place tomorrow and call. Please get back to all of your other friends." Samantha and Carolyn hugged, and they were gone. (They had to drive!)

There was a great deal of talking, quite a bit of alcohol consumption, and no small amount of shared sentimentality following Quincy's speech, as the entire mass of attendees began to move around our dinner area. Geoffrey was there, others from his staff, and Caddy Jimmy appeared drafted to assist in crowd control. Two doors to the outside, leading to a deck area were opened. As dinner guests accepted the outside invitation, the noise level fell and knots of small groupings began to form. Carolyn was with Emma who needed more of her time as the O'Sullivan's were scheduled to depart tomorrow afternoon. I was being left to guard the stairs into the main dining room area. I saw one of our waiters and asked if I might have a large tumbler of Johnnie Walker Black on ice. As I stood peacefully waiting, Mary Smith-Milton approached. Her drink was empty, and the returning waiter was dispatched to have it refreshed. She looked straight up at me, then, making eye contact, and I instantly recalled what Carolyn had said about that incident being "mesmerizing." It ever-so was!

"Ronan, although I am reluctant to conduct any business at an event like this one, I hope you can spare a few minutes. Oliver and his Chamber-mates are quite busy singing the praises of Northern Scotland, especially Nairn, Inverness and Dornoch. Dunsinane is also close-by as well, but I doubt many in this group would care," she broke her gaze, then motioned us closer to the bar where we stood to converse.

I knew Oliver and she were staying on for a few days, not what they were planning to do. I asked, "What are Oliver and you up to tomorrow?"

She smiled, making her look ten years younger, and somewhat attractive, "Geoffrey has facilitated our visiting Hearst Castle for two tours. We are planning to drive ourselves, and to stop at a restaurant with a grand view on the way back. But let me give you some good news. The hierarchy at Lloyds, mainly my boss, the Chairman, on my recommendation and our research, has approved your firm as our number one referral firm in Northern California, from its northern and eastern borders, south to Santa Barbara County and the northern edge of Kern County. You all will report directly to me or such person as I may delegate. Of course, more paperwork will follow."

I was bowled over by this unexpected news, thanking her profusely. But she held up her hand to forestall my further thanks, saying, "I wonder if we can have dinner Tuesday night to discuss some issues relating to our arrangements and others as well?"

I knew that Carolyn and I were planning to leave on Tuesday, but this was such a potentially big deal that my failure to meet as she requested so early in our relationship might be perceived as a failure to place appropriate importance where and WHEN needed. "If the weather is benign, perhaps we could conduct our dinner meeting on your deck. Oliver and I really enjoy the sunsets from your suite," she added.

I took quick notice of Geoffrey near-by. "Why don't we say 5:00 for cocktails. Please let me move quickly to assure that this all will take place. Thank you again!"

Fortunately, Geoffrey was able to accommodate this entire scheme as the Gordon's had agreed to move into the two bedrooms occupied by the O'Sullivan's and Emma's wardrobe. I had forgotten that. When I found Carolyn and gave her this news, she was pleased from a business perspective, but not at all happy missing our joint ride back up the PCH. However, by then, she knew it was potentially a very big deal.

Reggie Fox and his Ginger were standing not that far away from Carolyn. Ginger said, "Ronan, Carolyn did not appear at all happy with you. Is everything OK?"

"Not precisely. But Reggie and you should be the first to know that the Lloyds Legal Office has just given me notice that we are to be their Number One Referral Attorneys in

Northern California. The problem is I have to have a dinner meeting with Mary Smith-Milton on Tuesday evening and Carolyn has to leave for New York early Wednesday morning! Still, I feel compelled to attend that meeting with the new client here. If for no other reason than to show we appreciate this retention. A deferral to a later time in London just does not pass muster."

"Agreed," said Reggie, while Ginger added, "You do know that Carolyn did charm Ms. Smith-Milton during their first meeting. That may have helped in the process and you might just want to point that out to your lovely wife."

I went to have one last round with Quincy and the Brits before retiring for the night.

We sat outside with the O'Sullivan's until it became just too cold. They seemingly did not wish their time in this Paradise to end, but it would on the 'morrow. I turned off all the lights except one, then took Carolyn by the hand and led her through our bedroom to the deck off the side of our suite where we could stand alone and look up at an almost full moon. That night was too cold, but we stood for a full minute, then I turned her a quarter turn to face me and met her half-way, stopping to end in a long, warm kiss, and the words, "I shall always love you!"

We had lunch with Jerry and Samantha that next day at a corner table in the charming old section of Little Napoli in Carmel. Italian white with the Antipasto course, red Italian with Pasta, and took our time with some local social catching-up. (I greatly enjoyed my *penne* with vodka sauce.) After that course, the ladies broke into their own conversation and Jerry laid out very succinctly his reason for this meeting. He wanted to retain my firm to represent him and his associates in getting his whole plan, whatever it might be, up and running, Then, I explained my firm's new relationship with Lloyds Legal, including its potential for conflicts of interest. But I went on to explain that another entity existed, LTL Ltd., run by people with whom he was golfing that might just be the perfect vehicle for what he hoped to accomplish. I could assist in facilitating that arrangement as I would not personally be part of that operational loop.

In the end, we did agree that he could pay for my trip to London to facilitate the introductions and the process. (Later, Samantha insisted that Jerry include Carolyn and her in that trip. He agreed.)

We had a nice dinner that night in the Taproom with Manny and Esmeralda. I brought along one of our newer partners, Joshua Small, whom Manny had encountered on a few matters, hoping that he would make a good impression on our major business source as a newish partner in the firm, not just as a golfer. We had a splendid night, often referring back to our time in Ireland from last year, especially focusing on Waterville and our adventurous boat ride out to Skellig Michael.

Carolyn left very early the next morning with our SUV, taking all of my golfing equipment as well as her own. I was well up to see her off, while knowing that she was getting herself suited to New York time by changing her schedule to do all of her chores on East Coast time. She would continue to be early at all of her tasks once there in New York in preparation for her time in Paris. Carolyn was a tireless professional in the execution of her major career. When we parted, I realized I might not see her for ten days or more. Poor Mollie would be miserable going such an extended time with so very little interaction with her mother—her favorite person (as she should be!).

I spent a few hours that morning talking with Reggie about our CAL Board defense team, then about the Defense side of the American Civil Litigation Network (ACLN), in particular about our thoughts on members and whether each firm might be a candidate to do Lloyds' work in their primary jurisdiction. As someone who had practiced for more than twenty years now, Mary Smith-Martin might want a law firm recommendation or two from me. But I wanted to be very careful on this score, since I would be putting our firm's reputation somewhat on-the-line with any such recommendation, especially if one should fail.

On the ACLN Defense side, I felt confident in two of our co-founders, Fulton Finnerty and Liam Callahan, both of whom were fiercely effective in executing all of their tasks (Mark Westhoff was the Plaintiff's side co-founder; therefore, ineligible.). On the CAL Board defense team, there were a number of candidates based on well more than a decade of interaction in real litigation. Having done enough homework, I felt confident in raising this concept should the timing ever seem appropriate during our Tuesday dinner, set to start at 5:30 on our now-shared patio.

About 2:30, the in-house phone rang. When I answered, it was QC Mary at the other end. She called to advise that Oliver had decided to head back to London for a new matter of significance for the Chambers requiring his personal attention. He apologized for missing our dinner.

Geoffrey had caused the outdoor bar to remain stocked throughout our entire stay, and ice and other fresh set-ups arrived by 4:00. I had requested no bartender. I asked for the waiter to first appear about five. Mary Smith-Martin, QC arrived promptly at 5:30, dressed in a very charming pair of leather-like dark brown slacks and a slightly form-fitting dark burgundy top. She put out her hand which I took and then stepped part-way toward me. I took this to be an invitation to plant a European air-kiss on each cheek. When I finished that charade, she laughed, saying (without letting go of my hand), "I think we know each other well enough now that you can bestow a real kiss on my lips," and she took a step closer. Holding my hand all the while, she leaned upward enough to 'bestow a real kiss' on my lips. Mary backed away, her eyes sweeping over me as if to take my image into her long-term memory, then turned and found her place at the table, and sat accordingly. All of that happened in seconds. Nonetheless, for no explicable reason, I was a bit disconcerted.

QC Mary removed her sun-glasses to show-off her eyes. They were a deep blue, perhaps even violet. (Did she wear colored contact lenses?) She smiled, and spoke, "You seem somewhat abashed by my behavior. Please do not be. I may be a Queen's Counsel, but I am also a mature woman with very real sensibilities, and sensations. You, Mr. O'Neill, are an extraordinarily intelligent and composed gentleman. You will never have anything to fear from me. So, my I have a gin & tonic? Hendricks, please?"

"I make an excellent G&T. I am sorry I did not get to hear more about Oliver's fascination with butterflies. After all, they are exquisite creatures. A marvel of nature. With our planet evolving as it is, I wonder how long many of their different species will survive?" was my opening gambit, definitely not a response to anything she had said so far.

"QC" as I had been quick to nick-name her, after an initial sip, then a bigger drink, responded while reaching for a dinner menu, "I shall report your interest and your inquiry to Oliver. Please do not be shocked if he sends you a response."

My turn to smile, "I shall not. Perhaps he will wish to hear about how I came to live in this part of the world, initially it was environmentally driven." The waiter appeared, I checked with Mary and we ordered two appetizers which we could share.

Mary looked at the menu, then back at me, grinned, saying, "How American! May I please have a filet mignon, medium, no blood, as my main course. No hurry. I will have a small Caesar Salad afterward, light on the dressing."

I ordered the same, but my steak medium rare and a full-size salad to be split between us afterward. Also, a bottle of excellent Cabernet Sauvignon from the Napa Valley.

Her reaction to shift her chair somewhat closer and hold out her glass after our ordering, told me she had pre-conceived concepts that she wished to discuss. Her opening sentences told me that I was about to get a long version of her legal life. I quickly refreshed her gin & tonic, as she was talking. Then, I brought out another bottle of Napa Cabernet Sauvignon and sat it on the Bar. She was up to the time of being a squatter in her first chambers. My drink, I sat down and listened. She paused after about fifteen minutes, to take a few sips of her drink. "Will there be a quiz on this when you finish?" I offered.

QC's smile became a smirk, then a laugh, "You really do have a sense of humor, don't you?" Then she laughed before continuing, "Once I began to become established, I became known for explaining and ferreting out novel concepts used in fraud and other difficult to prove areas. Along the way, I met Oliver. He's such a nice man, extremely tolerant of me, and my many foibles. I had just started at Twenty Kings Bench Chambers, and my skill set appeared to overlap his quite a bit! One of the many minor Royals, a woman, had been thoroughly, and cleverly, duped out of thousands of pounds in investments and property, by a putative gentleman who managed to persuade her to have him become her business agent. Anyways, it was all very convoluted, but not necessarily germane. She hired Oliver, and he began having difficulties generating evidence, and interacting with his client. He asked me if I would assist with her case. I did just that and before very long, I was her lead Barrister. When things went our way, we got the other side to admit "fault in writing," but not guilt, criminally. This was accompanied by more than two hundred thousand pounds. Fifteen years ago, that was a great deal of money. We agreed to a non-disclosure of certain specified facts, but not to the ultimate outcome.

"My reputation got an immediate infusion among the mid-level Royals, and their friends in the lesser Peer groups, so many of whom are women, and I began to be in demand. Moreover, I split that handsome fee evenly with Oliver whose appreciation for my fairness, if not outright generosity, became known throughout London civil litigation circles. I did other work for Royals and before not much longer, I was asked to become a Queen's Counsel. I needed an escort for so many events. Oliver accepted that role. I needed a husband to attend other events. Oliver was not at all demanding. I asked him. He agreed. It suited him well. He is quite satisfied being Head of Chambers and calling me "his wife. We have separate lives. It's very convenient for both of us."

"So, you see, that's why I'm here. My last job at Lloyds, before its restructuring, was to deal with their biggest potential adverse outcome litigation matters. I travelled a great deal, worked too hard, but had a good overall life. Now, I am reinventing myself and Lloyds Legal. Quincy told Oliver so much about you that "I wanted to see what all the fuss was about." I saw that over the last months. By the way, Carolyn is a bonus. She is an utterly delightful human being. I'll stop there. (Pause.) My quiz is only one question: you get to come up with it at the end of this meeting."

I thought for a second to consider whether or not this was an extraordinarily round-about seduction on her part. Her 'quiz' comment certainly put me on the alert for the unusual. I said, "Wow! That's quite an adventurous life you've had, and it appears it will continue. But you asked for this dinner meeting, so please continue."

As she rearranged her posture, our waiter arrived with our appetizers. He set places for us elsewhere on the table, poured glasses of Rombauer Chardonnay from behind our Bar (Great Stuff!), and asked about the timing of the next course. I looked at Mary. She smiled indifferently, I asked him to give us 45 minutes or more, if he saw us still eating. He left.

"I wanted some time alone with you here in a different habitat. It seems that all of the things I hear about you are about your methods and your results, apparently so often out of the usual. I wanted to ask you how you came to be involved in insurance law?" Mary seemed sincere.

"Well, it's a bit of a long story in itself. I had done some work for John O'Sullivan's insurance company, Desert Mutual (also DMIC), defending their insureds. It was all fairly successful. That company had a senior person who knew the Risk Manager for a company named WALLBOARD in San Francisco which had its primary coverage of many years cancelled mid-term by its long-standing primary carrier, SF Casualty. WALLBOARD needed to get coverage really quickly, and that risk manager went to his friend at Desert

Mutual and persuaded them to write a primary Comprehensive General Liability (CGL) policy, but it had to exclude any asbestos-caused disease, like 'asbestosis.' DMIC had no underwriter available with the needed experience to create that exclusion at that moment. As a result, the WALLBOARD risk manager agreed to write it. SF Casualty ended up suing WALLBOARD, and also DMIC to contribute to its defense costs. I had done a very little bit of coverage and DMIC's usual coverage counsel had a conflict because they represented another insurer in similar, related coverage litigation. So, DMIC hired me. Against the advice of all the big firms defending the many excess carriers, we got our discovery done, and brought a summary judgment motion against SF Casualty and WALLBOARD.

"By the way, WALLBOARD was represented by the firm and senior attorney of the woman to whom I was engaged when I graduated from law school. Her name was, and is again, Sandra Allen. Her father's firm, then her successor firm, both of which represented WALLBOARD, have failed. Hers recently after WALLBOARD filed Chapter 7 Bankruptcy. With Carolyn's acquiescence, we have her working at our firm as a junior partner on one year probation. We also brought on one of her other partners and a number of her associates. All of them are highly competent.

"Oh! We won that motion. WALLBOARD and SF Casualty appealed. We defeated that. I was assisted on much of this by a young female associate, Mary Smith. She has been a full partner for years, and is the head of all of our coverage litigation. She is an excellent lawyer and a good person.

"Is she the one that you brought to London to assist you on your policy recovery matters? That name does not sound like what Quincy called her?" Mary asked.

I began to appreciate what an astute listener I had in QC Mary, "No, it was not. That would be Martha, another partner now. She has a scientific background and worked primarily in that area in London as well. Her availability in doing so, plus her intelligence made her an excellent fit for the Lloyds placement issues. She is returning after a slightly long maternity leave. She too is an excellent lawyer."

Mary looked over her sunglasses at me, "Are you telling me that I will not be working with you?"

"No, No! But I am generally no longer the lead attorney for day-to-day litigation matters on individual cases. I am involved in many of our firm's matters, and as such, my name appears first on every pleading as the senior-most partner, and our firm founder along with Reggie Fox."

Mary: "I had a very nice chat with him. He's older than me. By the way, you are not. He was in the U.S. Coast Guard. How did you meet him?"

Me: "I was in the Coast Guard Reserve, a JAG officer. You understand?" Mary nodded affirmatively, so I continued, "I knew him from that work. We had some crossover. I was looking for someone to hire to help run all the asbestos bodily injury litigation we had in our office. Fortuitously, Reggie got orders to rotate out of Coast Guard Island in Alameda, near our office, to Portsmouth, Virginia, to take over Fifth Coast Guard District Legal. Ginger, his wife, was very upset. They had three children doing very well in the Alameda school system. She did not want to go back East to all the negative factors that would entail. Reggie told me this while I was buying him a beer at The Fat Lady, slightly out of his way, going home. When I asked him what he wanted to do, he told me: retire and go to work in the Alameda area. With that

I offered him the job on my team, and I have never regretted it for a moment."

Mary took off her sunglasses, and looked at my eyes in that way only she could, "You really are something else. I keep thinking about how to use you to my benefit at Lloyds, but I could actually learn to like you very easily. I see why Quincy says you build loyalty. I think he means you instill it. Have you thought of how you might help me and Lloyds Legal?"

My turn to smile, and Mary smiled back, that nice smile I saw only once before, "I have. But I do not want you to think that I am trying to be aggressive. Something you said to me that morning at breakfast leads me to believe that you may be thinking that the big American defense firms which Lloyds routinely hired over the years represented a level of excessive built-in expense that might be unnecessary for your purposes going forward. After all, with computers and email, the capacity of smaller firms to do the same tasks as the larger ones is, in many cases, a gap that's been closed. In other words, smaller may be considerably more efficient, ergo, more cost-effective."

I looked at her, she was fixed on me, "Go on," she said.

"Well, I have had a great deal of experience dealing with other firms. I am a member of the Society of Insurance/Civil Defense Counsel (SIDC), an invitation only network of sorts open to counsel and their users. I have put together a network of defense firms for DMIC to do the CAL Board asbestos bodily injury defense work, and/or other insureds, and I am a co-founder, along with Reggie, and the first Board Chair of the American Civil Litigation Network (ACLN), past its embryonic stage, but still growing. Well, if you need law firm referrals, I am positioned to try to make recommendations. However, please recall that only the client litigation network provides some real first-hand experience."

With that, our discussions continued. I asked to be excused and called Lily, then Carolyn, then Mollie. It took awhile, but QC Mary was sitting where I had left her. She said I went for a short walk and just got back. Oliver called to say he's arrived safely at our home. Are you finished?"

I looked up to see no more sunglasses as the sun was well up the Coast now and getting close to the horizon. Me, "I am not certain how much more there is to add at this time. I have offered what I can. All you need to do is let me know if you wish me to do any of it, or anything else."

"In that case," Mary stretched in an almost feline manner, as she spoke, "Do you know the question you're supposed to ask?"

"I think so:" I said slowly preparing to gauge her reaction, "But I do not believe we should act on it, because of several reasons: first, I feel morally compelled to be faithful to Carolyn; and second, it could prove highly detrimental to our on-going relationships on other matters. That question was, I believe, 'Do you want to make love to me?' Please know, I am sorely tempted, but the time is past when I will give in to that desire again. I am sorry."

"See, that wasn't that hard, was it," as a new smile took over her face," the answer is "Yes, from the first seconds my eyes saw you in Lincoln's Inn. Even if we if do not act on that whim, shall we go inside? It's getting too chilly out here.

20

MY WORLD CONTNUES TO EVOLVE: BUSINESS CONCERNS OUTPACE LITIGATION

As I sat at my desk in my office in Jack London Square, Lily walked in with a pot of press coffee and a blueberry muffin. I came to the stark realization that my life as a litigator was slipping away to be replaced by one of undertaking a series of business-like legal marketing tasks. I told Mollie I would be home that night to take her to dinner. By 5:30, I was an hour behind on my departure and I still had one more task that needed to be finished. I asked Lily to step into my office, and asked her if she would go to my house, get Mollie and meet me for dinner at Trader Vic's in Emeryville (Not to far from where Lily lived). She left right away. I called Mercedes and told her what was happening. She put Mollie on the line, and she was thrilled from a remembrance of more than a year ago. Plus, Mollie really liked Lily. It was close to seven when they arrived at Trader Vic's, moments after me.

I was able to get a window table with a view of the City to the left and the Golden Gate Bridge to the right. I had Mollie sit next to the window where she would have an unimpeded view of the sunset under the Bridge in about 40 minutes. Lily sat next to her, sharing that view. I had ordered an Old-fashioned Mai Tai. Lily, who was driving had a Prosecco. Mollie a glass of ginger ale. I gave the menu to Lily and asked her to pick something for us to share. Not surprisingly, she went for the Cosmo Tid-Bits, that restaurant's premier starter of four or five appetizers, including huge fried shrimp and their special bar-b-que spare-ribs. She also ordered a salad for the three of us to share. We directed the conversation to Mollie: first, about her school day; next, about Pixar Studios, close by; then, about the views we were watching as the sun began to set seemingly into the ribbon of ocean visible under the single subtly curving deck between the towers of that world famous Golden Gate Bridge.

When the sun had set, I told them both the story of how I had first come to Sausalito because of the two oil tankers colliding under that bridge; and then, how I first met Mollie's mother when she was very young and living in the *Cote d'Azure,* in the same unit where her oldest sister, Maeve, stayed when she was in the area for awhile, as did a few other privileged guests; and where Carolyn kept all of her personal business records.

We ended the evening with an ice cream concoction. Mollie hugged Lily, as did I and she gave me a kiss on the cheek. We went home. "Better evening than I thought it would be," my mind said to itself. On our drive back, Mollie wanted to know why I hadn't married her Mommy right away. I tried to explain how that was a very long story. Mollie was not satisfied with that. "Oh, well!" I thought as we parked at our house in Ross. Patrick and Meaghan were home by then, and jealous of their little sister getting her own trip to Trader Vic's!

That next morning, I spoke with Carolyn, then Elsa from their shoot planning meeting with Maeve and Robert in New York. It was a short call because Sandra and I had a two-hour conference call with our North Carolina client's key people to go over a plan that I wanted them to adopt to try to end this litigation which it seemed they would never win. Neptune Fishing had painted itself into a series of corners in the conduct of its affairs in licensing uncertain chemical formulations from Ester-Tech, without adequate research or testing, nor any meaningful legal consultation before its contracting for huge commitments of time, money and other resources. As in the past, we expected any number of requested key participants to fail to attend this critical conference call.

From what Mason Eggars had told us, we knew that Leslie Worth, the GC of Neptune Enterprises, who was Mason's main contact, had received and read our letter because he told us about two conversations he had with her. In the second call, she allowed that she was pleased that we wanted to take decisive action (in the past he did mention that she was evaluated on, among other things, the amount of outside legal expense incurred anywhere among that conglomerate's subsidiaries); also, that our letter could be read as fixing the bulk of the blame for this disaster on Evrerson Harris, the CEO of Neptune Fishing. (He had been sent our letter, but we did not know going into this call if he had read it, or any comments he might have. The same was true for anybody above Ms. Worth at the parent "Enterprises level.")

Mason accumulated all of the client callers, and at 10:10, he patched Sandra and me into that call (my first actual contact with any of the client-types). I began right in, following the introductions of a great many executives, "I asked Mason to get as many of you all as possible to be on this call so we could hopefully achieve consensus on how to move forward. I'll call that the Resolution Plan, as we set forth in our letter, as well as how we all are to go about executing that plan. It seems to me that all of the key management from the Enterprise level are present as well as Mr. Harris and Mr. Small in Production from the Fishing subsidiary level. First, please allow me to ask if anyone had any specific disagreements about the asset/expenses listed in Enclosure "A" to our letter?"

Mr. Harris seemed ready to talk, but someone else coughed on the line, and his voice just seemed to stop. No one else spoke up, so I moved into the steps in the plan in the sequence we felt most likely to achieve a cost-effective resolution as possible in the relatively short term. This segment also included discussions not in our letter about what we might expect from the Ester-Tech side, and how we would deal with those tactics.

Adam Young, Senior finally spoke, "Mr. O'Neill, you sound like a man with a military background. If that's the case, why don't you tell us a little bit about it? You know the Citadel's just down the road a piece here in Charleston."

"Since it is you requesting me to do that, I shall do so. I have had the pleasure of being in Charleston on numerous occasions in my law practice; and, in my spare time, I did get a quick private tour of the Citadel. A great school with a magnificent tradition. I am a retired Commander in the United States Coast Guard Reserve. Most of my reserve duty was of the Judge Advocate General type. That's JAG Corps for anyone with a military background. On active duty, I was twice assigned to USCG Headquarters. At the first and rather quickly, I was detailed to report to Long Beach when the Executive Officer of the Coast Guard Cutter Point Arena was seriously injured and a replacement was needed in a hurry. My assignment at Coast guard HQ had been to assist in the gathering of 26 of the Guard's smaller cutters in Long Beach for transport to Subic Bay in the

Philippines. There, for combat retrofitting for ultimate deployment as an interdiction force to stop the smuggling of arms and men by the Viet Cong by coastal waters into South Viet Nam. I had served almost a year in the waters off that country's northern coast on the Point Arena when that cutter came under a two ship sneak-attack, suffering serious loss of life and damage. But, the survivors, mostly wounded, managed to make it back to our mother ship under Navy fighter cover. The CO was among those killed. The entire crew was decorated for surviving this surprise attack. After I recovered from my wounds, I was reassigned back to USCG HQ. for the balance of my three-plus year active-duty tour."

"What decorations were you awarded, having seen combat, besides the Purple Heart? No small award in itself!" from CEO Young.

"Well, the republic of Viet Nam gave me four, and I received a number of U.S. citations, the most notable, I guess, was the Silver Star." Silence hung for more than a few seconds.

"Commander, you appear to have been a war hero, and now you are a highly successful lawyer. You tell us what we are supposed to do to achieve the best possible outcome from this morass, and my son, Adam, Junior, will see that it is all carried out. If I am to have a role, please spell it out. I hope to meet you in person when his mess is over. Junior, you and Leslie see that my wishes are carried out. Thank you all!"

We spent another forty minutes or so on details needing to be undertaken. Suddenly, Leslie, Junior and the others-across-the-board were cooperative. Mason was being effectively by-passed. He did not object. Sandra joined in at the detail level and Leslie seemed pleased with that. Those two stayed on the line briefly at the end of the call. Junior spoke, "My father went to The Citadel, and did four years in the Army before resigning and going into, and building, this family business into what it is today. He was out when Viet Nam started. His middle brother was also out, but not his youngest, Joe.

"Joe was killed by a sniper while on a meaningless patrol in Nam. My father idolized that younger brother, and he considers being in the military a highly positive thing, but he was happy for me to go to Duke, instead. After all, I did get in. The point is you have a Silver Star, and that was a very big deal to him. At least for now, Ronan, you are the admiral in charge of this case. Good luck!"

Sandra was looking at me, when I turned to her. Tears were in her eyes, "Ronan, I love working with you. You are so kind, but something like today just makes me heart-sick that I lost you. I was such a fool all of those years ago. I'll get busy on finalizing those motions and trying to get a time-line calendar together to execute our plan. I'm terribly sorry I'm crying."

Sandra gathered her things and left. Lily came in with mail and messages. She looked at me in a funny way. I said, "Lily, I have told you that I was engaged to Sandra years ago. She broke it off, and I had a very hard time. She came to regret what she did, and now her being here appears to be a constant reminder to her. Today, some things that some of the clients said, I'm afraid those triggered that tearful outburst."

The next morning at 6:00, I told Carolyn in Paris what had happened. She was silent afterward, then said, "You have done more than enough by way of forgiveness for Sandra. Be careful. Be wise!"

— — —

Lily called to tell me that while I was on a call with the ACLN Board, Colleen Burke, our primary CAL Board contact attorney in Missouri, had called with a possible referral of some large, high-tech litigation against one of their clients in St. Louis. She asked me to call her right back as it was urgent.

Within a minute, I was talking with Colleen who was located in her firm's Kansas City office, "How are you and Reggie doing with that cluster of lung cancer cases there in Eastern Missouri?"

Colleen was a no-nonsense woman, "There going along. Depositions start soon and we'll be pressing hard on anyone's attempts at CAL Board product identification. But that's not why I called: I have this high-tech conglomerate that's a spin-off from an old-line conservative appliance manufacturing company that I have defended for its insurer a couple of times. It's called Admiral Electric Works (AEW, for short), and it has several subsidiaries one of which invents and manufactures all sorts of novel technical products, most of which are used in the newer types of evolving high-end products, many for the aerospace industries. It's a very profitable subsidiary, insured by American Specialty Lines (ASL, you know them)." I mumbled my assent, and she kept going, "AEW pays some serious premiums and for that reason has a right to choose counsel (It has a big retention, which includes attorney fees.), but you still have to report to both the client and the carrier. Anyway, that's enough background on that part of the relationship."

"The product involved is a highly technical specialized fire suppression deployment system for use in highly secret test chambers for space equipment and secret military aircraft. The main product is a foam-like substance placed on the inside surfaces of a test chamber which has a highly specialized secret formula that deadens all sound and allows that test chamber to mimic outer space. In the event of a fire in a chamber to preserve the test object and the entire structure, certain devices which are deployable metal pipe extensions are supposed to punch out pre-cut tubes of that foam to deploy sprinkler heads into the chamber to put out any fire. One of these systems was being tested, and the water was accidentally activated into its lines and a deployment took place with damage to all of the foam. Anyway, I am told, the plaintiff, North American Aviation & Space (NAAS), is seeking almost ten million dollars in damages for repairs and an undetermined amount for loss of use. Suit is being filed in federal court in San Mateo as the NAAS facility is located in San Mateo County. On my recommendation, AEW's General Counsel, Sophie Smart, a law school classmate of mine, has asked me to contact you to see if you might be interested in defending her entities "

"If you are, either she or her AGC for Litigation, Tom Winters, will get right back to you, probably today. I wish I could answer your questions about their case, but I have done my best to convey all of what I've been told. I am not certain I have been fully accurate. They are a very good client. What do you think?"

"Colleen, first, thank you for thinking of us. Second, I am more than pleased to talk with them, and I can be free the rest of the day, if need be. And third, I was so glad you mentioned their special relationship with ASL. If we were to work directly for ASL, I would have stopped your talking. We would not work for them with their track record for chronic delay in paying their defense counsel. Can you get in touch with your AEW folks and tell them I shall maintain availability today?"

We exchanged a few more pleasantries and I inquired about her potential willingness to get a referral to do work for Lloyds. I called Lily into my office, but first I asked if Martha was in her office. When she said Martha was here, I asked Lily to grab her and bring her along. If this matter was as scientific as it sounded like it might turn out to be, then Martha might be the best person to function as a co-lead defense counsel. (That would give her more to do as her lengthy maternity leave had caused Felicia Clark to essentially take over Martha's role on the giant GWF toxic lead exposure case.)

I went through what Colleen had told me. Martha actually smiled when I mentioned the possible need for her scientific expertise; also, that from what Colleen held out, we might hear as soon as today from someone in Admiral Electric's General Counsel's office. Martha, are you on board for this?"

Her "YES" was delivered promptly. Lily heard her phone ring and went to answer it. She called through our open door, "It's Ms. Smart and Mr. Winters from Admiral's GC office."

She buzzed and I picked up, putting the phone on speaker, "Hello, Ms. Smart and Mr. Winters, Colleen said you all might call as soon as today. I'm here with my partner, Ms. Walsh, who is our top lawyer on Science and Technology matters. Please tell us what we can do to be of assistance?"

"Hello, I'm Sophie Smart, and with me is Tom Winters, Admiral Electric's AGC for Litigation. Our company has been served on its own behalf and as the Parent of Specialty Technical Production (STP), one of its primary subsidiaries, which manufactures all different kinds of custom products used in non-standardized equipment (often also custom-made). The plaintiff is North American Aviation & Space (N2AS, said 'N, double A, S'), and involves two highly specialized test chambers. I trust Colleen told you all of this?"

I took this as a real query and responded accordingly, "Mostly, yes, and my assistant, Lily, has run a conflicts check, and we have none. However, Colleen only mentioned one chamber at the NAAS facility across the Bay. My partner, Martha Walsh is also here. She has a pre-law background in science and has been of enormous value in cases where those types of issues can drive a result. To answer your question, that's about all we know, so far."

"Well, what sorts of science have you been involved with?" asked Sophie Smart.

"We have done a great many years of product cases, even bodily injury claims, that call into issue a wide variety of science, from the simple Scientific Method to complex epidemiology. We have been influential at the state and federal court levels and in creating appellate decisions as well as at administrative agencies for shaping, or re-shaping, their policy decisions. Specifics are complex, but if you wish something specific, we should try to discuss one or two with you now," I responded.

Mr. O'Neill, this is Tom Winters. May I ask if you have done construction products cases? And what is the largest value case you have litigated to conclusion?"

Me: "Both interesting questions: first, the vast percentage of our cases have involved construction and the products involved. Second, the largest valued case which we won, after the first phase of trial, and post-trial motion and appellate practice was brought by the Los Angeles Unified School District to remove all of our client's products containing asbestos from their schools and other buildings, valued at more than five billion dollars. That was almost ten years ago now. Martha was instrumental in bringing that result about.

"Colleen mentioned testing chambers. We have never done those specifically, but we have extensive experience in fires, pumps, and large facilities, like United Airlines Maintenance Base facilities at SFO. Hopefully, you would find that sort of thing helpful."

Silence followed for more than a minute. I mouthed, "We are on mute." Then, "We think you all may be just what we need for this matter." A discussion of fees and payment methodology was quickly undertaken, then they allowed that STP would be copying all of its files, possibly relating to this Complaint, and sending them to us. I allowed that we had a process for dealing with client files and we would prefer the originals for production purposes and to account for every page in the need for privilege or redaction accountability (but they should keep their copies to use on the case as needed.). We had an outside service that worked with our office and was reasonable in its billings.

Ms. Smart then said, "Please call us, Sophie and Tom. You all are very impressive. I sense you routinely handle large, difficult matters. We shall send you the Complaint, contracts and Technical Manuals by overnight mail to allow you to become familiar with them. Tom would like to visit with you. Please get us an extension to plead. Thank you all for your time."

I turned to Martha after disconnecting, "If this is the N2AS facility on the Peninsula, it may involve the chambers used for Stealth testing. Let's see what they send. By the way, would you ask Deirdre if she would like to work on this with us? Might be a change she would enjoy."

In the weeks that followed, Martha and Deirdre became immersed in those STP documents. Tubes of blueprints showed up for the positioning of their telescoping sprinklers in the ceiling of a huge test chamber. It appeared that STP manufactured, and installed, the anechoic foam (A substance that was attached by a specialized glue to all of the surfaces of the welded two-inch thick steel walled test chambers to absorb sound and light, so the chamber would function like outer space. It never became clear if the air could be withdrawn from the test chamber, at least based on the documents STP supplied.) Part of this construction process was also installation of those telescoping sprinklers, primarily in the ceiling and upper walls, above the foam with anechoic plugs carved out of the soundproofing itself, then reinserted, to allow the telescoping rods to fully extend with a sprinkler on the end of each rod. The water pressure in the sprinkler system itself, when activated, was sufficient to cause the rods to move downward, pushing the plugs out, and in the event of a fire in the chamber, would then activate the sprinklers themselves to extinguish the fire. (This final activation was not supposed to occur when the system was being tested for its deployment. Each foam plug had a code allowing it to be restored into its correct hole in the anechoic ceiling after any test deployment. In the event of an actual fire, significant, costly repairs to the chamber would be necessitated.)

In that San Mateo County N2AS facility, the company attempting to test the water distribution in the system which it had originally assisted STP in installing, failed to follow the correct turn-off procedure to assure the pressurized water for the telescoping system's actual activation was to remain off-line for its test. As a result, the rods deployed, telescoping as they did so, and nothing kept the sprinklers from activating, allowing substantial water to come into contact with the much of the installed anechoic foam rendering that chamber unusable for about sixteen months while the entire test chamber was completely restored, then tested for its functionality. It was N2AS' largest such chamber and booked essentially solid for almost that one-plus year!

A similar incident took place in another N2AS facility in New Hampshire a few months later, but it was built on a turn-key basis by STP, enlarging our client's potential share of the liability for AEW. The San Mateo damages were $9.7 million for repairs and greater than $15 million for lost business. New Hampshire was a smaller chamber with repairs at $4.6 million and loss of use at $8.7 million. The complaint was more than 40 pages plus attached contracts and schedules.

Martha came to my office two days after receiving, reviewing, and initially analyzing their initial packet of several hundred pages. Her first comment was the most meaningful, "The Complaint, seemingly pleaded in grinding detail, is interesting for what it does not contain. There is nothing about N2AS or any of its subcontractors ever undertaking testing of either telescoping sprinkler system, as directed by STP's Telescoping Sprinkler System Manual (TSS Manual). The express warranty on the San Mateo TSS was 15 years, and the incident occurred in year 14. That warranty in New Hampshire was 10 years and the incident occurred in year 13. So, New Hampshire's claims should be time barred. For

San Mateo, our best defense would appear to be the failure to test, and I suggest that we take the position that such a failure voids the STP express warranty."

I was making notes, and looked up when she stopped, and said, "There's quite a great deal of materials and files which have been supplied. I got a date certain to plead in both matters 63 days down the road. I gave that date to Deirdre and Lily. With your thoughts in mind, I shall finish reviewing those initial materials. Is Deirdre finished sorting all of those boxes that arrived yesterday? I saw the PAPER CO. people here a few minutes ago. Are they setting up their process in the small conference room?"

"They are," Martha responded with a smile, "and a person from STP, named Lon Probst, was put in charge of assembling all of the papers and documents sent. Deirdre and I talked with him after reading his note in Box 1. He basically was overinclusive in his choices of what to send and he broke down generalized documents chronologically, keeping them all separate from job specific documents. He seemed bright and organized; AND, he's been assigned to be our continuing contact on anything we might need from STP by way of information or other help. He says they are all very project-orientated!" By the time Martha finished her statement, we were both smiling broadly!

Me, chuckling slightly, "Will miracles never cease? We have at last been blest by a client who gives us a contact who is organized!"

Martha, still with a wry grin, "But Lon says, 'not everyone at STP is as organized as he is.' So, documents may be missing, or mis-filed. Anyway, based on what he said, Deirdre is doing a final organization with PAPER CO. She's already run that format by Lon. They should be out of here tonight, if they can stay until they finish by about 9:00. OK?"

"Will someone from the firm stay?"

"Mary, Deirdre and I will all stay. We all agree about the safety issue."

"Great job! How does it feel to be back?"

Then we spent more than a few minutes on her baby pictures of tiny Michael Francis. She gave me an envelope with a note from Mary and her with about ten photos for Carolyn. I went back to reading the N2AS /STP contracts.

— — —

Felicia Clarke came into my office. Martha was with her. I got up and went to my table and sat so that they both faced the window with a view of the Alameda Estuary and whatever aquatic traffic might be sailing along it that day.

Martha was barely seated when she started to talk, "Ronan, I know my maternity leave was quite a bit longer than you probably imagined it would be when I first left, and that I was not always especially accessible while on leave. I think that was particularly true for the GWF matter because it seemed that Felicia and her helpers had a very complete grip on the matter under your guidance. Now, I wonder what am I to do on that matter? Felicia why don't you tell Ronan what the client's people have told you? Please."

Felicia looked back and forth between Martha and me, seemingly uncertain with how to proceed, but she finally started, "Andrea Parsons feels I have become the most knowledgeable of our lawyers about their case. Ronan, she understands your role. But she thinks to reinvolve Martha at this point where time and money would be needed to bring her up to speed, especially after being gone so long, 'would essentially involve a waste of fees. Her words, not mine.'"

Martha inserted, "I really cannot disagree. Which is why I wanted this meeting. Would you consider my involvement only in the science part of that case in a more limited role to be OK? If so, I think Mr. Nordquist would like that too. Moreover, I am certain Ms. Parsons would like to feel we were being responsive to her concerns."

I pondered for a minute, "You know, Martha, this new STP matter may utilize some real amount of time, but your asbestos PD work may be drying up. So, what would you do?"

Martha thought for a few seconds, "Cut my draw until I became more cost-effective?"

I shook my head, "Let's the three of us think this through a bit more closely. You two talk about this more and put together some specifics as to how you would minimize overlap. How about we do a 1:00 lunch next Monday at The Fat Lady?"

No sooner did they leave than I got a telephone call from London, QC Mary at Lloyds. We talked for almost an hour and I explained my thinking on law firm recommendations to her office. I used our recent experience on the *Neptune* matter in disguise to explain that depending on the nature of their role, referred counsel might reflect badly on referring counsel, or even vice-versa. She seemed to understand, but she still needed two referrals badly. In the end, I provided them, but I also agreed to help with her start-up with each. I did mention Colleen in Kansas city and her firm in connection with Missouri (while thinking: don't know where I'll get the time to do that. Then, a bell went off, and the word, Martha, appeared.)

QC Mary knew about Martha, having gotten an earful from Quincy on her many virtues, especially how Martha was clever at bringing people around to agreements without appearing manipulative. However, with her recent birth, Martha had failed to get to London for that final Lloyds Convocation. Moreover, Martha missed Pebble Beach as well. Yet, every extended discussion with Mary about Lloyds yielded a reference to Martha, but not that day. As we were about to disconnect, out-of-the-blue, I asked, "What would you think about using our Martha to assure that these referrals go as smoothly as possible. Perhaps the three of us could evolve a process to supplement the choice of counsel and to assure that the defense would be as outstanding as possible?"

I thought Mary had hung-up before I got started on expressing that last idea, but she was still there thinking, and finally asked, "Could your firm and Martha be associated with referred counsel, if need be? That way I would have access to you as well. Please let me think about it. Why don't you check and see what she thinks? I'll call you at the same time as today in two days and we'll finish this discussion then. Thank you so much!"

Martha was in her office when I sought her out the next morning. I explained my discussion with QC Mary at Lloyds Legal and how perhaps she could spend time here in the USA acting as an interface on matters with Lloyds utilizing her experience of years of interacting on science as well as the Lloyds market and coverage, plus she could work with our Mary when need be. The hope being that she could become the main interface between our office and

Lloyds on non-insurance matters. Her immediate response was what would I end up doing in the total scheme of things over future time. My response was that I would undertake less legal work, concentrate more on marketing, yet be available as a resource.

When I said that, Martha got up out of her chair and came over to stand in front of me. I felt compelled to stand. She reached behind her and closed the door to her office, then she reached up to my face with both hands, smiled ever-so-slightly, saying, "Does this mean that you are trying to set the firm up to allow you, and maybe Reggie to have reduced roles?" I nodded affirmatively. Her grip tightened, and she continued, "You still love me, don't you?"

"Yes, and I want you to have a lifetime of opportunity and to enjoy your son, and your Mary. This is the best I can do for now. The rest is what you make of it, if QC Mary at Lloyds agrees. Please say, 'Yes?'"

She pulled my face down to hers, kissed me deeply, and said, "Yes, but you need to be here for me as long as possible because I still love you too! I always will."

— — —

Several months had slid past since the Second USA/EU match at Pebble Beach. John and I got a note from Stanley Booth saying that he had two dates to play the Third Tournament at Royal Dornoch about 49 kilometers north of Inverness on a peninsula of its own name on the East side of Northern Scotland. The Links Hotel at the golf course, immediately by the starter's shack had 26 rooms and he had provisionally taken all 26 for the two sets of dates., either mid-April or early May. He also had associated dates at the Nairn Golf Club and that hotel for any extended stays. He looked for our feedback and if we wanted to see anything first, his office would make the arrangements.

Our calendars that far out would accommodate almost anything, although I had dates for The Society Annual Meeting as well as the ACLN National Meeting, both tentatively in the Summer months almost a year away. John had committed to come to the latter, a "City Meeting" in Chicago at the ESSEX House in June. (I paused my call with John after we had conferred and was fortunate to get Carolyn on the first ring to see if she wanted to go on a reconnoitering trip to Northern Scotland with John and Emily in late this July, one of her 'slow seasons?' To my surprise, she enthusiastically agreed.) John and I agreed on the needed details and we allowed that we would copy each other on all communications.

That night, Carolyn and I talked more about that trip. She once had a job up in that Inverness area decades ago when she was starting her swimsuit career. She allowed that the weather could be difficult, but the scenery was magnificent with the North Sea, the bays (loughs), crashing waves and the blueness of the skies! She had somewhat secretly harbored a desire to go back, so she jumped at the sudden opportunity to go!

In three days, Emily Anne and Carolyn had planned out a touring trip of Edinburgh, staying at the nearby Dalmahoy golf resort for two days, then north through the Highlands to Inverness, and finally on to Dornoch. For our returns, the O'Sullivans would go down the western section of northern Scotland from Nairn along Loch Ness to Glasgow, there to fly home. We would leave Nairn and go down the east side, stopping for a night in Aberdeen, another in St. Andrews, then onto Edinburgh for a return home from our original port of entry.

A few days later, QC Mary from Lloyds Legal called to talk about Martha in response to my e-mail I had sent her saying, among other things, that Martha was agreeable to our preceding discussion. In that call, I mentioned our trip to Scotland. She allowed that she was originally from Aberdeen. Perhaps, we could stay over an extra-night and she would join us for a round at her family's club. I asked if that would work well as a time for her to meet Martha, who had played for the USA in the first tournament in Ireland. We agreed to do just that. Lily made all of the needed changes for Carolyn and me as well as doing the bookings for Martha which included her flying down to London for follow-up meetings with Dr. Corbett McDonald and Julian Peto to catch up on the latest news about asbestos causation research and anything on lead causing diminution of IQ by virtue of lead dust exposure. The two of them had the most complete libraries of research: a worthwhile second task.

Sandra had managed to align the various interests in the Neptune companies, and to get the Ester-Tech counsel to agree to a private mediation, most likely in multiple sessions, to see if we could possibly get the two sides to a point where a resolution became a very real possibility. To facilitate this process, a hearing was set to resolve two motions by Neptune: first, that Punitive Damages were barred by the contract's language used to create that contract right, calling them, "A penalty." Second, that Liquidated Damages were barred by that same express language. We had a third motion in reserve on barring Attorney's Fees, but that seemed a risky initiative to undertake at that time if the mediation was to succeed.

Meanwhile, I spoke with Felicia and asked her to set up a brief call with the GWF executives after her running my idea to integrate the Neptune defective bait materials for use to isolate the GWF lots past our materials consultant and getting his tentative go-ahead on it. I also ran it past Strom Nordquist from GWF's insurer to explain the need for the steps we were taking to hopefully ameliorate GWF's potential continuing exposure from the fenced-in rubble areas they still owned (About four city blocks sprinkled around GWF's main facility). Meanwhile, both GWF and Neptune would have to know if this project was feasible, relying on their own materials expertise from among their people.

GWF's feedback was surprisingly fast: Andrea Parsons asked for a call ay 11:30 that very day. I was available for 90 minutes at that time. I asked Felicia, Martha and Deirdre to be on the call, and available when needed (I reminded everyone at the firm doing anything on either Neptune or GWF not to advocate any position publicly!).

When we took the call on our conference room speaker phone, I quickly told the GWF people who I had present. Andrea introduced their entire board, then three additional people and Stuart Brock, the GWF CLO.

She began, "Thank you, Ronan, Felicia, Martha, and whomsoever else at your firm who has worked to preserve GWF. This idea is truly interesting, and if testing bears out the potential promise you hold out as possibly existing, this idea may go a long way to insuring the future of our company. Now, Brock needs to say a few words on legal issues, and how we see them being handled in these close-quarters of your firm's dual representation.

Brock did just that, and it sounded very like the talks I had given over the past week or so. I asked Felicia to explain our firm's position on Mr. Brock's words. She did, "Mr. Brock's words are wise and they seriously echo the same admonitions given us by Ronan on multiple occasions about this very topic in this past week or so."

I polled the others from O'Neill Fox and they were in total agreement. Abraham Spence III took the floor, and he explained how they would be looking for one or more firms to assist in this novel undertaking. They had hired their own consultant to assist in that task and to assist in overseeing any testing of the Neptune materials. He added that they understood time was of the essence in all of this. The discussions continued for about forty minutes as myriad details were covered and a list of priorities for each entity was created.

Finally, Andrea Parsons closed, "Ronan, we want to thank you and the whole team at O'Neill Fox for your continuing support and insight on this matter. Please pass on our regards to Mr. Nordquist. As soon as we hear from you, we will begin to deal directly with the people at Neptune whom you designate. Even if this strategy fails as it moves forward, we will continue to appreciate these efforts.

Within two days, our Neptune team was assembled in that same conference room. Deirdre and I were the only two firm members in common with the GWF call. The five folks from Neptune all seemed nervous as they introduced themselves, until coming to their CEO/Founder, Adam Young (who did not use 'Senior" after his name). He stated, "Good to hear your voice again, Ronan. Your first agenda item is Assets at Risk. Please begin."

I nodded to Sandra and she went through each area of

claimed loss by both parties, and finished with the warehouses full of distressed (read 'useless') failed bait created with the Ester-Tech licensed formula as a component, all of the wasted storage space on a continuing basis, and other product and handling expenditures, plus claims for rebates, together yielded an eight figure number. I could only imagine Everson Harris cringing at this point.

When Sandra stopped, I quickly picked up the string of thought, "One question: if I could provide you all with a potential buyer for all of your useless bait, albeit not for use as bait, and at a substantial discount on its book value amount being carried, would you all be interested?"

Before Adam Young could speak up, Everson Harris jumped in, "Mr. O'Neill, I have never been a big fan of lawyers, but if you have something like that, please tell us?"

A moment of silence, then the Neptune CEO spoke, "Please tell us what you can?"

I proceeded very carefully. First, warning them that what we could say was limited for fear of creating any conflict of interest. I continued, "Our firm has another client that might have a very different use for that product you all seem to have created. An entirely different potential use. Since we represent you both as clients, we are in the position of an actual potential conflict of interest in going forward to explain the whole thing as it might be envisioned. So, before I proceed, I need you all to agree that what I tell you will not be used to assert that an actual conflict was created at some point in the future."

A few moments of silence followed: NO doubt—the mute button on the Neptune end.

Leslie Worth, the Neptune parent's General Counsel, spoke, "I have explained further at this end. And we all agree, 'No conflict exists for the rest of this call, now or going into the future.' Please proceed, Ronan."

Surprised I was suddenly on a first name basis, I did proceed, "Our other client is Great Western Foundry, located near Sacramento. If they can test some of your product, they could well buy it all for a present and future use. That would create cash for you on one hand and relieve you of on-going expense on another. No doubt that you would be unlikely to recover close to one hundred per cent of the book value, but it would have a possible long-range benefit, which might assist in a possible settlement with Ester-Tech. To avoid any further potential for conflict, their executives are prepared to deal directly with yours. I would suggest both companies' general counsel-types might initiate that negotiation."

Neptune's agreement followed after addressing a few minor questions. We gave them the needed GWF info sheet and Leslie Worth allowed she would send theirs directly to Andrea Parsons and Stuart Brock and that level would facilitate all further negotiations, with any further action by O'Neill Fox being severely limited to bare administration, if anything.

We then went into other areas to prepare for the upcoming mediation. After we hung up, Sandra shook her head and said, "This was such an amazing day. By starting with something potentially beneficial to them, you won over the whole Neptune team. We ultimately may get this thing to settle!" I just smiled as Sandra picked up her things and left, without further *adieu*.

While all of these tasks were being accomplished, I was working with the ACLN Board to add new members and to effectuate changes needed to accommodate the diverse member groupings. This was proving sometimes tedious for me, but Lily with her marvelous organizational skills was delighted to be involved. (She kept every nuance in perfect order for Reggie and me. So, I never complained to her.) As for that group's Annual Meeting in Chicago, the Midwestern leaders had all those preparations under control. (The meeting leaders' spouses seemed to lean a bit on Carolyn; but she never complained, even when she was working on her career out-of-town, or even out-of-country.)

– – –

Myriad other marketing and litigation matters were going on as well, chief among them, the new STP matter. Apparently, one of the defendants in that suit filed in the federal court for Northern California in San Jose, was not involved in any of the San Mateo test chamber flooding disaster. That party, located near Boston had just filed a Motion to Dismiss for Lack of Venue (in other words, that fire system testing company had no California presence and sought to have that suit dismissed in its entirety). From N2AS perspective, that moving company was the number two defendant on the New Hampshire chamber flooding event, making it extremely necessary lest STP, the number one, would try to shift all blame on an absent party. So, N2AS could not simply dismiss that party. The result was a sixty day stay from the court to try to have the parties work things out. This created a dilemma for N2AS. Martha and I conferred on how it might be handled, but decided to do nothing unless asked. Of course, we kept the client, its parent and its carrier fully informed, and they acquiesced in that we should proceed per our plan which Martha and I had laid out.

We had explained that these two cases were not going to go away easily. The records we had from both facilities showed nothing at this point to establish that N2AS personnel at either facility had undertaken any testing whatsoever of either telescoping sprinkler system (TSS). Moreover, the N2AS maintenance records for each chamber were skimpy, at best. Simply put, any testing to-date had only been of the alarm system, with no water actually entering each piping system so as to cause deployment; and in each instance, that alarm testing had somehow become the triggering event causing the TSS to deploy.

Each accidental deployment was only possible when water actually entered the entire system (to compress the air in the piping actually causing a designed deployment), and there was a manual shut-off valve on each system to prevent that very event from happening during any alarm testing. That valve either failed or was not turned on. Of course, neither valve had been produced as yet. We had made a formal request that all evidence be preserved, and had specifically requested an opportunity to have our defense team inspect each site, including all parts in use on each failure day. (We were fairly confident from our own sources involved in the repairs of each chamber that evidence was neither preserved intact, nor any real effort made to photograph or inventory all of the components removed, or replaced, from each damaged system. Our STP people on scene in each instance had not been briefed on making any type of record of evidence! Not great for our side, and another reason to do nothing additional at that point in time.)

With no real discovery, this was about the extent of our knowledge as to how each incident might have occurred. Then we waited almost three weeks to hear from the

Plaintiff's counsel seeking any agreeable input on potential resolutions for the New Hampshire defendant's motion. The long week in which we had agreed to accompany the O'Sullivan's to preview the courses in the Inverness area of Northern Scotland and to try out the area of the next tournament site was almost upon us. The next day, Sandra appeared and told me that Roger Salmon of Best, Smith & Salmon, counsel for N2AS, was calling to discuss options.

We listened to him for twenty minutes and he had expressed no truly viable option. Finally, I interjected, "Roger, we've been doing this a long time. No amount of willingness to stipulate to things will get this done. As your suit is currently constructed, you are staring a dismissal in the face with all the potential negatives which might follow. We have only one outcome to which we have authority to stipulate. You all need to move to sever your two claims into two separate actions, including a request that the New Hampshire claim be sent to the Eastern District Court in Boston, since you acknowledge that the New Hampshire defendant has its principal place of business there. That's what we can do. I'll be out of town for almost two weeks. Sandra will be around."

He had a few questions, thanked us, and said he'd get back. I told Sandra that Admiral Electric and STP should not want a second set of counsel for New England. So, it was paramount that the transfer be to Boston as too much travel time would be added getting to a federal court in New Hampshire. Also, I told her that if Roger filed a response to the venue motion, essentially admitting the need for the severance, that he would be worried about getting sued for malpractice if either claim turned out to be time-barred, afterward. She agreed with me, and we said our good-byes.

The Writ Petitions in the GWF discovery matter were

granted, with merits briefing to get underway. That time would allow Neptune to pursue its potential solution to one cash-bleeding area, if successful; the mediation would be getting started not long after I returned.

21

SCOTLAND: WHAT A DELIGHTFUL SURPRISE

Carolyn and I flew to Chicago and then on to Edinburgh. John and Emily Anne joined us for that long-leg of our two flights. We had a van meet us at the baggage claim, after being whisked through Passport Control, then Customs and on to the Dalmahoy. An aging estate still of great magnificence, just southeast of Edinburgh, in a countryside setting with a modern golf course as well as pastures with iconic cattle, also sheep, on the long driveway to the elegant Manor House, with many modern rooms attached.

Having arrived by mid-afternoon, Carolyn and Emma, as she asked to be called for this trip, had booked a tour of the Edinburgh Castle and the Royal Mile with dinner at its end in a fancy, but tourist casual, gastro-pub. A quick shower and change and we were on our way, finding ourselves amongst the last of that day's tourists to visit the formal rooms of the Castle, and its magnificent gift shop (deliveries easily arranged to the Dalmahoy). Not all of the shops and pubs on the Royal Mile were open, but enough for a couple of half pints and a few more souvenirs. The Capitol Gastropub was located two blocks short of Holyrood House, the Queen's Royal Palace and her seat for governing Scotland, but it was growing dark, so we cut our walk short.

John and I had decided to try at least one novel Scotch whiskey each day. We tried our first before that dinner. The one recommended by the barman from Islay was a bit heavy with too much smokiness, which I could not finish. So, I quickly followed it with a large pour of Macallan's 18, far more satisfactory. John followed my choice. Then, John and I settled back, sipped our drinks, and listened to the ladies as they aligned our meal and went on about a wide variety of topics. Carolyn had an endless repertoire of stories about all of the children, especially our Molly. John and Emma had no children, but she was on good terms with his three by his first wife Ruth. (Who was remarried having no desire whatsoever to leave New England and move to the desert. John did an hilarious imitation of Ruth telling him that "....if that's what you want to do, then you can go and do it, but you will be doing it without me!"). We all enjoyed John's sense of humor.

A one drink nightcap in a not very busy bar at the Dalmahoy, and we were off to bed. We both fell asleep almost instantly. When the phone rang at six a.m. to wake us, Carolyn struggled to answer it, but rejected my plea for a call-back in 30 minutes. She got up and made her way to a quick shower, then insisted I get a move on for our Scot's breakfast that was part of the "B and B" package that we had both booked (No reservations for tables!) and she feared a line of guests to be seated. Almost miraculously, I was ready within minutes of her, and we arrived at the Dining Rom at 6:36, nine minutes early. There was only one couple in line, then it was our turn. When we asked for a table for four, the Food Manager came over and explained that we all needed to be present to be seated. We listened patiently, then I interjected, "Might you get this Hotel's manager here right now, so we can clarify his policy which you have sprung on us?"

She looked askance, "What do you mean? This is very standard in the British Isles."

"Please get the Hotel Manager. It is not standard in London, nor Oxford. It is not in your advertisement for B and B; nor was it mentioned last night, when we asked for a reservation. No one at your front desk mentioned this process. We consider you in violation of good tourist procedure, and not being professional. Please get your manager," I said all of that in slow measured tones.

She looked at the people queuing behind us, and relented, taking us to a round window table for four, saying, "Please all come together tomorrow."

I responded, "When your Hotel Manager arrives, please send for me and I shall meet with him at your desk at this room's entrance. Thank you."

After breakfast, we had a very civilized discussion about the need for notice, and that rule enforcement without courtesy or understanding could very quickly undermine the goodwill needed for a hospitality enterprise. I suggested that his seating hostess, and the Food Manager, might have a nicer demeanor and a little prepared speech for people like us who were taken unaware of their seating protocol, like, "We'll seat you today. But in the future, we would ask that your whole party be present as our guests are seated on a 'first come, first seated' basis." He seemed to think for a second, then said, "That woman facing me looks famous?"

"She is, and she is my wife." I smiled at him.

He thought again, "Perhaps you will be my guests for dinner tonight?"

I paused, "How about a few drinks and bite or two after golf? We are set to go to a highly recommended seafood restaurant on the Glasgow Canal tonight, but thank you for that offer." We shook and parted amicably.

The Old Course at the Dalmahoy, although not on the coast, had many of the characteristics of links golf (although not nearly as well tended as was Pebble Beach). The grasses were all different and the areas off the rough were not much cared-for, and each of us lost at least one ball on an errant shot. We had a caddy for the foursome and he was incredibly helpful, but we were clearly suffering from jet lag and the eight hour time adjustment made the back nine (which was more difficult than the first nine holes) a fairly tedious experience. That said, our collective sense of humor was fully triggered on the 17th hole. Our caddy explained where we should try to put our drives as that hole had a ninety-degree dogleg to the right for the second shot. What he did not tell us on the tee was all about the hazards we were to face for the second shot.

Emily's ball was just off the left side of the fairway. Carolyn and John had shots from the middle of the fairway. I had driven mine a bit to the right with a gentle fade at about 200 yards, perhaps a bit too far. As we drove our carts to those balls, trees lined the right side of the fairway for the first 150-160 yards, then came a giant opening of no trees, but what emerged from the tree cover was an ancient stone wall, the likes of which we had seen on that course a few times, but not directly in the path of play. It was at least four feet high and in excellent condition. My ball was bout ten feet from that wall, right in line with the hole about 180 yards away, across a deep chasm, just beyond the wall extending close to 100 yards of carry. "Oh my!" was my first thought. The caddy looked at me and shook his head, saying, "I am sorry, Mr. O'Neill, but this wall is part of the course, so there is no relief."

My jaw felt like it had fallen-off. For only the second time on my life, I needed to hit my ball 180 degrees away from its intended target. As I selected my seven iron to hit that shot, I began to laugh, then I said, "How about high score on this hole buys our drinks afterward?" John laughed in response and those three readily agreed.

Emily was actually away, played her five-rescue club and drove to within twenty yards of that green, clearing all of the trouble. Carolyn hit her four iron about ten yards short of the green. The women were poised to win that hole and halve our match. John's ball was about fifteen yards further back than my ball. He chose his five-iron. He looked at me, shrugging his shoulders. I Said, "Why not go for it. No telling what's going to happen to me."

John had a clean line but for the wall. His ball strike was solid, but its flight was millimeters too low. It skimmed the very top of the wall and continued toward the hole only to die as it neared the far edge of the chasm. He asked our caddy what came next. To which, he replied, "The good news is there's a drop-zone. The bad news is it's not an easy shot."

I pitched my shot to within about ten yards of where Emily's drive had come to rest. Still my turn, I chose my five-rescue, hitting it too well, and off the back of the 17th green. Our caddy shook his head, then said, "Almost a great shot. Unfortunately, a result you may find unjust." At that point, I laughed, and the others joined in.

We drove along the wall for about another thirty yards, more trees on the right, then a break in the trees and the wall, and we turned right. The caddy was on the back of the Men's cart in the lead. The chasm was to our right. After going forward about twenty yards from the break, our caddy said to slide the cart slightly to the right and prepare to stop. Just ahead, on a precipice to the chasm were a series of small yellow stakes outlining a drop-zone. John got out of the passenger seat. Carolyn pulled the Ladies' cart slightly ahead of ours. As John took the seven-iron and walked to the hitting zone, Emma said, "Poor John, this is the reason I do not love golf. It can be such a cruel game."

John eyed his line to the pin which included much of the chasm, a brief green area, then a deep greenside sand trap, with the pin behind all of that. He strode to the place of his stance, placed his tee, then his ball. John stepped back for a last look at his line, two practice swings, then took his stance. He turned to the four of us, and said, in a calm voice, "Hitting four." His ball contact sounded good. His ball flew straight and true toward the elevated green. It seemed to carry over the intervening sand trap. We could not see it down, but our caddy, as he walked ahead, yelled back, "Great shot, Mr. O'Sullivan!"

We had a fine time finishing 17, and 18 was straight forward, ending with a tie between the teams. The Hotel's Manager was waiting for us when we left our carts. He greeted us by names, and was only too pleased to be asked to join us for the first round of cocktails. We talked The Golf briefly, but then he bent the conversation toward our occupations 'back in the States.'

His purpose appeared to be to get Carolyn to explain why she might be famous, but she had played this game for her whole adult life, and told him, "I invest in real estate refurbishments in Marin County, California. That's the area on the other side of the Golden Gate Bridge from San Francisco. I find it very interesting and satisfying."

After twenty minutes of varying chatter, including good places to stop suggestions on the highway through the

Highlands, the Manager asked for a selfie with the four of us to show his wife. (The next morning at our check-out, he was there to say good-bye, and introduce his wife, "This is my wife, Nancy. She wanted to meet Mrs. O'Neill whom she believes was in a *Vogue* Christmas issue shot in Paris under the name Carolyn Tyne. She also recognized you, Mr. O'Neill. The wife chatted for a couple of minutes. As always, Carolyn was gracious.)

After what had been a splendid evening and an early Continental breakfast, we departed the next day, for the Highlands, Inverness and ultimately Dornoch. We stopped at two distilleries on the way, well up in the Highlands about 75 minutes apart, and had a late snack in a pub on the southern edge of Inverness. The drive had far too many striking vistas to even contemplate listing them off. In all, we were quite happy with how the ladies had planned our foray northward. John asked me to take the lead on our final stretch of forty-something kilometers to the town of Dornoch. The road paralleled the shoreline as we climbed a gradual hill, slowly becoming a small mountain and to our right, overlooking an expanding body of water below. Becoming a huge bay. Carolyn was charmed, saying, "Oh, Ronan, this all so spectacular, more so than I had ever imagined it would be. That bay below is Moray Firth, guarded against invasion by Catholic Kings by the Black Watch Regiment, staged here and in a fort on the far shore with much artillery."

"You have certainly prepared as the historian as well as the navigator for this adventure. I love it," I told my beautiful wife, meaning every word.

"I also found a gentleman who is a member of one of our clubs and also at Royal Dornoch. Quite reasonable dues for Americans. He passed along some advice about the course, and caddies. He also said he would call the Golf Hotel and the Starter to tell them about us. Very nice man, Herb Scott." A pause, and she added, "He said to play our shots low, mind the wind and the greens tend to be hard and fast within two days after the last rain."

I smiled to myself as I listened to her go on about this and that. Finally, we began to round another turn and I could look across a different bay, smaller, and see a road parallel to the one on which we were driving. Carolyn, "This must be the Firth of Dornoch."

In a few miles, a sign announced the Royal Town of Dornoch. Underneath its name: The Birthplace and Generational Home of Andrew Carnegie. The entrance to the town itself was amazing, like going back more than 100 years. The stone buildings all multi-storied with slate roofs. The trees and foliage, large, robust and gorgeous—a postcard!

A Handsome sign read The Royal Links at Dornoch and The Dornoch Golf Hotel, Go Right.

We turned to the right. John was immediately behind me. In a few hundred yards, I pulled to a stop in front of the entrance to the hotel. Less than fifty yards ahead of my rental SUV was the starter shack for the golf course, out beyond it was the Firth of Dornoch below.

A footman came down the streps to greet us, "You all must be the O'Neil's and the O'Sullivan's. Mr. Scott called a few days ago to discuss your stay here with us. Please leave your keys and we'll see to your clubs, the cars, and, of course, your luggage. My name is Gary Stuart, an owner and a family member from around these parts for hundreds of years. Please come in.

Gary showed us to a desk. He bade all four of us sit and a real footman appeared with bottles of water and glasses, asking if we preferred still or sparkling. Gary allowed that all of our paperwork was in order and asked each lady to sign, acknowledging that they had made the arrangements. "We have upgraded both couples to two of our nicest suites, both have Firth views. Mr. & Mrs. O'Sullivan, you shall have Room 505. The elevator only goes to the Fourth floor, so I am afraid, you shall have to walk up one flight. Mr. and Mrs. O'Neill, I am sorry, but you will have to do two flights. Your suite, Room 605, is not quite ready. The prior guests were two avid American golfers. Perhaps you have heard of them, Michael Douglas and his wife, Catherine Zeta-Jones. They were only going as far as Nairn, so they were a bit slow in leaving. An utterly charming couple I might add. Please let me invite you all to the veranda for a glass to get the dust of your drive off while we bide a few minutes?"

Our introduction to Dornoch by Gary Stuart was typical of our time spent in this tiny idyllic corner of Scotland. We had gone into this mini-adventure not at all certain of what to expect, and our time there was so rewarding that we did not wish to hasten our departure in the slightest.

The number one highlight was the golf course itself, an up and down layout with obstacles of all natural descriptions guarding each hole: mini-canyons, marsh-carries, cliff-to-cliff shots, fairways of all different widths, and penalties aplenty if care were not exercised. On top of that were the views on the course itself, its surroundings with cliffs running down to the seas, the yellows contrasting against the differing greens of all of the alluring natural flora, the freshness of the sea air, and looking up into the clarity of the blueness of the sky. The Royal Naval Air Arm even appeared on a few occasions to salute the golfers as their jet fighters flew low, buzzing the fairways before reaching back out to the North Sea.

Then, there were the gracious, and often friendly, resident club members who were kind enough to invite us into their clubhouse and rejoice in Carolyn's befriending their fellow-member, Herb Scott of Napa, California, who apparently gifted many of them with bottles of ultra-high-end Cabernet Sauvignon, earning him a celebrated nickname of "that Generous Herb!"

John and Emma, like us, felt that this exploratory foray had served to validate Stanley Booth's choice of this course and this area as a superlative site for the third venue for our continuing international matches. These two added factors bought us more rounds from the Clubhouse members as apparently Stanley was a great favorite of his fellow-members as well as a benefactor of the Club itself. They also seemed truly fond of Yanks, with several women member golfers spending time with Carolyn and Emma (Apparently they were waging a crusade to add women's tee boxes on several of the ultra-long driving holes).

So, we spent two more days playing golf and one touring, then it was time to head down to Nairn. Leaving was difficult, but made easier by Gary Scott's presence, with his wife, and the knowledge that we would return in four months at the end of their short Summer season. A few photographs and they waived us away. Carolyn was bubbly as we drove away, "Virginia Stuart was so sweet. I hope we get to see more of them when we return. She knows who I am, but said she would keep it to herself lest the other women in the Clubhouse set become excited and pester me when we return. Did you ask if Gary was in any way related to the Stuart peers of Scotland?"

We chatted away and were in Inverness in seemingly no time. As we headed east out of that city, we stopped for lunch at a colorful pub recommended by Gary. Great view of the Firth and a pleasant greeting from our hosts, warned in advance of our arrival. The greeters were interested in our itinerary, which consisted of a round at the Nairn Golf Club, famous as a frequent host of the Walker Cup (essentially an amateur analog for the Ryder Cup, predating it as was the fashion almost a century ago) before the legitimization of professional golf through the heroics of Bobby Jones' Grand Slam (Jones was, and remained for his career, an amateur) and his ensuing rivalry with the first great American pro, Walter Hagen, who went far to preventing a second grand slam during the remainder of Jones's relatively short career. Of course, our local company were able to add British names to Jones' prime opposition, but no one contradicted the Walter Hagen effect on the game's changing fortunes.

These ever so polite Pub intervenors did offer a number of suggestions for our one non-golfing day. Two of which seemed worthwhile to the four of us, especially because they were so close to each other: a visit to Cawdor Castle and its gardens, one of the main sites of Shakespeare's *MacBeth*; and, Fort George, home base of the Black Watch Regiment, still active (Carolyn was thrilled with that prospect as a potential site for a future shoot. As she said, stirring Emma's enthusiasm, "That tartan pattern never goes out of style!").

We easily found the Nairn Hotel by following the signs to the golf course. It was a few hundred yards away on a knoll overlooking the Firth of Moray, as did that course. These were to be our last three days with John and Emma, but they were bound and determined to see Loch Ness and take a boat tour looking for that sea serpent. Our time together seemed as magical as that in Dornoch, and flew past. The Nairn Course was far different from lofty Royal Dornoch perched high on its peninsula, being difficult in its construction, particularly the small water channels, called 'burns,' crossing the fairways that would swallow a ball in play if not avoided (almost impossible to locate them if not an experienced player). That was what required a caddy! But it was the Cawdor Castle (magnificently decorated) with an excellent guide, not to mention the blooming formal gardens; but also, the Fort held us all in thrall. My being an American military officer was all it took to get us a private tour from a very senior sergeant. At the end of the three hours, we were well exercised and filled with that area's history from the English perspective (they still did not trust the Scots!). Carolyn could not wait to share her photos with *Vogue's* Robert as their prime magazine's European issue had trouble finding appropriate shoot sites in the British Isles.

Then came our parting: Quite frankly, Carolyn and I had become very fond of John and Emma O'Sullivan. So, when that morning came for them to head west toward Loch Ness and us a bit east, then south, to Aberdeen, there were a few uncomfortable moments in our parting, especially for the ladies. Emma was openly admiring of Carolyn and she carried their friendship on her sleeve. I never discussed this with John, lest he might perceive my thinking him jealous, or impute some negativity to their friendship in his eyes. At any rate, their SUV was loaded before ours and we stood outside the Nairn Hotel to bid them good-bye. After a lengthy verbal interchange, Carolyn moved quickly to John, put out her arms and gave him a hug of affection. I had never seen her do that with any business friend of mine, not even most in our firm. Then she went around to the passenger door where Emma stood. They embraced for a long minute. Carolyn backed away, but her hands still held Emma's shoulders, and we could all hear her words, "Emma Dear, we may be out of touch or a few days, but we'll all be home soon, and we'll be in touch no later than then. Have a great time exploring and be sure you make special memories with your John. Love you!"

With that she helped Emma into her seat and closed the SUV door. I was already shaking John's hand as he got himself ready to depart. (We had parted often so this was no big deal for us.) Then they were gone right down the street, one right turn and next stop the Inverness Circle and the road west to Loch Ness.

We departed not many minutes later, making a left turn where the O'Sullivan's had turned right, whereupon Carolyn opened up at last about Emma, in a slow, soft, thoughtful voice, "I believe that Emma does not know what it means to be married to John. I think she tries to love him, but he has so much going on in his life, and their ages are so different, that she feels their relationship is just not maturing into what she hoped it would become. She is afraid of him. Not in a physical sense, but intellectually and emotionally. I fear I have become if not her best friend, certainly her confidante. I'm not terribly comfortable in that role because of your business relationship with John. That's why the big hug for him. I've known him longer, and I do not want him to think I will do anything to influence Emma negatively toward her relationship with him. I hope you are trying to understand what I am trying to explain? I just feel so, ..so unable to break through to Emma."

When she drew in her breath, I interjected, "Carolyn, I am always more amazed by the things you do, and the life you lead, and that you include me so much in your time and create our interesting life together. When I see our Mollie, and I think of my Mollie, I can only tell you that between you and her, I was fortunate to have two saints looking out for me in my life. Now, I think what you are telling me is you will try to be a saint in the lives of the O'Sullivan's. I would never think of telling you not to do that, but I am asking that you be very careful. I still harbor the suspicion that Emma would perhaps like to have a physical relationship with you. I hope not, but that is a very dangerous area."

"Believe me, Ronan, when I say that you may be correct. But in Emma's case, she holds me in such regard that I believe she simply will not, perhaps cannot, bring herself to act on that feeling. Moreover, I am not certain that she consciencely knows that is what she wants. That's why I go to so much trouble to encourage our relationship as a very open, not secret, friendship; and, no more." I glanced over at Carolyn. She was shifted in her seat, talking to me in her most serious tone. As I looked back at the road, I thought to myself, "God, I love this woman!"

When I explained all of this business with the O'Sullivan's, as well as my adventures with the New Lloyds, to Dr. Arnaud, she spent a long session listening. She made notes. Finally, she offered, "I am not Carolyn's mental health care provider. But because of you, we are friendly. What you have told me is something that sounds to me, as if you wish it would all just go away. But, of course, you know that will not be the case. Let me just ask you to consider one thing before you leave, and we'll discuss it when next we meet: How many things that really matter of whatever nature has Carolyn gotten wrong in her dealings with you?"

22

ALL THOSE LOOSE ENDS

As we drove past the road to the Queen's Scottish retreat, Balmoral Castle with its huge mountainous estate, we began heading south. Aberdeen was not that far, and we arrived at our hotel a bit early for check-in. Not surprisingly, Martha was sitting in the coffee area of the lobby waiting as well. She had decided to hire an *au pair* to care for Michael Francis whilst attempting to expand our role with the Lloyds Legal Office. After all, an expanding workload on coverage issues would benefit her life partner, Mary Smith. She rose as we entered, hugged Carolyn with *faux* cheek kisses, and gave me a handshake, cheek -kiss, and half-hearted hug. "Oh, I am so tired. What a trip! The Red Eye to Heathrow was difficult, the connection rushed, but the taxi ride to here was crazy! The driver said this hotel was among the most centrally located in this city, but all the one-way streets make London look more sane than it really is. Anyhow, you two have found me." With that, a bellman of sorts appeared with a key and her suitcase. With little *adieu,* Martha departed to meet us at 3:30 in the Lobby whereupon QC Mary was to pick us up for a tour of her city.

Carolyn smiled, "Ronan, it's very sweet and thoughtful of you to include Martha in this Lloyds thing, especially after all of the effort you've put into it."

I paused a few seconds before responding (No flags about Martha in front of Carolyn.),

"You know that Martha was a major resource in creating the relationships in our science and medicine defense of CAL Board, especially all of the detail work and hours of preparation as expert witnesses for Julian Peto and Corbett McDonald. Plus, as a result of her limited input in organizing the Cheshire & Booth documents search, she has a great deal of knowledge and has come to understand the English more than the average American. Finally, I feel that if we can assist Mary Smith-Martin on American culture, that may help us beyond coverage and litigation. Maybe, if they become friendly, Martha may be able to have our firm enhance its role for Lloyds Legal. So, maybe this is all a bit selfish on my part."

Carolyn and I were riding up to our floor in their very small elevator as I finished that explanation. She looked at me. Smiled a big smile. Stepped right up to me, whispered, "You're so full of bullshit!" And, planted a big kiss on my lips that lasted until the elevator door was wide open.

The balance of our day was just great. Mary Smith-Martin was very proud of her Aberdeen. First, she took us on a walking tour which quickly disclosed why our hotel was so popular with the locals (There were a series of cut-throughs between groups of buildings which allowed our group to emerge onto several of that City's main streets without having to encounter heavy foot traffic and the barrage of automotive sounds on one of Aberdeen's very few two-way streets. Also, any number of stores, shops and retail complexes had entrances on both streets. Ultimately, we ended this walking foray at an outdoor memorial/museum featuring General Charles George Gordon, Commander of the British Forces at the Siege of Khartoum, Sudan, in 1884-85. A solemn place, but somehow I kept looking for a resemblance to

Charlton Heston from the biographical movie about that tragedy. Nonetheless: very moving.

Our hostess allowed that we needed a short break to allow the rush hour to dissipate. She was spending some time focusing on Martha and her recent motherhood. When we returned to the hotel, Mary said, "Tomorrow, I shall bring all of you to my club after breakfast. We shall play nine holes, then break for a light lunch. After the eighteenth hole, there will be a light cocktail hour, we shall change in the locker rooms, coats and dresses/skirts are required. The whole of the day, including dinner, will be my treat. Afterward, I shall return you all to here. Martha has agreed to join me for two additional days in London. Ronan, I do hope that will not cause any problems?"

"Tonight, I am taking you all to one of the most obscure, yet renowned, seafood restaurants in all of the UK, called The Silver Darling. I do hope you all shall enjoy it. It's my most favorite restaurant in the world!"

We changed to sporty casual for that dinner, and Mary returned at 7:00 to drive us to our 8:00 dinner reservation. The route was not anything like we were expecting. Within ten minutes, we entered the huge official Port of Aberdeen. Ships, piers, warehouses were everywhere as Mary maneuvered her SUV knowingly through them proceeding ever-eastward. Finally, after many minutes, we came to a finger of a jetty with a short pier, then a lighthouse at its very end.

Huge ships were tied up across this waterway on the far side of this harbor's entrance. Clearly, this was *the* seaport for the support of British Petroleum's North Sea Drilling Venture. Mary went slowly as we proceeded toward the lighthouse, then another structure, set back from that beacon, emerged. It was two stories with the top floor framed in glass, with each vertical panel topped by a triangular glass section moving upward at a forty-five degree angle to form a point topped by a sea creature wrapped around a pole of sorts. A small sign said Silver Darling, next line: Seafood. Mary pulled next to that building and parked. We exited the SUV, went inside and up a delightful curving staircase to a magically lit dining room where a table for four in front of a window overlooking that Harbor's entrance awaited us. I was stunned, "Mary, when you said unusual, that was a monumental understatement. I've never seen anything like this place!"

"Nor me!" chipped-in Carolyn.

The menu was incredible as was the maritime vessel show put on by the comings-and-goings of the vast British Petroleum North Sea fleet of crew boats (actually ships, by size) and drilling support craft. QC Mary, menu in hand, advised two courses each, and indicated that sharing, or tasting, of dishes was not frowned upon by the esoteric diners enjoying the studied pleasure of their meals amidst a very low level of conversation.

One glance of their Lobster, looking like Savannah-style, and I had my main course chosen. Appetizers included Oysters in Butter sauce, Clams and Mussels, separate dishes, both steamed, each said to have its own distinctive flavor. Whereupon, Mary held up her hand and suggested we start ordering our first course, each serving being a dozen or more; and, focus on our second. All except Mary opting for that Lobster. (We got that night's last three!).

Meanwhile, our cocktails arrived, and I asked for the wine list, an indication that I intended to pick up the tab for this feast. Mary, however, moved to intercept me. "Ronan, I appreciate your willingness to pay for this dinner, but with all of your travel, hotels, golf and other meals, this is the very least I can do. Besides, I have eaten many of the items on their menu and know well what is suited to accompany the choices made here tonight."

With that, Mary consulted with the restaurant's *sommelier* and ordered a series of wines, all whites, mostly French, one to accompany each choice ordered, or so it seemed. Mary pointed out that the Silver Darling's preparation was very deliberate, allowing all dishes in each course, where appropriate, to be served simultaneously. That would be true for our main course, but the appetizers would be served sequentially, with the intensity of flavor dictating the order of presentation and the accompanying wine.

For example, the Oysters were the first dish and as our final glass of wine was filled with the first bottle of French white, the lid of a large chaffing dish holding twelve oysters was removed, and its two attendants quickly placed three oysters on a plate the perfect size for each of us. Then the captain spooned a perfect amount of sauce onto each serving. A *"Bon Appetite!"* followed and we all began to immerse ourselves in an unparalleled culinary treat!

The conversations that evening were eclectic by topic, often tangentially related to someone's work, but never harsh, more explorational. The pace of the meal was slow enough to relish each course, but just quick enough to bring out the next dish in time to enjoy the next selected wine. What had turned into cocktails and four courses had taken us past ten o'clock. Still, I felt the need for something, I knew not what to put a capstone on the overall evening.

Mary spoke, "I'm fairly certain that no one wants to end this marvelous experience, but tomorrow is yet another day, and we have activities scheduled. So, if you all will indulge me, I shall put two small finishing touches for each of you and a final toast."

We all agreed with silent affirmation and four small plates with tiny portions of a cakelike object on each. Crisp, slightly sweet, more elegant with each of three bites and gone. As those plates were removed, they were replaced by saucers with small parfait glasses on each. Somewhat like a cross between ice cream and a popsicle in texture, yet sweet with a clarifying aftertaste, my palate felt cleansed, although not that it was in need of cleansing. Last came four small glasses, each containing a brown substance. Mary raised hers and said, "The English at sea had one drink that was consumed at every dinner, Commander, do you know the toast?"

"I'll do my best," was all I could respond, "Some years ago now, I had the opportunity to tour Lord Nelson's Flagship, HMS Victory in Portsmouth, I could imagine the officers gathered in his quarters at dinner the night before Trafalger, when he said, "We offer our Port wine in tribute to God, King, Country and Victory tomorrow!"

Mary smiled, and said, "Close enough. Certainly captured the spirit of the moment at the time when our nation ruled the seas. Thank you."

The next day was one more event than I was expecting. We did spend the bulk of the day at Mary's club, The Royal Links at Aberdeen. The golf was entertaining and the course's vistas ranged from gorgeous to spectacular, while the wind did play havoc with all of our golf games. Nonetheless, a successful stopover on our trip. I was greatly encouraged by QC Mary's invitation to Martha to stay on for a few days in London and to spend her time shadowing Mary whilst learning some of the operating details of Lloyds

Legal (I was to learn, eventually, that this time frame also proved to be the beginning of Mary's seduction of Martha, lasting over a period of years!).

Carolyn was feeling a mother's need to see her Mollie, and upon our return to our room asked if I would mind cutting some of our time short to return home. If she could get it arranged without great cost in travel time or money. Meanwhile, I had received a multi-page fax from Lily with a note from Felicia Clarke (quickly becoming a highly dependable *wunderkind)* which asked what she could do to help. I picked up the telephone and called Felicia (wo was the back-up for Martha and me on the N2AS matter while we were in Scotland). The Santa Clara Judge had tentatively agreed to sever the two insulation-destruction events in the single North American Aviation & Space Complaint into two separate cases and refer the New Hampshire claim to the Eastern District of Massachusetts (Boston). But only if all parties agreed to so stipulate. I told Carolyn what was happening, then called Felicia. Carolyn finished a call with our airline and shook her head: NO. I spent thirty minutes with Felicia. I did stress that cost-wise, Cayuga Mutual would be better off with our firm in Boston than bringing a second firm up to speed on the myriad details involved. Also, if a call was needed with Strom, I could get that done from Scotland as it was only a five-hour time difference.

By the time Carolyn and I arrived at St. Andrews, Felicia and I had completed all of the elements of our task to file Specialty Tech Products (STP)'s Stipulation timely and she was in touch with Ramona Kingsley to act as our local counsel in Boston. (When next I spoke with Strom, he offered that Felicia was an incredibly helpful young attorney who had a grip on what litigation issues were important to him and the ability to explain options for dealing with those issues.) We relaxed and toured the somewhat ancient town and had dinner overlooking the Old Course.

We enjoyed our last days together as just the two of us, but were delighted to be greeted by Mollie and Elsa at SFO, both awaiting us as we escaped U.S. Customs with no hold-ups!

As I may have mentioned in passing, Carolyn's avocation continued to be the restoration of once grand older houses in Marin County. Before we departed, she had made several inquiries and brought two of her sub-contractors to inspect a huge house with magnificent views on a Tiburon hillside westward-facing across an inlet in Richardson Bay separating the Tiburon Peninsula from the western mainland of southern Marin County at Mill Valley. Carolyn had left her real estate agent with a Limited Power of Attorney to negotiate, and if possible, close the purchase of that house which had been devastated by wind-driven rain leaking into the spaces in the walls through the window framings facing westward, causing serious dry rot throughout the walls and supports of the house (a massive rebuild!) Carolyn called it a 'million-dollar view' and she paid well less than that to take the house off the hands of the sellers who had unwisely trusted their son to act as their general contractor in building their huge precious retirement home.

On our flight home, she told me about that deal and how she looked forward to her new undertaking in Tiburon. I could only smile: she had her condo in Sausalito, our home in Ross and "our second home" in San Anselmo, and now this. For some years by-that time, she had me as a very silent partner backing her on any needed financing. But then, there were the eight or ten that she had already rehabbed and sold at huge profits in all but one case, and she did not suffer a loss on that one. (She always put some of her after-tax profits into the trusts or each of our children.) She added, "If Patrick Tyne does get paid to play professionally, I intend to let him invest in these enterprises as a relatively safe avenue to preserving some capital for him. What would you think?"

My response, as I reached over and gave her a quick kiss in our seats, "You have had great success sizing up your ventures and I have no reason to think you will fail with any one of them. But we have a history and you have built capital to undertake these types of ventures. Would Patrick become an entity investor, or just be in a single deal? I think that might prove important. What about you?"

"I feel explaining one deal is the best way to start. Our entity would require too much explanation, and his interest might be so small as to discourage him. We could do one or two deals, then talk entity, especially if he leaves his capital in place. Do you agree?" Carolyn gave me her small endearing smile. She had me.

— — —

Sandra and I had our initial session to mediate a resolution of the Neptune litigation. We were both on reasonably good terms with Amanda Tatum, lead counsel from Prescott & Sievers, LLP, Ester-Tech's counsel. In one of our pre-mediation calls, Sandra and I suggested that each side make a somewhat formal presentation of its opening mediation statement utilizing an electronic format, including multiple screens to give a life-like affect to each side's case, but not have the actual parties engage in commentary, rather limit that to the lawyers. After a week's reflection, our opposition had a few conditions, which we accepted, so it was decided to go forward, with the presentations on Day One, negotiations on the second day, and a third day, if needed/based on some progress. Absolute privilege was a cornerstone of the agreement.

Our mediator, retired Judge Isadore Greenberg, a highly experienced jurist and quite given to creating compromise in unpromising bitterly contested situations, was attending in the Plaintiff's counsel's office that first day. Adam Young, Jr. and Leslie Worth, Neptune's EVP/CFO and its GC, as well as Everson Harris, Neptune Fishing's CEO, would attend from our office. Ms. Tatum and her founding partner, George Prescott III would attend with Abdul Singh, plaintiff's sole owner and chief witness from their office in San Francisco.

Hyatt had purchased a small hotel on the Alameda Estuary at the west end of Jack London Square and our client guests stayed there. The proceedings were to begin at 10:30, allowing final presentations that morning, based on our final exchange of positions last Friday at 4:00. Being on East Coast time, the three guests had a very early breakfast and walked around the Square only to confront the very end of that morning's farmers' market which took place four days/week immediately to the east of the Square's buildings for several city blocks and just to the west of the main line of the Union Pacific RR, running across Webster Street on Third, right next to our office building.

The clients were in our lobby waiting when I arrived at 8:40. They could not wait to discuss all they had discovered at, and about, Jack London and his Square. We were enjoying our coffee in our mid-sized conference room overlooking the Estuary when Sandra joined us. We got to our client's opening positions by 9:30, and we agreed Sandra would make the entire presentation while I would be in reserve to take their comments and to do any needed counter-balancing to Ester-Tech objections/opposing positions.

Much to Ms. Tatum's obvious distress, her client, Mr. Singh, had demanded that he give his personal account of all that had transpired along with the e-mails and texts which he selected for the Power Point which his counsel had largely shared with their Friday position disclosure.

The number of notes passed to me, almost exclusively from Mr. Harris, disputed most of Mr. Singh's positions. I coded them and inserted the two-digit code on my document of their Power Point. When time came for the Plaintiff's damages, Ms. Tatum took over. She said virtually nothing new, so we were able to address their positions quickly after our opening statement from Sandra and the lunch break, which we each did.

Having agreed that we would retire for the balance of the afternoon without verbal input from the clients, both sides would begin tomorrow with their initial demand and offers on the first hand. A few minutes before 6:00, we five agreed that the time had come to repair to Scott's Seafood on the Estuary in the heart of the Square for a West Coast seafood dinner. I closely limited my alcoholic intake as I would drop Sandra at her co-op in the City, then drive to Ross using that route. We had a pleasant evening listening to stories of many of Neptune's successful ventures. Sandra had quite a few glasses of wine. I sensed she would have liked to stay, but persuaded her to leave with me. On the way to her home, on the Bay Bridge, she allowed, "Junior is a very handsome, well-spoken gentleman. Did you know he was separated from his wife?"

I thought for a minute before answering that, then, "Well, that must be true since she's probably in North Carolina. Who told you that?"

Sandra smiled, making a face I had never seen before, "Why Leslie Worth did. Without my asking. What do you think I took from that?"

I decided to let that dog lie right there!

When I got home and told Carolyn about Sandra's comments, she could not stop laughing. It proved contagious!

— — —

EPILOG

Some of the bigger cases in which I was involved as well as the various networking organizations, not to mention O'Neill Fox, all made the transition up to, and through, the millennial shift. Most of the people in my life grew older, and a few departed for good.

As I sit here bringing this novel to its end, I feel that at the most, I have one more in me. For that reason, I will tell you that with some small assistance from me of a legal nature, Carolyn was able to rebuild her huge house on that western-facing hill in Tiburon, and to sell it for a profit of well-more than one million dollars. After sharing three hundred thousand of that profit as a bonus with her three main subcontractors (building an ever-stronger bond for the future), she was looking at two more places: one with a bay view on a northeast facing hillside in Tiburon and the other on the steep Belvedere hillside overlooking Sam's party-deck, with a wharfage view of Downtown Tiburon.

Carolyn and "the girls" insisted that we take the family to Paris again for a final Twentieth Century Family Christmas. Three of those women now worked with Robert on French *Vogue* shoots part of that time. Robert had Christmas dinner with us at *Le Meurice's* dining room as did the Bignons. Patrick Tyne and Elsa went on to visit her family in Stockholm afterward that very evening. (Patrick for only two days as he needed to get back to Princeton to complete his final basketball season.)

We stopped in London for a few nights and took the rest of the family, including Maeve, to see *The Lion King* and then to dine at the Ivy in SoHo. We talked about seeing Princess Diana there some five years before, without Prince Charles, celebrating her birthday with a group of male friends. She had been all smiles that evening and took a moment to acknowledge our group of six, including Quincy, Will, Bradley, Madeline and Carolyn sitting nearby, by nodding to us and broadening her smile. None of us ever saw her alive again after that night at the Ivy.

TIBURON CHARACTERS

(Includes most Carryovers from SAUSALITO, MILL VALLEY, ROSS & SAN ANSELMO)

These pages display the main, recurring characters from SAUSALITO, MILL VALLEY, ROSS, SAN ANSELMO and this novel, TIBURON. The organization is by relationship to Ronan, then by place or event.

THE O'NEILL'S and Other MAJOR CHARACTERS

Robert Emmett O'Neill, Ronan's father, who dies in SAUSALITO

Mary Katherine (Kate) Garrity O'Neill, Ronan's Mother, Twice Widowed

Rose Mary (1940), Meaghan & Mary Clare (Twins, 1948), Ronan's siblings

Ronan Joseph O'Neill (1943), Autobiographer

Margot Arnaud, M.D. (UNK-2018), Ronan's psychiatrist for forty-three years; on her death,

> Ronan received all of her notes & tapes from their therapy sessions.
>
> Those materials provide much of the basis for these novels.

Mollie Phelan (1945), Ronan's Wife and Mother of their four children;

Highly successful applications designer in start-up days of EDP/teleprocessing;

Her brother, Chad (1943), a basketball teammate of Ronan at Georgetown;

Her father, a widower, marries Kate later in life (dies in ROSS)

Ronan & Mollie's Children: Maeve (1977), Robert (1979), Patrick & Meaghan (Twins, 1981)

Au Pairs: Yolanda (their first); Ingrid Johannsen (into *ROSS;* then in SAN ANSELMO), her sister, Elsa in ROSS and SAN ANSELMO); Gustav and Ludmilla, Ingrid & Elsa's Parents, and Helmut, their Brother (in ROSS); Esmeralda and Mercedes, Yolanda's Daughters (in ROSS and TIBURON)

— — —

Sandra Allen (1949), UC Hastings law student, becomes engaged to Ronan (in SAUSALITO);

Her father, Ken, senior partner in San Francisco law firm; (dies in MILL VALLEY):

Both serve as lead counsel for Wallboard Corp.

Ronan assists her in creating her own firm after her father dies.

Carolyn Tyne (1956), a fashion model and Ronan's first acquaintance in SAUSALITO with whom Ronan becomes evermore romantic; they marry after Mollie's death in ROSS.

Unknown to Ronan for a brief time, she has a son by

him, Patrick (1973)

Lisa/later Lisette- Carolyn's mentor and first lover, works in Paris

Vera—Carolyn's Connecticut lover and Patrick's "other mother"

Mollie—after marrying Ronan, their daughter born in SAN ANSELMO

Patrick Tyne, illegitimate son of Carolyn and Ronan (1973)

Raised in Connecticut on Carolyn and Vera's farm; Relocates to Sausalito with his mother, and meets Ronan for the first time, shortly before Mollie becomes fatally ill (ROSS).

Attends Princeton, Basketball All-American (SAN ANSELMO, TIBURON).

Marries Elsa Johannsen, Ingrid's sister, while playing for the NY Knicks, and retires to attend Yale Law School (BELVEDERE).

Maeve O'Neill, Ronan and Mollie's oldest child, and outstanding student

Begins Stanford at age 16, after 'advanced learning career' at SF University HS;

Becomes infatuated with *haute couture* photo-staging. (MILL VALLEY & ROSS);

While on family trip/Carolyn shoot in Europe offered an apprenticeship at *Vogue* by *Robert*, its most senior layout planner/managing photographer, lives in Paris part-time with Jean BIgnon, M.D., Head of INSERM, & his wife, Camille, and splits her continuing formal education with the *Sorbonne*.

(SAN ANSELMO, TIBURON)

Joel Tinker (1942) marries Elaine, Sandra's law school roommate, both UC Hastings grads.

Ronan's best friend and classmate during USCG active duty days. Lived in Sausalito. Assisted Ronan in getting his first law job at Klein Kelly in Oakland. Moves to D.C. to practice law to accommodate his wife's career and maintains long friendship and working relationship with Ronan and Klein Kelly.

Ronan's Team at O'Neill Fox (formerly Klein Kelly) at Jack London Square, Oakland

Reggie Fox (wife: Ginger), Partner; Phil Hassard (marries O'Neill nanny Ingrid in ROSS), Partner; Mary Smith, Partner; Martha Walsh, Senior Associate (Ronan's long -time mistress), becomes Partner in ROSS, (Has son. Michael Francis Walsh with Mary Smith, her S.O. in TIBURON); Joshua Small, Junior Partner in SAN ANSELMO, becomes Partner in TIBURON); Felicia Clarke, (Associate Attorney in ROSS; becomes Junior Partner, then Partner in TIBURON); Deirdre, Senior Paralegal; Lily Lynch, Senior Team Administrative Assistant.

Jerry Klein & Sean Kelly, original founding partners of Ronan's law firm (retire and sell their interest in the firm to its other partners in SAN ANSELMO)

— — —

Tinker's Team in D.C.: Mace Snow, older litigator; Tod Clifford, younger litigator; both partners

— — —

O'NEILL FOX NETWORKS

Society of Insurance/Civil Defense Counsel (SIDC)—Invitation only/Vetted/Honorary Organization –Ronan becomes a member in **MILL VALLEY**; Other Partners follow

American Civil Litigation Network (ACLN)- firm membership by invitation, following vetting

Ronan invited to be a founder and ACLN's first President (**TIBURON**).)

OTHER CO-FOUNDERS:

Fulton Finnerty (Abby) Pagliotti & Finnerty, Jersey City

Liam Callahan (Serena) Spruce, Callahan & Epstein, Chicago

Mark Westhoff (Barbara) Westhoff & Gordon, Atlanta

— — —

RONAN'S MAJOR CLIENTS

DESERT MUTUAL INSURANCE COMPANY (DMIC) - Scottsdale, Arizona (**WHOLE SERIES**)

Charles Ezra Sewell, President (CEO)

John O'Sullivan, Senior Vice President & Chief Actuary (COO, becomes CEO in SAN ANSELMO) 2d Wife: Emily Anne (Emma); Sean (Bud), son, Ohio State (TIBURON)

Dudley Chisholm, Vice President, Chief of Claims
Larry Decker, Assistant Vice President – Claims
Emmanuel (Manny) Garcia (wife: Esmeralda), Senior Manager, Major Claims, ultimately becomes SVP of Claims
Geraldine (Gerry) Dwyer, Chief, Casualty Claims (leaves for The Hartford, becomes EVP of Claims at Connecticut Indemnity (CI) in SAN ANSELMO)
Angela Lenovo, replaces Gerry Dwyer at DMIC
Richard (Richie) Goldberg, Claims Coverage

CAL BOARD PRODUCTS, INC. (CAL Board) – Sacramento, California (Ronan's major client along with DMIC, its Insurer):

Austin Smith, JD, Vice President and General Counsel

HANEY PUMPS, INC.—Auburn, New York (Largest Submersible Pump Manufacturer in U.S.A.)

Carey Crawford, VP and General Counsel

GREAT WESTERN FOUNDRY- Roseville, CA (Century Old Railroad Car Equipment Supplier)

See Below for Participants

CAYUGA MUTUAL CASUALTY INSURANCE, Seneca Falls, New York

Strom Nordquist, Western Regional Senior Adjuster, Glendale, CA

CONNECTICUT INDEMNITY (CI)—Glastonbury, CN (Spin-off from The Hartford)

Gerry Dwyer, Senior Executive Vice President (for Claims)
Phillip Stanczak, Vice President (for Claims)

— — —

RONAN'S MAJOR LITIGATIONS AND ASSIGNMENTS

WALLBOARD Corp. vs SF CASUALTY et al. ("*Wallboard*") {In SAUSALITO & MILL VALLEY}

Iconic Insurance Coverage case, venued in San Francisco
Coordinated with four other similar matters under Order of CA Judicial Counsel

WALLBOARD Corp. – San Francisco; Millard Granger, former Risk Manager

SF CASUALTY, San Francisco, immediately prior primary insurer (to DMIC) of WALLBOARD for multiple decades.

Hon. Isadore Greenberg, Judge, San Francisco Superior Court, jurist on the *Wallboard* and ultimately all other California Coordinated Asbestos Bodily Injury Insurance Coverage Litigation

Ken Allen, National Coordinating Counsel and Lead Trial Attorney for Plaintiff WALLBOARD
Sandra Allen, Ken's Partner and daughter, Co-Lead Attorney for WALLBOARD
Ronan O'Neill. Lead Trial Attorney for Defendant DMIC

— — —

Other NATIONAL COORDINATIONG COUNSEL (NCC) for Certain Other Defendants

NATIONAL GYPSUM – Abbott & Tweed, Philadelphia
Alicia Goines, Lead NCC Coordinator
Leonard Tweed, Co-Lead NCC

UNITED STATES GYPSUM – Bigstrom & Steel, Philadelphia
Fred Talcott, Lead NCC
Melinda Sykes & Adam Morris, Co-Lead Counsel

W.R. GRACE – Black, Weiss & Marsh, New York City
Alan Maycroft, Lead NCC
Dexter Wells, Co-Lead Counsel

INTERNATIONAL ASBESTOS BROKERS—Williams, Spencer & Wright, Philadelphia
Brad Eustace, Lead NCC and Lawyer Liaison to Third Circuit Court of Appeals

— — —

ASBESTOS IN BUILDINGS MAJOR CASES ("BUILDINGS CASES")

***MULLEN* CLASS ACTION**, Martinez, California Superior Court {**In MILL VALLEY**}
Dismissed on Defendants' Joint Demurrer Motion.

Judge: Hon. John Kendall

Marvin Jones, Plaintiff Lead Attorney

Ronan O'Neill for CAL Board, Co-Lead Defense Attorney

Ken Allen for Wallboard, Co-Lead Defense Attorney

– – –

LOS ANGELES UNIFIED SCHOOL DISTRICT ACTION (*LAUSD*), Los Angeles, California Superior Court, Central District **{In MILL VALLEY & ROSS}**

Judge: Hon. Bernard Weitzman

Charlie O'Reilly, Plaintiff Lead Attorney

Abel Stoneman, Co-Lead Attorney with O'Reilly

Avery Schein, Glass, Schein & Shea for National Gypsum, Lead Defense Coordinating Attorney

Rod Gorman, Glass Schein, Co-Lead Defense Trial Attorney

Ronan O'Neill for CAL Board, Co-Lead Defense /Trial Attorney

– – –

CONSOLIDATED SCHOOLS CLASS ACTION (SCHOOLS), U.S. District Court, Philadelphia, PA. **{In MILL VALLEY, ROSS & SAN ANSELMO}**

Judge: Hon. James McGirr Kelly, Article III Judge

Hon. Marvin W. Oliver III (succeeds J. Kelly after his Recusal by Third Circuit)

David Berger, Lead Attorney for Plaintiff Lancaster

School District
Ron Motley, Lead Attorney for Plaintiff Spartanburg School District
Scott Kelly, Lead Local CAL Board Attorney
Ted Darrow, Co-Lead Local CAL Board Attorney
OTHER NCCs, above, plus Ronan O'Neill as NCC for CAL Board and
Ken Allen and Sandra Allen as NCC for Wallboard

Consultant for CAL Board to US EPA:
ARCHIBALD COX, former United States Solicitor General and Law Professor, Yale Univ.

———

CENTRAL WESLEYAN COLLEGE CLASS ACTION, replaces the dismissed {**In MILL VALLEY**} **CLEMSON UNIVERSITY CLASS ACTION (COLLEGES),** U.S. District Court, Charleston, SC. {**In ROSS & SAN ANSELMO**}

Judge: Hon. Solomon Blatt, Jr. replaces
Hon. John Anderson, District Court Judge, Charleston, SC
Ron Motley, Lead Plaintiff Attorney, Charleston, SC
Arthur Miller, Harvard Law Professor, appearing specially for Plaintiff
Josh Smoulders, Lead Local CAL Board Attorney, Greenville, SC

———

OTHER LOCAL CAL BOARD ATTORNEYS

WA: Tom Felix
NYC: Reggie Black
OR: Lucy Baines.
NJ: Barry Brown
AZ: Bob Hoover
MA: Ramona Kingsley
TX: David Simms.
NC: Mason Eggars
MD: Alan Kinnard
MO: Colleen Burke
NV: Joyce James

— — —

EXPERT WITNESSES

FOR THE PLAINTIFFS; Irving Selikoff, M.D., Epidemiologist, Mt. Sinai, NYC

And other Medical Scientists, many associated with Mt. Sinai Hospital

Consulting for CAL Board:

Jeremy Nobel, M.D., Harvard School of Public Health

Sir Richard Doll, M.D. (wife: Eugenia), Epidemiologist, Oxford, UK

Mary, his Executive Assistant, Ratcliffe Infirmary, Oxford

Julian Peto, Ph.D. (SO: Edna), Mathematics, Oxford & U. of London

Alison McDonald, M.D., Epidemiologist, U. of London

Jean Bignon, M.D. (w: Camille; s: August), Chief Physician (CEO), INSERM, Paris

ALSO FOR CAL Board: J. Corbett McDonald, M.D., (wife: Alison) Epidemiologist, McGill University, Montreal & University of London, Schools of Medicine/Epidemiology

— — —

DMIC REINSURANCE POLICY RECOVERY PROJECT/LLOYDS INSURANCE MARKET In SCOTTSDALE, AZ, BOSTON, MA, LONDON & PARIS (IN MILL VALLEY, ROSS, SAN ANSELMO, TIBURON & BELVEDERE)

WELLINGTON CHASE, Brokers for U.S. Clients/ London Placements with Lloyds Brokers,

(Defunct, Undertook DMIC Reinsurance placements over many decades to Lloyds Placing Brokers)

CHESHIRE & BOOTH, LLOYDS Placing Brokers, The City, London

Stanley Booth IV, Chairman of the Firm

Frederick Booth, one of Stanley's sons, Policy Document Search Leader

Grayson Turnbull, Jr., Retired Employee and Consultant to DMIC for their Search

Edgar Booth, another son & #3 n the firm to his father

PIERCE FIELDS, Solicitors, The City, London, for Cheshire & Booth

Frederick Pierce, Jr., Senior Partner/Grandson of Founder, For Cheshire & Booth

Christopher Rice, Partner

FOR DMIC: TWENTY KING'S BENCH WALK CHAMBERS, Barristers, The Temple, City of London

Quincy Franden-Jones (Q), Senior Barrister For DMIC

Wilfred Smythe, Chief Clerk of Chambers

Oliver Martin, Q.C., Head of Chambers (Tiburon)

Wallace Wilkens, Barrister

ALSO for DMIC: THORNTON, CAMPBELL & THORNTON, Solicitors, Lime Street, The City, London

Bradley Campbell (wife: Gabrielle), Senior Partner/Founder's Son,

Madeline Myles, Bradley Campbell's Executive Assistant and

Eventual COO of Long-Tail Litigation, Limited (LTL Ltd.), London, in ROSS

Added in SAN ANSELMO, also acts for Connecticut Indemnity (CI)

LLOYDS (NEW) LEGAL, Lloyds of London, Lime Street, The City

Mary Smith-Milton, Q.C., Head of CLAIMS LEGAL for LLOYDS, wife to Oliver Martin (TIBURON)

POTENTIAL 'NEW LLOYDS' INVESTOR: JERRY MILTON (w: Samantha), Venture Capitalist, Carmel

— — —

BOSLEY HOBART, JR. et al. vs HANEY PUMPS, INC. ("BO HOBART" Case) {In ROSS}

JUDGE: Hon. Hiram Forestall, California Superior Court Judge, Calaveras County in San Andreas

Ruth HOBART, Lead Plaintiff, *Guardian ad Litem* for/and wife of
Bosley HOBART, Jr. ("BO") Plaintiff, severely incapacitated in water pressure tank explosion

James (Jim) Downing, Walkup & Downing, San Francisco, Counsel for the Hobarts

Carey Crawford, VP and General Counsel for Haney Pumps, Auburn, NY

Ronan O'Neill, Lead Counsel for Haney Pumps
Strom Nordquist, Senior Adjuster, Cayuga Mutual Insurance, Pasadena, Primary insurer for Haney Pumps

Ross Weatherbee, uninsured installer of allegedly defective pumping system,

Including the Haney submersible pump and the water pressure tank supplied by Haney

Stanley Pressure Tanks, Kansas City, MO, alleged actual manufacturer of the subject water tank

Cross-Defendant of Haney Pumps
Howard Shein, San Francisco, Counsel for Stanley Pressure Tanks

— — —

HECTOR ROBERTS et al. vs. HANEY PUMPS, INC. ("UAL SFO MAINTENANCE BASE" Case) {In SAN ANSELMO}

Court: San Francisco Superior Court Master Calendar – No Single Judge Assigned Until Trial

Hector Roberts and wife, Plaintiffs, Master Plumber/Pipe Fitter, United Airlines Maintenance Base, San Francisco International Airport (UALMB/SFO)

Antonio Amaretto, Amaretto Law, Counsel for the Roberts

Haney Pumps, same as HOBART case, above.

Co-Defendants: UALMB site: General Contractor: Shane and Wilcox, Los Angeles

Mechanical Subcontractor: Bravo Brothers, So. San Francisco

Haney Pumps Mechanical Engineering Consultant: Chad Darwin, Bechtel, Corte Madera

— — —

ENVIRONMENTAL DEFENSE FUND and NATURAL RESOURCES DEFENSE COUNCIL vs. HANEY PUMPS et al. (SAN ANSELMO, TIBURON)

Judge: Law & Motion: Alameda County Superior Court, Oakland Branch: Hon. Robert Oberholzer (UC Hastings '74)

Plaintiffs: Acting as their own Counsel

Defendants: Multiple Submersible Pump Manufacturers selling indirectly in CA to end-users.

Lead Defendant: Haney Pumps, largest seller of submersible pumps in CA.

Board Chair & CEO: Charles Sherman

Board Vice Chair: Thomas Weller (Outside Board Member)

Client Contact: Carey Crawford, Haney VP/GC

Lead Counsel: Ronan O'Neill with Partners Mary Smith and Martha Walsh

Other Counsel: Joel Tinker with Partners Mace Snow and Tod Clifford

Other Defendants: ALL but two other Pump Manufacturers with CA submersible sales

United States Senators from New York: Patrick Moynihan (D) and Alphonse D'Amato (R)

ROSEVILLE LEAD-EXPOSED CHILDREN vs. GREAT WESTERN FOUNDRY, INC. (SAN ANSELMO, TIBURON)

Court: Sacramento Superior Court, Hon. Ezra Quinn, Presiding Judge

Hon. Helen Winters Appointed Single Judge for All-

Purposes (TIBURON)

Plaintiffs: Young, Scott & Little, Ephraim Scott & Will Little, Lead Counsel for all Children and Their *Guardians ad Litem*

Defendant: Great Western Foundry (GWF), alleged owner of toxically contaminated property

Board Chair, President (CEO): Abraham Spence III
Executive VP (COO): William Graham
VP – Finance (CFO): Andrea Parsons
General Counsel (GC): Stuart Brock
Lead Defense Counsel: Martha Walsh, with Ronan O'Neill: 2d Chair: Joshua Small (SAN ANSELMO), succeeded by Felicia Clarke (TIBURON)

Primary Insurer: Cayuga Mutual, Seneca Falls, NY by Strom Nordquist, Western Regional Claims Manager, Pasadena, CA

— — —

ESTER-TECH VS. NEPTUNE FISHING, INC., NEPTUNE ENTERPRISES (TIBURON)

U.S. District Court, San Francisco, Hon. Erin Brown, presiding
Plaintiff: ESTER-TECH, a California corporation, Abdul Singh, CEO & sole shareholder

Lead Counsel: Amanda Tatum with George Prescott III
Prescott & Sievers LLP, San Francisco

Defendants: NEPTUNE ENTERPRISES, Principal/Holding Owner, Wilmington, N.C.

President/CEO: Adam Young
XVP/CFO: Adam Young, Jr.
General Counsel: Leslie Worth
AGC for Litigation: David Pounds

NEPTUNE FISHING, INC., 100% Subsidiary, Major Fishing Gear Supplier, Wilmington
President: Everson Harris
CFO: Mildred Gamble
Product Development: Eugene Peters

NC Counsel: Mason Eggars, with Regina Isaacs, Wilmington
Lead Defense Counsel: O'Neill & Fox, Sandra Allen with Ronan O'Neil

— — —

NORTH AMERICAN AVIATION & SPACE (N2AS) VS. ADMIRAL ELECTRIC WORKS, INC., SPECIALTY TECHNICAL PRODUCTS, INC. (STP), and FIRE SAFETY & TESTING, INC. (FST)

U.S. District Court, San Jose, judge unspecified

Plaintiff: NORTH AMERICAN AVIATION & SPACE, San Mateo, CA

Lead Counsel: Roger Salmon, Best, Smith & Salmon, San Francisco

Client Defendants: ADMIRAL ELECTRIC WORKS, Kansas City, MO

General Counsel: Sophie Smart
AGC-Litigation: Tom Winters

SPECIALTY TECHNICAL PRODUCTS (STP), Austin, TX, Subsidiary
Designated Client Contact: Lon Probst, Round Rock & Austin

INSURER: AMERICAN SPECIALTY LINES INSURANCE (ASL), NEW YORK, NY by
Albert Cook, Senior Adjuster, over $1,000,000 SIR, NYC -both entities/one claim

MO Counsel: Colleen Burke, Burke & O'Brien, Kansas City & St. Louis, MO
Lead Defense Counsel: O'Neill & Fox, Martha Walsh with Ronan O'Neill

ABOOKS

ALIVE Book Publishing and ALIVE Publishing Group
are imprints of Advanced Publishing LLC,
3200 A Danville Blvd., Suite 204, Alamo, California 94507

Telephone: 925.837.7303
alivebookpublishing.com

www.ingramcontent.com/pod-product-compliance
Lightning Source LLC
LaVergne TN
LVHW050918080826
845145LV00001B/126

* 9 7 8 1 6 3 1 3 2 2 7 0 9 *